Tex Miller Is Dead

Found Families Book One

Kelly Elizabeth Huston

Watermount Publishing

Praise for Tex Miller Is Dead

"It has been such a joy to read TEX MILLER IS DEAD and easily my favorite read of 2023 so far… Y'all. Y'ALL! I just loved this book. It's a quirky, genre-bending romcom with the King of Imaginary Friends, a romance that will grip your heart, side characters I want as my friends (hello, Laney Li!) and ultimate the happy ending that left me with a smile." — Sharon M Peterson, author of *THE DO OVER*

"KE Huston's TEX MILLER IS DEAD is an imaginative, fast-paced romp across all my favorite New York City spots, in which a novelist whose muse skyrocketed her to the bestseller list is also standing in the way of her finding IRL love. Filled with delicious banter, quick wit, and a lot of sparks, readers will zip through TEX MILLER IS DEAD, rooting for our heroine to learn to experience life outside the pages of her books. A fun read from the get-go!" — Lisa Roe, author of *WELCOME TO THE NEIGHBORHOOD*

"…my cheeks are still sore from snickering my way through this clever, witty story. Kelly Elizabeth Huston's tongue-in-cheek humor had me reading straight through the night! Humor aside, the storyline itself is unique and intriguing… I am so looking forward to the next novel by Kelly Elizabeth Huston." — Kyle

Edited by Ash White | Cover and format by Watermount Publishing

ISBN: 979-8-9877885-0-9 (e-book) | ISBN: 979-8-9877885-1-6 (paperback)

Library of Congress Control Number: 2023903202

Visit www.kellyelizabethhuston.com for author information

To the man who has carried so many of my rocks for over twenty-five years. Thank you for helping me make my writing fantasy a reality.

1

Tex Miller was dead. Okay, not quite dead, but he was about to be, and I alone would be responsible for it. No, this wasn't my first attempt, but it would be the last.

The airport-wide announcement that played on repeat chimed in again:

Welcome to Charlotte-Douglas International Airport. For your safety...

The time and place were not by chance. I knew what I was doing, but if I had any hope of success this time, this is how it had to go down, in broad daylight, public, with my escape a hundred yards away and thirty-five thousand feet skyward. Plus, there'd be free cocktails; first-class still had *some* perks.

The March sky gleamed brilliant blue, and the sun's harsh reflections bounced off the shiny silver of fuselages and wings parked in neat diagonals. The severity of the glare flooding the concourse compelled me to wear sunglasses. Weepy eyes will do that. Sure, there were other reasons a woman might don dark glasses indoors. *Let people wonder*, I thought. I knew the real reason. The telltale sting of tears made me wince, but I sucked back any sadness. The joyful squeal of a toddler cut through the busy airport's white noise as he pounded the window glass, yanking me back to the task at hand.

There would be questions, of course.

"Why?" His dying voice rasped more air than sound.

"Yes, Tex. That will be first and foremost, I'm sure." I rolled my eyes at his banal question. For over twenty years, I'd endured the man—his bravado, his boisterous snark, and now?

"No, Callie, I'm asking. Why? Why are you doing this?" His words came louder now. Was this some show of force? One last desperate grasp at clemency?

"You know why."

"Wasn't I good to you, Cal? Didn't I provide for you? Make first-class possible?" How completely Tex-like to take on sweet sincerity in these last moments. It's why his fans adored him, the *Commander of hearts. Please.*

"You did, Tex. You did all that and more, but let's give credit where it's due. We had a good run. But I need more. Decades of lonely days and nights, it's no way to live. And frankly, I don't want to share anymore." I cringed at all the melodrama, only to have him double down in B-movie-like agony.

Tex wheezed a listless, death-rattle gasp. The truth was, if I could have taken him in my arms, I would have. I'd hold him, kiss him, ease his suffering. Then again, if I could do those things, we wouldn't be in this predicament now. There'd be no reason to kill him, would there? Even in his last breaths, Tex was beautiful, rugged in a way that made most women swoon, and with enough swagger to turn men's heads too. And the critics would no doubt wonder why the fan-favorite got taken out at the top of his game. Yes, there would be questions. Hell, there might very well be wailing in the streets.

"I love you, Callie."

I stopped typing. "Nope. That's not helping, and it won't change anything."

"I know, but it's true. It's always been you, and I needed you to hear me say it," Tex coughed.

The giggle rose out of me. A subtle shoulder shake at first, but then it bubbled up stronger until I couldn't contain it. The inappropriate guffaw echoed in the cavernous airport corridor. Heads turned. I composed myself; now was not the time to draw attention. Sure, I was the only one who could see him, hear him, but that didn't make me crazy. He was my muse, for God's sake. Still, people judge, so best I keep him on the down-low.

"I've made you laugh thousands of times over the years. I thought I knew all of them. The fake, the genuine, that *snort* when it sneaks up on you. But that one's new." He grimaced in what looked like pain. It wouldn't be long now.

"I guess it's hearing those words from your lips. I've imagined them more times than you ever made me laugh. They don't feel the way I thought they would, but it's how I know it's the end."

"Wait, Cal. Maybe not. Maybe it could be a beginning."

"Don't be silly, Tex. Declarations of love come at the end. You know that. It's how the story arc goes."

Flight 515 to JFK, New York. This is the final boarding call for flight 515 to JFK, New York.

"That's my ride. Thanks, Tex. I mean it. And I am sorry it had to end this way. Goodbye." I gave the slightest pause before hitting send, initiating the next phase of my assassination plot, almost sure it was the right thing to do. *Almost.* To compete with the man was a losing battle. Tex Miller demanded all my time, all my space, all my air. But I had other stories to tell. At least, I hoped I did.

Laptop closed, I slipped it into my leather carry-on and wobbled a moment getting out of one of the airport's signature rocking chairs. Steadied, I slung the strap over my shoulder and dashed for my getaway gate.

"Just in time, ma'am," the gate agent remarked as I scanned my airline phone app to board the plane. Hurrying down the gangway, I chanced a look back. What did I think I'd see? Police? A hoard of screaming, angry fans? No one followed. With one step onto the plane, relief washed over me. I gave a polite nod to the flight attendant in her tidy blue uniform and ducked into my bulkhead window seat.

"Killer?" the woman asked with inquisitive eyes.

"What?" I jolted from my short-lived respite.

"Cocktail?" she asked again.

With a furtive glance around, I leaned toward her. "It's eight in the morning."

She shrugged. "I thought I recognized the look."

"Whiskey. Neat." A fast but quiet blurt. *That's for you, Tex*, I thought. "Coffee, too, please. Black."

"You got it." As she navigated the tight quarters to pour my drink, the phone, still in my hand, vibrated. Given the email I'd just sent, the name on the screen drew no surprise.

"I'm on the plane. Can't talk," I answered.

"You can't do this, Callie. You just can't." Laney Li half-shouted and Laney *never* shouted.

"It's done. Tex Miller is dead." I ended the call and powered down the device. Handing me my whiskey, the sky waitress's wide eyes caught mine. "You didn't hear that. And I'll take another one of these as soon as you can make it happen." I emptied that glass, another first-class perk, in one fiery gulp.

As soon as the plane touched down, I booted up my phone, and it pinged with an immediate text message, the Around Town Car

Company letting me know my scheduled ride would wait for me at baggage claim. I had no doubt. My man Bernard was on the job, after all. Bernard was my driver. Well, not mine alone, but since I've been making trips to New York, Bernard has been my man. I was so beholden to Bernard that in the twenty-some years we've worked together, there have only been three instances when I found him unavailable to drive me: his daughter Maisie's high school graduation, her college graduation, and her wedding day. On all three occasions, I changed my travel plans. No, I wouldn't say my life revolved around Maisie's schedule, but you could.

Whenever I fly to New York City to meet with my literary agent Laney and my Watermount Publishing editor, Celeste, I fly into JFK. Bernard always waits for me with his shock of white hair under a black cap, atop a black suit, holding a placard with C. AUSTIN written in neat block lettering. I've made this trip nearly every month for twenty-two years, but this is what we always do. When we first met, he was still a ginger, and I was a brunette in my mid-twenties, and by our third introduction, I began greeting him with a daughterly peck on his pleasingly pudgy cheek. Twenty-two years in, this custom has stuck as well. I couldn't say for sure, but I imagine I'm as old today as he was the day of our first meeting, or close to it. But, with a little help, my shoulder-length wave is still brunette.

From atop the escalator, I used my vantage point to scout out Bernard, but to no avail. The crowd, made of every make and model, buzzed below, harried and huge, but no black suit, no black cap. Pulling out my phone again, I stepped off the moving staircase and out of the fray to check messages. Three new voicemails, all from Laney. Those I ignored. I also received yet another confirmation text from the car company. The repeated contact was unusual compared to my visits over the years, but I assumed Around Town had implemented some new policy after a nervous traveler insisted on frequent updates.

I brushed off the momentary concern and set my sights on claiming my luggage, a roller bag I didn't care to hassle with on the plane. A growing jumble of suitcases chugged around the serpentine beltway as more bags skidded down the slide extended from the ceiling. Eyes on my bag, I waited patiently amid the scurry of more eager patrons, realizing just how *un*hurried I was to get to my destination. Laney's stern face popped into my mind, and my stomach tightened at the angry image. Laney wasn't only my agent; she was my best friend, my only friend. She'd come around once the initial shock subsided. Wouldn't she? Celeste would be a different story. Distracted by my wandering thoughts, I snapped to when I realized my bag had gone by and hurried to chase it past the carousel's next curve.

With my suitcase retrieved, I again looked around for my man Bernard. In twenty-two years, he'd never been late.

"Aw, what's the matter, Cal? Feeling abandoned? Left behind?"

I nearly tripped over my own feet, spinning to see Tex, his tall, muscular frame in a casual lean against a backlit car rental advertisement. "Dammit, Tex," I growled through a clenched jaw.

"As I live and breathe." He filled his would-be lungs while giving his limbs a broad stretch, like a man reborn. His crooked grin tended to catch my breath and did it again. "But imagine how *I* feel? You left me gasping my last breaths on page 437, Calliope Jones. Talk about abandonment issues. Dare I ask what happens on page 438?"

My fleeting concern for Bernard rebounded and escalated to full-blown worry. I headed to the exit, leaving my problematic protagonist in my wake, very much *not* dead.

2

Outside the terminal doors, a damp chill met me. Tightening my scarf, I stepped toward a familiar car with its Around Town logo in the back window. When the driver's side opened, a man who was most definitely *not* Bernard exited the vehicle. I stopped short and looked up and down the loading zone in search of another black town car. To my relief, Tex had gone *poof* again.

"Ms. Austin." It was a statement, not a question. The man hurrying around the front of the vehicle to greet me knew who I was.

"Yes?"

"Good morning." The tall stranger dressed in a black suit, but no black cap, opened the rear passenger door.

I stood my ground. "I'm sorry. Bernard is my driver. Bernard is always my driver. I schedule my vis—never mind, but Bernard is my driver."

"Oh, not this morning, ma'am. I'm to take you to Watermount Publishing." The man gestured to the back seat.

"There must be some mistake." Realizing I stared at him a moment too long, I fumbled for my phone to show the man proof. "See, Around Town texted my confirmation. Twice."

The driver nodded. "Yes, I—we—*they* texted to confirm your ride, but with me." His chiseled jaw, with a near-black day-old beard, clenched before he steadied himself with an emphatic, "Bernard is unavailable today."

"Well, that's not possible. Bernard wouldn't cancel on me, not without letting me know, anyway. In twenty—"

"Twenty-two years," the man interrupted. "Yes, ma'am, I know. Bernard told me. Let's get in the car where it's warm. I can explain." His granite features softened; a polite smile flickered as he reached for my luggage.

I took a tentative step in the direction of that warmth as a cold wind gusted down the airport roadway. Again, I stopped, cautiously standing an arm's length from the chauffeur. "How did you know it was me?"

"Pardon?"

"When I came out, you said my name. Not in question, just my name, like you knew it was me. I could have been anyone."

"Bernard let me know what to look for. There was no question when I saw you exit the terminal, Ms. Austin."

"Really? What did he say that made me so—easy to spot? How did he describe me?" I stood closer now and had to tilt my head a fraction to meet his midnight-blue eyes.

He bowed his head an inch and cleared his throat. "*Uh*, tall. He said you were tall." Something new flashed in his look, a brief devious grin I thought I'd seen before, and it said he didn't plan to share any more than he had already.

"Ah. Lucky for you, there's such a notorious dearth of tall women coming and going from JFK's terminal eight." I eyed the man askance with my own quick smirk and ducked into the car, pleased with my efforts at a little harmless flirting with a man likely ten years too young. Too young for me, anyway.

Having deposited my suitcase in the trunk, the driver situated himself behind the wheel, texting while he did it. Back to his steely expression, he spoke into the rearview, "Shall we?"

"No." Hoping for another peek at his grin, I offered him mine. "You said you would explain." Worry reflected at me when he gave an anxious glance at his watch. "We have time," I assured him. "Plenty of time." But now I couldn't be certain something wasn't amiss.

"Bernard called out sick this morning." My substitute spoke over his shoulder. "And with rain coming, there could be back-ups. I don't want you to be late, ma'am."

"Okay, call me Callie, please." My Bernard-worry rebounded for the third time. "And I don't mean to be rude. Truly, I don't, but that doesn't sound like Bernard. Not at all. And your name is?" The burgeoning angst in the car belonged to me now. And all the ill-advised flirtation ceased.

"Sorry. Andrew, ma'—Callie. People call me Drew."

"Drew? Where the *hell* is Bernard?"

Drew unbuckled and rotated in his seat to look at me. His well-mannered smile had faded, and dread flooded his narrowed eyes. The crease between his dark brow indicated something dire, and the conflict to share or not waged in his stare. I couldn't quite place what I recognized in his kind face as I awaited his answer, but a familiarity tugged at the back of my mind while my concern skyrocketed.

"M-miss Austin. Callie. Bernard suffered a heart attack early this morning. He—"

The words *heart* and *attack* crashed into my chest. "Where is he? Take me there, please."

"But—"

"Now, Drew," I barked, then tried to calm my tone. "I don't care where. Just get me there, please."

"Yes, ma'am." Drew buckled his seat belt.

"Thank you." I dialed Laney, but the call went straight to voicemail. "Laney. Change in plans. Bernard is—sick. I'll text details when I know more. Handle the meeting, reschedule the meeting. Whichever. I'll be in touch." I ended the call with a trembling thumb. "Where are we going, Drew?"

"He's at Bellevue. On 1st Ave."

"Is that good? Is that a good place to be? For him, I mean?" I struggled for a deep breath.

"Well, it's—yes, it's good. Are you alright?" We spoke to each other's rearview mirror reflections.

Twinges of guilt for my silly attempts at banter moments earlier snaked my insides. "No, Drew, I'm not alright. I'll be alright when I know Bernard is alright." With that, Drew gunned the gas to speed through a yellow light as we exited the access road to the Van Wyck Expressway.

The dreary cold mixed with the pang of fear was all too familiar. I grew up an only child of wonderful parents in upstate New York. No, I didn't begin life a southern belle. The community was small, close-knit, and rather poor, but a great place where children ran free dawn to dusk in summer, schools performed well-above average, and parents volunteered with soccer leagues and scouts. It wasn't until I moved from the small town that I realized how much we had—and how much we didn't.

My world turned upside-down when my long-distance runner dad dropped dead of a heart attack at thirty-seven. I was twelve. Mom did her best after that shock, eventually marrying a man named Gerry after we moved to Buffalo to be nearer to family.

Gerry was never my father. Nothing untoward happened, no neglect or abuse. But I had grown fiercely independent by high school, and my focus zeroed in on my schoolwork and escaping the gray skies and dirty snow mounds on the edge of Lake Erie to any greener, sunnier locale anywhere. The wet chill on the way to Bellevue served as a reminder of some of what I wanted to escape all those years ago.

The stop-and-go traffic said we had a long trip from Queens to Manhattan. I blamed the two shots of whiskey for the headache creeping up the back of my neck into the base of my skull. Eyes closed, I rested my head, hoping the rhythmic thud of street seams would lull me into a catnap, but my concern for Bernard wouldn't allow me to relax while my ricocheting nerves and pounding heart told me I should have foregone that third cup of coffee on the plane.

I opened my eyes to find Drew staring back in the rearview mirror. His gaze quickly shifted to the road while his ears betrayed him, turning pink. I shut my eyes again.

"*God*, Cal, you should take something for that headache. You never could handle the dark liquor."

"What was that?" I snapped, bolting forward, twisting to see Drew's face.

"Excuse me, ma'—Miss Austin?" Drew flinched at my harsh tone. "I—didn't say anything."

I sat back; fingers massaged my temples. The headache made its way above my ears, and my creation's poorly-timed pop-in didn't help matters.

"Come on, Cal, you didn't think I'd go down that easy, did you? *Please*," Tex scoffed. "And now this bombshell?"

"Stop. Stop talking," I hissed a whisper.

"Miss Austin? Are you—? Should I pull over?"

"Not you, Drew. Sorry. Just get me to Bellevue. Thanks." Hands clasped in my lap, I glanced at the passenger seat to my left.

"Hey, babe. Seriously." Tex shook his head with a laugh. "Don't act surprised and snag yourself some painkillers from your satchel there." He pointed to the messenger bag at my feet. "Bernie keeps a fancy cooler of water bottles up front. I'm sure the new guy's got one too. Surely, he'll toss you a water so you can down some vitamin I."

I pulled my bag to my lap to rummage for the travel-sized bottle of ibuprofen and I poured four pills into my palm. Drew handed me a bottle over his shoulder without me asking for it.

"See? There ya go. Take a breath. You know I'm here to help you." Tex wore his serious face.

"That's *new*," I groused at the dashing adventurer next to me as I grabbed the drink. "Since when?"

"Yes, it is." Drew sat straighter. "I, *uh*, Around Town bought a new brand. If you prefer the other, I'll be sure to have it stocked before your next ride."

"Oh, no. Drew. I don't care. That's not necessary." I washed back the handful of pills with a silent reprimand for engaging with my phantom friend when we were around others.

"Okay. Also, I'm sorry to do this, but in all the chaos this morning, to get to you on-time, I didn't get fueled up like I should have. I'm gonna need to make a quick stop. To be safe."

"*Jeez*, new guys—am I right?" Tex complained with an exaggerated eye roll, then sipped from the lowball glass of whiskey he now held.

"No worries, Drew. It happens."

"And would you like me to deposit your suitcase at your hotel? I'm happy to handle that for you." My man Bernard had clearly trained the new recruit.

"Let him take it, Cal. You know how you hate to hassle with a bag."

"That won't be necessary, Drew. I'll keep it with me." I shot a subtle sneer in Tex's direction. We pulled into a fuel station, and my driver exited the car to fill up.

"You're being particularly stubborn today, aren't you, Ms. Jones?" Tex cocked his head of dark curls and swirled his drink.

"I'm stubborn? And what the hell? Why are you wearing a tuxedo?" I jeered at his sudden costume change.

"Why, *in-deed*? You know how this works, Cal. I don't dress m'self."

"You have to stay quiet now. Better yet, go away. Bernard is—don't make trouble, please." The driver's door opened and Drew slid in behind the wheel. I looked back at Tex, but he'd vanished. "Thank goodness," I muttered.

"Just a few gallons. I apologize for that." We sped into the dark of the Midtown Tunnel. "And I wish you would reconsider letting me keep your bag, so you won't have to worry about it throughout the day."

"You're right, Drew. Thank you. Please excuse my erratic behavior. The day's been—trying." We shared another brief eye-lock in the rearview.

The town car swerved into the U-shaped driveway of the hospital's main entrance, and I opened the door before we came to a complete stop. I slammed it and bolted toward the revolving entryway of Bellevue but staggered to a halt when my brain caught up to my feet. Hurrying back, I tapped on the front passenger window; it opened. "Thank you, Drew. Sorry to mess with your day. I'll make it right with your boss. Promise." I gave a weak wave as I spun back into a gallop in search of news of Bernard. If the chauffeur spoke to me, I didn't hear a word he said.

3

Automatic doors led me to a huge atrium. The glass ceiling soared five stories, and the echoing landscape tilted when I looked up at it. Eyes closed, I regained my balance and reminded myself to breathe before searching out directions to the cardiac care unit and my man Bernard Pierce.

Stepping off the elevator, I nearly ran into a woman pacing in the hall waiting area. "Mrs. Pierce." I reached out to take the petite woman's hand. She was smaller than she appeared in pictures Bernard had shared, but I'd know the almost-lilac tinted hair anywhere. "I'm Callie Austin. I'm—"

"Ms. Austin," she replied in a hushed gasp. "Yes, I know who you are."

"You do?"

"Of course I do. Bernard has spoken of you for years. How did you—"

"How is he? Where is he? May I see him?"

"Slow down. He's fine. They got to him quickly, even though he drove himself here, the old coot. He had an all-nighter here in Manhattan last night, but you know he can't resist when you have a scheduled visit."

"Oh my God!" I reddened at my inappropriate volume and lowered it. "I didn't know. I would never expect him to—not ever. He should have—" Bile inched up my throat as a wave of nausea hit. "Mrs. Pierce, I am so sorry—"

"Moira. Please." She gave my hand a firm squeeze with a sad smile. "Have a seat. You're shaking, dear."

"When can I see him? Is Maisie here?" I half fell into a chair.

"Maisie just left to see to Joe Jr. He's teething, the poor lamb. Can I get you a coffee?" It seemed the gentle woman also needed someone to care for.

"No, no more caffeine for me just now, thank you."

"Okay. So, they got to him quickly. From 'door to balloon,' as they say, took less than one hour. Before I made it here from Queens. Remarkable, really. He's resting now. Sleeping, finally."

I took a much-needed deep inhale and realized I still had a tight hold of Moira's hand. My chest ached under the weight of fear on the woman's face. "Is there anything I can do? For either of you. Anything? Please, name it."

"Oh, surely, you have things to do. Reasons you are in town. We wouldn't think of holding you up." Moira patted my arm.

"As it happens, my day has cleared entirely." As the words came out, my phone pinged. I pulled it from my coat, and without looking at it, turned it off, depositing it back in my pocket. When an elevator opened, Moira looked past me. Drew exited, holding two lidded paper cups.

She beamed. "You came back."

"Come on now, Mrs. P. I told you I would." The chauffeur kissed Moira's cheek. "How's the old man? Mais still here?"

"You missed her. She headed home for the baby." A phone rang, Moira's this time. "Speak of the angel." Moira patted my arm again and walked away to take the call.

Drew and I stood with blank stares at one another for an awkward moment before he offered me a coffee. "Here. I brought you a cup."

"That was kind, but no more caffeine for me, thanks."

"I sorta got that jumpy vibe in the car. Made a judgment call and ordered you decaf." He urged me to take the cup again.

"Well, I take it black so—"

"I know. Bernard has that on record. No cream, no sugar, and now, just for today, no caffeine." Third time's the charm.

"Oh, thank you." I took the beverage, sipping it immediately. While I drank, Drew's gaze followed Mrs. Pierce down the hall. I squinted at his profile, trying to decipher why he seemed so familiar.

"What?" He brushed his fingers across his nose, and then his hand ran down the front of his coat and tie. "Is there something on my face? Did I spill on my shirt?"

"What?" *Oof.* Caught gaping again.

"You were staring. At me."

"Sorry. Just a bit dazed, I guess. The morning has been a whirl."

"Yeah," Drew agreed.

"Well, don't let me keep you." Needing some distance, I escaped to a waiting area chair.

"You're not keeping me. I'm here to—"

"No, I won't be needing anything today. I cleared my schedule." I took another swallow and waved him off.

"Well, since you were my charge today, I guess my schedule just cleared up, too. And the Pierces are family, so I'll be staying—you know, just in case." Drew took a seat, setting his coffee on the table between us.

"Just in case what? Is there something you aren't telling me?" With new panic, I jumped to my feet again; he followed suit.

"No. Just in case you change your mind and need to—want to—go somewhere. Anywhere."

"Jeez, Drew." I sat again, and after the briefest hesitation, he followed. I rubbed my nose, trying to rid it of the distinct hospital smells of industrial cleansers and sickness. A constant squawk overhead summoned medical staff in codes I didn't understand and under all that noise droned the steady hum and occasional *tink* from a flickering fluorescent tube light above us. It promised to be a long day.

Laney needed an update. A text reply told me she opted to reschedule rather than handle Celeste at Watermount without me. I should have known I'd have to make my case to my agent *and* editor and sighed in my frustration.

"Everything okay?" Drew set down a months-old People Magazine.

"Super," I chirped my sarcasm. "Sorry. I hoped that someone had disposed of something for me, but they didn't."

Drew leaned toward me with a solemn look and whispered, "You mean—like a body?"

I snorted a laugh, then blushed at the indelicate noise, but the speck of inappropriate humor brought brief relief.

His face twisted, trying to keep his feigned frown, but he gave way to real sincerity. "I meant what I said before. You're my day today, so if there is anywhere you want to go, or anything you need, I'm your man."

I stiffened. "Bernard's my man. And I'm not going anywhere until I've seen him." The words rang harsher than I meant as my eyes returned to my phone. After a few minutes of nothing but hospital racket, Drew stood to walk away. Dread rushed me. "Drew?"

He stopped and met my eye. "I'm not going anywhere, Callie. Just seeing if I can get an update. I won't be long."

I blanched with a hard swallow. "Thanks." I tried, but no smile surfaced. As Drew left, I rose to take in the view. A mounting drizzle added to the somber mood of the day. The panorama featured a cluster of apartment high-rises with the East River beyond it, but the gloomy sky didn't do the scene any favors.

When Moira returned, I squeezed her arm and asked, "Maisie alright? You?"

"She'll be fine. I fibbed and told her these were the hardest parenting years. When Joe Jr. turns twelve, I guess I'll have some explaining to do." Her snicker at her own joke compelled the grin I couldn't muster earlier. "Drew's talking with her now. He can always talk her down, better than Joe, even."

"Drew said you all were family."

"Oh, not blood, but yes. Same neighborhood growing up. He and Maisie were in the same class. They were quite close."

"It's sweet how Bernard has taken Drew under his wing."

"His wing?" Moira squinted.

Behind us, Drew cleared his throat. "Gotta stay hydrated, right?" He handed us each a bottle of water. "I saw they had your brand, so—"

"My brand? Wow. Bernard really is teaching you everything he knows, *hm*? To be honest, I'm not that picky. Truly. Please don't think I'm that kind of client."

"Well, at Around Town Car Company, we aim to please. You need only to ask." Drew grinned like a TV ad man while he spouted the familiar slogan Bernard often repeated.

"*Ha*. You even sound like him. You couldn't have a better mentor. No better man to show you the ropes. What am I saying? Of course, you know that already, right?"

Drew looked at his smart black leather wingtips and then at Moira before nodding to me with a humbled, "I do. No question. Bernard is the best driver on the team."

Moira *hmmed* with a head tilt to Drew before she looked at me.

"Time for a nurse check-in." Moira scurried toward the nurses' station.

After much prodding, I convinced Drew to find himself something to eat. "Really. Give me your number, and if anything changes, I'll text. Promise. I have some calls to make, anyway."

"I've got your number. Here's me." My phone pinged with a text alert. A car emoji appeared on my screen.

"Cute."

"I try." He shrugged. "Sure, I can't get you something?"

I wiggled my phone. "Some privacy? Important business to attend to here. Don't need you hearing *where* I bury the bodies. You know." I angled my head toward the elevator. He smiled, buttoned his suit coat, and backed away.

Eager for distraction from those dark blue eyes, that chiseled chin, the boyish grin, I texted Laney to see if she had time to talk. My phone rang seconds later. I updated her with what little information I had while letting her know I would be out-of-pocket for the rest of the day. The cardiologist said the first twelve hours were critical, and I planned to stay close until I saw Bernard out of danger. I apologized for the changeup, but Laney had no interest in hearing it. My best friend knew of the old man's importance to me. Celeste and Watermount could wait.

"I think you can tentatively reschedule us for tomorrow."

"Should I arrange another car now that Bernard is out of commission?"

"Well. No. Bernard's—protégé of sorts picked me up this morning. Feels right to keep him if he's available." All in the name of professional courtesy. Maintaining good client-to-company relations, keeping ailing Bernard's boss happy. Oh boy, who was I trying to convince? "Of course, I don't need a ride from the hotel to Water—"

"Hold up. Protégé, *huh*?" Laney interrupted with a lascivious tone.

"*Ha.* Yes. Which implies he's young, and he is. Younger, anyway."

"Trainable."

"I suppose."

"Submissively obedient."

"Well, those words mean the same—wait. What? O-kay, mind out of the gutter." Heat sprouted in my chest. So much for distraction. "Will you make those arrangements? His name is Drew."

"Arrange for your new, young, *hot* driver to be at your beck and call this week? Yes, that I can do. With pleasure."

"Who said—I didn't—I never said he was hot." I rolled my eyes but knew Laney simply meant to lighten the mood.

"Well, is he?"

My pause said all Laney needed to hear, and more than I intended to say. She let loose her loud honk of a laugh as she hung up.

"Who's hot?"

I spun around, nearly tossing my phone in startled surprise. Tex appeared extra broad-shouldered in a Naval Commander's service dress blues.

"No one for you to concern yourself with, Tex. And no one is hotter than you." I walked past him, taking a seat where I'd left my coat. "Just ask your egomaniacal self." I cocked my head with a teasing sneer. Tex lifted his chin with a blue-eyed wink, indicating beyond me. A nurse with a quizzical look stood in a doorway. I quickly placed the phone to my ear, "And then *I* said, that's what *she* said."

The nurse typed on a tablet and walked down the hall. I shook my head, exasperated by my imperceptible pal. Keeping the phone to my ear, I asked, "Why are you here?" I knew the answer, of course. Tex always came when I needed him. For over twenty years, whether or not I wanted his company.

"I don't know. Guess I got to thinking how we met and felt a little nostalgic. The smell of antiseptic in the air, the constant yelp over the PA, the sticky magazines full of celebrity gossip from last summer." Tex's playful tone ebbed as he admired his military cap. "It's been a while since I wore my uniform."

"Not since that first day."

"Hey, keep that thing to your ear if you don't want someone coming along with their giant net to drag you to the psych ward." He pointed to my phone.

I lifted it back to the side of my head. "Aye, aye, Commander," and gave a two-fingered salute.

My dad's heart attack left me a death benefit to help pay for my college tuition, so I worked hard, got good grades, and excellent test scores. That combination meant I had several notable options to choose from my senior year of high school. My desire to leave snow country wasn't a secret, so, while an upstate New York Ivy and an esteemed Boston area college both turned my head, the University of Virginia won my heart when I visited on a spring weekend. Cherry blossoms floated through the air at the same time a foot of snow dumped on both New England and the Mid-Atlantic.

A death benefit. That's what they called it.

Charlottesville had lots of appeal: all four seasons, small-town charm at the foot of the Blue Ridge Mountains, and a rich history just three hours from both Washington D.C. and Virginia Beach, plus a top twenty law school I thought for sure I would attend. The easiest decision I ever made.

My visits to Buffalo were rare and short, but the last trip stretched four weeks, the time it took for pancreatic cancer to kill my mother and me to see to her end-of-life requests.

She went fast. From diagnosis to death, a blink of an eye and yet her agonizing slow-motion demise couldn't have been more prolonged. The dichotomy teased the worst kind of irony. Much of that too-fast passing of time, my mother slept, drugged into unconsciousness. The only way to combat the pain. After the first week, I insisted the doctors allow her to go home. She could sleep, stoned on morphine, in the comfort of her own bedroom.

Each day, a fresh horror unfolded, and I wished she could share her saving grace—the elixir drip to her vein. Hospice provided care, and I held her tight while Gerry, her husband, didn't handle things at all.

I'm not sure how it all started. Mom slept, and Gerry watched TV. I, unwilling to leave her side, opened my laptop, and words began to flow. Naval Commander Theodore "Tex" Miller appeared and whisked me away on an adventure. So, while my classmates partied and crammed for the LSAT, I wrote and fell in love with a man who didn't exist, and my mother wasted away to nothing and then died.

Like the living dead, I staggered through the last semester of school. Passing all my classes, I finished on time, despite deferment offers by caring professors and a supportive dean. I was done with academia and wanted out. Law school no longer appealed to me, so I buried myself in a dumpy two-room apartment off a Charlottesville side street and spent days and nights with no one other than Tex. It was the best of times; it was the worst of times...

"Callie."

"Yes." Startled, I placed my phone to my ear as Tex drew me to the present. He pointed over my shoulder.

"Ma'am? Mr. Pierce is awake."

I jumped to my feet, grabbing my coat. Tex disappeared.

"Miss. What are you doing here?" Bernard lay frail, a terrifying, sickly pale.

I simpered. "You know I love a good view. And the East River on a cloudy day—well, you can't beat this vista." I gestured to the window and its closed blinds. "Give me a second." I pulled out my phone again, texted Drew as promised, and placed it back in my coat pocket. Filling a cup of water, I held the straw to give Bernard a sip. "So, what's new?" I forced a chipper tone.

Bernard wheezed a pained laugh, then coughed. When he settled himself, I offered more water. He refused. "I know somehow you will convince yourself this is your fault, Miss. But you need to put that thought out of your mind. And I'm going to be fine. Maybe cutting back on the job some, but—"

"Yes, now that you've been grooming your replacement, the timing couldn't be better."

"My replacement?"

"Not *replacement*. No one will ever replace you. I mean your mentee. Your *apprentice*? I don't know what you call him in the driving biz."

With a knock, Drew's handsome face poked in the opened door.

"Were your ears burning, Drew? We were just talking about

you."

"Oh, Miss—" Bernard clutched my hand.

"Like I said earlier, Bernard's the best. I lucked out with this guy." A buzz came from inside Drew's coat. Phone in hand, he backed toward the door. "Sorry, gotta take this. I'll be back, old man. Don't go anywhere and, *uh*, don't wear yourself out with too much talking. Rest." He raised a brow at Bernard and bowed out of the room.

I took a deep breath, the first satisfying one in a few hours. "Moira will be here any minute." When the rain moved through, and clouds hinted at glimpses of blue sky, I had encouraged her to get some fresh air.

Taking another sip from the straw, Bernard spoke, "You certain you're okay, Miss? I know you had a meeting. I do apologize for this bother."

"Bother? Don't even think of apologizing, least of all to me. You take care of yourself." I nodded at the troubled eyes staring back. The fear of losing the man gnawed deep in my gut, and the thought of it happening without knowing if he knew me, *truly* knew me, caused heartache. "Bernard, we've been together for more than twenty years, right?"

"Twenty-two this May, Miss."

"And—do you—know who I am?" The question sounded stranger out loud than I thought it would.

"You're Callie Austin, no?" His brow furrowed.

"Yes, I'm Callie Austin. But—do you know who else I am?" I watched the man, but the answer wasn't obvious in his face. "It's just we've never spoken about it. In all these years, with everything we've shared, it's the one thing we never talk about, and well, it's fine either way. I mean, I have no expectation that you know—or even care. I just wondered."

"I would never burden you with the fact of my knowing, Miss. It seems obvious to me you have meant to live an anonymous life. I will always respect that."

"Thank you, Bernard." The sweetness of the old man's statement in his gentle lilt brought a wave of calm, but that wave surged, an abrupt rise and fall, surprising my insides. "Wait. So you *do* know who I am?"

Bernard chuckled with obvious discomfort while patting my hand. "Yes, Miss. Moira and I are big fans. We've read them all. But Maisie's the biggest. She's read them many times. They do love that Tex Miller. Love him like he's real and theirs alone to love. A wee bit odd to me, but I do enjoy the stories. That Calliope Jones sure tells a right fine tale." He winked.

Like he's real and theirs alone to love... the words stirred my anxiety again, and I shuddered hearing them. "Yes, he was—is—very—popular."

Moira rushed into the small, equipment-packed space, and I hurried out of the way of the couple's reunion. Heat prickled under my wool coat as I peeled out of it in my escape to the hall. I leaned against the wall and then bent over, hands on my knees, trying to ease the new swell of post-traumatic panic. Sucking in air, I blew out a long, steady stream.

"Whoa. You alright, ma'am?" The nurse I encountered earlier hurried to my side. "Let's get you in a chair. Do you have any health issues?"

"No, I'm fine—"

"Hey! Are you o-? Is she okay?" Drew jogged down the hall to the seating area, where the nurse checked my pulse.

I waved him off. "I'm fine. He's okay. Go see him."

"I'll be just a minute." He hesitated but trotted back toward Bernard's room.

"Well, I'll say it." The nurse muttered, still gripping my wrist, eyes on the second-hand sweep of her watch. "Girl, he *is* hot."

She wasn't wrong.

4

Too exhausted to fight me, Moira caved when I urged her to lie down on the sofa-like contraption in Bernard's room that pulled out to something tantamount to a twin bed. It was the sort of hospital furniture meant to dissuade significant others from staying the night, but Moira refused to leave her husband. Once she settled, I informed Drew his day with me was done. And the incessant ring of his phone said he had other responsibilities. I was there to help but only for a short while. They needed to take the support while I could offer it. It didn't feel like nearly enough.

Daylight faded as food services delivered meals to the cardiac care ward. I fetched soup and a sandwich for Moira and found her awake after four hours of rest, just feet away from her spouse. Bernard woke again, too, and the three of us chatted while Moira ate and Bernard picked at the bland option his condition allowed.

Comforted that some color had returned to his cheeks and knowing Moira wouldn't leave his side, I said my goodbyes.

"I have a meeting tomorrow morning, but I will come to see you when I finish. Whenever that is."

"I don't suppose I have much on my schedule tomorrow, so whenever you would like to visit will be alright by me, Miss. But don't you make any special effort about it." Bernard patted my hand in a fatherly fashion.

"Moira, if there is anything you need, please let me know."

"Thank you, dear. Thank you for being here today."

I kissed Bernard's cheek and wished the couple a quiet night. In a slow trudge toward the elevator, I dug in my shoulder bag for my phone to order up a ride to my hotel.

"Callie?"

"Tex," I grumbled, face in my bag, still scrounging around my oversized purse.

"Who?" Drew stood in the waiting area.

"What? *Drew*. Hi, I was about to—*text* someone. What are you—why are you here?" I stammered my way through the confusion.

"That text wasn't going to be on a rideshare app, now, was it?"

"*Hm*, maybe?"

Drew knitted his brows. "I'm gonna try really hard not to take that personally. Shall we?" He gestured toward the elevator. "I'll run ahead and pull the car to the front. I parked in the south lot. It's a trek."

"No, thank you," I replied, shoring up the bag on my shoulder.

"What do you mean, 'No, thank you'? I'm here, and I have your luggage. Why won't you take the ride?"

"Oh, I'm taking the ride. I just would rather walk to the car if that's alright. I've been indoors all day and could really use some f—" Before I finish my sentence, the *loudest* hunger rumble I had ever heard roared from my stomach. Both our eyes widened at the prolonged gastric gurgle.

"Food? You could really use some—food?" Drew asked through a broad grin that caught my breath.

My second unseemly snort of the day joined in the noisemaking. "I am hungry, yes." I pressed my hand to my abdomen.

"This works out perfectly, then. After you." He held the elevator door, and I stepped inside, too hungry, too embarrassed, and too tired to put up any resistance. Drew tolerated my slow pace as I enjoyed the cool evening air despite the lingering whiff of East River. In the dark, I chanced a look at my walking companion, reminding myself we had only met that morning. Whatever about him rang familiar tricked me into thinking he was someone I knew, someone I'd known long before the start of that Tuesday.

When we arrived at the town car, I stalled briefly, reluctant to get in, except I knew it put me one step closer to my hotel where I could eat and take off my pinching shoes.

"So, food." Drew opened the rear passenger-side door. "How do you feel about a parked car picnic?"

"A what?" Halfway into the vehicle, the mouthwatering aroma of chilis, garlic, and lime hit me. Drew closed the door and trotted to the driver's seat to hold up a large paper sack with a grease-splotched bottom.

"It's Taco Tuesday at my favorite food truck here in Kips Bay. Two for one, so I got us a bagful. I hope you like Mexican." His optimism radiated in the dim glow of the car's courtesy light.

"Well, right now, I'd eat my left arm, so yeah, Mexican sounds great. You really shouldn't have, though. Talk about above and beyond. But does your boss have rules about eating in the cars?"

Drew handed me two paper-wrapped street tacos and a stack of napkins. "Yeah, so, about that—"

"Nope. No worries, Drew. Your secret is safe with me. I won't tell a soul. Promise."

He grinned with a *hmph*. "Yeah? You're quite the secret keeper, *huh*?"

"You have *nooo* idea," I mumbled with a mouthful of the best taco I'd ever eaten. Tangy juices and crema mixed in my mouth, resulting in something near euphoria.

"In that case..." Drew leaned toward the cooler sitting on

the floorboard of the front passenger seat. Flipping the top, he produced two bottles of ice-cold beer and popped the caps off each. He handed me a bottle across the center console to my seat in the back. I took it gladly.

"You know, you've got some pretty big shoes to fill, young man. But—this is an excellent start. Cheers!" We clinked bottles and both enjoyed a long swig. I relaxed as the dome light faded, and Drew pressed an overhead button, allowing the moon roof to drone open. I relished another bite of taco and the skyward view as the sliver of a waning crescent appeared.

My statement on shoes was well meant, but now, all I could think about was getting out of my Jimmy Choo heels. I stretched my long legs across the back seat, flexing my ankles. Distraction came as a quiet phone ping deep inside my bag. I stuffed the last bite of taco in my mouth, crumpling the wrapper as I chewed. Drew's hand snaked over the seatback, beckoning me to give him my trash. "Thank you," I said, rummaging for my phone again. It was Laney.

Laney Li: *Around Town guaranteed their services for the week, but not the driver. Guess the young hottie has other bookings. Sorry.*

I disguised the day's third snort with a polite cough and replied my thanks. "What a day," I sighed, lounging with a sated belly after the last swallow of my beer.

Drew nodded. "Is there anywhere else you need to go tonight?"

I bolted upright. "No, just my hotel. You know the one? How rude of me to keep you. You must have things to do, a family to get home to." Flustered, I brushed non-existent taco crumbs from my coat and hurried to buckle my seat belt.

"Yes. I mean no, ma'—Miss Austin. Wait. Yes, I know the hotel. No to the other—"

"I should get to my hotel. Big meeting tomorrow and—"

"I'm not trying to rush you, Miss Austin. My apologies."

"It's Callie, remember? And I'm the one who should apologize. Sprawled back here with all the forbidden food and drink. I forgot myself for a second. I didn't mean to be disrespectful of your time."

He opened his mouth to speak again but must have thought better of it. Instead, he wiped his hands with a napkin and tossed the crumpled wad aside to buckle up too. We rode in an unnerving silence to my Flatiron District hotel. Our day began with friction, and it seemed it would end that way too. I leaned my head against the window, its coolness offering a modicum of relief to my flushed face, chastened by that last exchange. The night-time light concealed embarrassment as I reached for the wallet in my bag.

The car veered into the hotel loading zone. By the time Drew reached my door, I already stood on the curb.

"I may be new at this, but I'm pretty sure you're supposed to let me open that for you." He stepped around me to retrieve my bag from the trunk, then circled back to offer me the pull handle. "Yep. They teach that on the first day of Chauffeur School. It's Driver 101, the most basic of fundamentals."

"Is that before or after they teach you when to fuel up?" I asked with a straight, curious face.

"Ouch." The poor man put his hand to his chest, looking wounded.

I looked at my sore feet on the shadowy sidewalk. "Oh jeez, Drew, how many ways can I say I'm sorry tonight?"

"*No*, I was—kidding." Drew ran his fingers through the dark curls on top of his head, those navy eyes wild in his rush to ease my concern.

I lifted my chin with a wink. "Me too." But a sudden falling feeling in my stomach made me look away. I cleared my throat.

"Thank you again for stepping in today. You're gonna do well in this job. Here."

He flinched a subtle inch as I slipped a folded one hundred-dollar bill into the fine fabric slit next to his suit coat lapel. "I—can't accept this." He fished the money from his pocket.

"You can, and you will. You bought coffee and water and dinner to boot, not to mention the much-appreciated company. It was nice to meet you, Drew." I walked toward the hotel lobby door.

Drew unfolded the crisp bill. "A hundred dollars? Miss Austin, people will talk."

Admiring the man standing in the streetlamp light, I exhaled at his self-assured smirk. With flashes of the knowing grins of Laney and the cardiac care nurse, I decided the fact that Drew was unavailable for the week was probably a good thing. It also made me bold enough to make one last quip. "For the last time, it's Callie. And Drew, hate to break it to you, but *people* already are. Goodnight." I waved over my shoulder and hurried to the door, knowing full-well I'd be kicking off my shoes in the elevator.

Once in the quiet lobby, I beelined to the hotel's sleek front desk. I chose this hotel for the convenient location and the wonderful views, not the initial warmth of its staff. And it's a good thing too.

"Callie Austin checking in. Apologies for the late arrival. It's been a day."

The young man behind the counter ignored me. I wasn't sure if he had even heard me by his lack of reaction. My picture ID and credit card ready for use, he took them, still with no verbal recognition of my presence. The absence of customer service was not unfamiliar to me, but I knew once he saw my reservation details, his demeanor would change in three, two, one...

"Ms. Austin. Yes. Welcome. How are you this evening?" Immediate eye contact and a near-smile accompanied the attitude shift.

"I'm well, thank you."

"Yes, we have you in the Park Suite as requested, staying four nights on the thirty-eighth floor. Will you need extra keycards for this visit?"

"No, not necessary."

"I'd be happy to make any arrangements for you during your stay. Spa treatments? Theater tickets? Restaurant reservations?"

"I'll keep that in mind, but nothing now, thanks."

"We have a phone number and email address on file for you. Do you prefer calls, texts, or emails for communication?"

"Text, I suppose—Tofer?" I pointed to his name tag.

"It's short for Kristofer. With a K and an F."

"Of course it is."

"Yes, if I can do anything to make your stay more enjoyable, please don't hesitate to call—or text," he spoke the words through a tight New York City smile.

"Oh, I won't." I scooped up the envelope containing a room key and spun on my heel to head to my room and a hot bath.

From my suite's window, I had a view of Madison Square Park in front of me, the Flatiron Building to my left, and further away to the right, the Empire State Building. That night, the iconic skyscraper stood in its signature white, but for decades, the tower lights have maintained the tradition of changing color to celebrate events and organizations throughout the year. The colors were fun, but the signature all-white had always been my favorite.

I could see Watermount Publishing from my spot, too, and I'd welcome the quick trek to my morning meeting despite the tough task the appointment would include. I loved to walk the streets of this city.

Weary from the day, I slipped into a hotel robe while the bath filled for a much-needed soak. Classical music played through an under-the-counter speaker as I stepped into the stone soaker tub. Sudsy and almost too hot to bear, the water covered me, and I relaxed in the thick, perfumed foam of luxury hotel bubble bath. Steam swirled off my feet as I sank and stretched my toes to the end of the bathtub. A light knock tapped on the door. With a slight sigh, I called, "Enter."

Tex traipsed in, holding a cocktail. He sang the Billy Paul classic with an admiring leer at his non-existent reflection. "*Me and Mrs. Jones, we—* You know, as a grammarian, that wording should really bug you."

"Okay, Tex."

"Would you look at that? It's not just any man can pull off a robe and jaunty ascot with this much flair, Cal. I'm just sayin' it's a shame you want to put an end to all this."

I snorted at his hubris. "Boy, I definitely broke the mold with you, didn't I? What's with the giddy mood?"

"What? We're in New York again, and Bernard is going to be right as rain. What's not to be giddy about?" Tex leaned against the sink counter. "You stress out over the littlest things."

"A heart attack? A heart attack is a little thing?"

"No. You're right. I'm sorry." Tex bowed his head, chastised. "I wish you didn't worry so much, Cal."

"We can't all be Mr. Cool-as-a-Cucumber, Commander."

"That's why you need me. Because you're always as nervous as a nun in a cucumber patch." Tex's sayings tended to make me laugh out loud. "Now, there's that laugh I love to hear."

"Time to go, Tex."

Standing upright, Tex moved as if he planned to untie his robe.

"*Don't* even think about it, mister." I shooed him out of the bathroom. My visitor huffed and exited through the pocket door.

A second later, a muscular, bare arm reached in to hang the robe on the hook inside the entry. I cleared my throat and sank deeper into the suds to enjoy my bath.

5

I enjoyed an excellent night's sleep; then again, I always slept well. Since infancy, my ability to fall asleep fast and stay that way for at least eight hours had been a blessing. When a flicker of a dream caught my breath, the room got warmer, but I shook off the passing fantasy, relieved I'd be *walking* today—no need for town cars or handsome, albeit evidently, inexperienced drivers.

Determined to remain barefoot for as long as possible, I padded around shoeless, picking at my breakfast while I enjoyed my complimentary newspaper. So much better than reading news on a screen. A single crocus decorated the tray, the deep purple petals barely hiding the stamen's bright yellow-orange. A reminder of impending springtime. That notion prompted a smile at the same moment a New York City Public Radio announcer droned something about the coming weekend and snow. I ignored it. My return flight to Charlotte took off on Friday.

I poured another half cup of coffee, squinting at the Louboutins that taunted me from my closet. In a moment of self-aggrandizement, I wondered if I had what it takes to make a pair of Nikes more fashion-forward than frumpy. I shrugged, reasonably confident I didn't.

The morning trek across Madison Square cleared my head as I prepared for the difficult conversation about to take place. At least that was the intent. From the outside, it was a regular meeting.

Every month or so, Celeste and I met up, Laney always keeping guard. We'd talk numbers and plot lines, deadlines and cover art, the mutual hand-holding that assured everyone the well-tuned production line still churned out the beloved product. But today Celeste would learn the factory was shutting down. And while I had dreams of reinvention, there was no guarantee the savvy Celeste and Watermount would be on board. Still, dueling driver images rattled me: a poor pale Bernard versus a certain confident grin accompanying sexy, dark blue eyes that had no business interfering with the day's agenda. A mini-groan whimpered out of me, and I redoubled my efforts to focus.

Watermount Publishing was a relatively small publishing house with a broad mix of books and a fast-growing market share. With seventeen imprints, they issued both fiction and non-fiction. The firm had been a welcoming environment from day one for my genre-bending *Tex Miller* saga of a romantic adventurer who liked to leave you in suspense in settings all over the world. And despite the enormous sea-change in the industry over the last twenty-two years, Watermount and I stuck together. It was home. Plus, they obliged me in wanting to live that anonymous life Bernard so eloquently mentioned. The book world landscape continued to morph, but Watermount remained steadfast, and so did I. Both of us made concessions along the way, but in the end, it had been lucrative for all involved. Unfortunately, we might have reached the end of the road.

Snippets of my airport conversation with Tex played in my brain.

Him: *"Wasn't I good to you? Didn't I provide for you? Make first-class possible?"*

Laney Li, my literary agent, could say the same.

Me: *"We had a good run. Let's give credit where it's due. I'm sorry it had to end like this."*

It's so damned convenient when a writer can reuse her words.

I caught my reflection in the polished brass-framed doors of Watermount Publishing's building, the portal to whatever I had to confront next.

I remembered the first time I stepped off the elevator, a wide-eyed twenty-four-year-old, without a clue. The first face I saw belonged to Laney Li. My agent was ten years my senior, and smiling did not come naturally to her, but that day, she showed off her version of ear-to-ear.

"Are you breathing? You need to be breathing. Breathing is important in these types of meetings. Other meetings—not so much, but the first one—"

"I'm breathing, Miss Li," I interrupted.

"Call me Laney or Laney Li, never Miss Li." She pulled her focus from her pager. "Relax. Today is just about them seeing you, your face, and how they can sell it with the book. You look great, by the way."

"Oh, no. Thank you. But I have no intention of—I can't—won't sell my face today—or any day. Please, I just want to sell my book."

"I don't understand. Why don't you—"

"It's too personal. My writing. It's personal and sad and I don't—I can't share that with anyone but Tex—I can't share that." The still-grieving child inside me was incapable of imagining such a public thing while the inexperienced (barely) young adult had no interest in gaining any sort of notoriety. The speed at which everything changed only made matters worse and my oblivious resolve more stringent. I didn't know what I didn't know, but if I could control one thing, if I could claim authority over any aspect of my life careening off its rails, I would cling to it as long and hard as I possibly could.

"What about interviews?"

"No. No interviews. God no. They'll want to know about the inspiration. Probably ask about my parents, my past, my process." My panic grew. "No. Absolutely not. None of it. I don't want any of it, Miss—I can't. None of it, Laney Li."

Laney didn't offer me comfort or try to change my mind. She simply stared past me and her *mind went to work. "Never sell your face?"*

"Never." I lifted my chin to steady my breath, hiding my fear. "I'm afraid I have to insist."

"Like never *ever?" Laney's brain went into overdrive, and that marked the end of my contribution to the conversation. "Interesting," she said, but not to me. "What a wild angle. No public persona. Huh. I can work with that." She paused. "Yeah, I can work the* hell *out of that." And a plan took shape, a plan that took on a life of its own, and quickly erased mine. I couldn't have been more relieved.*

Watermount Publishing occupied the top two floors where offices and conference rooms filled the bulk of the space, plus a beautiful lobby and reception area designed to make visitors feel like they were some place special.

On the ground floor, I climbed a short flight of stairs to a familiar small conversation spot, a potted palm, and the elevator that would deliver me to the publisher's penthouse, but a fresh addition joined the scene. A young, sandy-haired woman smartly dressed in a pinstripe skirt, a crisp collared-shirt, and tie under a cashmere sweater sat in one of the leather club chairs, arms and legs crossed, with her chin resting on her chest. The low hum of a snore buzzed. I had a feeling she might be there for me. Inspiration struck. A stall tactic. I pressed the call button.

When the elevator doors opened, a sharp grunt behind me said my lobby companion woke. "Oh, shi—" the young woman murmured. "Um, Miss Austin? Are you Miss Austin?"

Without turning around, I replied, "I am, but by all means, don't let me disturb your naptime."

"I'm sorry. I've been here, waiting—the better part of an *hour* for you."

Her blunt reply surprised and maybe amused me. "I'm sorry to have put you out..."

"Elsie. My name is Elsie Murray," she tried to back-pedal—a little. "And no bother, but my boss insisted I greet you upon arrival. You must be someone important."

"And you, Elsie Murray, must be new." I took in her freckled face and sharp eyes that seemed to play opposite to one another. A sweet, naïve optimism camouflaging an eagerness to prove her smarts—and fast. "Let me guess. Celeste's new intern? First week? No, you're exhausted. Must be week two."

"Yes, ma'am." Her jaw clenched. "On all counts."

I let the *ma'am* thing slide. Her mental self-flagellation read clearly. I sympathized with her. The challenges she faced as a young female in this city and this industry were no joke. "Don't fret, Elsie. Your on-the-job-snooze-secret is safe with me. Here." I pulled a twenty-dollar bill from my wallet. "Go get me a venti, nonfat, no whip, double-shot, white chocolate mocha, extra hot. Get yourself something too. You'd be wise to make it caffeinated."

"Sure, but I need to see you to my boss first."

"Elsie," I tsked. "Don't tell me you've already forgotten how important I am."

The poor kid blanched.

"I'm joking. Relax. I've got you covered. Hurry, though." I spun her to face the exit, and the dubious intern took slow steps toward the stairs. When she glanced back at me, I gave an enthusiastic thumbs up and shooed her away as I stepped into the lift. The doors closed between us.

"That was nice."

"Jeez, Tex! Don't sneak up on me like that." It shouldn't have surprised me to see my fictional hero. Showing up when I got out of sorts was kind of his thing. And his thing was happening a lot lately. "And I *am* nice."

"Yeah, but it was generous to give the kid a break. Allow her some fresh air, a chance to stretch her legs, not to mention buying her coffee. But since I *did* mention it—who's the mocha for? Not you." Tex leaned in the corner, relaxed in jeans, Allen Edmonds shoes, and a button-down under a leather jacket.

"You know it's for Laney Li. A peace offering."

"Aw, why? Did you two have a fight?" His tone sounded more snide than concerned.

"No, but we're about to." Unable to stall any longer, I pressed the button for the top floor. "And I need you to stay out of it. Hey, why no tux today?"

Tex pinched the bridge of his nose with a huff. "It's like you don't even know how this works. You're the one who—"

"Yeah, yeah. I know. It's just you look so good in a tuxedo. I guess I wanted one last glimpse."

"Callie, I look good in *everything*."

"See that? That right there. If your fandom had any idea the ego behind your rakish good looks, unassuming intelligence, your charming wit, no way they'd love you as much as they think they do now. *Hm.* That gives me an idea..."

"Oooh. Plot twist. Love it. Care to share?"

"Aw, Tex. It's like you don't even know how this works," I parroted. "You'll find out. And you just might wish you had it as easy as page 437. Now scram," I yipped the last bit louder than I meant as the elevator opened. I swatted over my head. "There's a fly in here," I declared to the puzzled receptionist. With a glance, I was pleased to see Tex had followed instructions, at least for the moment. "Callie Austin here to see Celes—"

"Callie," Laney bounded from her seat on a long sofa of tufted, burgundy velvet, her ever-present phone in hand. Much like all-consuming social media, having my eyes, ears, and thumbs glued to a phone never interested me. Luckily, I had Laney to keep me in the know.

"Laney. Why are you out here? Has our meeting changed?"

"No. I just thought maybe we should have a minute." Her deceptively slight frame rose to kiss my cheek, but her petite stature was a feint. Laney Li was a force, and if you didn't know it, the razor cut of her unexpected platinum bob served as first warning, even before she opened her acerbic mouth. "We good?" She gritted in a whisper directly into the brunette waves at my ear. "Maybe a quick powder before—?"

"Relax, Laney. Everything's gonna be fine. Just because Tex—"

"*Tsh, tsh, sh,*" Laney interrupted, waving her hand across her throat. "Not here," she mouthed. "Madison," my agent snapped at the receptionist. "We're going to the restroom."

In the publishing world, knowledge equaled power, and well-trained front desk personnel tuned in to all conversations from their small spot in the Watermount realm. That "spot" comprised a raised mahogany counter that gleamed under warm halogens. Hard to say how many skills any of those young people learned, since, whenever I came to the office, a brand new receptionist held the post. The turnover surprised me, but old receptionists often became new assistants hoping to climb the ladder from there.

Laney's brute strength dragged me down the plush carpeted hall to a unisex bathroom. Once inside, my anxious agent slammed open each stall door to be sure we were alone.

"Are you okay?" Her tenor sounded like genuine worry. "Is Bernard? That must have been scary—for you."

"Yes, he's the closest thing I've had to a father since I was a kid. Of course, until yesterday, I didn't know if he knew who or—what I am, but there you go. But yes, I'm fine. And I'm sure he will be too."

"Good. Glad to hear it." In one breath, Laney's attitude turned one-eighty. "Now what the *hell* do you think you're doing?" Per usual, Laney didn't shout. She didn't need to. Her glower communicated more than any raised voice could ever hope to convey.

I stared at the agitated woman. Letting her seethe wasn't the most prudent choice, but other than reiterating the exchange between Tex and me, I hadn't planned a speech. Funny how you can't write both sides of the dialogue in real-life conversations.

"I'm trying to take back my life, Laney."

"Your life? Your beautiful, creative, private life? Your five-star hotel suite and downtown Charlotte penthouse apartment life?"

"Uptown Charlotte." My correction reflex slipped.

"What?"

"It's *Uptown* Charlotte. Downtown Chicago. Midtown Manhattan. Uptown Charlotte. And yes. That life. I love you, Laney. You're the *little* big sister I never had, and I appreciate all you've done for me, and that's been a lot, but just because I don't want to write about Te—"

"*Tsh tsh sh!*" Laney's hand sliced at her throat again.

"This isn't easy for me either, so I need my best friend *and* my agent to have my back in there."

"Dammit, Callie. You had to pull the big sister bit, didn't you?" Hands to her hips, Laney's softening face focused on the mosaic-tiled floor before sighing, "I've got your back."

"Great." We stared at one another. "Now what? Hug it out?" I opened my arms to welcome her.

"In twenty-two years, have we ever hugged?"

"Not even once, Laney Li."

"Well, we sure as *hell* aren't starting today."

As she spoke, a timid knock tapped on the door, followed by the muffled low-pitched summons of Intern Elsie. "Ms. Austin? Shi—. Are you in there?"

Laney yanked open the door, startling poor Elsie with the force of it.

She almost swore again. "You're not Ms. Austin."

"Not by a lot, kid. You in the habit of knocking on doors clearly labeled for you to enter?" Laney pointed to the unisex sign. She enjoyed providing a teachable moment for young professional women.

"No. Are you in the habit of hijacking clients to hide behind—"

"*Hey*, Elsie." I couldn't interrupt fast enough. "I'm here. And we haven't seen your boss yet. You got something for me?"

Elsie thrust the venti cup in my direction.

"Hand it to short stuff there. She needs it." With impressive defiance, Elsie kept direct eye contact with me and handed the cup to Laney.

"Give us a minute, Elsie." Laney let the door glide to a close in the intern's face. "I like her," she mouthed with admiration.

No surprise. Gumption appreciates gumption. "Nonfat, no whip, double shot, extra hot," I informed her. "Now, you wanna hug me, don't ya?"

"If there was bourbon in it, I might—Nah. Still not a hugger. You ready?"

"I'm ready."

Laney opened the door again. The intern hadn't left her perch just across the restroom threshold. I couldn't help but chuckle at her moxie. Trying to channel my inner-Elsie, shoulders back, chin lifted, I followed her and Laney to a posh conference room.

The inside wall of frosted glass had the words "Watermount Publishing" etched in the center, and, in smaller font, the names of the imprints surrounded it. The impressive view out the opposite window wall was high above Madison Square Park. A dark inlaid table sat at the center of the room, anchored on each end with floor to ceiling bookshelves lit to display the company's decades of publications. A mid-century Sputnik-inspired, muted brass fixture highlighted a tray holding a Waterford crystal pitcher of water and matching glassware. Cut-glass gleamed center stage on the enormous table surrounded by cushy high-backed leather chairs. I loved the smell of this room. Something about the combination of books, furniture polish, and Chanel No. 5 elated me. I don't know who wore it, but she—or he—had been wearing it since long before I ever got there. It was intrinsic to the environment, part of the atmosphere, and very much a harbinger of good things.

"Callie. Welcome. Can we get you anything? Fizzy water? Cappuccino?" The greeting came from Celeste, my editor. Celeste had started as a brand-new intern about the time I first stepped off the elevator. After ten years of ascending the ranks, she became a full-fledged editor and took over for Charles Watermount, my original editor, who signed me all those years ago. He took a monumental chance giving me a shot, and I will always be grateful for the opportunity he made available to me. More so, that he let me do it my way. Celeste is a couple of years my junior and a dynamo darling in the publishing world, but we have never quite seen eye to eye. Still, with Laney's big-sisterly (some might say barracuda-like) help, we have managed a fruitful relationship for nearly twelve years.

Whenever I visited the office, the meetings began the same way. Celeste, with her jet-black pixie and Givenchy power suit, offered me fizzy water or cappuccino, and I'd say, 'I'm good, Celeste. Thanks,' and the meeting commenced. I loved a ritual.

"I'm good, Celeste, thanks. Your Elsie has been so accommodating. Most promising intern I've met in my twenty-two years here. You'll want to take good care of her. She just screams '*poachable*.'" I winked as the blush bloomed on the fair-skinned, barely twenty-something, but noted a hardly perceptible nod and took it as thanks.

Celeste pursed her thin lips, letting the insinuation slide. "Then let's jump right in. We have some rather exciting news to share."

"Oh, so do we," I countered, "but, please, you go first." I didn't intend to antagonize the woman but needed to shore up my position before dropping the end-of-Tex news.

"Great. So we are all aware of the changing paradigm that is the publishing world. So many platforms now and all types of media linking arms and collaborating in myriad ways. We're always looking for new, exciting projects that might benefit our current clients and draw in new ones. I find myself at multiple social engagements weekly, it seems, meeting execs in all aspects of media."

Laney fidgeted in her chair, an uncharacteristic state for her.

Celeste continued. "A few weeks ago, I met someone from The Luna Network. Are you familiar?"

Laney cleared her throat in an exaggerated cough.

"Sure. Some sort of television channel, right? Like HBO? Movies, but with their own programming too. And an app, I think. Though they probably all have apps nowadays, I imagine."

As my attempt to appear informed fizzled, Laney coughed again. I reached for a glass and the pitcher to pour water and slid it to her with enquiring eyes.

"Exactly, Callie. Cut to the chase; they are looking to go big. They want to compete, and they are ready to throw *a lot* of money into a new production of a multi-episode, multi-season Luna Network original series, *Tex Miller*."

"Jesus H. Christ. That's it. Meeting over." Laney flew to her feet. "This is not how this is done, Celeste, and you know it. Any proposals for my client go through my agency and me. Those prepared to create the product should present their offers. Not some proxy. This is a book publishing house where you publish my client's *books*. I vet any and all discussions regarding other production avenues first and present them to my client when and how I see fit. My agency has its own books-to-film resources. I'm not sure what the intent behind this ambush is, but it's amateur hour. Let's go, Callie."

Laney walked out while I scrambled to my feet. Grabbing my bag, I gave an amused, wide-eyed Elsie a sheepish wave and trotted after my agent, who waited for the elevator. The doors opened. Tex reappeared, wearing his mostly unbuttoned tuxedo shirt. The suit coat hung on one arm, and he still wore jeans, but no shoes, with his curly locks wildly disheveled like the rest of him. His expression begged, "*What the hell?*"

"Don't say a word," I blurted at him before I could catch myself.

"Oh, I wasn't planning to," Laney said, then took a long draw on her mocha and stepped onto the elevator. I followed.

We descended in silence except for the clicking sound of Laney's red-tipped fingernail tapping the screen of her iPhone. Faster than the seconds on a clock, the ticking warned of the impending detonation of a bomb. I feared the explosion was a foregone conclusion, but the exact moment of the boom was uncertain, as was the size of the blast radius—new Laney Li territory.

"Would you like to go to The Bar?" I dared to ask on the sidewalk outside Watermount's building.

"Which bar?" Laney's face was back in her phone.

"The Bar, that's the name of the bar at my hotel."

"That's right. I remember. Wow. They really flexed their creative muscle on that one. How's the food? I'm ravenous."

"It's excellent. British cuisine."

"Insert oxymoronic joke here," Laney quipped.

Relieved to hear her sense of humor was still intact, I sped toward my home for the week, eager to put a bit more distance between Laney and Celeste. The sun rose higher, but the temperature remained nippy, making the short walk a brisk one. The long, southern stride my five-foot-nine-inch frame afforded me proved inconsequential to Laney's five-foot Manhattanite version. I had learned a few habits in the twenty-two years of frequent visits to New York City, most of them compliments of Laney, but it never took long to slow down when I returned to the less hurried pace south of the Mason-Dixon. Truth be told, I loved both locales and knew my luck at being able to partake of both. Most of all, I enjoyed the good fortune that no matter where I was, Laney Li always had my back, all five feet of her. But honestly, that's all anyone would ever need.

6

We entered the hotel lobby from 24th Street. I stepped aside to allow Laney access ahead of me and took the opportunity to look for Tex in the late-morning swarm of pedestrians at the crosswalk. Sensing the precarious situation, he must have opted to make himself scarce. I never said he wasn't smart.

"Who you looking for?" Laney barked, more out of habit than anger.

"Me? No one. Want to stay in the lobby bar or head upstairs to the one attached to the restaurant?"

"Upstairs. Food."

"Right. Let me check on Bernard. I'll meet you in a few."

Laney never actually stopped moving. A shark to the core. She made her way past the flickering fireplace and up the modern curved staircase to the next floor while I made a quick call to Moira.

After learning all was well at Bellevue, I took a seat next to Laney at the bowed bar in the otherwise vacant wood-paneled room. I opted to wait for her to speak rather than provoke any harsh response. With her usual Scotch neat in front of her, Laney deliberately fingered her way through a bowl of nuts, eating only the cashews. In no hurry, I grinned, pleasantly surprised when the bartender brought me a martini without me having ordered one—just a little dirty, extra dry, with the requisite three olives. Exactly how I liked it. The fact the clock read before noon should have given me pause but remembering the morning drinks I downed on the plane the day before made me wonder if this might be my new normal.

"Thank you." I slid the glass closer with a nod to the barkeep. He simply gestured to my nut-sorting friend. Still, I waited for Laney to speak first and bided my time, taking a sip of my cocktail.

Laney's phone rang with the name Celeste popping up on the screen. My agent declined the call. Once upon a time, doing such a thing would have troubled me, but not today. I took another swallow.

"I love it when the little spitfire gets all *ballsy*, don't you?" Tex sat on the other side of Laney as I choked. For a time, a *long* time, Tex only came around in my solitude. These more public pop-ins were escalating, and he clearly enjoyed the mischief-making.

"What are you doing here?" Startled, the words tumbled out before I could stop them.

"I'm eating cashews and blowing off your publisher. What's it look like?" Laney replied but didn't stop her snacking. Tex laughed and smacked the bar, causing me to jump in my chair. "You okay there, Callie?" Laney asked, tossing another cashew in her mouth.

"Am I okay? Are *you* okay? Never seen you walk out of a meeting like that." I swirled my bamboo pick of olives in my glass.

"That was good, right? Dramatic?" Laney dusted salt off her fingers and pushed the cashew-free bowl toward Tex as if she knew he had taken the seat. Tex eyed the remnants with a wary glance at me. Laney emptied the glass that sat on the cocktail napkin in front of her and signaled for another.

"Bad. Ass," Tex exclaimed with momentary admiration. "Now, move these deadly nuts away from me before I go into anaphylaxis." Tex had learned of his peanut allergy in book three. It wasn't pretty.

"Yes. Very dramatic," I spoke to Laney, rolling my eyes at Tex. He grew more anxious by the second. "Jesus," I mumbled. "Will you hand me the nut bowl, Laney? Please."

She did, and I set it as far away on the other side of me as I could lean.

"Now what?"

"Now what? You tell me. That was your agent buying you time, oh author-mine." With a quick peek at the bartender polishing glasses at the far end of the bar, Laney lowered her voice. "You're the one who wants to put an end to one of the most beloved book characters of modern time. *You're* the one who is trying to kill the sexiest, smartest, most charming man any of us could ever hope to meet." She continued at regular volume. "And I say that as an aging lesbian."

"God, she gets me. She *really* gets me." Tex leaned back in his bar-height chair.

"Shut up." I meant the comment for both of them.

Laney loose her loud honk of a laugh and downed the second Scotch. If I hadn't seen her pint-sized body handle liquor before, I would be concerned.

"Seriously, what now? This isn't the first time someone has approached us about putting, *ahem*, you-know-who on screen. I don't think it's possible. Never have."

"Oh, I know *you* think it's impossible, and you have done your damnedest to cock-block any attempt at doing it with your 'artistic sensibilities.'" She air-quoted at me. "I'm sure you'll do the same this go-round, but I wanted to give you a minute to consider without Celeste putting any undue pressure on you. That was ridiculous. Luna should have made that pitch. And they should have done it through me. That's just facts."

It's true. More than once studios expressed interest in putting

Tex on a screen, both big and small, but projects never got off the ground. The reasons varied, and I may or may not have held some responsibility for a number of those failures. And as time went on, the likelihood of any movie or television production company finding success seemed less and less, much to my relief. Tex Miller stories were big and broad and took place all over the world, and their grandeur was a huge part of their appeal. Readers dove in whenever they cracked the spine of a Tex Miller book, and many remarked that work stopped, dishes and laundry piled up, children went hungry whenever the latest novel hit the market. It only made sense some other medium wanted to feed an already eager fandom. Multiple studios claimed the franchise would be a hit and several generous offers to make it come to fruition came our way.

One stumbling block was casting. In the early days, names like Hanks, Ford, Costner, Cruise, and more got thrown around. Later years saw some of those names again, but added, Damon, Affleck, Bloom. More recently, Heughan, Egerton, and *any* Hemsworth got tossed into the mix by Hollywood scuttlebutt magazines, blogs, and shows. As the creator of this character, you'd imagine my delight with a pool full of the aforementioned actors considered for bringing Tex to life. To be sure, the prospects were head-spinning. And by that, I mean nauseating, heart-palpitating, head-pounding, and stressful. The truth was, I didn't want it. No, I couldn't have it, and I put a stop to it, with the help of the barracuda who sat to my left.

Sharing Tex on the page was one thing. I took pride that so many enjoyed reading Tex's adventures but depicting him in any other way would only lead to trouble. No known actor would ever be all things to all people. No one who had previously filled the shoes of Indiana Jones or Forrest Gump or Jason Bourne or Thor could ever do the same for Tex Miller. At least that's how the scenario ran in my head.

No. Tex Miller would need to be plucked from obscurity. A *nobody* had to fill those shoes, but what dashing, intelligent, charming thirty-something with acting talent was still a nobody? Add to that, he had to be at least six foot two, blue-eyed, muscular, with a chiseled chin. And even if, by some dubious chance, some casting director found that man, what studio would back an unknown with the pile of cash needed to do the stories well? Mission impossible.

Laney's phone chirped again. This time it was a text, also from Celeste.

Celeste: *Expect a call from Jason Steinman at Luna. You should take it.*

Laney looked at me as Tex hovered over her shoulder to read the screen.

"You want my advice?" Laney asked, fully capable of keeping her thoughts to herself if I said no. Tex gave an exaggerated nod.

"Of course." I stirred my martini, then slid the first salty olive off its sword and chewed.

"You're in town. Take the meeting if Mr. Steinman can do it this week. That lets us know how serious Luna is. Listen to what they say. Hear their demands, counter with yours." She moved in closer, speaking softly again. "Like all the other times, we'll go in as representatives for the talent they will only know as your pen name Calliope Jones. We'll be there on a fact-finding mission to report back to Ms. Jones, so there's no pressure in the room. We walk away, and I'll call them shortly afterward with a 'thanks, but no thanks.'"

"Field triiiip!" Tex hollered with a slap to the bar again, making me slosh my drink.

"You're not invited," I scoffed, mouth full of another olive. Why did I let Tex provoke me?

"Invited? Of course, I'm invited, Callie." Laney gave the bartender the international sign for 'check, please.'

"Right, of course. Just—testing you." I finished my drink with a glare at Tex.

Laney looked at me sideways. "What's with you today?"

"Didn't we say we were eating? Your cashews and my olives hardly constitute a meal."

"God, no. They're holding a table for us in the restaurant. Let's go eat and see if this Mr. Steinman—" Laney's phone rang. "Well, well, the devil's got ears. Laney Li," she answered. "... yes, Jason. I heard you might call... sure, but my associate and I would need to... today? Two o'clock?" Laney's wide-eyes asked me for confirmation.

I gave a lackluster shrug.

"That works," she continued. "... No, don't send a car. We will find our way there. Just send the address. Two o'clock today. Thanks, Jason." Laney ended the call, shaking her head.

"What's wrong?"

"Probably nothing. It's just Jason Steinman sounds—eager. Don't stew. That's my job. But now I gotta fly to do a little digging before the sit-down. Sorry to bail on lunch. I'll meet you at the meeting spot. I'm sending a car." Laney hopped off her stool and kissed my cheek. "Don't stew," she reiterated as she trotted out of the bar.

Tex disappeared, too, and I returned to my suite to kick off my shoes.

Back into the day's version of devilish high-heels, I threw on my cashmere car coat and a scarf the graying skies told me I would appreciate. My charging phone signaled a text, and sudden butterflies reminded me of my agent's apprehension earlier. *"Jason Steinman seems... eager,"* Laney had mused with an unfamiliar headshake. A second alert pinged. Grabbing my mobile and bag, I headed for the elevator and my ride to The Luna Network.

It wasn't until I got to the elevator I read my texts. The first was only an emoji. A car emoji. The second read:

Drew: *And like last night, I'm not rushing you.*

I'd like to say the elevator's descent made my stomach flop, but truth be told, I had yet to get on the elevator. A blurred reflection on the brushed stainless-steel sliding doors startled me. His face wasn't clear, but the figure stood, a tall man, wearing a black suit, black cap.

"Why the hell are you—?" I spun in alarm.

"Wearing this *ridiculous* get-up? I have no idea. Part of the plot twist you mentioned, I presume." Tex leaned against a console table, arms and legs crossed, dressed like a chauffeur. A mellow ding announced the elevator's arrival. I entered it, giving my own gentle headshake. Tex vanished.

The lobby replayed a similar scene from the morning, but I paid little attention walking straight to the exit, searching for fresh air. Before I pushed through the glass door, I jerked to a stop at the image of a tall man leaning, this time, against the town car I knew was my ride for the day. Black suit, black cap, arms and legs crossed. My stomach lurched again.

I exited the building with a plastered smile. A clean-shaven Drew pushed himself off the car and flicked his cap's brim—a gesture I was sure he'd learned from mentor extraordinaire Bernard. "Good afternoon, Callie."

"Good afternoon, Drew. Didn't think I'd be seeing you again. I heard you had other commitments today." Something warned me to avoid direct eye contact, but that blue was too striking to ignore. A dark sea where I'd get lost. Drown, even.

"Ah. I just go where I'm told, and a Laney Li told me to come here. I gotta say, she was rather adamant." He stood stiffly at attention, hands behind his back. "At first, I thought she was your assistant maybe, but then the way she made her um, *requests*, I—well, now, I'm not so sure."

"*Ha.* Me either, Drew. Hard to say, most days. It's best to think of it as a partnership." I shifted gears. "I see you're wearing the cap today."

"Yes, I couldn't find one—it—*mine* yesterday."

"I see. Found your razor, too."

He rubbed his chin. "Yesterday started off with a—"

"Yes. Of course—" I waved off his explanation, not wanting to think about Bernard's medical emergency. I must have frowned.

"You don't like it? The cap?"

"On you? Actually, not so much. It doesn't really suit you." I shrugged.

He bent his head, slowly removing the hat.

"*Calliope Grace*, what is wrong with you?" I scolded myself aloud. "I'm sorry, Drew. I'm not usually so candid with strangers, but with you, it's like I have no sense of—"

"Manners? Tact? Basic social niceties?" His raised brow intimated the questions weren't rhetorical.

Tickled the young driver had the courage to admonish me, a

snort oinked out, earning a glimpse of his boyish grin. "I was going to say, 'no sense of when to keep my mouth shut,' but your suggestions work, too." We stood motionless in an awkward pause before I hurried to reach for the car door handle. Drew beat me to it.

"This feels like we got off on the wrong foot. Again."

"Two for two. Batting a thousand." I focused on the upturned toe of my shoe.

"What do you say we try again? Good afternoon, Callie." He opened the car door.

"Good afternoon, Drew. Love the cap. You should wear it *all* the time." I stifled a laugh and ducked into the car. After closing the rear door, my driver walked around the front of the vehicle, his hand in his hair, an obvious tell that revealed his unease. When he opened the driver's side, he tossed the black headgear to the passenger seat and climbed in after it.

"Calliope, *huh*?" Drew seemed determined to move beyond the rough start.

"What?"

"Your name is Calliope? Callie is short for Calliope?" We conversed via the rearview again.

"It is, but I never use that name. I mean—no one calls me that. Ever." The line of questioning made me nervous, and I chastised myself for the loose tongue.

"It's unusual. Greek. It means 'beautifully-voiced.' Ovid called Calliope the Chief of all Muses." Drew conveyed some pride with his Classics lesson. The baffling combination of charm, wit, and confidence that emanated from the driver grew more confounding with the added intellect. It was an unfair judgment, and I knew better than to articulate it, but the man's potential seemed like—more. His striking good looks didn't hurt, either.

Why did he choose this path? Or was it somehow chosen for him? The questions weren't unfamiliar to me, but in my wondering, our eyes locked a beat too long.

"Yes, well, my mom's side of the family has some long ago roots in Greece, but I was often told they named me for an obnoxious musical instrument that makes loud noises when you push hot air through it, so I guess that basically makes me a walking paradox," I countered with a cheeky grin.

Drew had a sweet laugh, genuine and infectious. I couldn't help but join in when he did it. "Well, I like it. It suits you. And you can take that any way you like, Calliope. Shall we?"

"Sure. Thank you, *Andrew*."

"No one calls me that, but my mother, and even then, that's rare."

"I could say the same, but my mom's dead now so—"

"Oh, I'm sorry." Drew turned his noticeably paler face to me.

"Don't be. It's been a long time, and I wouldn't be the woman I am today if she lived, so, without that, we'd have never met. Silver linings, Andrew." I opted to focus on the mounting traffic as I spoke his name again.

"*Hm*, is that moniker gonna stick?"

"I think so." I pointed to my wrist. "Tick-tock, Andrew. Tick. Tock." We pulled into Madison Avenue traffic, heading north toward Midtown. A few blocks past the park, we came to a stop in Koreatown.

"This hold-up shouldn't take long. I'll get you to your meeting on time." Andrew gestured to the map app displayed on the dash.

"It's fine. They can't start without me." I took in the city's mid-afternoon bustle rather than the seductive reflection distracting me from the lion's den I was about to enter.

"So, Calliope *is* the boss, then."

It was as if Drew—Andrew—sensed my need to focus on the work. I smiled, nudging my concentration to the imminent meeting. "Sort of, but today *Callie* is just the messenger, the go-between, so to speak."

"That sounds—confusing."

"Not most days, but sometimes, yes. Today? We'll see."

Andrew gave a curious look in the rearview, but traffic moved, so he redirected his gaze.

My New York visit was speeding by, having lost the day before to Bellevue. With any luck, this would be the only meeting with The Luna Network, but I also needed to have a serious conversation with Celeste. That wouldn't be an easy one. Add my visits to Bernard, and the obligations quickly usurped my time. I chided myself for including Bernard on my to-do list. Visiting him was no bother. If I had my way, I'd go to him now, instead of enduring this charade with Jason Steinman.

My phone rang. "I'm here, Laney. Pulling up now. Relax," I assured her as Andrew exited the vehicle.

"Just checking. Wanted to be sure your fledgling driver knew his way around the city. Any more word on Bernard?"

My car door opened. "No, but I'll see him later today." I reflexively took the hand offered me as I scooted out of the back seat. "And I'll see you in about ten seconds, Laney Li. Hanging up now." I ended the call. "Thanks for the lift." On tiptoes, I rose, kissing Andrew on the cheek. "Whoops. Sorry." I let go of his hand, taking hurried steps toward the building door. Despite my embarrassment, I turned back. "See, what happened there was—I always give Bernard a kiss on the cheek, coming and going, and I was just thinking about him and talking on the phone, and I was kinda on autopilot so... We can forget that happened, right?" My stomach rose and fell on the wildest non-elevator ride of its life.

"Sure," came Andrew's quick reply.

"Great," I sighed.

"Actually, probably not, no." His hand ran through those dark curls as he shook his head.

"Right. No hard feelings if you feel the need to get a sub for my next ride—if you're feeling unsafe with the *cougar* client. *Oh God,*" I muttered. Yeah. I just called myself a cougar. "I gotta go." Giving a hitchhiker's thumb over my shoulder, I spun on the heel of my Louboutins and bolted to the sanctuary of the building vestibule. Laney sat in the small public lobby near the bank of twin elevators, phone in hand. I pushed the call button several times in rapid succession.

"You okay?" Laney joined me, thumbs still tapping her screen.

"Ye*p*." The strained pitch and overstated plosive of my reply said otherwise. I focused straight ahead as one of the rundown elevators rumbled its way to retrieve us.

"Cuz, you don't *seem* okay." A tired *dong* chimed, and the doors parted a few inches, stalled, and then lurched to open. We climbed on board.

"I might have—just kissed the driver. It's *fine*." I gave an exaggerated wave, waiting for the lit numbers to show our ascent.

"Might have?"

I whined. "No—I did it for sure."

Laney pressed the door-open button, ducking her head into the lobby for a look. "The Baby Driver? You kissed the Baby Driver?"

"Oh stop. He's not *that* young, Laney."

"Sure. *Now* he's not that young."

"No, really. He's not, and he's—"

"Whatever helps you sleep at night, Mrs. Robinson." The doors squealed closed as Laney hit the button for the tenth floor. "And, to be clear, we'll be revisiting this topic *very* soon. But for now, I need your game face."

7

THE ELEVATOR DOORS JUDDERED open on the tenth floor. If stepping into the lobby at Watermount Publishing felt like arriving in some fancy, magical land that made you feel special, doing the same at The Luna Network was like getting hurled into a frat house the day after finals, but mere minutes before scheduled demolition. Tattered motivational posters papered walls of flaking paint in what could have been an ironic art installation. Ceiling tiles were missing, and the furniture looked second-hand, low-end, office-quality. Not a stitch of burgundy velvet anywhere. A pungent mix of burnt popcorn and coffee hung in the air, and certainly, no smoke detectors worked to warn us to vacate the premises in an emergency. My red-soled shoe stuck to the dingy, threadbare carpet, and I rolled my eyes as Laney raised one shoulder and returned her focus to her phone screen.

A lanky, young man in skinny jeans and a tight cardigan rushed us from an office down the hall. "Are you the decorators or the pitch people? By your *fab*ulous look, I'd guess decorators, but that makes you way early."

I took a deep breath, then coughed, regretting it. "We're here for the Tex Miller meeting."

"*Ah*. The pitch people, then."

"Well, that implies we are the ones pi—"

"This way, please." The greeter skipped away, yelling, "Jason!

The pitch people are here."

We followed to an open area where three mismatched sofas sat in an open-ended, square configuration. "Take a seat. Jason will be here in a jiff." Our host left us, heading back the way we entered.

"Is this a joke, Laney? Is Celeste punking us? Is punking still a thing, because this is—well, this is *excellent* work. Truly." I made zero effort to lower my voice.

"Hello, hello. Welcome to the war zone. I'm Jason. Jason Steinman. You must be Laney Li." The short and prematurely balding Jason shook Laney's hand with the rabid enthusiasm of an underdog politician. "Please, have a seat. And you are?" My arm got the same assault.

"I'm Callie Austin. I work with Ms. Jones."

"*Oooooh*. The enigmatic *Mizz* Jones." Skinny Jeans returned from the hall. "I swear, before it's all said and done, you are going to tell me *everything* about her... or him. I just *have* to know."

"Down, Cyrus. Don't pester the visitors," Jason hissed while sliding his glasses up the bridge of his nose. "And Ms. Austin, Callie, may I call you Callie?"

I nodded.

"As we told Celeste, our entire staff here will sign any non-disclosure agreement Ms. Jones would like to send our way. Whatever she wants. As a matter of fact, that is the phrase of the day here at Luna, NYC. '*Whatever Ms. Jones wants*.'"

"Oh, I'm sure that won't be necessary, Jason." I continued to scrutinize our surroundings, certain I could find the hidden cameras.

"Wonderful!"

"What she means is," Laney finally joined the conversation, eyes still glued to her phone, "there will be no need for any NDAs because we won't be telling anyone anything of any consequence about Ms. Jones. Not his or her name, not his or her location, not how he or she takes his or her coffee."

Jason stiffened and adjusted his glass again, while Cyrus ushered us to the dormitory-inspired couches, pouting. If I had questions, it was clear now, Laney would play the role of Bad Cop in today's little melodrama. This relieved me to no end.

"Okay, then. As I said, the key phrase here is 'whatever Ms. Jones wants' so while we walk you through our vision for this mighty project, please keep in mind we've set nothing in stone. We can be flexible, *will* be flexible. We want this venture to be how Ms. Jones would have it be so, whatever—"

"Whatever Ms. Jones wants, yes, we get it." Laney finally looked up from her phone, but then gave a passive-aggressive glance at her watch. I stifled a quiet cough to cover my amusement.

"So, as you can see, we are in a rebuilding phase here at Luna," Jason continued. "And when I say rebuilding, I want you to know we mean rebuilding at every level and in big, *big* ways. Better infrastructure, better programming, better bandwidth, better marketing."

"Streaming services are the wave, and we here at Luna want to harness the power of this tide and make a big splash." It was Cyrus' turn to speak, and his contribution included bright eyes and broad hand gestures.

I tuned out the men while continuing to explore the rehabilitation project Luna called home. It was a pre-war building with lots of character hidden behind added walls, grimy carpet, and water-stained acoustical ceiling tiles likely installed decades ago. Maybe The Luna Network knew what they were doing. Perhaps these young people could make a go at competing with the big kids at HBO and the like. Twinges of guilt seeped into my gut. Sure, we came to hear out their plan. I'd listen to their pitch, but it was a fool's errand for Jason and Cyrus. Nothing would come of it. And what was I going to do about the afternoon's Andrew debacle?

"What a *dump*." Tex stood next to the burned-out Mr. Coffee doing his best Elizabeth Taylor doing her best Bette Davis. I kept my composure. "Seriously, Callie, we can do better than this. Can't we?"

I eyed him warily.

"*Ah*, right. Just sit there pretending to listen to them while you're really thinking about... who are you thinking about?"

Laney's hushed tone pulled my wandering mind back to the meeting. "Jesus H. Christ."

Cyrus clapped his hands and bounced in his seat like a small child at a birthday party. Jason wore a broad smile, and all three of them stared at me. Jason had been speaking for several minutes now, and I apparently missed something important. My widened eyes implored Laney to say something, anything that would clue me into whatever slipped by my preoccupied brain. The silence quickly approached uncomfortable.

Laney cleared her throat. "And that's the production cost. Per episode. For how many?"

"Like I said, we just don't think you can do Tex Miller justice in your typical ten or thirteen. The saga of it all, the different locations. Sixteen is what we're thinking, but that's just for starters. So at $10mil per—"

"$160 million?!? To produce it?"

"Yes, well, season one," Jason clarified.

If I had been trying to mask my surprise, it was an epic failure, but in truth, I was too stunned to disguise my reaction in any way, shape, or form. I found myself on my feet, and Laney followed suit. The two men bounded from their spots of grungy, clashing polyester plaid.

"Well, this has been a most interesting initial meeting, fellas." Laney took charge. "Thank you for your time and for seeing us in such short order. We will relay this preliminary information to Ms. Jones. Let's be sure you send everything we went over today and any other thoughts, or ideas, to me—"

"Yes, to her," I added, pointing to Laney in an effort to appear articulate. Laney pulled me by the wrist toward the elevators while I tripped over an extension cord and collided with the corner of one of the decrepit sofa frames.

"Great shoes," Cyrus clucked.

"Thanks." I grimaced as I rubbed the knee I had bashed into the furniture. "We'll be in touch. *She'll* be in touch. Laney, that is. Laney will be in touch. Soon. Maybe. Probably." I forced myself to stop blathering, wincing at my unprofessionalism and the pain shooting down my leg.

Jason and Cyrus followed us to the exit, and in a moment of cosmic mercy, elevator doors jerked open as soon as I hit the call button. Laney and I hurried on board. Per usual, Laney kept her face in her screen while I gave an inappropriate thumbs-up as the doors closed. Neither one of us spoke the whole jolting ride to the ground floor. Out on the sidewalk, the radio silence continued. I looked up and down the block, not sure what I hoped to find.

"You up for a little walk to the Club?" Laney asked while looking down the street. "Not a block and a half. That way."

We crossed 5th Avenue to head east on 44th Street.

8

LANEY LI WAS BORN and raised in Lower Manhattan, but for four years, she called New Haven, Connecticut, her home while she attended Yale University. The Yale Club was a private restaurant, meeting space, gym, boutique hotel, and more, available to any Yale graduate willing to pay the dues. The Virginia Club of New York found residence at the Yale Club in the mid-1990s. UVA alumni, prepared to pay the price of admission, had a home away from home whenever they visited with all the benefits of a Yankee Eli while being a Rebel Wahoo. Laney and I complemented each other in many areas of our working relationship, but our alumni connection was kismet. A private place to conduct clandestine talks with no interruption proved ideal for our often-secretive arrangement. There was also a super hush-hush women-only poker night. They met monthly behind a bouncer-guarded door with an ever-changing password for entry, but sometimes those feisty gamblers got a little too—well, Laney *loved* it.

We spun through the revolving door under the awning on Vanderbilt Avenue. After showing our requisite identification, we ambled our way to the Bulldog Bar. It was early for any sort of dinner rush, but we sought the quiet. The cocktails that came with it were a bonus. A taproom invited us, big and bright, with barrel vaulted ceilings painted out in antiqued Yale blue and gold.

We ordered drinks at the bar, then went in search of a discreet spot, somewhere out of the way of the after-work crowd that would arrive soon. Again, it felt way too early for alcohol, but my noontime martini was long-gone, so somehow I convinced myself a Bloody Mary qualified as a legitimate midweek, late-afternoon drink, and given the adventure of the last thirty-six hours, I needed it. Laney and I entered a large sitting room of white plaster columns, Palladian windows, and leather sofas with coordinating wingback chairs arranged in conversational groupings around the space. Laney gestured to a corner location to conduct our business just as I spied the back of Tex's head of dark curls as far from us as he could get. He held up a newspaper opened wide. As if anyone other than me reads a newspaper anymore. I rolled my eyes.

"What's that for? The eye roll?" Laney asked, as she made herself comfortable on the sofa.

"Nothing. I thought I saw someone."

"Who? That guy over there?" She gestured to the other end of the room.

"Wait. You see that guy over there?" I took the third big swig of my drink.

Laney sipped her Scotch. "You know, I'm not a woman who frightens easily. I can hold my own in pretty much any situation. I keep up with my Krav Maga. But you? This trip? You're scaring the crap out of me. Of course, I can see that man over there."

Snorting in my unladylike way, I plopped down on the sofa next to my agent friend. The gentlemen put down his newspaper but remained facing away from us. Laney held her finger to her pursed lips. I snorted again, already feeling the warm fuzzies of my drink. It was the second snort that made the man turn to see his disruptors.

"Shit," I whispered as I slipped down the smooth leather, but there was nowhere to hide. Laney's head snapped in his direction while he gave a tentative wave over the back of his seat.

Laney didn't take her eyes off him and, barely moving her lips, asked, "What's happening? Who's that guy? Why's he coming over here?"

Before I could answer, he spoke to us. "Thought that was you. I'd know that snort anywhere." Andrew casually folded the newspaper and tucked it under his arm. "Hi, I'm Drew." He reached down to shake Laney's hand.

"Driver Drew? Baby Driver Drew?" Laney's gaze ping-ponged between him and me.

"Baby what?"

"*Laney.* Yes, this is Andrew—*Drew*. He's been driving me, *uh*, I've been riding. No, he's been my chauffeur here lately." I sucked down the rest of my drink.

"*Uh-huh.*" Laney stared at him, her mouth open.

"Funny running into you here. You both Yale grads?" Andrew crossed his arms, almost dropping the newspaper as he did it. The fumble betrayed his effort to appear casual.

"*Uh-huh,*" Laney repeated her eloquent reply.

"*Oh*, no. Not me. UVA. *Wahoowa!*" I cheered too loudly with a raised fist.

"*Ah.* Well, I won't interrupt. Nice to meet you, Laney Li. Put a face to the name—and the adamant requests." He winked at me and I slid further down my seat, muzzling a laugh.

"*Sit,*" Laney barked.

I thumped her shoulder.

"I'm sorry. Won't you please join us, Andrew?" Her invite included an over-the-top hand gesture.

"Drew's fine. Really." He smiled at me and sat.

"I need another drink. Cal? What are you drinking, Drew?"

"Nothing for me, thanks. I'm—driving today."

"Of course you are. Back in a flash." My agent scurried off to the taproom.

My head swirled. Kissing my driver had embarrassed me. Luna's offer had shocked me. Add the guzzled cocktail and my Laney and Andrew orbits colliding at the Yale Club—wait. What the hell was Andrew doing at the Yale Club? After too much dead air, I gave an anemic, "Hi."

"Hi. I didn't know how long you'd be. And we didn't talk pickup strategy."

"Yeah." I nodded.

"That was my fault. I got thrown by the—"

"Kiss? Sorry about that. Again."

"*Nooo*. Perks of the job." Andrew bowed his head as his ears reddened. "You should have texted. I'd have been there quickly. I've got a nearby parking garage, so this was a convenient spot to wait."

"Convenient? So how is it you—"

"Sometimes, you just know one won't be enough," Laney interrupted me as she returned with a tray carrying two drinks for each of us.

"Are you celebrating? Was it a worthwhile meeting?" Andrew leaned back and crossed his ankle over his knee. Evidently, he planned to stay and chat.

Laney handed me a drink with a needling prod. "Yes. Tell us, Callie. Was it worthwhile? Are we celebrating?"

Making quick work of my second Bloody Mary, my eyes watered from the spice. "Let's not bore the poor man with our business talk," I wheezed through the potent horseradish and took another gulp.

"She's right. Tell me about you, Drew? Eli, I take it?"

"I am, been out fifteen years now."

Who was the enigma now?

"Good God. You *are* a ba—He *is* a baby. Thirty-five for me. L'chaim." Laney raised her glass.

I crunched on the celery stalk decorating my drink.

"Which college, young man?" Laney faked a business tone.

"Saybrook. You?" he replied, mimicking her feigned seriousness.

"Calhoun—I guess that's Hopper now." She corrected herself.

And with that, my agent and my chauffeur took off on a rehash of their university glory days. They got more and more animated talking about campus life, academic challenges, and something called Bladderball while I got drunk before four o'clock on a Wednesday. This was not how I saw the day going.

Thirty minutes on and my third Bloody Mary down, the restroom beckoned me. I considered excusing myself, but the newfound Yalie pals, engrossed with their nostalgia, might have forgotten me. I got to my feet but quickly found myself back on the sofa.

"Easy there, lightweight. I'll have you know, Drew, I have taught this woman many things over our twenty-two years of friendship, but how to hold her liquor isn't one of them. All good, Callie?"

I winced. "It's not the liquor. It's my leg." I pulled up the cuff of my woolen trousers, revealing an ugly, bruised, and grossly swollen knee.

"Jesus H. Christ. Is that from the sofa at Luna?" Laney sat her glass on the table, leaning for a closer look. "That's not good. Prop it up here. How did you not realize it was this bad?"

From behind us, Andrew trotted in with a bar towel and a plastic bag full of ice. I hadn't noticed him leave.

"Here." He knelt beside me, gingerly placing the makeshift ice pack on my knee.

I hissed.

"Sorry. We should probably get that looked at." Andrew grimaced.

"Oh, no. I don't think it's as bad as all that. I mean, I walked here. Remember?" I pleaded with Laney for backup.

"Yeah, you walked here after being thrown for a pretty serious loop, and it wasn't your first loop of the day, if you'll recall." Laney's head gestured to Andrew with exactly zero cunning.

"*Laney Li*," I shushed through a clenched jaw. Andrew chuckled from his spot on the floor.

"Get the car, Baby Driver. We're taking her to the hospital."

Andrew still held the ice to my knee. "You heard the boss. Hold this." He placed my hand on the compress. "I'll be right back, Calliope." He took off to get the car.

Laney's wide eyes grew wider. "Calliope? You told him—"

"No. Not exactly. Can we not do this now? Help me to the door."

"Jesus H. Christ."

9

Although not the closest emergency department, I asked to go to Bellevue. If I had to be at a hospital, I wanted to be where I could see Bernard. No one fought me. The effort to get into the car prompted a throbbing ache, and I was glad for the three Bloody Marys that made the pain tolerable. Sobering up wouldn't be fun.

Laney darted from the car as soon as we arrived at Bellevue.

Andrew shook his head, arriving too late to open her door. "It's like you people don't even know how this works," he joked.

My head jerked back in surprise. "What did you say?"

Before he could reply, Laney jogged back to the car, pushing a wheelchair to make my transport easier on all of us. As she wheeled me away from the car, my driver hurried around to the driver's seat.

"Andrew," I called from the chair.

"Hey, don't worry, I'll find you." With a reassuring nod, he ducked into the car and pulled back into traffic.

"Okay," Laney grumbled. "There is much more going on here than I know about." And she wheeled me toward the building.

"You might be right, Laney Li." My goofy grin was short-lived as a searing pain shot down my leg.

The diagnosis? A hairline fracture of the patella. A cracked kneecap. This came after some considerable maneuvering by several medical staff, including a series of x-rays from every possible, painful angle.

By the time Bellevue finished with me, the sun had set long ago. To add to *this* lost day, I was sober, hungry, in pain, and all of that made me cranky. Emergency services had fitted me out with a knee brace, crutches, and a wheelchair, reinforcing any age insecurities with a vengeance.

"I hate to leave you like this, but I've got another client thing and I'm an hour late." Laney, a multitasking wonder, talked and texted at the same time.

"What? Another client?" I clutched my nonexistent pearls.

"Yes, dear. You're my most important and favorite client, of course, but there are others. Mama's gotta eat."

"Yeah, well, you'll eat very well if this Luna thing takes off."

"*Ha.* As if." Her thumbs stopped. "Wait, are you considering it?"

"No. Maybe. I don't know. Not sure this is the moment to be making big life choices."

"Knock, knock." Andrew shook the curtain of my less-than-private exam bay. "Laney summoned me, and just in time to save you from making big life choices."

"My hero." Was I getting too comfortable with the young chauffeur and our banter?

Laney looked at me with a furrowed brow. "Okay, you two. Get home safe. Take the pain meds, you'll need 'em. I'll check in with you tomorrow. Thanks for sticking around, Baby Driver. I trust your overtime pay is good." She kissed my cheek and disappeared through the curtain.

"You've been here the whole time?" I sat straighter in my hospital bed with a fleeting thought of lip gloss.

"I saw Bernard for a bit. He's better. Sends his regards. Made me promise to see you safely to your hotel." Andrew sat and glanced at his watch.

"I'm sure I can catch a cab. This is New York. Cabs and wheelchairs happen all the time."

"You have a ride. I promised." He dismissed my idea. "Does it hurt much?"

"Oh, it's just a hairline—"

"I know." Andrew held up his phone, showing me a long text. "Laney filled me in, along with all the instructions we are to follow tonight. Getting you settled in, the medicine to take, how many pillows to prop under and around your leg. My marching orders are long and detailed."

"You can ignore all of that. I'll be fine. Just as soon as they let me *outta here*," I half-shouted, leaning around the fabric enclosure. "Surely you have someplace to be. Two late nights in a row and your significant other might start to wonder."

"I'm kinda married to my work these days. Not much time for a social life."

"What? A good-looking guy like you?"

Andrew's ears turned pink in that way I'd seen more than once. "What about you? Is there a mister out there wondering, '*Now, why hasn't Calliope called?*'"

"Ms. Austin? Are you ready to blow this pop stand?" My nurse Nancy fluttered through the curtain, interjecting before I could reply to Andrew. "*Oooh*, hey, Honey." She shot Andrew a flirty glance, then gave me a big wink. "I didn't know your Boo had shown up. Hey, *Boo*."

Surely she wasn't serious. *Surely*, she saw the age difference and...

"Here's what we got." She read from a tablet. "Brace on the leg. Crutches. Wheelchair. Happy pills, but just a few. I see you refused any here, but if you want to sleep tonight, take them."

"Oh, I sleep fine."

"Up to you, but tonight and tomorrow is all you get. They're heavenly, but they are from the devil, and you're gonna want some food in your belly first." Nancy continued down the list. "Instructions. These are for Boo." She handed the pharmacy bag and paperwork to Andrew. "We've arranged a follow-up for you when you get to wherever home is. Unless you have questions, that's it. Get outta here. Stay off your feet, but with a Boo that looks like that, I don't imagine that's such a burden. *Mercy*." Nurse Nancy flew out through the drape as quickly as she had appeared, leaving both Andrew and me a little redder in the face.

10

BY THE TIME THE town car pulled up to my hotel, my knee ranked a good eight and a half on the ten-point pain scale. I didn't know how I would get to my suite or how I'd manage once I did. But I knew the effect pain medication had on my mother, so the idea of taking any felt like a non-starter, but I doubted whether I'd sleep without some relief. My lifelong ability to sleep whenever and wherever never included a broken bone. I didn't relish the new role of damsel in distress, and to call me irritable may have been an understatement.

"Tofer is probably on the desk this evening. He can help me to my room. You really have surpassed any interpretation of your job description today, Andrew."

"I know Tofer." Andrew turned off the car ignition.

"You do?"

"It's good business for us car guys to know the desk staff, concierges, and valets of the hotels. Tofer, short for Kristofer, with a K, right?"

I gave a lame grunt. It's all I had in me.

"Calliope, I've got detailed instructions from two women who are far more intimidating than you, not to mention a promise to Bernard, so I'll be following orders tonight. I suggest you try to relax a little and get with the program." Andrew exited the vehicle and stepped inside the hotel to speak to the valet. A moment later, he removed my variety of mobility aids from the trunk. Leaning over the wheelchair push handles at my opened door, he made a serious but optimistic face. "So this next part—not gonna lie. It's gonna hurt, but we're doing it. Real fast, and then it will be over. Okay?"

I squinted at his encouraging face. "Alright, Andrew," I exhaled. "And to show you how much I appreciate your honesty, I'm not gonna lie either. Chances are, saying things like that to women is to blame for your lack of a social life. I mean, I'm not a hundred percent on that, but I'd guess it's not helping your game. Like—at all."

Andrew's chin hit his chest, and his shoulders shook with a laugh. His genuine smile was endearingly crooked and again, somehow familiar. "Did you slip a pill while I wasn't looking, Calliope?"

"Nope. I'm naturally witty."

"You are and then some." He reached into the car. "Ready?"

It was fast, and it hurt, but I felt relief, no longer confined to the car. When he wheeled me through the vacant lobby, only Tofer stood at the front desk.

"Ms. Austin. An Elsie Murray from Watermount Publishing made a delivery. I had it taken to your room. Mr. Statheros." Tofer gave a thoughtful nod to Andrew. "If there is anything I can do..." Tofer stood a little straighter, letting the rest of the statement hang as Andrew and I headed to the elevator.

"Thank you, Tofer," I said as we sailed by.

"What floor?" Andrew asked.

"Thirty-eight."

"Nice."

"I like a view. Statheros? Is that Greek?"

"Sure is."

"So that's how you knew about my name?"

"That and Yale. We Elis are just wild about Ovid." The doors slid open on my floor, and I pointed him in the right direction.

"3815." Panic spiked. What if Tex was around? I winced at the notion as I handed Andrew the key card.

"I'm sorry you're hurting. We'll get you some food ordered up so you can take a pill soon."

"I'm not sure I'll be taking a pill. Not a big fan of narcotics. But if I'm ordering up food, I'm ordering for two. It's the least I can do for all your help today. And I know I'm not as scary as Laney Li or Nurse Nancy, but you really shouldn't fight me on this."

"Thought never crossed my mind," he said, gently rolling me over the bump of the door threshold.

"Nice digs. You weren't kidding about the view." Andrew took in the skyline while he removed his suit jacket and rolled up the sleeves of his somehow still-crisp white dress shirt. "Where should I put you?"

My mouth went dry as he faced me, loosening his black uniform necktie. I struggled for my words. "Crutches. If you could—hand me my crutches. I'm going to change—somehow. Why don't you order dinner? The menu is there. I'll take a burger. Medium. The usual fixings."

"Sounds great. I'll make it two." Once I stood, Andrew handed me my crutches. "Would you prefer I go while—"

"No, there's a pocket door. Make yourself comfortable. There's a half bath if you..." I pointed a crutch in that direction. "I'll be back." I struggled my way to the bedroom and rolled the door closed behind me. Underestimating the thorny position I had put us both in, I bumped my head against the door frame in frustration. Crutches were new to me, and I dropped one trying to maneuver past the bedroom desk. It slammed against the furniture with a resounding *smack* of hollowed aluminum tubing. "I'm alright!" I shouted and hobbled to the bathroom to change into my pajamas. My modest button-up PJs and the oversized hotel bathrobe brought some relief, but my reflection showed the dark circles under my eyes, indicators of how my whole body felt. I washed away the day's grime from my face and, with an exasperated sigh, flipped the light switch and limped into the bedroom. The bed turned down, side lamps lit, I saw Andrew in my bed, naked, at least from the waist up.

"What the *hell*—" I closed my eyes tight while trying to keep my balance.

From the other room, Andrew called out, "Calliope? Everything alright in there?" By the end of the question, his anxious voice was just on the other side of the pocket door.

I opened my eyes to find *Tex* in my bed. "*Don't* come in! I'm fine. Stay out there," I hollered.

"Are you sure, Calliope? I can call for help."

"No. I'm fine, Andrew. Be out in a minute." I whispered to Tex, "You can't be here."

"*Ah*, yet here I am. You know what this reminds me of? Book three, or is it four?"

"It's four—" I knew he knew the answer.

"When the cheeky orangutan took off with my pants just as the deadly Russian arms dealer-slash-seductress—"

"Yes, the fans loved that part." I couldn't help but grin.

"The fans love *all* my parts, Callie."

"Go, Tex. Go now." I wobbled to the door with one crutch.

"What's going on out there, Cal?" Tex looked as perplexed as I felt.

"Nothing, and it's none of your business, anyhow." The bed was neatly turned down again. Tex was gone. I took a deep inhale and slid open the door. Startled, Andrew stood on the other side. Out of heels and slumped over my crutch, I observed his height. It wasn't often someone made me feel petite.

His shoulders dropped, and he exhaled at seeing me.

"I'm fine. The food here yet? I'm starved." A firm knock at the hall door sounded as I brushed by him and the Tex-induced commotion.

"Excellent timing." Andrew jogged to the door while I shuffled to the sofa. A young man wheeled a cart, and Andrew instructed him to set up the meal on the coffee table rather than the one for dining, so I could remain semi-reclined with my leg propped. I signed the bill but noticed Andrew slipped the man a stealthy cash tip. I didn't mention it.

Four covered plates sat on display, and Andrew noted my curiosity. "So whenever I got hurt, playing sports or whatever, my mom would always make me a sweet treat to help me feel better."

I smiled at his sharing.

"What? I'm the oldest and the only son."

"I see."

"Whatever." He shared his boyish grin. "It seemed appropriate here too. But I didn't know what you might like. If you're a fruity dessert person or a chocolate dessert person. So I got one of each." He lifted the two lids to show me a poached green apple tart drizzled with honey and a dollop of ginger ice cream, and chocolate almond mousse paired with a raspberry coulis.

"Well, I like both fruity desserts and chocolate but never together. I think chocolate mixed with fruit is an abomination in any form."

"Wow. That's a rather stout opinion about sweet treats."

"I have *stout* opinions about lots of things."

"This may come as a surprise to you, Calliope, but that is no great surprise. You ready for your burger, or will you just dive into the apple tart?"

"Burger, please." I sat back on the linen sofa cushions with an airy whimper.

Andrew draped a cloth napkin across my lap and handed me a plate piled high with a burger and fries. He took a seat across from me in an armchair.

"Help yourself to a beer from the minibar."

"How about for you?"

"Just water, please. Thanks."

He returned with a bottle of water for each of us and handed me one he'd opened, along with the bag of happy pills. The ache knifed my leg, and I knew a pill would be necessary soon. We ate in silence for a few minutes. The burger was tasty, but the meal lacked the charm of the previous evening's car picnic. Thinking back on it, I'd gladly exchange the knee pain for my sore feet from that night. I tore open the bag to get at the bottle. "Here goes nothing," and swallowed two yellow ovals with a gulp of water.

On the top floor, no street noise polluted the suite, something I usually appreciated, but the quiet that night was disconcerting. Half my meal left on the plate, my appetite was plainly gone. I waved off Andrew's concerned look. "Please. Keep eating. Eat it all. And let's talk. Distract me from the throbbing. Tell me more about Yale." *And how a smart, funny, hardworking, and God, oh-so-sexy grad found himself driving a glorified cab—Calliope Grace! Don't be such a snob.*

"I think you heard enough about Yale today. Your friend Laney is quite the storyteller." He took another bite.

"Thought that was my job."

"*Hmm?*"

I sipped more water with a shrug. "Nothing."

"You want to tell me about your big life choices? Your worthwhile meeting today?"

"*Ha.* It's funny. I came to New York this week to end a thing. Finish it. But it just won't die—like some horror film villain. Just when you think it's safe..." I twisted to see my bedroom door, afraid Tex overheard but saw no sign of him. My voice sounded a bit muffled, and my limbs grew heavy. A pleasant buzz rolled across my forehead, and a warmth came over me like a cozy quilt, making me smile. "*Hmmm.* Nurse Nancy was right."

"Was she? You feel some relief?"

"I do. Although I also recognize, a few minutes too late, of course, that I've put myself in a precarious position now. In a hotel room with a male stranger."

"Stranger? Haven't we moved beyond that? I mean, I hope so. Though I think it's way past time I confess—"

"Nah. I trust you. No friend of Bernard's would ever do a woman harm." I closed my eyes and breathed deeply.

"It doesn't feel very chivalrous to leave you like this." I could hear Andrew stacking dishes, cleaning up the remnants of dinner.

"Oh, you don't need to worry. I have my constant companion." My loosening lips and tongue got away from me.

"Yeah? Who's that?" Andrew's voice drifted from further away now.

"My pal Tex never leaves me alone for long. Like ever. *Whoops.* I shouldn't have said that."

"Tex? You mean Tex Miller? Didn't mean to snoop, but I saw some books on the entry table." His voice was nearby again.

"Those are for Maisie, the super fan. A gift. First editions. *Oh boy.* Don't tell me you're a fan too."

"A fan? I've read some of it. I know fans though, and they are—"

"Zealous? Fervent? *Rrrabid*?" I put some growl in the last

descriptor.

Andrew agreed with a chuckle. "They sure put the *fan* in fanatical. Let's just say you don't exactly strike me as being much like those—enthusiasts."

"Enthusiasts. *En-thoooos-iastsssss*. That's a funny word."

"I think it might be time for you to sleep, Ms. Austin."

"Ms. Austin? Are we back to that? *Uh-oh*, have I made you uncomfortable? Is that line of professionalism getting blurred, Mr. Statheros?" I floated now and couldn't open my eyes.

"Don't concern yourself with that. I'm a big boy."

"*Hmm*, I've noticed," I agreed, over-enunciating. "*Big* and *boy* being the operative words," followed by a gasp at my inappropriate chatter. "Calliope Grace! Can you just—stop—talking?" For a moment, I resented Andrew didn't bother to temper his laugh, but sleep was coming fast now.

"How about we see if we can get you into bed?"

A giggle, entirely unsuitable for a woman my age, snuck out of me. "Andrew, now you sound like Tex. *Hm.* Come to think of it, you don't just—" And that was the last thought I had before morning.

11

I woke to a knock at the door, but my surroundings baffled me. An extra blanket pulled from a closet tucked me into my spot on the sofa, and I struggled to piece together the end of the evening. The murky memory jerked me upright, compelling a howled expletive in pain. Flashbacks of the day before boomeranged, along with the agony in my knee as I hobbled to answer the door.

"Miss Sailor-mouth is awake," Laney spoke into her phone. "I'll call you back." She hung up. "Morning, Mary Sunshine. I'd ask how you're feeling, but I—and the rest of the thirty-eighth floor—just heard."

"What are you doing here?" I limped away to collapse on the sofa again.

"Oh, Callie. You little minx. You don't have to play coy with me. Baby Driver called after his walk of shame." Laney plopped on an ottoman across from my lounge spot on the sofa.

"What? Whoa. Nothing happened. We ate burgers. Talked."

"Alright. I know. But this lady can dream, can't she? Besides, Tall, Dark, and Youthful made it abundantly clear there was no funny business. I mean—and really. Like *that* would ever happen."

"What's that mean? *That* would never happen. *That* could happen. I mean, it didn't, but it *totally* could. 'That would never happen.'" Incredulous, I couldn't stop repeating myself.

Laney laughed her loud honk. "Settle down. I just meant it

would never happen because of your knee. You being in pain. That's why that would never happen. Sheesh."

"He called you."

"Just to say you were snug as a bug on the sofa. Kind of reminds me of—"

"Yeah, book one? When she gets the fever, and he stays late into the night until it finally breaks?"

"Yep. That's when I fell in love, you know. When I had to get your book to a publisher because I knew the rest of the world was gonna fall in love with him, too. Hard to believe it's been almost twenty-two years and twelve epic tomes later. What a wild ride, Calliope Jones. Thanks for letting me tag along."

"Hey. I couldn't have done it without you, and why are you talking like it's over? I haven't made my decision yet."

"Haven't you, though?"

"If there is one thing you've learned in our twenty-two years, it's don't rush me. I need a day. At least. Can you give me a day, Laney Li? I'm asking for one damn day."

She stood, repositioning the pile of pillows *someone* had placed around my injured leg. She had a look about her I didn't recognize. I wasn't sure what it meant to convey, but it made me uneasy. She cleared her throat and took my hand as she perched on the corner of the coffee table.

"I have no doubt I have been a good agent to you, for you. I've made some great deals, negotiated excellent terms. Hell, I have hidden your identity like freaking WITSEC. But I'm not sure I've been a very good friend. You've been unhappy for a while, and I didn't see it, or if I did, I ignored it, wished it away. And that was wrong."

My best friend rose, needing distance from the discomfort I knew this kind of heart-to-heart provoked. I could probably count on one hand the number of people who made it past the tough exoskeleton of Laney Li, but if you were lucky enough to find yourself among the chosen few, her gooey center might just swallow you whole. It wasn't something many got to see.

"I know we talk, play telephone Scrabble, and see each other every month, but when we aren't together, I have my wife and our cats and other clients and a very full life. But you? You go off to him, just him. And as much as we'd all like to think he's real, he's not. Which means you go off to something imaginary. Unreal. An intangible, and I think it's beginning to break you. Jesus, I think it's been breaking you for a long time, and I let it happen. You are one of the smartest, funniest, most beautiful, creative women I know, and you share it with no one... except you share it with everyone, but no one knows it's you. And I get why Calliope Jones wants to stay a recluse. But Callie Austin needs to find a life and share it. Get a dog, get a girlfriend, get a boyfriend, whatever, but something real, something tangible that can touch you back."

She returned to my side with a reassuring nod before she added the next bit. "And if you can balance that with Tex Miller, praise be and pass the gefilte fish. We'll carry on, and the saga continues. I'm here for it as long as you'll have me. But if that means killing Tex Miller—then we *kill* the son of a bitch." Laney squeezed my hand and stood. "This might feel like the moment where we hug, but you know that's not happening, right?"

"Yes, I know." My eyes stung, and my throat tensed in an invisible grip.

"Take the day. Take a week. Take all the time you need. I can handle whoever is beating down the door. That's my job, and I'm damn good at it, but I promise to be a better friend. Right now, take care of yourself. Call me when you decide, then we'll make a plan." She let go of my hand and walked out the suite door, letting it *clunk* closed behind her.

My head rested against the window wall, and I hugged a down pillow.

"You know I'm not the problem, right?" Tex relaxed in the armchair across from me; one ankle rested on his opposite knee.

"*The* problem? You mean, I've only got one?"

"No, you've got a few, but ain't none of 'em me."

"Don't talk like that, Tex. It doesn't suit you."

Tex groaned. "It's like you don't—"

"Like I don't even know how this works? But I do."

"Your Dad died. Your Mom died. Bernard almost died. The people closest to you die."

"Oh, but not you, Tex."

"Exactly. That's what makes me so great. I've scaled mountains and buildings. Jumped from helicopters and buildings. I've crawled through crumbling mineshafts and—*ahem, buildings*—"

I laughed.

"It's like that lady writer who solves all those murders. You'd think, at some point, everyone would stop inviting her places because people wind up murdered wherever she goes. Disaster follows me, but like a cockroach, I'm indestructible."

"You are a dashing cockroach, Tex Miller, and you saved my life. The least I could do is keep saving yours."

"What you need to do is start saving *yours*." And Tex disappeared.

I crawled off the sofa, not gracefully, but I did it. With the help of a crutch, jeans and a sweater made my outfit for the day. The Nikes I'd pined for most of the week completed the ensemble. And with my hair pulled up in a ponytail, it all made for a decidedly dressed-down day. I considered my options, but no question, I knew what I wanted. And who. If nothing else, Andrew Statheros was a mystery. A smart, funny, kind, and sexy mystery, and I needed to solve it. So, with the perfect excuse, I texted my new driver.

Callie: *Available today? If not, no worries. I think there's an app I can use.*

My heart thudded in the few seconds I had to wait for a reply.

Andrew: *Don't you dare. Give me thirty minutes?*

I smiled.

Callie: *Deal.*

While waiting, I autographed the books Elsie brought from Watermount and bagged them up again to take to Bernard for him to give to Maisie. I called the front desk for help to get to the ground floor. Unwilling to take chances with the knee, I kept the wheelchair and crutches with me, with hopes I'd graduate to only needing crutches by Friday. The young man who delivered last night's dinner knocked on my door to assist me. Loaded down with the bag of books and crutches, we arrived in the hotel lobby. Andrew hurried in as the bellhop wheeled me to the door and stopped short with a quizzical head tilt I couldn't decipher.

Looking squarely at me, he said, "I've got it from here, Cisco." He slipped my wheelchair attendant a twenty-dollar bill.

"Thanks, Mr. St—tatheros. Any—time." Cisco tripped backward with a flustered wave and stumbled toward the front desk.

"The tip I gave you Tuesday evening was for you, you know?" I teased with a gentle scolding.

Andrew hunched his shoulders. "I'm a big believer in paying it forward," he deflected, moving off that topic. "I missed the dress-down memo."

"Didn't you hear? It's Casual Thursday. You'll need to take that tie off if you plan to drive me around today. Tell your boss I insisted."

"Luckily, the boss is a big believer in the client always being right." He loosened his tie and undid his top button as he asked, "Sleep well?"

"I did. Thank you for—"

"Better safe than sorry." He dismissed my attempt at praise. "Where to today?"

"I've got a delivery for a Mr. Bernard Pierce, so Bellevue Hospital, please." I waved off Andrew's curious look as he eyed the tote of books in my lap. "They're just some books—"

"I know. We talked about them last night. They're for Mais."

"We did? I mean, yes, they are. For Maisie."

"Shall we?" Andrew wheeled me to the waiting town car while I tried to remember the content of our conversation the night before. I cursed the pain meds.

With another beautiful day, I couldn't believe my luck on this early March trip. Andrew asked about my knee and made polite chit-chat about the spring-like weather on the short ride to the hospital. I was eager to see Bernard and hoped to hear an excellent report on his condition. We soon learned the hospital planned his discharge for that afternoon, so we were lucky to catch him when we did. His color had improved, and the delight he showed when Andrew and I entered his room was more than any I had seen outside pictures of Maisie's big day celebrations. My heart eased to see that look of joy and the camaraderie between Bernard and Andrew. In my worry, I hadn't fully appreciated Andrew's concern for his friend but saw the relief in his entire demeanor now. It only spurred my growing fascination.

"What's in the bag, Miss?"

"Oh, just some books. For Maisie. I thought she'd like them."

"Not just books, Old Man. These are first-edition Tex Miller books. Ms. Austin must have some pretty good connections to get her hands on these." Andrew lifted the Watermount tote from my lap and placed it on a chair. He pulled out a book and opened it. "Whoa. And would you look at that? They're autographed. Maisie's gonna flip." Those blue eyes twinkled with an air of mischief.

Mouth open, Bernard's wary eyes moved from Andrew to me. "Yes. Very nice. Maisie is quite the fan. Thank you, Miss."

"No thanks necessary. Glad to do it, really—"

"Looks like a party in here." Moira elbowed her way through to reach her husband's side. Kissing his cheek, she grinned. "You look even better than you did this morning. Ready to go home, you old coot?" She turned her attention to Andrew and me. "Hey, you two. It's nice to see you. Here. Together. Sorry to hear about your knee, Ms. Austin."

"Calliope's been a champ. Hasn't slowed her down a bit," Andrew piped up, giving my shoulder an affectionate squeeze.

"*Calliope*?" Bernard and Moira asked in unison.

"*Ha*. That's my name. Don't wear it out." I sing-songed as a flush inched up my neck. "We should probably get out of here so you can get on your way home. I hope to see you before I leave town tomorrow, but if not, I'll keep in touch and catch you on my next visit." I hoisted myself out of the wheelchair to give Bernard a kiss on the cheek. "Take care of yourself." When I fumbled my way back into my transport, I caught a new look on Andrew's face. His easy, impish grin had vanished.

Bernard patted my hand. "Will do, Miss. Will do."

We all waved as Andrew backed me out of the hospital room. Heading toward the elevator, we encountered the nurse who had taken my pulse the other day. "What happened here?"

"Oh, I'm a klutz," I chortled.

She winked as we rolled past, and my heated blush bloomed

again. What could these people possibly be thinking? The nurse, Bernard, and Moira? My cougar client quip from the day before ricocheted and with it a pang of humiliation when I realized how ridiculous the two of us must look together.

Neither Andrew nor I spoke as we rode down the elevator and to the car parked at the south lot, the site of our Taco Tuesday dinner. The quiet unnerved me, but letting the traffic sounds and water splash of a nearby sculpture fountain fill the void seemed the safest bet as he wheeled me to my car door and opened it. Something had changed and fast. Surely, reality had hit Andrew, too. I pulled myself to standing but lost my footing, stumbling into the open door between us; he caught me under my arm in the misstep.

"So—you're leaving tomorrow?" He stood near enough that I had to crane my neck to meet his gaze. The sun shone behind his head, forcing me to squint to protect my eyes, while flashes of auburn sparked when it landed on his dark chestnut twists. He didn't look at me like I was too old for anything.

I swallowed hard. "I am. Yes. Tomorrow." It's not as if this was news to me, but I recognized my disappointment in saying the words aloud. "Tomorrow night, actually." But the addition didn't help. I ducked into the car to avoid the heat I'm sure I only imagined radiating from his stare, chiding myself for my apparent inability to speak in full sentences. Andrew loaded the wheelchair and crutches into the trunk.

"Where to now?" he asked from behind the wheel, speaking to the rearview.

"*Hm*. I guess—nowhere."

"What?"

"I don't have anywhere I need to be. I have the day off, it seems. Well, I've got a big decision to make, but... and Laney is with other... people today. You can take me back to the hotel. You must have other things to do. Places to go. People to drive." I took a sudden interest in the snaps on my jacket.

"Yeah, sure, of course." He pushed the ignition button and put the car in gear. We inched along in the parking lot until his abrupt brake-stomp stopped us. "*Uh*, no. Actually," he added.

"No?"

"Nothing pressing. A couple of stops here and there if that doesn't bother you, but—"

"O-okay," I accepted his offer before he'd even made it. "Oh, sorry. It's just I usually have time to walk about the city when I visit, but I'm not in the best of shape for that today."

The crooked grin reappeared. "I know just the thing. And it coincides with a stop I need to make." We drove up First Avenue, both smiling at the new plan.

My phone pinged with a text from Laney.

Laney Li: *Ok, not your babysitter, but Watermount sent flowers because of your knee, but the front desk said you left the hotel. A young man named Cisco confided a Mr. Statheros picked you up. A Mr. ANDREW Statheros. The plot thickens. I officially say DO everything I wouldn't do, you know, cuz I'm a fifty-something-year-old married lesbian. Then I want ALL the lurid details.*

I shook my head and emitted my signature snort. Andrew never looked my way, but I caught his chuckling reflection as he maneuvered through the Upper East Side traffic. In less than twenty minutes, he pulled into the entry of a parking garage at 76th Street and 5th Avenue, adjacent to Central Park, and hopped out of the car, waving at the lot attendant. Bending inside my opened door, he asked, "Think you can stroll the park with crutches alone, or do you want the chair?"

"Just the crutches, please." My pleasure at the prospect reflected in his face.

"You got it. I'll let you off right here and drive in to park. Save you some steps."

"You sure there's a space?"

He looked over his shoulder, then back at me. "Guaranteed. Let me grab your gear. Leave your bag."

Andrew jogged out, stopping to speak to the attendant. I couldn't make out the genial conversation, but it included a fist bump. He joined me on the sidewalk without his tie and wearing a leather jacket he'd traded for his suit coat.

"Friend of yours? Someone good for a car guy to know?"

"Yeah, something like that. Let's get into the park, and then we can take it easy while I tell you all about it. Those crutches might wear you out."

We crossed 5th Avenue and into the park. Andrew was right. Walking on crutches exhausted me, but I enjoyed the outdoors and the company. When he pulled a bottle of water from his coat pocket, he playfully pointed to the label showing "my" brand and opened it for me. I rolled my eyes at his teasing as I drank. When I said I was ready to continue, he pointed the way.

It wasn't long before we arrived at the bronze statue of Alice in Wonderland, depicting the Mad Hatter's tea party, a perfect resting spot.

"I love Lewis Carroll," I gasped when we rounded the curve leading to the sculpture.

"The Mad Hatter is supposedly a caricature of George Delacorte, the philanthropist who commissioned the work in 1959," Andrew explained.

"Wow. Yale has really paid off for you, hasn't it?" The detective in me dove right in as we sat on a bench to admire the artwork.

"*Ha*. No. This one I owe to high school. I liked the smart girls who read a lot. Bringing them here was a cheap date that scored some good points." He handed me the water bottle.

"Smart girls who read, like Maisie?" My question didn't include eye contact.

"No. Maisie and I never—well, no. Anyway, I thought you'd like it."

"I do. Very much." My suddenly dry mouth appreciated the water.

"Calliope, I've been trying to tell—" Andrew's ringing phone interrupted. "Sorry, work call. I need to take it. Excuse me." He walked away with the phone to his ear.

A young woman power-walked up the paved path, pushing a stroller with a toddler on board. The young boy kicked his feet and pointed, excited to get freed to play. He climbed under the giant toadstool, and using the smaller ones as steps, he stretched his arms and legs to inchworm his way to the top of the big mushroom that served as the tea party table. Proud of himself for conquering the summit, he stood to wave his hands overhead at anyone who might pay him attention. Getting satisfaction from me, he plopped on his bottom and slid down the polished slope of the sculpture, hitting hard on the ground below the three-foot drop. He did not land on his feet. Momentarily stunned, he took inventory to see if he was, in fact, okay. I held my breath. Deciding he was fine, he spun around and attacked the mushroom step stools to do it all again.

"Sometimes, it's best to let them fall," the young mother called to me across the way from her perch on another bench. "It's how they learn not to be afraid. The fall rarely hurts him, but never taking the leap? Well, who wants to live like that? Am I right?" That's when she eyed my crutches and shrugged. "Guess it doesn't mean you won't get banged up every now and again. But some scars will make you a more interesting character in your own story, won't they?"

"Are you a writer, by chance?" I asked, but sometimes we're just easy to spot.

"Guilty." She dipped her head.

"I bet you're good at it."

"I hope so."

"It won't always be easy, but don't stop. Don't give up."

"I don't think I could, even if I wanted to." She laughed, but it was the kind of scary truth that required laughter; otherwise, she might cry. I knew the feeling.

Andrew cleared his throat, and I blanched, wondering how long he'd been standing there. "Knee giving you trouble?" he asked, noting my wince.

I simply nodded.

"Plan B, then."

"What's that?" I asked.

"Let's get in a boat."

"A boat?"

"I know. Touristy, right? But you can be outdoors and moving and not hurting your knee. What do you say?"

"You're gonna row us around that lake over there?"

"Well, I could get some red striped t-shirt-wearing guy to do it for us, but then I wouldn't feel like a real man."

"Row on then. I wouldn't want to bear witness to your emasculation."

"See, now it was girls using big words like that in high school that got me to places like this in the park." He grinned when I looked at him askance. "Maybe not *that* word, but you know what I'm saying." He offered his arm to help me to my feet.

A weekday in early March meant rowboat traffic was at a minimum. Pairs of mallards dotted the lake, and the sun danced on the rippled wakes made by their fluttering feet below the surface. In warmer weather, the park attracted many more visitors, but at this time of year, it surprised me that this tranquil space existed in one of the largest cities in the world. I enjoyed myself and emitted a sigh.

"You okay over there?" My rower paused his stroke to remove his jacket.

"Are you kidding? This is the dream. A beautiful day spent with a strapping young man oaring me around a lake."

"*Hm*. Hard not to notice this isn't the first time you have referenced my—youth."

"I'm sorry." I inched up onto my elbows. "Have I offended you?"

"Offended? No, but it's disappointing to know you're ageist, that's all." He resumed paddling with a side-eye look full of playful arrogance.

I let go an uninhibited laugh. Worse than my snort, but I didn't care. "Ageist? *Um*, is that something someone like *me* can be about someone like *you*?"

"God, you have a great laugh. And, yes. Ageism goes both ways, you know. It surprises me how many rooms I walk into where people make assumptions because of my perceived youth."

"Oh, there is nothing *perceived* about it. You are young, Mr. Statheros."

"Well, I don't feel so young, and I know it's impolite to ask, so I won't, but I see little difference in our ages, if I'm honest."

"Liar," I tsked in mock-surprise.

Andrew let go of a full belly laugh, and I joined him.

"Seriously. I'll wager you aren't ten years older than me."

"I bet I am."

"So what? So when I'm eighty, you'll be ninety. It's just a

number."

I relaxed on a pile of pillows on my end of the boat. Eyes closed, I enjoyed the sunshine's warmth on my face with the intermittent quack of ducks floating on the cool breeze. "I'm just saying, I'm not sure your eighty-year-old self will enjoy being chased by a gaggle of ninety-year-old women at the old folks' home."

"And I'm just saying if *you* were there, I'd let you catch me."

I giggled like a schoolgirl from my reclined position. "Oh, boy, Tex. You are in rare form today."

"Tex?"

With a gasp, I bolted up and leaned in a combined motion that sent the boat topsy-turvy. The jostling rolled my injured leg into the side of the craft as water splashed over the hull. "Shit!" I grabbed my knee as the pain exploded.

"Whoa. You okay?"

The rocking subsided, but the damage was done. Choppy waves churned into the paths of addled waterfowl, squawking their displeasure as they fled the mayhem.

Whether from the pain, the undulating lake, or my embarrassment, nausea welled up in me. "To tell the truth, I'm feeling a little queasy. I think I'd like to get off the water now."

"I'll get you to dry land."

"Thanks."

The beauty of the day faded as we neared the shore. The sun dimmed, and the temperature dipped, both in a matter of minutes. If I could have blinked myself to the safety of my hotel suite, I would have teleported in an instant. Neither one of us spoke as he sculled to the dock. Andrew disembarked first and with a noteworthy show of strength, pulled me from the boat. Our bodies collided as I landed on one foot and caught a musky trace of his efforts. God, I liked it but hopped away. The quick-release put more space between us.

My crutches waited at the mooring, and the dock attendant handed them to me. "Did you enjoy your outing? So nice on a day like today. Not so crowded."

"Maybe a *little* crowded," I mumbled, then "Yes, it was nice. Thank you." I limped down the berth, unsure how to extricate myself from the mess.

Andrew hurried to guide me up the concrete stairs, but I refused his help.

"You're being particularly stubborn today."

I spun around, pointing a crutch at Andrew's chest a few steps below me. "Alright. Knock it off. I don't know if you think you're clever or what your game is, but I've had enough."

"I—I didn't say anything, do anything, Calliope."

"You didn't just—" I looked around. Other than the boat worker, no one stood near us. I put my hand to my head, dizzy.

"Have you eaten today? Let's get you a bite to eat."

"I can't, Andrew. I didn't bring my bag. Someone said to leave it in the car, and since I can't seem to speak in full sentences or function like an adult when you're around, I have no money, no credit card, no ID, no phone. What is with me?"

I hobble away from the dumbfounded man standing on the stairway. But with an abrupt stop, I swiveled to face him. I took a deep breath and hung my head. "And now, I've just yelled at my only way outta here in a demoralizing and very public way. Andrew, I apologize for my outburst. This really has been the most discombobulating week of my life, and I'm not sure why you drew the short straw and have to endure it, and I'm sorry. If you could, please just take me back to my hotel, and I will compensate you for your time and your expenditures for the last few days, and we—never have to see one another again."

With quiet patience and unexpected kindness, Andrew took two steps toward me, closing the gap to a more conversational distance. "Are you done?"

"I am."

"A few things then. On the plus side? You found full sentences again. And I'm not sure if there are any hard and fast rules about how an adult is *supposed* to function, so maybe lighten up a bit. And while I'm sorry you felt the need to yell at me—publicly—and that your week has been *discombobulating*, my week has been—pretty extraordinary, and on the not-so-plus side, the thought of never seeing you again makes me feel kinda lousy, actually. But if you insist I take you back to your hotel, of course I will, but not before I buy you a sandwich and or anything else you may like from this renowned dining establishment. I mean, it's a landmark. Not to be missed. I bet if we get a little food in you, we can chalk all this up to low blood sugar and not give it another thought."

Andrew put his hands in his pockets and waited for a reply, but I had lost my sentence-making skills again. I managed, "Extraordinary?"

With an eager nod, he replied, "Sure. What with my favorite tacos and the big tip, the out-of-the-blue kiss on the cheek, and the best burger I've had in quite a while, this week has been—aces." His frank tone made my head spin.

Opting for a simple, singular focus, I lumbered away from him. "Where are you going?"

"Didn't you mention a sandwich?" I called over my shoulder.

He skipped a couple of steps to catch up to me. "I said—other stuff, too."

"One thing at a time, Andrew. One at a time."

12

Boating on the Lake in Central Park predates the Civil War, but the landscape along the shore has changed through the years. The current version was thanks to Carl and Adeline Loeb. The Loeb Boathouse opened in March 1954, and the landmark restaurant celebrated its anniversary throughout the month, hence the early spring boat ride availability. With indoor and open-air dining, it was a favorite spot for momentous celebrations, romantic dinners, and afternoon snacks with kids for locals and tourists alike.

Well past any sort of lunch rush, a few tables lingered over drinks, enjoying the view and warmth on an afternoon that quickly cooled from the day's earlier mild temperatures. As soon as a hostess showed us to a table, I excused myself to the restroom.

When I exited the bathroom stall, Tex leaned by a wall-mounted hand dryer, legs crossed at the ankles, fingers in his ears.

"I know, I know. Inappropriate. But here I am." Tex shrugged, then took the opportunity to admire his non-existent reflection in a mirror. "Aren't you supposed to be meeting with Celeste or those Luna-tics? See what I did there? Luna-tics? Cuz Luna—"

"Yes, Tex. I get it. You're clever. And I know I have decisions to make, but I don't like to be rushed."

"Rushed? You couldn't move at a more glacial pace if you were actually made of ice." Tex snickered into his fist.

"Is that some sort of Ice Queen joke? Because I'm frigid?" I scowled while he arranged his chestnut locks on the top of his head.

"Just as long as we both know who's really making the jokes here, Cal. I speak the lines I'm given."

"And yet, so often, it doesn't feel that way."

"*Hmmm.* I'm not sure how that's my problem. Now you should probably get out there before *you-know-who* thinks you're doing something untoward in here."

"Like talking to an imaginary narcissist with magnificent hair and bad jokes?"

"Or that. It is glorious hair, though."

I hit the button to dry my hands, noting my playful ponytail and pink cheeks were a refreshing look, and pushed through the door to rejoin you-know-who.

Andrew stood when I hobbled to the table. He pulled out two chairs, one for me, one for my leg.

"Feeling better?" Andrew indicated my knee.

"Nothing like a little potty break to recalibrate. Yeah, and jeez, that's not something I should say again, like—ever. What looks good?" I opened the menu, relieved to have a place to hide, while I chastised myself for saying the word *potty* out loud. A moment later, a tap rattled the laminated tri-fold in front of my face. I peered over the top edge.

"Are you hiding?"

"Hiding? Me? From you? Maybe."

"Why?"

I set down my menu. "The better question is *what*. What is it you think is happening here?" I tilted my head, imagining a power shift with the posed question.

"We're having a meal together and not for the first or even

second time." He held up three fingers. "But I think it's cute you're nervous."

"*Ha.* Please. I'm forty-six years old. I haven't been 'cute' in a *very* long time."

"*Ah-ha!*" Andrew sat back in his seat.

"Cat's out of the bag. I'm forty-six."

"You said ten years. I'm thirty-seven."

"Oh, well, one year makes *all* the difference."

"*Excellent.* Kind of arbitrary, but I'll take it." He shrugged with his crooked grin.

"You are awfully self-assured." I folded my hands, enjoying the new dynamic.

"That's my Yale training."

"Training?"

"Yep, Yale drama."

"Really?"

"Yes."

"You studied *theater* at *Yale*?"

"Lots of greats came out of Yale drama. Streep, Newman, Foster—"

"I know."

"I mean, it's kinda known for it. It's a *good* program."

"I *know*," I reiterated with a nodding smile. "I'm impressed, is all."

"Oh. Anyway, one fundamental of acting is the improv, and the answer is always, '*Yes, and...*' You lean into whatever gets thrown at you. That and fake it until you make it."

"So, driving is just your day job. You're an actor." The puzzle pieces fell into place.

"Oh, no. I'm not an actor. Not anymore."

Hm. Maybe not. "What happened to leaning in?"

"Life. Life happened. And I leaned in a different direction." His focus returned to his menu, and I was sad to find our banter ceased. It seemed I'd crossed a line I hadn't seen coming.

"I'm sorry. I didn't mean to pry." I touched his hand across the table in apology. He tried to hold mine, but I pulled away, scanning the room to see if anyone noticed the exchange.

He didn't acknowledge my inadvertent snub. "Don't be. You mentioned you wouldn't be the woman you are today if your mom hadn't passed away. My dad's death, about sixteen years ago, did the same for me. And while I sure wish he was still around, I wouldn't change the outcome. I miss acting, though. I was good at it, but I guess I do a little acting every day. Hell, we all do."

A server scurried to the table. "Don't mean to interrupt, but do you care to order?" She only had eyes for Andrew.

"Yes, I'll have a hot tea, Earl Grey, please. And the grilled cheese with tomato-bacon jam." I handed her my menu while Andrew grinned at me and ordered the same. He shook his head as the waitress walked away.

"What?" I asked. Surely, he recognized the young woman's gawking.

"It's just I wanted the grilled cheese, but I thought if I ordered it, you might make another crack about my age, so I was happy you ordered it first. But I've just decided that jokes be damned. I'm leaning in. Which means we need to clear the air, Calliope."

My stomach lurched at his use of my name, and any chill vanished, replaced with the prickling start of stress sweat. He knew. He knew, and for the first time in my life, I was about to be confronted with my lie. Again, I took in the nearly empty dining room. Still eyeing my crutches, I saw no way to make a quick getaway. We were about to clear the air whether or not I wanted to, and at that moment, the best course of action was to get out in front of it.

"Okay. I need you to understand—" I jumped in to explain but got vetoed.

"No, please let me get this out because I never meant for it to get this far, and I've been trying to figure out how to—explain. Deceit was never my intention. Honestly, and Taco Tuesday, I tried to tell you, but then—I didn't, because then Wednesday wouldn't have happened, and then Wednesday night there were those happy pills, so that timing seemed bad. But I knew if I was lucky enough to see you today, I would definitely tell you, but then you said you were leaving tomorrow, and I thought, *What's one more day?*, except I knew that wasn't right. But every time I thought, *Now! Tell her now,* you would do or say something, or the phone rang, and I didn't want to mess up anything that was happening here, except I know nothing can happen here if we aren't honest. So, just to be clear, I did what I did because I enjoyed spending time with you, and I wanted to continue to spend time with you, which I now realize may seem kind of creepy. Stalker-ish?" Andrew finally took a breath.

"*Hm*, just how big a fan are you, Andrew?"

"What? Fan?"

"And how did you know? Did Bernard tell you? I know Laney wouldn't, but you didn't meet her until after Taco Tuesday, so..."

Andrew cocked his head. "I don't think we're talking about the same thing."

"Of course, Moira probably knows," I spoke over his last comment. "She could have said. She has no allegiance to me, but I'm pretty sure Maisie hasn't been told. Was it Moira?"

"No. It wasn't anybody. Well, it was you, really. Maybe a smidge of help from your pal Percocet."

"Me?"

"The way you talk. Your vocabulary. The way you mentioned his name. Your name. The books in the bag. I added two plus two plus two. It wasn't rocket science, but—"

"So you've known but just didn't say anything, and I've been riding around with you thinking one thing when things were really something else."

"Yes. And no."

"What does that mean?"

"It means, yes, I've known who you are for a while now, and I didn't say anything."

"And the no part?"

"I'm not a driver."

"What now?" A chill hit me. My inner-thermostat had officially gone bonkers. Confusion fogged my brain, and I wondered how I could have gotten everything so wrong.

"I'm not a driver. Yes, I came to pick you up that first morning because I knew Bernard was supposed to pick you up, and Bernard's talked about you since I was a little kid—whoa, okay, so, that there—not really helping my case. Let's—let's forget that last part." His fingers tugged his curls before he continued. "So, I threw on a suit—forgot to shave or fuel up—but I wanted to be sure you got to your meeting and figured I would have someone else pick you up afterward, but then—"

"But then you thought, mysterious, celebrity recluse and—"

"No, no, I didn't know then. Then I thought, 'Wow, this woman is smart and funny, and so beautiful, and she loves Bernard fiercely,' and then that little snort you do and I—"

"I need you to get up now," I blurted while my shaky hands rearranged silverware, moved my water glass, strangled my napkin.

"What?"

"I need you to get up and walk over there, please. Go look at the water or go to the restroom. Just go somewhere that is not here."

"But why?"

"Because I need a minute, and I can't get up and storm off like a normal person would. Too much furniture and crutches, and it would be awkward and probably noisy. Just go, please." The words tore from lips in a near-whisper as my mind reeled.

Andrew's chair screeched as he pushed backed from the table. I pointed toward the water. He opened his mouth to speak but tossed his equally choked napkin on the table and walked away.

Cosmic lightning struck when I watched him move to the portico rail. How had I not realized it before now? Obviously, I had on some level, some subconscious layer of my psyche, but now it was so clear. The similarities between the men were undeniable, and not just from a physical standpoint, but in every way. Both were smart and kind, with a charisma that attracted men and women alike. Was it possible my creation existed in the real world? Of course not, but even so, what was the universe trying to say by putting this man in front of me at the very moment I aimed to end the other? I looked at the one facing the water and replayed Andrew's confession. His beautiful confession.

The waitress delivered our food, and I asked her if she would let my friend know to come back to the table.

Andrew did a slow walk to where I sat.

Still feet from one another, I said, "Hi. I'd get up, but I have a hairline fracture of the patella, not because I'm old or anything, but sometimes a bit clumsy. My name is Callie. Calliope Austin. I'm a writer, and you might have heard of my books, but that's not important. And you are?" I put my hand out to shake Andrew's in introduction, hoping he would play along with another do-over.

He did. "Andrew. Andrew Statheros. Nice to meet you." He shook my hand with an amused squint. "May I—join you?"

I gestured to the chair, and he sat.

"So, what do you do, Andrew?"

"I own a car service. Around Town Car Service. My dad started it, now it's mine."

"You *own* a car service." I smiled, mystery solved. "Around Town? That's a good one. The best."

"Thank you." He nodded with a shyness I hadn't noticed before, then he added, "And parking lots."

"Excuse me?"

"I own parking lots. Several, actually. Not sexy, but it's a decent living."

I snorted at his unvarnished delivery, and I buried my mouth in my napkin.

"That is, though," he added. "Sexy."

"What is?"

"*Everything* you've got going on over there, Calliope Austin."

The white napkin at my face could only highlight the flush a sudden warmth told me climbed my neck and onto my cheeks. "We should eat before it gets cold." I pointed to his sandwich.

"Does it feel cold in here to you?" His heated stare said he knew the answer.

I swallowed hard. "Nope. No, it does not."

We each picked up our sandwiches and dipped them into their accompanying tomato-bacon jam. Buttery bread crunched, and cheese oozed with the salty sweetness of the preserve. I didn't know if it was about eating the decadent version of a childhood treat or our lack of confidence in continuing what we had started, but conversation halted. A restaurant shift change began, and preparations for the dinnertime seating were underway. Andrew didn't appear to notice the uptick in the activity as silverware clanged and chairs skidded.

"So, what are you gonna do?" Andrew sat back, wiping his hands on his napkin.

"*Hmm*?" I chewed a mouthful of sandwich.

"Your big decision. Is it something that might bring you to town again? Sometime soon?"

"I don't know. It could, I suppose. Laney is—" Mid-sentence, Andrew's phone rang.

"Sorry. I *am* working today. I work every day." He pulled the phone from his pocket, giving a puzzled look at the screen. "This is Drew... Yes, she is... she *is*..." Andrew chuckled. "Yes, she is, no doubt about that. One moment." He handed me the phone. "It's for you."

Laney had tracked me down. Since I abandoned my phone with my bag in the parked town car, my agent friend fretted, searching for me as the sun set. First came a reprimand for not carrying my phone—not the first time she'd given that lecture. Once she finished the scolding, she explained how Jason and Cyrus had more plans they would like to discuss. Also, an executive producer with serious interest wanted to share his thoughts on the project and introduce his team to Ms. Jones's team. And to show how earnest they were about moving forward, they would love to meet the next day to give us more "food for thought" to take back to our "boss."

Meanwhile, Andrew watched me from the other side of the table. He stared without a sound, hardly moving, but those dark eyes seemed to take in every strand of hair, each line on my face, the curves of my brow. Moving down the bridge of my nose, he lingered on the dip of my cupid's bow. No smile or frown, just a slow gaze, like he hoped to memorize every inch. I had never felt more seen.

"Hold on a sec, Laney Li." I put the phone to my thumping chest. "*Yes, and*, hm?"

With a glint in his eye and a slight tilt of his head, Andrew nodded. "Lean in."

I put the phone back to my ear. "Laney—*yes, and*... It means, set it up for tomorrow. Let's hear what they have to say... Yes, I mean it... no, just some Earl Grey, why?... Text me the time... I think I can arrange one... no, I'll handle it on my end... I'm sure. Bye, Lan—"

She ended the call. Handing the phone to Andrew, I said, "I'm gonna need a lift to a meeting in the morning."

"I can arrange that. After we have breakfast." Andrew pushed his plate aside and folded his napkin.

"Wow. You have some pretty high expectations of how the rest of this evening is going to go."

"What? No, I—*NO*! I meant I would drive to the hotel to take you to breakfast. In the morning. Not—"

I laughed at Andrew's wild eyes and reddened ears. "Just kidding. I knew what you meant." The joke ebbed the tension. "We should probably get out of here, though."

We took our time strolling to the parking garage, but the crutches forced an end-of-day fatigue, and my knee ached with a relentless throbbing. The temperature dropped further with the sunset, but my nascent fascination with the company I kept distracted from both the pain and nip in the air. Easy conversation flowed as we talked about what we loved in the city, and he asked me about my home in Charlotte. While it seemed a ridiculous comparison, I couldn't help telling him about my beautiful hometown full of street art, theater venues, and fantastic dining. "You should check it out someday." Again, I was thankful for the nighttime light hiding my blush.

"I might do that. I don't travel near enough. I can blame it on work or that I can go to Italy, China, Korea, you name it, in a matter of blocks from my loft, or because I don't feel comfortable leaving my mom and sisters for long, but the real reason is probably—"

"Probably what?"

"I don't know. Travel, travel for fun, doesn't seem like a solo activity. I mean, you go somewhere you've never been before, and you want to say, 'hey, look at that,' but if you're alone, who do you say that to?"

I nodded. "I travel to the places I set my books, so I guess *I* say it to anyone who reads them. But I understand the sentiment."

On the ride to the hotel, I sat in the back seat, despite knowing Andrew was no longer my hired driver. It allowed me to stretch out my leg.

"Why don't you let me help you up to your room? You've had quite the workout today."

I agreed, glad to have an excuse not to end the evening yet, if only for a few more minutes. "That'd be nice. Thank you."

Andrew wheeled me through the lobby. Tofer, staffing the front desk, nodded his tacit approval at seeing us together again. "You had another delivery, Ms. Austin. We placed them in your suite."

"Thank you, Tofer. Good night."

Our stroll and car ride had been so full of conversation, the elevator's quiet loomed. Soft music played, a New-Age spa sound that, for me, had the opposite of its relaxation intent. Tension climbed again in the unbearable warmth of the lift. I handed Andrew my key as we rolled up to 3815. It took him four fumbling swipes to earn a green light and gain entry.

I stripped off my coat and tossed it aside before I pushed out of the wheelchair as the heavy hotel door clunked closed behind me. My inner voice begged me to relax and breathe as I reached for the crutches Andrew handed to me.

"All set there?"

"All set. Thanks." *Sentences, Callie. Full sentences.*

"Nice flowers. You must be important."

"They're from my publisher," I shrugged. "I'd prefer chocolates."

"But no fruit centers, right?" He added as his hands slipped into his pockets.

"Never." I scowled.

"So, breakfast?" He grinned.

"I'd like that. Nine o'clock?"

"I'll be here." Andrew tipped his head towards the door, then moved that way.

I followed, unsure how the next part would go, and yet I'd convinced myself we both felt it. The attraction was real, palpable even. When he made a quick turn toward me as if to speak, but then said nothing, I knew I wasn't wrong. We stood too close for there to be any other conclusion. I didn't know if he could tell, but inside I trembled, glad to have the crutches to help stay upright. It had been a while—a *long* while. And just when I should have *leaned in*, as his head lowered, mine did too—foiled by doubt.

His soft lips brushed my forehead, and everything stopped—sound, my heart, breathing.

"If—you don't want this to happen," he whispered, "now's the time to say." Andrew's mouth skimmed my temple, his rough end-of-day stubble grazed my cheekbone. I kept mum. Another kiss feathered my cheek. "Calliope?" His fingers tucked a lock of hair behind my ear, then stroked under my chin.

The clean scent of his neck mixed with the smell of his leather jacket revved my nerves, but I still couldn't make myself speak. Lifting my face, our noses barely touched once, twice.

"God, you're so beaut—" Our lips met before he finished the thought. A brief, gentle impact followed by another, then another. Each grew stronger and longer than the last until I let myself tumble into the desire. I dropped the crutches—one banged against the door, getting caught on the handle, the other hit the floor with a loud *thwack*. My hands held his face, and I melted into his sweet mouth. As his hands slid from my shoulders down my back, I pulled at the nape of his neck, overruling my head and telling him I wanted more. He pulled closer, wrapping his arms around me as lips parted, tongues meeting for a tender but earth-shaking caress. Both of us breathless, it ended as it began—soft, short kisses, followed by his lips brushing my cheek, then a whisper, "That was—"

"Perfect." I found my voice.

A low hum tickled my ear, "I was going to say 'nice,' but your word is better."

"Remember, words are my thing," I quipped, still trying to steady my breath, standing on one foot as I held onto the zipper edges of his jacket.

"Maybe not *just* words."

"Well, I'm a bit out of practice." I hid my eyes in his chest, intoxicated by the bergamot that drifted off his skin while he rested his chin on my head.

"If I'm honest—"

"Always, please," I interjected.

"I've been out of the game lately, too."

"I'm glad we could help each other out, then." I pulled back from our embrace. "We did pretty well for people who've been riding the bench."

He agreed. "Not looking to push this metaphor too far, but care to give it another—?"

I didn't let him finish the question. Like the first kiss, the second began with innocence, but I tugged at the opening of his coat as it escalated. He gripped the curves of my hips with a strength that startled a slight gasp from me. I clung tighter with an encouraging hum, enjoying his gentle nip at my bottom lip. With only one leg to steady me, balance gave way. Arms wrapped around one another, Andrew stumbled with a minor thump into the door. My braced knee collided with one of his. Another gasp, this one louder and in pain, ended the kiss.

"I am so sorry, Calliope." He apologized in a husky murmur.

"No, no. That—*ouch*—that one's on me," I gritted as I pressed against him. Finding my footing, I hopped backward while he held me at the elbows. His face was a mix of want and shame. "And totally worth it, by the way." I grimaced through my wincing, watering eyes.

Andrew picked up my tossed-away crutches and handed them to me. "I should probably go. Before I injure you any further."

I hated he was right. Not about hurting me, but he needed to leave. My aching knee and throbbing center said so. Composed with the supports back under my arms, I eyed the floor and gave a little laugh.

"What's funny?"

"It's just, last night, you hung around to be chivalrous, and tonight, you're leaving to be—chivalrous." I teased with a demure grin.

"I'm leaving because I'm about out of chivalry and *wow*—that didn't sound right. Sorry, it's just—" The fingers pulling his hair gave away his frustration.

I couldn't help but snort. "Don't be. I'm flattered, but yes..." I stopped myself from reaching for him. "You definitely—need to go. Now."

One hand on the door lever, he slipped the other into his pocket. "Tomorrow, then. Breakfast?"

"Yes," came my quick reply.

"Nine?"

"Yes."

"Good night, Calliope." He moved to leave.

"Andrew?"

"Yeah?"

I chanced one more chaste but lingering kiss. "Thank you for a wonderful day. Good night."

Andrew backed out the door.

13

Tex sat on the edge of my bed, and he didn't look well.

"I could have used another hour of sleep, Tex. It's not like you to wake me this early when we aren't writing."

"It's not like you to not say goodnight. Ever."

"Didn't I?"

"You did not, and you know it."

"What's this about? The meeting today?"

"Which meeting? It seems to me you have two."

"I have breakfast, then a meeting. And the first one has nothing to do with you."

"Doesn't it, though?" Tex pulled at the curls on his head and stood.

"You know what this reminds me of?" I remained in bed.

"Book five? The imposter bit?"

"Exactly, Tex."

"One of your more unbelievable plots." The dig was a valid one.

"And yet—?"

"And yet, the readers loved it. No accounting for taste." He shook his head, baffled.

It was too early in the morning for a one-star review on a book I wrote a dozen years ago. Particularly not one orated by the novel's hero.

"Tex, you sat there yesterday and told me you weren't the

problem." I sat up, turning down the covers in a neat fold at my waist, eager to get to my protagonist's point.

"That's right." Tex paced a slow back-and-forth at the foot of my bed.

"Well, if you are trying to tell me you are the *solution*, I'm sorry, but that just can't be."

Tex stopped. "If *I'm* trying to tell *you*? Come on, Cal. You know how this works."

I rested against the headboard, then gave it three gentle thumps. When my eyes opened, Tex had gone. Sliding back down into the sheets, I rearranged my propping pillows around my knee. "What the hell was that about?"

I dozed over the next hour. Floating in and out of consciousness, I dreamed of Andrew's powerful grasp of my body, the soft tickle of his tongue. The mere thought of his dark sea eyes on me lit fires that hadn't burned in more time than I cared to admit. But as the sky lightened, my impatience to start the day ballooned, and I wished I had said eight o'clock for breakfast.

Back to business wear, I opted for a low chunky heeled boot rather than my usual pumps and pulled my hair back into a ponytail again. I liked the look but couldn't help but wonder if it represented some delusion of youth. When my phone pinged at eight forty-five, I almost fell over trying to get to it to read the message.

Andrew: *Here. I'll be up in 5 minutes to get you. Ok?*
Callie: *Yes.*

Three minutes later, he knocked. With one crutch, I glided to the door to greet him. The first several seconds included a stuttering, overlapping mash-up of half sentences.

"Good morning!" we said in unison.

"Wow, you look—"

"And look at you all—"

"Yes, is that ok—"

"Of course, just different. You look great."

"Hi," we spoke at once again, then leaned to give each other awkward kisses on the cheek. An unnerving silence followed all that commotion.

I cleared my throat. "Well, that was worse than I thought it would be."

"Yeah, weird, right?"

"Little bit." I nodded.

Andrew turned and walked out of my hotel room, the heavy door closing behind him. At about the count of three, a knock sounded. Taking a deep breath, I opened it again. This time, I smiled as Andrew cupped my face and placed a tender kiss on my eager lips. Far too brief, but a sign of better things to come.

"Hi," he whispered, his thumb stroking my cheek. "Better, right?"

"So much better," I squeezed the words out.

"Breakfast?" he asked from an agonizing closeness.

"Probably," came my dazed reply.

Andrew laughed.

"I mean, yes. We should—go to breakfast." I patted the cashmere scarf draped across his chest. "Where to?"

"One of my favorite Greek spots, and it's near your meeting. We should get going. Laney sent me another long text of instructions."

"Oh, God. I haven't told her. She still thinks—"

"I know, and it's fine. She'll know in time, but not now. Let's go eat. I'm starved."

To my ear, the last comment didn't sound like it had anything to do with food.

"Let me grab my coat." I sailed off for my bedroom, buoyed

by the charming visitor and my newly honed skill of one-crutch walking.

"You'll want it," he called after me. "It's cold out there. They say snow is coming, but such is life in the Mid-Atlantic in March."

My coat lay on the neatly made bed. Nervous energy had me pulling it together earlier. But now, Tex, decked out in full ski gear, including goggles, lay there too.

"Remember in book two, the snowstorm hits?" Tex leaned back on his elbows, kicking an alpine ski boot in the air.

"Jesus, Tex," I hissed. "I wrote it. Of course I remember. Why are you doing this?"

"I need you to remember, Callie. What happened?"

"The sun came out, and Tex Miller saved the day. Same as in book one and three and four. You see the pattern, right?"

"But what happened? The sun came out, and what?"

"I get it."

"Say it, Cal," Tex practically growled.

"There was an avalanche. The snowstorm hit. The sun came out. And then there was an avalanche." I shoved one arm through a coat sleeve.

"Book two, right?" Andrew asked from the doorway.

"Christ, *yes*, we covered that," I barked, but the ski bum Tex had disappeared.

"Calliope? You alright?"

"Yes." I shuffled to where Andrew leaned in the door frame, embarrassed he caught me in my imaginary tête-à-tête. This time I made the first move. A poorly timed and desperate act to cover what just transpired. A hint of concern seeped into Andrew's look as I tilted up to kiss him. His initial response was uncertain, stilted. But with a lusty yank on his scarf, I demanded more, and he responded in kind. Any reticence disappeared when, letting my crutch fall, I untied that scarf and wrenched it to the floor.

Momentarily off my feet, Andrew whirled me past the doorway, slamming me against the wall on the other side. Our needy mouths crashed. Unwilling to let go, he pressed against me. The swift forcefulness startled us both, lips parted, eyes locked. Neither of us moved except for the synchronized rise and fall of our chests as we both struggled for breath. Not breaking our gaze, he swept away wisps of my hair tousled by the commotion. Restraint and craving warred inside me.

The next kiss slipped back to the tender version. His lips, warm and soft, teased mine with a few playful brushes against my mouth. When his tongue grazed my lip, I tugged at his hair to encourage him. Bending further, his mouth found my neck, lingering on an erotic spot I never knew existed. My hand slid across the wall, grasping the door frame for balance. *How was this happening?* As he gave the skin just under my ear a pleasurable bite, I lost myself.

"Jesus, Tex." The name panted from my lips before I could stop it. Andrew froze. Our breaths still rasped as he pulled away to look at me. His shocked expression cleared any doubt he heard what I said. "Shit," I muttered. Wrecked by the look in his stormy eyes, I closed mine to block the image. The metal buttons on my coat cuff scraped along the plaster when I let go of the molding and hopped to steady my stance. My first thought was to make a joke, crack-wise, ease the tension with my wit and good humor, but no funny came. I kept nothing in my arsenal for this and as the seconds ticked by, the vacuum only made the situation worse. "It's not—"

Andrew put up his hand with a vehement headshake. He bent to pick up the scarf I had tugged to the floor just moments ago.

"I'm going to—get the car—to take you to your meeting. Take your time. You've got some." He bowed down again, this time to collect my crutch. I put my hand on his as I took possession, but he recoiled, not wanting to be touched. He walked out of the bedroom, and I watched him all the way to the hotel corridor door. When he stopped with his hand on the lever, I thought he would turn around, talk to me, yell, something, anything. Instead, he heaved open the door and left, never looking back.

"He's gone, you son of a bitch. Happy now?" My shouted summons echoed in the large room. "What? No snark? No rolled eyes?" I thrashed out of the one coat sleeve, overheated first because of Andrew, now because of Tex. "Seriously? You're gonna ignore me? That's not how this works. You don't get to disappear. Not show up. We had a deal." I paced in panic. Grabbing a water from atop the mini-fridge, I cracked open the glass bottle, and flung the cap. "Tex! Where the hell are you?" But then it became frighteningly clear. I tumbled hard onto the sofa and took a drink. "Oh, no."

<h1 style="text-align:center">14</h1>

I drained the rest of the water bottle, then sat shell-shocked. How had this happened? How did I allow Tex to intrude? In an intimate moment, no less. And now this?

He warned me. Raised an avalanche alarm, but despite that, I missed it. Now what? How would I fix it *this* time?

With the unexpected success of my first Tex Miller novel, life changed almost overnight. Laney tried to brace me for it, but it wasn't the kind of experience you could fully grasp until you were in the midst of it. I was lucky, though. I chose anonymity, much to Watermount Publishing's dismay. And Laney took that decision and ran with it. All the way to the bank.

Of course, this occurred before the internet boom. Sure, the internet existed. There was AOL and *you've got mail*, but nothing like what exists today. Yes, lucky for me. But while my publisher desperately wanted to market my face along with the book and the ones to follow, they settled for the exact opposite. The *"Who is Calliope Jones?"* scheme proved just as successful a ploy, maybe more so. And my initial quiet desire to remain unknown snowballed, completely taking over my life. I couldn't see any other way.

Cabs and limos whisked away sunglasses and scarf-wearing stand-ins at opportune moments, men and women alike. *Page Six* and other rumor rags dropped blind items. So many scents permeated the landscape, making it impossible for the bloodhounds to decipher any truth. The enigmatic *Calliope Jones* was born and cloistered away in one fell swoop, leaving an adoring public to scratch its collective head.

Laney had been right. She had been a good agent for me. That first book offer was actually a three-book deal for a series with the protagonist we all know and love, Tex Miller. Barely twenty-four years old, it was a fantastic gig to get, and if I didn't realize my luck at that moment, I soon did.

But with all that luck came expectation and a lot of pressure. The first book needed to sell well. Fortunately, it did. Then came the need to write, revise, edit, and produce book number two in short order. Strike while the iron is hot, is what they said. Don't give your fans time to find another new favorite hero or, worse yet, forget about Tex entirely. Stress to get book two finished ran high. Full of gratitude for what the publishing world had given me, I wanted to please it further. But by the same token, I wanted out. I couldn't take the pressure. The push to write well and write fast overwhelmed me, and I didn't want to put myself through that for the rest of my life. Decision made, my barracuda agent went to the mattresses for me and got me out of my contract with Watermount, provided I completed the second book.

I dug deep. I argued with Laney, and occasionally, I cried at the desk of poor, grandfatherly Charles Watermount. But the worst fight was the battle with Tex himself. He refused to go quietly, and he played on every doubt I had about offing him in the first place.

The plot had our hero stuck in a snow squall, unable to save his beloved, but when the storm subsided, and the sun came out, the danger hadn't passed. Not knowing his better-half was already safe, he ventured out to rescue her. Spoiler alert: An avalanche fell, and the world lost Tex in a tragic end. Local law enforcement deployed search and rescue ski patrols, followed by a recovery effort, but to no avail. No one could find Tex Miller.

They say truth is stranger than fiction, and maybe that's true, but while it appeared Tex Miller was dead, I wasn't so sure. All I knew was I couldn't find him either. Anywhere. He had disappeared, vanished, gone silent. And losing him was like losing my father and mother all over again, only somehow worse. There I was, contract canceled, my second book unfinished, and I was once again totally alone. Nothing I did could conjure my hero. I spent days and nights in an agonized depression spiral, falling into a dark hole, unable to crawl out to find light. So, I did what any woman worth her salt would do if her hero went MIA, if her savior had been captured by cowboy bandits, whisked away by thorny, winged dragons, or kidnapped by the grim overlords of a rival biker gang. Wallowing in despair wouldn't win the day. I hitched up my word processor and rescued him right back.

Book number two did better than the first, and with Tex Miller resurrected, Watermount and I penned a *new* deal. Industry insiders applauded Laney Li for her hardball tactics and mad-agenting skills in getting her client a bigger, better contract with some of the best-*undisclosed* terms ever heard of in the business. Publishing deal aside, Tex and I made our own pact. I would continue to write anonymous blockbuster books, starring him, and he wouldn't leave me again. Ever.

And for twenty years, give or take, it worked. Everyone was pleased. I wrote laser-focused and produced novel after novel on my timetable, at my speed. And I did it, convinced my success came in huge part to the titillating secret identity of Calliope Jones. Being found-out would surely mean the death knell of Tex's success, the end of my livelihood, and the utter disappointment of those few closest to me. But on my forty-sixth birthday, a day spent alone, I was done, finished with this one-sided marriage. If there were more stories in me, great. If not, that was fine too. Financially set, royalties would continue to hit my bank account for decades to come. I was confident, but somehow, I think Tex was less so. He thought I would change my mind. I had done it before. This time would be no different.

Enter Andrew Statheros, and suddenly our hero was no longer so sure I would change my mind. Not only that, but now our hero was nowhere to be found.

15

When I reached the glass door to my pickup spot, Andrew leaned against the car, much like he did the second afternoon of our week's routine, except this time he wasn't in costume. This time, he wore street clothes and a sad scowl that said he wasn't over the incident in my suite's bedroom.

"You don't have to drive me, Andrew." I tried to meet his eye, but he avoided mine as he opened the car door. "Seriously, this is just—"

"Give me your crutches. I'll put them in the trunk."

I did as he directed, then balanced on the curb using the car door for support. He continued around to the driver's seat, not helping me into the back. His refusal to help hurt almost as much as needing assistance in the first place. Pulling my messenger bag strap over my head, I flung it with enough force that it smacked the far-side window of the interior, landing on the floorboard with a clattering thud. I hopped and slid into the seat, careful not to show any pain. The ride could have been a quick one, but with the threat of wintery weather, the world spilled out onto the streets, 5th Avenue, in particular.

"Andrew?"

His eyes flashed to the rearview but didn't hold there long. He didn't reply.

"That's fine. You don't have to talk to me, but you can't keep me from speaking so…" Head back, I focused on the moon roof, remembering the waning crescent I enjoyed on Tuesday night. Now, four days later, there would be no moon at all. At the moment, that timing read like ironic poetry.

"I'm sorry for what happened upstairs. Not all of it. Just that last bit. The rest of it—well, the rest of it was—amazing. Too fast? Maybe. Too soon? I don't know, I have no idea what the timetable is like these days. But that's not something I do, like *ever*. So, thank you, I guess? For throwing an old lady a bone and—*wow*, now that phrase sounds a whole lot dirtier than I ever thought before. *Huh*." I grimaced, pondering the unfortunate expression but caught the glimmer of Andrew's begrudging grin in the rearview mirror.

"What I mean to say is—I like you. I like you a lot. I think you're funny and smart, kind, and hardworking, loyal and—hot. That's right. I said it. You are an incredibly handsome man, and you kiss like—well, not like someone who has been out of the game for a while, that's for sure." The recent memory stoked more inner heat, and my wool coat became sudden overkill.

I forced a slow inhale before I broached the apology. "Moving on to the part I am sorry about, and I am, truly. I don't know what else to say. I mean, anything I'd say would sound nuts, and maybe it is, but I can say in twenty-plus years, Tex never made me feel like you've made me feel in the last twenty-plus *hours* so…" A guttural grunt of frustration rumbled out of me. "*Argh*, this is weird because I *never* talk about him to anyone, *ever,* and now, of course, under the circumstances, I recognize you probably should not be my go-to on that score. Right. Stupid. Sorry."

I pinched my bottom lip and focused on the streetscape crawling past us. "I understand it should be as simple as you're real, and he's not, except it's not that simple, and I don't want to be dishonest about that. It's complicated. Anyway, thank you for making me feel attractive. Crutches and all. I haven't felt—well, thank you. And again, I am sorry, but just for that last bit."

We had half a block to go, but traffic moved mercifully fast. As soon as we pulled up to The Luna Network building, I grabbed my bag and hoisted myself out of the back seat to avoid Andrew's snub again. I held myself up on the car door when he handed me my crutches. The wintry cold snap was real but looking up at Andrew warmed me all over. Part lust, part shame, all disappointment. My stare shot to the ground, and I winced as my throat tightened.

"It was nice to have met you, Andrew Statheros. Good luck with—everything." I straightened up and kissed his cheek. That time with intention. Andrew didn't speak, but he didn't pull from me either. I lingered for a moment but, accepting defeat, retreated and shuffled into the building lobby.

Laney waited, and like that first visit, I hit the elevator call button several times in rapid succession. One elevator opened, and she trotted to my side as I pressed the cracked number ten for our destination. When the elevator lurched, Laney pulled the emergency knob. We came to a hard stop, knocking me into the wall. No alarm sounded, but it didn't surprise me.

"What now?" Laney leaned against the car railing.

I let a slow breath go. "Let's just say, when you've been out of the game for a while, and you take the opportunity to get off the bench, chances are when you step up to the plate you're gonna have more strikes than hits, and well, you *really* oughta have all the players' names straight in your head."

"Wow. That's a lot of metaphorical baseball, and I'm saying that as a diehard season ticket-holding Mets fan and I don't even get *what* the hell that last part was supposed to mean. Are you ready for this?"

"*Yes, and...*" I hit the release on the emergency stop, braced for the rest of the jagged climb.

Luna's offices looked an even bigger mess than two days earlier. True demolition had begun. We wandered, unaccompanied, down the hall to the sofa configuration I blamed for the bruises on my knee and my sore armpits. The suite was decidedly more crowded this time. People sat, stood, leaned everywhere. A wide range of employees, all wearing small wireless phones attached to their ears, held briefcases and laptops. Everyone spoke, though obviously not to one another. Chaos vibrated, but it hushed when Cyrus yelled, "They're here, everybody!"

All eyes popped up at Laney and me standing next to Jason Steinman and the megaphone Cyrus. You could have heard a pin drop, but instead, we heard the second elevator ding. Silence followed, then:

"*Calliope?*" Andrew's stage-whisper call echoed down the hallway. "*Calliope?*" He repeated, louder this time as he came closer, still not visible to the crowd. "Calliope?" Came the third full-throated plea as he rounded the corner and stopped short, meeting a sea of wide-eyes. I waved with a forced smile. Taking quick note of the crowd, he sped ahead. "You, *um*, left your phone in the car. *Ma'am.*"

No one moved.

"Probably fell out when you—"

"Who the *hell* are you?" Jason Steinman erupted.

Cyrus grabbed Jason's arm and squawked, "Oh. My. Gawd! Look at him. Those eyes, that chiseled chin, and that hair! He's Tex *freakin'* Miller!" Then he grabbed my arm. "And *gurl, yooou* are Calliope Jones!"

"Okay. Eyes here, people." Laney didn't skip a beat. "I'm gonna need everyone, and I mean *ev-er-y-one,* to power down all electronic devices immediately." She pulled a folder from her bag. "We've got

NDAs for you to sign, effective, say, two and a half minutes ago. Pens out, people! Consider any knowledge of this little scene here officially embargoed."

I held up a finger, asking Andrew to give me a minute as the chaos resumed. After Laney's declaration, his face read some combination of confusion and concern, but he nodded and stepped around the corner out of the war zone's escalation to DEFCON 2. I stood in front of Laney, waiting while she juggled more balls than I could count.

"This got interesting in a hurry." Laney continued typing into her phone. "I mean, I do not know what's happening, but it's interesting."

"Yeah. Could I have a minute to talk to—"

"Your Baby Driver, who by the way, is *neither* baby *nor* driver."

"How'd you know?"

"Um, Google? I've known since yesterday."

"Oh. Wait, Andrew said you sent him instructions—*this* morning."

"Yeah," she honked while she typed. "What are the chances the hunky millionaire parking mogul actually picked up my dry cleaning?"

"Laney Li." I glared, having forgotten my agent's inability to forego a good hazing.

"Just having a little fun. Go, but be quick. We need to wrangle these folks, and soon."

I swung around on one crutch, down the hall and to the elevators where Andrew waited. He handed me my phone.

"Thanks." I looked back over my shoulder as Laney shouted more orders.

"Your agent is kinda badass, isn't she?"

"Not the first time someone described her in those—exact

words. Wait, how'd you know she was my agent?"

"Um, Google?" Andrew looked at me sideways.

"*Hm*. I really gotta look into that." We both gave a weak laugh, but I wasn't kidding. "So, I've got this thing." I gestured around the corner. "It's probably gonna be awhile. They just had a little bombshell moment, so it could take a minute to get back on track."

"Sorry about that."

I shook my head. "Nah. It's fine, I mean, I don't know that for sure, but don't worry. Laney will handle it."

Andrew nodded. "Still—I'm—"

"I'm flying home today," I blurted.

"Yeah. I know."

"Are we—alright? I hate to leave with us—*not* okay."

"Does that mean if I said we weren't okay, you'd stay?"

I smiled. "No."

He nodded again. "Well then, I don't know what we are, except only three days old. An unusual three days. A very full three days, but three days—"

"Technically, today is day four, but I'll yield to your point. Sorry about that amorous blitzkrieg earlier."

"*Ha*. It's not like you were there alone."

"That's for sure." I flushed at the memory.

"How about a ride to the airport? Maybe we grab dinner? Talk?"

"Four days. Four meals. If this were a book, someone might take all this eating for symbolism, but *yes*," I hurried to accept his offer. "I'll take that ride. I don't know how long I'll be here, and I still have to pack."

"The island's not that big. You know how to find me. Also, it's snowing."

I took a step backward, feeling pulled in two directions.

"Oh, this is Laney's." He grabbed a bundle of hangers draped in plastic film, dangling from a stray nail in the wall. "I picked them up on my way to you this morning." He shrugged.

I gave a feeble wave from under my agent's dry cleaning and started toward my meeting. "Hey, Andrew." I spun around to see he hadn't moved from his spot. "Thank you."

Andrew put his hands in his pockets and lifted his chin in a silent reply. I headed into the lion's den to meet my new normal.

16

"Where is our ride? I have seen four silver Honda Accords in the last thirty seconds, and none of them have been our car. How is that possible? This is why we use a service. Which is an oh-so-elegant segue into—what's the deal with Baby Driver?"

Laney and I stood outside the Luna building. Snow had been falling for hours, and I wondered whether my plane would depart on time or even at all. I had doubts.

"To start, we're gonna lose the nickname," I replied, avoiding Laney's eager eyes.

"Are we, though?"

"We are if you want to know anything."

"Done. Now dish."

"What is it you want to know? Never mind, I know what you want to know, and I don't have that information to share. We spent the day together. Visited Bernard. Strolled Central Park. He rowed a boat." I kept a lookout for my rescue rideshare.

"He *rowed* a boat?" Laney gave me a shove but then caught me with a quick grab of my arm. "Sorry. Crutches. I forgot."

"He rowed a boat. We ate a sandwich. He took me back to my hotel."

"And?"

"And this morning, he picked me up at my suite. We were supposed to go to breakfast."

"*Supposed to?*"

"Yes, but things got a little heated, in the good way, but then they got heated in a bad way. Things got said. And now we are in some weird limbo spot where I'm going home today, and that's that. End of story."

"End of story? Why do I hear a but coming?"

"End of story. *Except now*, I've had some time to reflect."

"Oh, no. *That's* never good. Don't reflect. Don't overthink. For the love of all that is good, Callie, don't get in your own way."

"He walked out. He shut down."

"The man took a breath and came back. *And* scrambled to keep your cover. Sometimes taking a beat is a good thing."

"Whatever. I'm flying home today."

"Maybe. Maybe not." We both looked skyward.

Our ride pulled to the curb and not a minute too soon. Traffic inched, but Laney was good about not having public conversation, no matter the topic. I enjoyed the return trip to my hotel with nothing but the random honks of Manhattan drivers and the salsa music playing low behind my head. The rhythm made me think of Taco Tuesday, and I couldn't help but lament what a difference a few days made. It hit me. I would miss Andrew Statheros, no matter how this day ended.

"You coming in?" I asked as we neared my drop-off.

"No. I'm going home. Two years ago, I got stuck in that March blizzard. Lesson learned. Be safe. Let me know when you get home, but I'm betting it won't be today." As she said the words, a gust blew across the car, wafting snow and forcing the Honda to swerve. The driver, Laney, and I sucked in a collective gasp.

The hotel lobby bar bustled with Friday night happy hour. Tofer staffed the front desk, but his usual cold discourtesy warmed to something near kindness when I stepped to the counter.

"Ms. Austin. How are you?"

"I'm well, thank you, Tofer." I wasn't sure what to make of his chummy demeanor.

"Alone this evening?"

I looked around. "Seems like. So, I have my room booked through tonight because I knew I had a late departure today. That's not looking likely. Is it going to be a problem to book tomorrow, too, just in case?"

"No problem at all. We are happy to have you. I've sent another delivery to your room, and we've extended happy hour tonight. It's a blizzard thing. You should check it out." Tofer's look put me more on edge.

"I've had a long day. I think I'm going to confirm my flight and—"

"Flight? No flights." He shook his head.

A text from my airline said the same, but it was the only new message. I held up the screen as if to show him. "I see that. A hot bath it is then."

"Probably should check out the happy hour first. Upstairs version, though." He pointed straight up with his pen.

"I'm really not—"

"Take the elevator. One flight up." Gesturing to the elevator this time, he grinned. The Cheshire Cat sprang to mind. Then I understood.

"Thank you, Tofer."

"You're welcome, but I'm sure I don't know what for."

When I exited the elevator, one flight up, music filled the corridor along with low tones of quiet conversation, a far less frenetic version of the bass-thumping scene below. Through one doorway, muted pink banquets sat empty in front of a welcoming blaze in the ornate stone fireplace. Candles flickered on vacant tables in the dark wood-paneled space. Another arch led to an unoccupied billiard room in hues of vibrant purple, including the table felt and the funky Victorian light fixture hanging above it. The Bar, where Laney and I drank cocktails earlier in the week, was where I found Andrew. He sat on the end barstool, chatting up the bartender. A mellow mood hummed with an old jazzy tune playing underneath the hushed exchanges of the few guests enjoying drinks. I watched him unnoticed, feeling my overthinking acutely. Damn Laney and her advice. As I approached the bar, the familiar mixologist lifted his brow, and his chin went with it.

Andrew turned and nearly jumped out of his chair. "You're here."

"*You're* here." I hopped a step, catching my crutch on a stool. "*God*, I hate these things." My mood got off to a ruinous start.

"Have a seat. I saved one in case you showed up." His manner, sweet and gracious, made our combination a tricky one.

The barkeep slid an ice-cold, slightly dirty martini with three olives in front of the chair. "It's true. He fended off many offers of company to hold that seat for you, Ms. Austin."

"Did he now?" I appreciated the bartender playing wingman for his end-stool patron and softened a little.

"Callio—Callie," Andrew opted for a more prudent, public name. "This is an old classmate of mine. Jonathan. We were at Yale together a *long* time ago."

"Not that long ago." I took a substantial swallow of my drink with an exaggerated wink over the rim. "Nice to meet you, Jonathan. You make an impressive dirty martini, second only to your memory."

"That's why he makes an even better Hamlet," Andrew offered.

"Shut up, man. You were the head of the class, by far. And always a class act. Callie, I've heard a lot about you today. Flag me down if you need anything. Hey, Drew. Great catching up and—good luck." Jonathan walked away as he wiped his hands on his apron.

Still unsure of where we stood, I sipped my martini instead of saying the wrong thing.

"How was the meeting? Unless you can't talk about it." Andrew asked, undeterred by my prickly mood.

"I can talk about anything I want. It's my deal. But I have nothing to say about it now. I mean, I haven't gotten my head around it yet, and it's confusing and scary, and it seems to be moving kinda fast. And I don't like to be rushed. So I'm gonna need everyone to exhale and let me think." I focused on the eclectic collection of artwork around the room. A bright flicker bounced off a picture glass, but Andrew's voice pulled my attention.

"Are you talking about work stuff or—"

"I don't know what's happening here. I don't know why you're here. They've canceled all flights, so I won't need a ride tonight, and I bet you knew that before I did."

Andrew swirled the liquor in his lowball glass in a way that made the hairs on the back of my neck stand tall. I shivered. He put his hand on mine, but when I pulled it away, he downed the rest of his drink. Out of the corner of my eye, I noticed another flash.

"Okay. I wanted to see you. Spend more time with you. Get to know more—about you. I wasn't sure I made myself clear earlier. I mean, I don't think that I did, and I meant to, so I wasn't real happy about how we left things."

"You know what I'm not real happy about? I'm not happy about people who disappear. For any reason, but particularly if it's because things have gotten uncomfortable. You don't just walk out. Or give me the silent treatment. You don't just vanish. Grown-ups talk." I directed my little rant at my martini glass and immediately regretted the grown-up comment. I also recognized this wasn't all about Andrew and finished my drink too quickly.

Andrew laughed, and I sat back, surprised he'd found humor in the situation. "Come on, Calliope," he began through his chuckle. "This coming from the woman who made *me* get up from the table when she couldn't adequately navigate the furniture to escape an uncomfortable moment at the Boathouse? And that's the last age crack. Stop. No more. I don't care how old you are, and I think last night and this morning were *pretty* good indicators of *that*. And in the car, you rattled off a list of things you think of me, and none of them were about my age, so let's stop using that as an excuse, some kind of obstacle. We have plenty of those. Six hundred or so, once you hop a plane. And by the way, I have my own list. A list of things I think about you, and I look forward to sharing it sometime, but it's long and growing.

"And another thing you should know about me is I don't scare easy, but you're right. I shouldn't have walked out. I messed up, and I apologize, but a man has his pride." Andrew signaled Jonathan for another round while I sat stunned and tried not to slip off my chair. Turns out, the fired-up guy had more to say. "And tell me if I'm wrong, but it sure feels like there is something worth exploring here, and if you say otherwise, it'll be a lie, and you know it. I wouldn't have waited here, and you wouldn't have come looking if we didn't both feel it."

There is something about the third sip of a second martini. Not some colorful, fruity concoction served in a martini glass—something more berry than booze—I mean a grown-up drink. No age crack intended. That third sip of that second drink is the sweet spot, at least for me. Under normal circumstances, I feel pleasantly warm, at ease. I waited until that third sip before I responded to Andrew's heated but level-headed rebuttal to my feeble tirade.

"You're right." I smoothed out the edges of my cocktail napkin.

"Excuse me?" Andrew slanted with an impish tilt in my direction.

"I said, you're right. Accurate. As in, *not* wrong."

"I *know*."

I snorted, and my shoulder delivered a playful bump to his. He took my hand resting on the bar. It wasn't the first time one of us had attempted it, but it marked the first time the other didn't withdraw. I watched the interaction as his thumb stroked my fingers, then gave a gentle squeeze. I squeezed back. Catching each other's reflections in the mirrored wall holding the backlit shelves of liquor bottles, we smiled. Neither of us let go, hands or eyes, until, by my count, a third white light sparked. This one lit up directly behind us, aimed at the mirrored wall. A young woman I thought I recognized took a picture with her phone.

"Sorry," she quipped. "Wanted a picture of that liquor bottle there. The tall one." She pointed before trotting away.

"That was weird." I let go of Andrew's hand and took hold of my drink.

"We're in a New York City bar. Things don't get any *less* weird than someone taking a picture with her phone. It's a citywide pastime."

"Right. Of course."

"You okay?" Andrew held my hand again.

"Yeah. Long day. Long week. I miss my—" I stopped, pressing my lips closed tight.

His grasp on my hand eased. "You miss who? Please tell me you have a self-sufficient goldfish or maybe an oddly personable philodendron at home."

I leaned into his shoulder again. "Not a *who*. A *what*. I miss my—bed. And for a second, that felt like something I shouldn't say—to you."

"*Hmm.* This would probably be a good time to let you know there is nothing you can't say to me. That's one of the items on my list—your list. You speak your mind. I like that. A lot."

"I'll be sure to keep doing it, then."

"I have no doubt."

"Any other bullet-points you'd like to share, from your—my list."

"Maybe later. For now, it's day four, and we haven't eaten yet. No symbolism intended. There's a room through there. A fireplace and candlelight, and it looks like a perfect spot for a first date."

"A first date?" A catch in my throat surprised me.

"Is it something I said?"

"No. I just think my mom would have gotten a big kick out of me meeting a nice Greek boy."

We dined in the firelight and candle glow, and it didn't feel like any first date I ever had. Hours passed, and I paid no attention to anything going on outside the two of us. Other than the server who took our order, it was just Andrew and me.

Ordering off-menu, I had a simple omelet: smoked cheddar, ham, and spinach. Andrew ate scallops. I learned how he grew up surrounded by sisters and cousins in a rowdy Greek life that wasn't far off from a Hollywood interpretation. He heard about me losing my dad early and growing up with my head in a book in Western New York. We talked about how he was going to be a New York stage actor, and I planned to be a trial attorney, and how none of that happened. Life had us lean in different directions, and we were glad for it.

We agreed on most things, and when we didn't, we sparred. It was riveting. Sometimes he chose the opposing view just because he liked to argue with me. And while I appreciated hearing his real opinion eventually, the quarrel brought back memories of debate in college, and I loved every minute. But at eight o'clock sharp, Andrew's phone vibrated. His employees were checking in, and work duties called.

When he rose to take his calls elsewhere, I encouraged him to stay. The weather had seen to the restaurant's low turnout. There was no one else around to bother, and I didn't mind his divided attention. He sat at the table to take his calls, and though he had said the parking lot business wasn't sexy, I'm not sure I agreed.

"It's not bad out there. Connecticut is getting nailed, but it looks like it skirted us. A few inches. It'll be gone tomorrow. Crisis averted." Andrew reported after hearing from his garage chiefs around the boroughs.

"Great!" I cheered. "I haven't been *longing* for my bed in vain, then."

Andrew picked up his phone again but returned it to the table. He patted it and then folded and refolded his napkin in front of him. I gave a questioning look. His fingers drummed the table. "I thought I'd give my mom a quick call, but now I have an image in my head that makes that call feel—untimely."

Adoring his pink-tinged ears, I threw my napkin at him. "You said I could say anything."

"Could, not should, Calliope." He relaxed his put-on scowl.

"Well, while this has been great, I have a flight to book, and you have Mom and parking details to see to—and so there is no wondering or second-guessing, this greatest of first dates should end here, cuz—it's a first date." I shrugged.

"I agree."

"You do?"

"I'm not saying I like it, but, yeah. Slow is best. But I won't let this greatest of first dates end without knowing when I'll see you again. I mean, after your ride to the airport tomorrow."

"I don't know."

"*Hm*, that doesn't really work for me."

"Well, there's talk of scripts. I've agreed to consider writing samples. Baby steps all around, I guess. They're planning to send them to me. Maybe I could come back for them. In a month?"

"A month?" Andrew's brows shot into his curls.

"Thank goodness for phones, right?" I stroked his fingers.

He nodded, watching our coupled hands.

I crutched my way to the elevator, where we decided the evening should end. I would text him when I had my flight time and meet him at the curb. He agreed. No need for any mushy goodbyes that would wait for tomorrow. We said goodnight with the sweetest of first-date kisses, equal parts determined and hesitant to put the proverbial toothpaste back in the tube.

In my room, I found a box of chocolates with a note:

Calliope:

Sorry I was a jackass. I like you too. A lot. And I promise—no fruit centers. Andrew

Crawling into bed, I noted my knee felt on the mend. My flight was later than I wanted, but Andrew would pick me up at ten o'clock, and I would be in my Uptown Charlotte apartment before sundown. I lay in the dark, thinking about life at home. A part of me was eager to get back to it—while the looming six hundred miles of obstacles plagued my thoughts. And they weren't the half of it. The stillness of a well-insulated hotel suite could make for an eerie atmosphere. Though very much alone, I whispered, "Goodnight, Tex."

17

I HAD ROOM SERVICE to thank for not being late. Cisco made the delivery that included a bright red tulip with a brilliant yellow center. The contrast to the gray and white outdoors struck me. I hobbled around in a rush to pack the last of my bag and get ready for my ride to the airport. Tex remained missing in action.

Cisco returned to help me to the lobby. While we waited at the elevator, my phone pinged. I assumed it was Andrew, but when another ping sounded, then another, and another, I dug for my phone, cursing my large, deep bag. The texts were not from Andrew.

Laney Li: *Don't panic!*

Laney Li: *I've been on it since 8 this morning.*

Laney Li: *Don't speak to anyone until you talk to me.*

Laney Li: *It's him they're after, not you... at least for now.*

"Shit," I murmured, eyeing Cisco. The doors slid open, and we stepped inside. On the way to the ground floor, I reminded myself to breathe and staggered on my crutches through the lobby's morning chaos directly to Tofer at the front desk. "Do you live here, Tofer?"

"Ms. Austin. Sometimes feels like it. I saw the—are you alright?"

"Not sure. Wait. Saw what? Is there—I mean—I got—" I showed my phone to the man.

"Ms. Austin," Cisco interrupted. "Your bag is in your town car for the airport."

"Thank you, Cisco. Tofer?" I turned back to the desk attendant.

"Click this, ma'am. It might explain." Tofer texted me and offered an apologetic wince. "I look forward to your next visit."

I spun and hurried for the door through the crowd to find Andrew. Andrew was not there.

"Ms. Austin." An enormous man in a black suit and black cap opened the rear door for me.

"Where is he? What's happened? Is he alright?" I fought to keep the panic out of my voice.

"Mr. Statheros sends his regards and this." Thick fingers pulled a note from his breast pocket.

I slid into the back seat. Heart racing.

Calliope, I'm sorry. You were right. It was weird. Laney said I shouldn't come for you, and I shouldn't call or text until I heard from you. Please call me as soon as you can. I never meant for any of this. I feel awful. -A

I clicked the link Tofer texted to me:

OGLER.COM- Gimpy & the Greek God
Ogled! You never know who might come out to play in the snow, but indoors, Oglers were on the prowl last night, and we hit pay dirt. Mr. Andrew Statheros, one of the city's most eligible bachelors, was on the scene at a quiet trendsetter bar in the Flatiron District. Oh, no, ladies! He was not alone. Witnesses said Statheros was with a tall brunette on crutches. Ouch!

```
Ponytailed gal pal, or is it something
more? Only Aphrodite knows. The two looked
cozy with drinks at the bar, followed by
a private fireside dinner for two. The
Zeus of Parking Lots has been missing in
action, not gracing our humble pages since
his nasty break-up with a certain socialite
our legal department forbids us to name.
Our records say it's been over a year.
Time flies. Who is this new woman? Has
she nabbed Adonis, or is the joke on us?
Pictures don't lie. Meanwhile, we'll be
shaking every olive tree to get to the
bottom of this. Stay tuned.
```

The post included grainy pictures, but the blogger spared my face. Andrew wasn't so lucky. I texted Laney.

Callie: *CALL ME*

I appreciated the tinted window as we rode up Madison Avenue until I caught my reflection in the darkened glass. A violent yank on my hair tie brought tears to my eyes. No more ponytail for me.

"Any problems on the way to the plane?" Laney rarely bothered with the typical greeting proper phone etiquette might suggest.

"No. I took my hair down. I had to keep one crutch, though. My knee is throbbing. I'm fine."

"Smart. Like the early days, *huh*? Making sure no one looked your way."

"Can't say I missed it. What do you know? Is Andrew—Drew, alright?"

"He's not my concern, but he'll be fine. All signs point to him as *Ogler*'s target, but I don't like the timing. I'm holding seven NDAs, and the ink's not dry. They all saw the two of you, and anyone could see he wasn't just some driver with your phone. I don't like it."

I remained quiet on my end of the line. A flight attendant handed me a glass of water with a polite smile. I couldn't help but be suspicious, but my throat appreciated the cold wet. Mind reeling, desperate for answers, I offered the best I had in logical help. "There was hotel staff too, and the bartender was an old college friend of his—if it is just about him. What else do you know?" I forced myself to ask the vague question Laney knew I wanted answered.

"Just what's on the internet. Don't read it. It's likely some combination of gossip, guessing, and innuendo. And it was over a year ago. If you want the truth, best to go to the source. I don't know the guy, but what I've seen I like. With you, I mean. I like him with you. And I don't like anyone."

"Thanks, Laney. Gotta go. They're closing the doors. Contact me if anything changes."

The plane landed in Charlotte two hours later. I retrieved my bag and staggered to a cab lane for a ride to Uptown. It was good to be home. No one looked for me here.

I lucked out with a chatty cabbie. Southern hospitality, I suppose. He welcomed me to Charlotte, and I thanked him without divulging my local resident status. We talked about the weather and daylight-saving-time as I made a mental note to change the clocks that evening. I had one whole day to decompress before facing the world on Monday, and even then, my schedule was light, only an appointment with an orthopedist to follow-up on my knee.

On the elevator, my stomach rose and fell, eager to see if Tex waited for me on the top floor. Maybe the change in venue would lure him from hiding. Perhaps he'd been waiting at home all along. Another disappointment levied itself, and I chucked my crutch, flinching at the clank that echoed in my vacant flat. My roller bag made a makeshift aid to help me limp through my apartment, straight to my bedroom, where I flopped on the king-sized bed with a grunt. Crawling under the covers seemed like a good idea, but my stomach growled, and I wanted out of my clothes. I hoisted myself to standing, shuffled to my closet to strip down, and redressed in loungewear meant for Saturday nights spent home alone. My walk-in housed a lamentably vast array.

At almost five o'clock, I opened the refrigerator, wondering what to whip up to satisfy my hunger. Lucky me, I found all I needed to recreate my dinner from the night before: eggs, cheese, ham, and some wilting baby spinach. Another omelet would hit the spot, but it didn't help my wandering thoughts. And what was that strange sensation in my chest?

I stepped onto the kitchen balcony. There were four balconies in all. The kitchen, the dining room, the living room, and the main bedroom each boasted one. I've mentioned I like a good view. The sinking sun glinted off the modern glass and new steel construction down the block with a blinding flare that reminded me of that damn camera flash. Stepping back inside, I poured a glass of red wine and dialed my phone.

"Calliope, what took you so long?"

While used to skipping phone niceties with Laney, I wasn't up for it with Andrew.

"*Hello*, Andrew. Want to try that again?"

"Sorry. Hello. Where are you? *How* are you?"

"I'm home. I'm fine."

"Were you delayed? I thought you'd be home long before now."

"I've been here a while."

"And you didn't call?"

"I'm calling now."

"I was worried."

"Well, my world got rocked for like the fourth time in as many days, so I needed a minute. And let's not forget this last one involved the media, which I have actively avoided since you were in junior high, so…" I may have been angrier than I realized.

"Wow. Back to that, are we?"

"Yeah. Back to that. Maybe. I don't know. No. Andrew, I'm sorry." I didn't know if the fault belonged to him, but he was the easy target.

"No. I'm sorry."

I limped into my library and flipped the switch to the fireplace. Curled up on a leather sofa, my braced leg stretched long, my wine went down easy, and I let go of a long exhale, sinking deeper into the couch. I longed for every sense of Andrew: his touch, his smell, his voice in my ear, but neither of us spoke.

Finally, he got brave, tackling the six-hundred-mile obstacle. "What are you doing now?" The quiet question warmed me.

"Drinking a glass of red wine, in front of a fire, on a well-worn leather sofa in my favorite room."

"That sounds nice. Why's it your favorite?"

"It's different from the light and airiness of the rest of the place—which I also love. But this room is wood-paneled, with beautiful millwork. Even the ceiling is coffered and stained. It's dark and cozy, and everywhere I look, there are books. Floor to ceiling, practically wall to wall. There's a clock that ticks. It's weird because usually such a thing, a ticking clock, would irk me, get under my skin. But this clock, in this room, calms me. My heart meets its beat. Syncs to it, somehow."

Andrew didn't respond. We sat in the stillness, and the clock marked the passing of time with the occasional sound of his breath on the other end. When his breathing changed, I knew he would speak.

"I don't know what you know, what you've read but—"

"I know nothing. I haven't read anything," I interjected. "That's not accurate. I read the *Gimpy and the Greek God* post, but that's all. Google really isn't my thing. Besides, Laney Li says it's all gossip and guessing and innuendo so..."

"I always liked her." He probably aimed to lighten the mood but missed.

"Look. I'd be a fool to think you didn't have a past. I mean, have you seen you? That your past proved worthy of social media, gossip column attention... well, that is also *really* not my thing. But you don't owe me any explanation. We're, well, you and I are not even a 'we.' The solution is simple. I'm here, you're there. You won the six-hundred-mile lottery. You're off the hook."

His breathing changed again.

"Gee, *thanks*, Calliope." His sarcasm stung, and somehow I had offended him. "I appreciate you—*uh*—letting me off the hook. Such a relief. I spent the day freezing my ass off, pacing a crappy eight-by-ten office in my Queens maintenance shop. Stomach knotted waiting for your call so I could blow you off, cut and run, disappear, you know, because things got uncomfortable for a minute."

"Wow, there's some Yale drama for you. I'm giving you a break, but if you'd feel better telling me, go for it. I'm listening."

"It doesn't feel like a conversation we should have on the phone.

We should be face to face."

"It also doesn't feel like a talk that's going to wait a month, and let's be honest, my coming back to New York to see you is an incredibly *stupid* move, and we're smart people." My tone became immediately upbeat. "Look, before anyone's feelings get hurt or whatever, let's not, you know—make a thing out of it. Thanks for the interesting week. Okay. I'm gonna hang up, and we're okay. No harm, no foul. Rest easy. Okay? Okay. Bye." I hung up the phone and took a sip of wine. I did *not* feel okay.

18

I took Sunday to decompress, wandering my condo in pajamas. Music played, and I had a book opened wherever I sat as I followed the sun from one balcony to another throughout the day. Tex still refused to show his face. Even so, I took comfort in being in my own home, surrounded by my own things, my own quiet.

Monday morning began with laziness too, but I prepared for an afternoon appointment for my knee. I wasn't exactly eager to face the world but knew it was a necessary evil. Besides, the sooner I could lose the leg brace, the better. The orthopedist's office was nearby, and I used an app to get a ride. I only thought of Andrew for a moment before pushing his image aside. That may have been a lie, but it's one I would keep telling myself. What was the second rule? Fake it until you make it?

The new medical complex gleamed with fountains and flag poles. Glass prisms reflected rainbows, and I imagined myself a geriatric Dorothy Gale limping toward a multi-colored Oz. Bellevue had scheduled my appointment at the Sports Medicine division of the healthcare conglomerate, where I would meet with Dr. Joseph Kelley. Dr. Kelley came highly recommended, and Laney saw to it that I got on his schedule and quickly. I was lucky he had an opening, since he also served as one of the physicians for the local NFL franchise. Thankfully, it was postseason. While waiting in an exam room for the good doctor, the hanging diploma delighted me. He'd attended none other than the University of Virginia. Was it fate?

After a quick knock, a young, blonde man entered, and gave me pause. He wore light blue surgical scrubs that pulled across the bulges at his biceps and quads. He was a hulking presence, and I couldn't help but stare. When he reached for the white lab coat hung on the door and slipped it on, it answered my immediate question. The coat clearly displayed *Dr. Joseph Kelley* embroidered over the breast pocket with the medical facility's name on it. His grin was toothpaste commercial quality, and his handshake breathtakingly firm.

"Hey, do I know you?" His fresh face beamed as he pointed at me, then checked his tablet for my chart information.

I snickered. "I don't think so, but I went to UVA."

"Wow! *Wahoowa!*" He bellowed with the enthusiasm of a frat boy on game day.

I reciprocated in a much milder fashion.

"No, I know you. Twelve West."

"Yes. I am Twelve West." I looked at him sideways, unnerved that he knew my address.

"Eleven West." He tapped his chest with his stylus. "I've seen you around. Not a lot, but I never forget a pretty face or a good gait. You wear heels a lot. Good heels. Your rear foot pronation at heel strike is excellent."

"I'm sorry. My what is what?"

"Your foot and ankle dynamic during stepping. It's good. Now let's look at your knee."

Post examination, pleased with the state of my knee in general and my patella in particular, Dr. Kelley felt reasonably sure I could get away with an at-home exercise program and a few more weeks in the brace. Relieved to get such a stellar report, I hopped off the exam table, feeling no pain at all. Fake it until…

Standing in the facility's glass atrium, my phone primed to order a ride home, the young doctor sailed by then stopped short. "You headed home by chance? I am and can give you a lift."

I looked around, surprised he spoke to me.

"Yes, you, Twelve West."

"*Uh.*" My phone pinged in my hand with a text from Laney.

Laney Li: *You're welcome*

As a big believer in signs, I shrugged and accepted the doctor's offer.

Dr. Kelley's car was a sport utility vehicle, a fancy one loaded down with all manner of sports equipment. "Excuse the gear. Between medical stuff, the NFL gig, the kids' lacrosse I coach, and a grown-up soccer league I play in, my car is full."

"Your calendar, too, I presume."

"I keep busy. What about you? Your chart says, 'self-employed.' What's that mean?"

"I'm a writer," I stated bravely.

"You mean—like books?"

"Yes, like books." I gave a slow nod.

"Oh, I'm not a big reader." He shrugged with a curled lip.

"Well, wherever would you find the time?" I let the man off for his oafish remark.

"True that." He ignored the out and piled on. *Charming.*

We parked in our building's garage and entered through the rear of the building lobby. Still dressed in scrubs, he held the door, and I brushed by one of those bulging biceps and marveled at its size. "Thank you, Dr. Kelley."

"Oh, please. Call me Dr. Joe."

I snorted at his request, but quickly realized he meant it. I bowed my head to hide my amusement and lost my limping balance for a moment. Dr. Joe caught my arm to steady me. When I righted my stance, Andrew Statheros stood near the elevator several feet in front of us.

"Careful there. Those crutches can kill ya." Andrew lifted his chin, showing off his crooked smile.

"What on earth are you doing here?" My disbelief robbed me of any witty greeting, but I couldn't help but return the grin.

"Thought we needed to have a face-to-face that wouldn't wait a month, and you said coming to New York was—what was the word? *Stupid*, I believe you said." Andrew offered his hand to Dr. Joe. "Hi. I'm Drew."

"Yes. Drew. Andrew Statheros. This is Dr. Joe. Dr. Joseph Kelley. My doctor. For my knee. He lives here with me—in the *building* with—in *this* building—where I live—also." I tried to slow my chatter. "He's one of the team doctors for the Panthers. Football. So—*that's* cool." My clenched grin and wide eyes gave away my flustered state.

The two men shook hands for longer than I thought necessary. Knuckles were white and not just mine.

"Oh, and my knee is healing, so—good news there. And apparently, my pronation is spot on, so—I've got that going for me too," I rambled.

"Thanks for taking such excellent care of the patient, Doc."

"You bet, Drew." Dr. Joe looked at me. "You all good here, Twelve West?" He gave a quick glance to Andrew, then back to me.

"Me? Oh. Sure. Thanks."

"Going up?" the doctor asked.

"Not just yet. You go on ahead."

The elevator doors opened as soon as Dr. Joe hit the call button. I gave silent thanks to the universe's charity for putting a quick end to that uncomfortable introduction.

"Nice guy," Andrew offered as he slipped his hands into the pockets of his jeans. "Seems a little young. You sure he's a *real* doctor."

"Yep. Very nice. *Very* young. But with very little appeal to me." I failed to keep a straight face. "How'd you find me?"

"Laney Li." The meaning of her last text read differently in this new light. "I'd have gotten here sooner, but I had arrangements to make for work, and Laney took some convincing to give up your address."

"Yeah, I'm surprised she did."

"I can be pretty persuasive." He took a step toward me, and I had no doubt.

"You've got that right? Still, she's a tough nut." I stood my ground.

"Tell me about it." He took another stride in my direction.

"And—why are you here again?" The temperature rose, and with it, the pitch of my voice.

"I heard it was a great city. Street art. Theater. Fantastic dining. Plus, I met this woman who drives me a little *crazy*, and she's here so..." He stood very close to me now.

"Crazy, *hm*? Not sure that's a word we should throw around. Given, you know," I made the international sign for 'cuckoo' at my temple.

"I flew six hundred miles for a second date. That's gotta be worth something." He gave me the grin with all the boyish charm. *Real charm.* I couldn't help myself and tilted up to give his cheek a peck. "I didn't mean that, but I'll take it."

"Can't help but notice you came empty-handed."

"What? You want more chocolate? If you want more chocolate, I'll find you more chocolate."

My lips wanted more *Andrew*, as I rattled my brain with a

floaty feeling something in the back of my mind told me might be trouble. "I meant a suitcase."

"I parked it in my hotel room up at the corner. Nice one. It's new, I think."

"It's Charlotte. Everything's shiny and new." I hit the elevator call button.

"Yes, even their doctors," Andrew joked.

"Oh, stop."

Andrew complimented my home as I gave him a quick tour of the public spaces, including the library and three of the four balconies. When I offered a drink, he declined. Playing the merry hostess, I tried to hide my nervous energy, but found no luck.

"Make yourself at home while I freshen up a bit." I said as I scurried off to lock myself in my bedroom to get ready for our impromptu date. After thrashing at my hanging clothes like they had done me wrong, I chose an outfit with ballet flats I swore I would never wear and cursed my knee for demanding sensible shoes.

Pleased with the outcome of the quick makeover, I dialed my phone. "Pick up, pick up, pick up!" I begged. Thankfully, she did.

"I already said, 'you're welcome.' Why are you calling me?"

"You're lucky I can't reach through this phone and throttle you, Laney Li."

"What? Little ol' me? What's the problem?"

"Problem? Let' s see. He's here. I'm here. We're—here."

"That's a problem, how? He likes you. You like him. He looks like him. You—"

"Seriously? Okay, the last time I—well, you know. You had bangs and owned a Blackberry."

"Jesus H. Christ, okay, I have *not* been a good friend. Yep. I see that now. Not sure how I can help from here, though. Time to step up to the plate. That's all the metaphor I've got." Laney hung up.

Exiting my bedroom, I limped the full length of the apartment, checking each balcony along the way. The setting sun reflected off the neighboring structures in a brilliant fifteen-minute light show at this hour, this time of year. I realized it was an hour later than usual. The thought reminded me of the library clock, and I knew where I would find my guest.

I crept with intentional quiet. Andrew sat on the well-worn leather sofa in my favorite room. His eyes were closed, but his regular breathing hinted he was awake. I leaned in the doorway, watching. A perfectly twisted curl hung down, grazing his dark eyebrow. It fell to the side when he bent his ear to his shoulder in a neck stretch common for weary travelers.

The nervous, out-of-practice coward in me half-hoped, if I left him alone long enough, he might fall asleep. The ravenous cougar, starved for affection, wanted to pounce on him right there. I focused on the clock. My heart synced to it, and remaining perched against the pocket door frame, I cleared my throat.

"Great room." He didn't move from his spot.

"Told you."

"It smells like you."

"Thank you?"

"It's a great smell, so you're welcome. I hope you don't mind that I took a seat. I heard talking; it sounded heated. Not the words, just the tone. I came in here so I couldn't eavesdrop."

"It wasn't him."

He paused. "I didn't ask."

"No, but you said I could say anything to you, so I'm saying that."

"Alright."

"He hasn't been around since that morning. At all."

"Is that unusual?"

"Very."

I entered the room to sit in an armchair across from him. With one leg curled under me, I propped the braced leg on an ottoman. Leaning into the corner of the wingback, I folded my hands in my lap, my eyes focused on my fingers. The room got the morning sun, so by late in the day, the already dim space was even darker. The lack of light felt appropriate.

"Is it weird if I ask questions?"

I gestured for him to continue, then flipped on the fireplace. Again, if this had been a book, someone might take the sudden illumination for symbolism. I waited for his next words.

"Has it happened before? His disappearing?"

"Once. Book two."

His dark brow raised. "That was a long time ago."

"Yeah, you'll want to avoid doing the age math. I wish I had."

His shoulders bounced with a silent chuckle. The clock ticked, and my heart kept time. I had never spoken like this to anyone. And in the past, the mere thought of it made me anxious. But now, I talked, Andrew listened, and my heart kept steady.

"What will you do?" He'd quit laughing.

"To get him to come back? Or if he doesn't?"

"Either. Both."

"I don't know, Andrew. Navigating new waters right now. Lots of new waters."

"Am *I* water in this scenario?"

"You are *a* body of water in this scenario, yes. Just one of a few."

"And that body of water is—?"

"Beautiful, warm, inviting—scary, a drowning hazard."

"Oh, I was doing so well for a second."

Despite my forward talk, my heart continued clock-like. I

wanted to sit with him, fireside, on my favorite sofa. Feel his arm around me, my head on his shoulder, breathing *his* smell. That seemed like something couples do. Except we weren't a couple, not yet, not really, and I needed to get through the next part before coupling was even on the table.

"And the other new waters? What are—"

"They're not my focus at the moment. They're not threatening to breach levees anytime soon."

"Whoa. Threatening? I'm not—" He straightened, then leaned forward.

"Sorry, poor choice of words. Occupational hazard. I usually get more than one draft. I don't feel threatened. Promise."

We both inhaled and his silhouette relaxed in the fire's glow.

"If our first date was the greatest, this second is kinda weird. I can't reiterate enough how out of practice I am."

"I think you're doing fine."

"How about you tell me something?"

"Like?"

"How about the socialite that *shan't* be named? The Macbeth of girlfriends past?"

"Ho, boy. I think I'll take that drink now."

"I thought you'd never ask. Stay there." I kicked off the ballet flats and padded off to the kitchen. On my return, I served two generous pours of red wine. Despite the pull to sit near him, I returned to the wingback, noting his disappointment. I knew it was the prudent move. Seconds ticked by, and the gravity of the situation became clear.

When he finally spoke, he was quiet and only had eyes for his wineglass. "What do you know?" he asked.

I intended only to listen, but it was clear Andrew needed help. "I know what *Gimpy and the Greek God* told me. It was a little over a year ago, and it was 'nasty.'" I used the requisite finger-quote bunny ears. Andrew's laugh felt forced. Not from a place of dishonesty, but one of hurt, and I regretted opening an old wound.

"Well, not much of that is true."

"Which? The *nasty* or the *little over a year* part?"

"It was much more than a year ago, nearly two actually, and any nastiness that took place was not at all public. Anything seen—caught on camera—was by design, and it happened long after we were over." He sipped his wine.

"I don't understand."

"We were together, then we weren't, and then several weeks later, we staged a scene for the society pages. It's not that uncommon."

"O—kay, and why'd you break up?"

"Is that important?"

"I don't know, is it?"

"It's just not something I should talk about."

"Oh, God, don't tell me you signed some sort of non-disclosure." NDAs. Finally, something I understood about the 'realities' of high society.

His gaze shot to me. "I didn't, though they tried, and while we're at it, I didn't sign the one Laney pushed on me either."

The tension changed, and not for the better. "I didn't ask her to if that's what you're implying. I wouldn't have, and I didn't, and I won't. *Ever*." Our eyes locked, with nothing but the steady sound of the mantel clock. Or was that my heart?

"I apologize. I shouldn't have snapped at you or assumed you were involved in that."

"You should know, when it comes to me, Laney will always have my back. Always. But if it means stabbing you in yours, she won't think twice. Good for me. Bad for anyone thinking of being my enemy."

"Laney doesn't need to protect you from me."

"Apparently, she agrees. She led you here, didn't she? I'm not sure there is any higher praise. You've been green-lit, as they say." I put up my hand in a pretend defensive pose. "By her. I'm still conducting due diligence."

"Feels like I just lost some ground."

"Why? Because you defended your honor? Or because you're willing to stay quiet to defend someone else's? Even if she doesn't deserve it. Either way, ground gained. I can read between the lines, and I don't need to know anything you don't need me to know. And should circumstances change, I will do my best to listen with an open mind, just as you have done for me. Seems fair."

"And what if I have more questions—about—?"

"Tex? Ask away. If you haven't run for the hills yet, I'm ready to let my freak flag fly." That won me a grin.

"That's intriguing in more ways than—"

"Down, boy. But seriously, shouldn't date two be Putt-Putt with wings and beer."

Andrew stood while setting his glass on the coffee table. He gave himself a small stretch. Had the clock sped up? His shadow extended across the wall of bookshelves behind him as the firelight bounced. He reached out, silently asking for my hand. I gave it. Pulling me to my feet, I hopped twice, balance tested in more ways than one.

"You got your footing?" He squeezed my hand, then let go and stepped back toward the sofa.

"What are you doing?" I stood confused by the distance between us.

"Sounds like you're jonesing for some mini-golf and Buffalo Wings. You can take the girl out of Western New York, but... It's your town. Lead on." He gestured to the door. Head cocked, I stared at his grin, highlighted by the flames. "Did you think I was getting you on your feet for some other reason? Something more—"

"I did. Guess I read that wrong. Like I said, out of practice." I reached for my wineglass, but before I could get it, Andrew grabbed me at the waist, pulling me to him fast, but didn't put his mouth on mine, only held me tight. "Andrew?" I breathed his name.

"Yes?"

"I would like nothing more than for you to kiss me—" He pulled me closer still. "But—I can't sleep with you—tonight."

He relaxed his grip.

"It's not that I—"

"Wait, I'm confused," Andrew interrupted. "I don't— understand. I mean, sure, I've been out of the dating scene for a while, and the vernacular is in constant flux, but does Putt-Putt mean something different in North Carolina than it does in New York?"

My snort got away from me, and I hid my eyes in his chest. He wrapped both arms around me. When I pulled away to see his face, it was kind but serious and something like adoring.

"I hear you. Slow. I get it. I kinda like it." His sweet kiss had me wondering if I had meant a word of what I'd said.

While there was no Putt-Putt, there was a lively evening at a local watering hole around the corner from my building. Well, as spirited as it gets on a Monday night before March Madness. Andrew and I laughed and ate, shot pool, and threw darts, continuing to get to know one another with inexplicable ease. At the end of the very late night, he saw me to my lobby elevator with promises of lots of calls, emails, and texts, and a less-than-chaste kiss that left me a breathless puddle with swollen lips and six hundred reasons to be disappointed. Despite the wonky start, date number two knocked it out of the park.

As quickly as he appeared, Andrew was gone. He had businesses to run, and employees counting on him, plus social media hounds to convince he wasn't worth pursuing. It was another earth-quaking day in a series of unexpected moments, beginning a week ago with Bernard's heart attack. Who knew the roller coaster was just getting started?

19

Tex was still on mute, but most days, I handled it well. I opted for a different approach and began talking to him about a new writing project, even if he refused to respond. Not new Tex Miller, because without him, that felt impossible, but a fresh story altogether. Possible plot points, the kind of characters I was considering, intriguing settings, times, and places I could delve into and explore. Still, he refused to come to me, which meant I made little progress. But I had other ways to spend my time.

"I hate it when you hold on to the *U*, Callie," Laney groused through the phone speaker.

"Oh, here we go again. You're the one who taught me that move. What's it you say? Don't hate the player—"

"Yeah, yeah. So what'd you score?"

"Hold on. Still doing the math."

"You know, if you do it on the app, the app does the math for you."

"I don't like the app. Any apps. So you do it your way, and I'll do it on my old school board spread out on my dining room table and then input the—"

"*Just* get on with it, Callie. Where are you playing your word?"

"Off that *C* you left hanging out there at the end of PHALLIC."

Laney honked. "Man, I love a theme night."

"QUIXOTIC, triple letter on the *X*, plus a triple word score.

Could have been worse. I had to use a blank for the second *I*. Comes to 129 points, thank you very much."

"That's it, I'm out."

"Sore lo—"

"Watch it, Austin."

I snorted, pushing aside Laney's and my current game of our version of Scrabble where we each got all the letters, then sipped my wine. "Hey, are we ready with scripts? What's the holdup?"

"I think they're trying hard to woo the writer with, you know, *good* writing. Give them a minute. You have a reputation for being hard to please."

"I have a reputation? *Nooo*, Calliope Jones has a reputation."

"Speaking of reputations? Anything you care to share?"

"My reputation remains in good standing as does my holding out record—"

"Jesus H. Christ. I served him up on a cracker and still you—"

"Not helping, Laney. What's the word up there? By word, I mean gossip, guessing, and innuendo."

"All's quiet, but that just means your Greek God is wisely lying low. Chances are if he raises his pretty head of curls, he will get seen. It's a relentless business. Back to scripts. The EP, that's an executive producer for you dilettantes, would love for you to hear rather than read it, but I can quash that. No need to pack a bag."

"*Uh*, not necessary. I could maybe—"

"Okay, stop. You're just gonna make a fool out of yourself. I'll arrange it, but we are doing this my way. Got it?"

"Yes, Laney Li."

Another month passed, and I still hadn't heard from The Luna Network. Television production had the same hurry-up-and-wait attitude as book publishing.

"They want it just right, and they want to do at least four episodes to give you an idea of the story arc. They've got their shit together. This could really be something, Cal. You need to prepare yourself for that. You may not be able to say no this time." Laney lectured in stern agent-mode.

"Oh, I think if I've proven anything, it's that I can say 'no' like nobody's business."

"*Hmm*, something tells me we aren't talking about Tex Miller anymore."

"Let's not say his name." The snap was not how I ever spoke to Laney.

"You okay, Callie?"

"I can't write," I confessed.

"What's that mean?"

"I. Can't. Write. Three words. Not hard words. Three easy, *monosyllabic—*"

"Whoa. What's with the sass?"

"I don't know." I let dead air hang before I continued. Laney knew not to fill it. "You know how I've mentioned Tex and I—well, we write together? Sort of."

"At *Agent Academy,* they teach us never to mock the talent. Whatever the artist says goes. Ours is not to reason why."

"Yeah, well, this talent is rudderless without her muse, and her muse is a dashing cockroach that's gone missing. Like for a while now."

"How long?" Laney asked, all glibness gone.

"Since that morning in New York when things got heated in the good way, then heated in the bad way and—"

"Okay, I get it. This happened before?"

"Nope. Not really. Not like this." The answer came close to true.

"So, what are you thinking?"

"I think I have never been more scared in my professional life." With a deep inhale, I held my breath, then let it go in a long steady stream. In a spectacular display of her twenty-two years of hard-won wisdom, my agent remained silent on her end of the line. "Don't worry, Laney. And—thank you for listening to me."

"No problem."

"Bye, Lan—"

"Callie?"

"Yes?"

"You know there is no *Agent Academy*, right?"

"Yes, I know. Bye, Laney Li."

20

THE PHENOM 300 TOUCHED down at Teterboro Airport. That was doing it Laney's way. She made sure The Luna Network took good care of the 'talent,' and I went along for the ride, with some exceptions. The hotel was *my* pick, and I planned to stay at my usual. I was also beholden to Around Town Car Service, and nothing would get in the way of that. But a private, eleven-seater business jet qualified as *good care* I could get used to.

It was early May, and I had high hopes of seeing tulips in Central Park, but more than that, I wished to see Andrew under the radar, for both our sakes. We'd logged more than a few hours on the phone in March and April, video chats, countless texts, and emails. We joked about my sudden appreciation for technology. The thought of breathing the same air made breathing all the more difficult, while the notion of his touch made me positively giddy.

I walked down the canopied airstairs onto a carpet strip that led to a black town car on the tarmac. My roller bag in tow, I hurried to the vehicle. The hulking man in a black suit, black cap, standing guard at the rear passenger door was familiar. The driver made Andrew's six feet, two inches look short and my man Bernard absolutely petite. I smiled on my approach as he reached for my luggage.

"Hello," I shouted over the small aircraft's engine-slowing whine, surprising the behemoth by taking hold of the immense hand he extended. "We met last time I was in town, but I'm sorry. I didn't get your name that day."

"Dante, ma'am." He hesitated but then shook my hand. "You should get in the vehicle." He gestured to the rear door I blocked while I persisted with our get-to-know-you chat.

"Please, Callie is fine." A breeze gusted across the expanse of pavement, blowing my hair in my face. "Or just Miss if you want to stand on principle, but I'm not so formal." My nervous energy spilled out all over poor Dante. "I've known Bernard for years. That's what he calls me. Miss. I like it." I stepped aside, turning, so the wind blew my tresses out of my eyes.

"Yes,—Miss. You should get in the car." The driver opened the door, then rounded the back to deposit my bag in the trunk.

I ignored his instructions to continue our conversation. "How is he? Bernard? I knew he wouldn't be getting me today, but—" I'm sure Dante replied, but a firm yank of my arm from inside the car found me, on my back, in Andrew's lap, with his eager lips devouring mine.

Two months of long-distance foreplay was enough to make anyone eager to get in the game. Andrew was stealing second before I ever heard, "Play ball," but I was all for getting in some field time. The unanticipated kissing went on for some time, but when I regained my senses and came up for air, I gasped, asking where Dante was.

"He's waiting outside until I give him the high-sign to get in."

"Andrew!" Still draped across him, I swatted his arm.

"I know. Sorry. I've just been wanting to do that for weeks." He raised his hand to rap his knuckles on the window, but I pulled on his neck for another quick go at-bat. He obliged me with a long, slow kiss, the likes of which I had imagined for nearly two months, except so much better. I relented a minute later.

Lips tingling, I slid to my side of the backseat with a sheepish wave to Dante after running my fingers through my wind and Andrew-tousled hair. He buckled his seat belt, eyes stoically front.

"You know where I'm headed?" I asked Dante.

"I do,—Miss."

"I'm not in any hurry. So feel free to go the long way."

Dante's eyes shot to Andrew in the rearview. Andrew took my hand. "You heard the woman." He brought the back of it to his boyish grin with a craving look almost too much to endure, but I was determined to find a way.

"So, tonight—" Andrew began, nuzzling close.

"Oh, I have to go to this Luna thing. Some spacey network relaunch party. Laney says I gotta show my face. Not for public, but for 'industry relations.'" I air-quoted with a shrug.

"I know." Andrew's brow furrowed as he pulled away a few inches. "I'm going to be there too."

I gripped his hand tighter. "Yay. Fun. Wait, not fun? What's that look?"

"I'm going to be there to take the scent off you. Or us, I guess. Laney arranged it. She didn't say?"

I said nothing, only stared. I should have known *Laney's way* included more than a private jet. A familiar knot tightened in my gut. A knot that meant I had relinquished control in a way that could have unforeseen consequences. Fallout I wouldn't see coming.

"I'll be there, but we can't interact, except maybe a brief introduction. That way, the cameras won't follow you."

I remained quiet.

"This way, you should be in the clear this week. It's a precaution. You said I should do what Laney said. And she's the pro."

"Sounds like you have an affinity for faking it for the cameras, too." The snark slipped out.

"Calliope. Tell me not to do this, and I won't. One word from you, and I'm out."

"Are you bringing a date?"

"Not an actual date."

"Wow. A fake date. Young, probably. Right? Age-appropriate, anyway?" My age anxiety didn't take long to resurface. "Wait. Does she even *know* she's a fake date?"

"Of course she knows."

"But she's reliable? I mean, she's—whoa, she's *what*, exactly?" My imagination shifted into high gear.

"She'll be convincing."

"Oh, super. I can't wait to see what that looks like."

"No, I mean she's a pal from school. Yale. An actor. It's acting."

I looked out the tinted glass as we crossed the Hudson River. Somewhere in the conversation, I let go of Andrew's hand and wrung my own. The sick sensation from my twenties, when all the anonymity began, returned. I knew Laney hired people for the express purpose of taking the focus off me. But I never imagined we'd still be doing it this many years later. I certainly never thought we'd force someone I cared for to take part. And I couldn't help but wonder where the hell Tex was in all this.

I took Andrew's hand again and laced my fingers in his. Eyes on the horizon, my thumb stroked his palm until he sandwiched my hand in both his. I pulled away. The rhythmic thump of the tires on the pavement joints slowed as we neared the end of the suspension bridge. The altered rhythm calmed me. I knew the situation was of my making. Andrew's involvement in the ruse was for my benefit. The blame lay elsewhere. I recalibrated. With a squeeze of his knee, I sighed. "Sorry. It's just—I feel bad for you, is all." My hand inched up his firm thigh as I kept my eyes on the approaching city.

"For me? Why?"

"Because—well, I'm gonna look *amazing* tonight." I bit the lip of my devilish smirk.

Andrew thumped his head on his headrest, seizing my hand to kiss it again.

Our goodbye came too soon. One last kiss would be all we'd have for the night, and I made the most of it. In hindsight, it was an unwise play. Time to hit the showers, cold showers. Andrew remained behind the safety of darkened windows while Dante brought my suitcase to the curb and I exited the vehicle.

"I'll see you in two hours, Miss. I'll be your ride to the event tonight." Spry for his size, Dante's kind eyes sparkled with some bit of knowledge I hadn't learned yet, but I thought I glimpsed approval. Clearly, Andrew Statheros garnered loyalty from his employees. Like Bernard, Dante appeared more like family than personnel.

"Excellent, Dante. I'll see you then." I lugged the roller-bag indoors, ready to check into my suite.

"Ms. Austin. Glad to have you back." Tofer beamed, at once hospitable, and I wondered about the change. "We have everything set up for you, just as requested. If there is anything you need during your stay..."

Tofer continued with the welcome spiel while he handled the paperwork and made a card key. When another guest completed his transaction with another desk clerk and walked away, Tofer's demeanor changed. He spoke quietly, his eyes never leaving the computer screen.

"Please accept my apology for the mess during your last visit. I can say with confidence our staff was not involved, but I do promise to take better care. Discretion is important to us, and we want our special guests to feel secure in that. Thank you for allowing us to make amends."

I nodded at the young man who, while trying to save his business face, was also making a personal apology. I knew he meant every word he said. "Thank you, Tofer. You are *very* good at what you do, but I assure you I don't know what you're talking about, so think nothing of it." I winked and headed to the elevator and the thirty-eighth floor.

21

THE MEATPACKING DISTRICT, ON the far west side of Manhattan, has been a neighborhood of change since the mid-nineteenth century. Named for the industry that saw its rise during the Industrial Revolution and then the more salacious characteristics of the darker days of the 1980s, today it is an example of gentrification—full of art galleries, nightclubs, and the High Line Park. Real estate has skyrocketed with the development of trendy boutiques and large-scale residences in century-old slaughterhouses of brick and glass.

Of course, all this revitalization came with headaches, too, making it the quintessential spot for The Luna Network to put its revival on display and for me to have to circumnavigate some media scrutiny. But damn, if I wasn't going to look good doing it.

When I stepped into the lobby from the hotel elevator, my head snapped at an exaggerated cat-call whistle. On a bench, Laney appeared to be immersed in her phone, her silvery-blonde hair even edgier than usual. I stood directly in front of her, forcing her to look straight up to meet my gaze. She didn't.

"What? No call, no text, no 'I'm on the ground, see you soon'?"

"You're on my shit list, Laney Li, and you know why, so I wasn't much for chit-chat."

She tilted to give me a wicked leer. "Would it help if I said the way you look tonight would make a good dog wanna break its leash?"

I couldn't help but soften. "Yes." I kissed her cheek as she got to her feet.

"Don't you need a bag?" She noticed my empty hands.

"I've got lip gloss, ID, a credit card, room key, and two twenty-dollar bills. I'm a simple girl with simple needs—and *pockets*, my friend." The black halter jumpsuit housed everything I needed, and I carried a matching shrug for wearing to and from the glitzy soiree, to cover the ample skin displayed in the back. My plan for the evening was to see, be seen, and get out. The less time Andrew had to take part in the charade, the better, and Laney was about to hear all about it.

"I didn't tell you because of the whole 'shoot the messenger syndrome,'" Laney admitted.

"Sounds like you're the architect, not the messenger." I had saved some snark for Laney.

"Tomato, *tomahto*."

Delight for the fancy night out mixed with the anxiety of what it all meant, and I surrendered to whatever Laney's next scheme might bring. We played catch-up while waiting for our ride—two besties, getting silly before a Saturday girls' night out. If anyone proved that age was just a number, my gal pal topped the list, and I couldn't appreciate our time together more.

When Dante arrived, I introduced him to Laney and promised her that conversation, within reason, was safe in his presence. She was wary, but then she always was. She kept talk to a minimum.

"You know Andrew's date?" I dug for information.

"I met her."

"Anything I should know?"

"Don't let her appearance throw you, but there is a method to the madness."

"What's that mean? Does she have a shaved head? A peg leg? A face tattoo?" High on New York City, my best friend, and Andrew Statheros, my mood ran more buoyant than Laney *pretended* she could bear.

"Seriously, Callie. We get this right tonight, and you don't have to worry as much. I have my doubts, though, seeing as you weren't on the ground thirty seconds before you were making out in the backseat of a car like a couple of horny teenagers." Her tone sounded like an irritated reprimand while she gave me a surreptitious fist bump with a wink.

That elicited a cough-covered laugh from Dante. I caught his eye in the rearview. With my own wink and a pretend scowl, I barked, "Eyes *front*, Dante. Mind your business."

"Yes, Miss," he snickered.

"Calliope Grace!" Laney came as close to a shout as she ever had. "This evening can do us a lot of good and freeing you from the limelight is one of them. Stay away from Mr. Statheros and if he confronts you, do not smile, blush, bat your eyelashes or give lingering looks. There will be cameras everywhere."

I gave her a reassuring hand squeeze.

The Luna Relaunched event took place on the penthouse floor and rooftop bar of an up-to-the-minute Meatpacking District hotel. Dark decor with neon lights created a spacey feel designed with The Luna Network in mind. Indoors the music boomed with a driving beat, hammering the chests and eardrums of all the glamorous party people. I couldn't help but think of my library clock with wistful thoughts of home. Once through security and the coat check, Laney pulled my arm to speak to me.

"What? I can't—" I pointed to my ear.

"Only drink what I give you, and don't put it down." She made a grave face.

I nodded, trusting her vigilance while hoping she worried for no reason.

The dance floor, surrounded by white leather half-moon-shaped booths and midnight blue tables, sparkled in the party light. Throbbing techno-music drove a grooving Cyrus to stop center stage, compelled to "vogue" for eight beats. He laughed at his retro moves, then sashayed toward me.

"You need a drink, doll," he said with a playful hip-check, followed by an admiring look at my shoes.

"Laney's getting me one, thank you."

"Isn't this fabulous? Everyone is gonna want to be part of the new Luna. You should too. It's going to be—*H-ot*!" Hot had two syllables the way Cyrus sang it.

Laney arrived with what looked like a vodka up with a twist.

"A classy drink, for a classy dame. Cheers." We clinked glasses. I took a sip and coughed a little. "Strong?" Cyrus asked. "Pace yourself. It's gonna be a long night. See ya 'round." He gamboled off toward a ringside table.

"Water, Laney? Really? First of all, I toasted with it, and everyone knows that's bad luck and second? I'm gonna need more than water to get through this."

"Don't be superstitious. Leave the paranoia to me. And you'll get something more, just on my timetable. Now, go. Mingle."

I had no idea who most of these people were, but sprinkled about, I saw the familiar faces of the would-be Tex Miller production team. One such guest introduced me to a writer colleague who was very excited about a hush-hush project he was "scripting for." The young man wasn't at liberty to tell me more, but a subtle wink from our mutual 'friend' told me what he was up to. I wished him luck. We would meet again on Monday, and I hoped he wouldn't be uncomfortable at that moment.

The Executive Producer arrived, surrounded by an entourage of up-and-comers. His gregarious hello to me turned heads. I hoped he would tamp that down for the rest of the evening, but people noticed.

Celeste surprised me when she approached, but then I remembered she mentioned how she made the rounds at these types of media events.

"Callie. Small world." It wasn't. She didn't ask me why I was there because she was already well-aware. More than anything, she enjoyed thinking she knew more than most. Information was power, and Celeste had it in abundance—and she always wanted more.

All in all, I handled the evening well. Initially, anyway. The music volume faded at some point, though it still pounded my ribcage. My cheeks had never endured so many kisses by so many in so little time, but I knew that was a byproduct of the environment. After each interaction, my eyes found Laney perched in her out-of-the-way spot, always with her eyes locked on me. It was like finding my home planet between each alien encounter on this spaceship voyage.

The one time I couldn't lay eyes on my safe-station was the moment I came face-to-face with Andrew Statheros and his date. It's not like I didn't know it would happen, but somewhere in the neon glow and cosmic dance music, I let down my guard, forgot, dropped my game face. It wasn't so much his broad shoulders in a crisp white shirt, radiant purple in the black-light shining around the vast room, or his naturally tanned skin, even darker in the otherwise low glow of the club. His curls were more playful tonight, roughed up, untamed. No, I enjoyed seeing all that and did my best to remain stoic in my reaction to it.

The challenge came with the woman on his arm. An hour earlier, Laney had clearly said, "Don't let her appearance throw you." That had been a warning, but in my giddiness, I missed the signal. Someone should have said something. Cautioned me outright. The woman stood five foot nine inches, but in heels, like me. She had long dark brown hair with a gentle wave, like mine, and brown eyes the color of—you guessed it—yours truly. Her build, though slimmer, was me ten years ago, and if I knew what to look for, I bet her rear foot pronation at heel strike was spot-on too.

"Chug-a-lug!" Like a genie-granted wish, Laney planted a real vodka twist in my shaky hand. "There's more where that came from, so down the hatch."

I did as she suggested. The stunning couple continued their walk toward us in a bevy of camera flashes I hadn't noticed before that moment. No use denying the beautiful duo was picture-worthy.

"Laney Li?" Andrew shouted over the party noise from a few steps away. "Laney Li. Drew Statheros. And this is Stephi Chase. You and I met at the Yale Club a few months back."

"Yes. Of course. Drew. Good to see you." The two leaned into one another, kissing each other's cheeks in greeting. "This is my friend, Callie. Callie Austin, this is Drew Statheros. And, Stephi, was it?"

As if on autopilot, I extended my hand to shake his.

"Nice to meet a friend of Laney's." He took my hand but also leaned in to kiss my cheek. Instead, he groaned in my ear, "God, you weren't kidding. You're *killing* me," then pulled away to gesture to his date in introduction. There was some friendly banter, but I never said a word, momentarily inebriated by the downed vodka and the rasped desire Drew Statheros had growled in my ear. The striking twosome walked away. Too soon, yet not soon enough. Palpable relief washed over me.

"Breathe," Laney demanded through her pained smile.

"Is it over yet? Can I go home, please?" I pleaded through a plastered grin.

"Let's get another drink. Head outside. You're gonna love this view. New Jersey never looked so good." We linked arms, walking to the rooftop terrace. An outdoor bartender poured our drinks, and I kept my eyes fixed on the Hudson River and Hoboken beyond it. Tower-heaters dotted the open-air space, negating the cool breezes of the early May nighttime. A bead of stress sweat rolled down my breastbone as Laney handed me a drink.

"What am I doing?" I exhaled the question with the harshness of more vodka.

"You're enjoying a stunning view on a gorgeous night." She gave an uncharacteristically grand gesture to our surroundings.

"No, what am I doing here? Like this? Why are we doing this? So no one knows who I am? Does anyone really care? Do I care anymore?"

"That's a lot of questions. Why? So you can have a sort of normal life. Does anyone care? Twitter and Reddit both say, 'yes.' Do you care? I don't know, but I think you do, and this is just an adjustment we need to make. We'll figure it out. But if this show takes off, yeah, it's gonna get harder again. People are going to be looking for you, for *her*—for Calliope Jones. And if you want her to stay hidden, then folly like this will have to continue. And you hanging around with someone who attracts attention, like our boy in there, is not good for your anonymity. Don't shoot the messenger."

"Right. And let's not forget the part where it all goes away if the world finds out. Bye-bye readership. So long royalties. Because chances are, the Tex-love isn't about my writing."

"Stop. You're stunning tonight, but Imposter Syndrome? It's not a good look. Get over it."

I gulped the rest of my drink. "Have you found out how *Ogler* got their intel?"

"No."

"Did his date have to look like…"

"It could come in handy, and she doesn't, not in the face." Laney sipped her drink.

I looked at her askance.

"Did you see her chin?"

I shook my head. "*Uh*, no?"

"*Exactly*!" Laney clinked my martini glass while I snorted.

Laney and I made one more lap of the party. It gave no indication of slowing down, but Laney assured me we had done all we needed to do. When I ventured out to the coat check to collect my shrug, more people were coming than going. The crush at the large walk-in closet grew as more patrons got in line, and the sole attendant took her time. Music pulsed overhead in the dark corridor, claustrophobic in the closeness of it all. When a hand touched my bare back, I flinched before seeing Andrew next to me. He kept that hand on my skin for far too long.

"What are you doing?" I nonchalantly sidestepped away from him.

"I'm getting Stephi's jacket. Come to my place." We didn't look at one another as we stood side by side, inching our way to the coat check.

"What?"

"Come to my loft. It's a few blocks north."

"How?"

"Dante."

"I can't."

"You can." He gently nudged me toward the Dutch door and the employee behind it. His thumb stroked the round of my bare shoulder.

"I can't." I flinched from the tenderness of his touch again.

"You can, for a little while. One drink. I'll be a complete gentleman."

I stifled a laugh. "I *can't*." The coat-check girl reached for my claim ticket. Flustered, I handed her a twenty-dollar bill instead, and she quickly placed it in the tip jar. I caught her smile as I chanced a look at Andrew, dropping my voucher as I did it. He knelt to pick it up and gave it to the young woman, who turned to collect my wrap.

"I wish you would." His face begged, and the weighty gaze made me so dizzy with desire, I forgot myself and placed my hand on his chest. I fingered a button on his dress shirt, mesmerized by his stare.

When the woman returned with my shrug, she cleared her throat, bringing me back to Earth. I grabbed my garment. "I'm so sorry," I whispered and pushed by him in search of Laney.

"Cal," Laney stepped into my line of sight. "All good?"

"Yep. It's warm back there. Where am I taking you?"

"Nah, I got a car coming. Poor Dante's been sitting around all night. I'm not about to make him drive to Brooklyn. A man that size, I want to keep on my good side. Unless you're up for another drink somewhere?"

I looked back toward the coat check. "Uh, no. I'm pooped. Flight and all today. Of course, no commitments tomorrow. Not until Monday morning, right?" Maybe my distraction appeared like fatigue. But more likely, my friend let me off the hook to assuage my guilt and poor choices without calling me out in case I followed my heart instead of my head. For once.

"Yeah, but I get it. Get some rest. Maybe brunch tomorrow?"

"Mimosas and carbs? Yes, please."

We rode the elevator down in silence and kissed cheeks as she hopped into her rideshare that had pulled behind Dante's parked town car. Dante waited at the rear door for me. I pulled my shrug around, feeling the cool night air in earnest now. Ducking into the vehicle, I was disappointed to find the back seat vacant. Somehow, I'd convinced myself Andrew would be waiting there for me. I shook it off.

"Did you have a nice time, Miss?"

"Yes, thank you, Dante. Hey, I had asked about Bernard earlier, but we were—interrupted. How is he? Do you know?"

"He's doing good. Real good. Comes to the garage a few days a week. Mr. Statheros has him doing some office duties. Scheduling rides and maintenance, and such. Drew's the best boss."

I agreed with a nod into the rearview, my face highlighted by a streetlamp ahead of us.

"Where to, Miss?"

I looked at my reflection and Dante's enquiring eyes. "My hotel, Dante. Please."

"Yes, Miss." He put the car in gear and pulled from the curb. For twenty minutes, we rode through town in stop-and-go traffic. It was Saturday night in the city that never sleeps, and plenty of cars and people were on the streets to prove it.

"Dante?"

"Yes, Miss?" He spoke half over his shoulder.

"Would you—could you—hand me a water, please?"

The man leaned to pull a bottle of water from the cooler in the front floorboard and handed it to me over the seat. I drained the fluids as we pulled up to the loading zone at my hotel, then cursed with my head pressed to the headrest while Dante exited the vehicle to open my door. As I stepped out, Dante gave a slight flick to the brim of his cap. My feet didn't move, but my gaze rose from the pavement to look the man in the eye. "Don't hate me, Dante."

Dante lowered his chin and seemed to read my mind. "Not a problem, Miss. I'm headed that way anyhow. Hop in."

We sped back to the Meatpacking District.

22

Dante parked near a large industrial elevator in a well-lit, spotless underground garage and escorted me out of the vehicle.

"This will open directly into his apartment with this key." He handed me a heavy for its size, short steel elevator key on a length of chain. "Put it in the lock for the sixth floor and turn it. The lift is slow, but it will open directly into his loft."

I nodded at his instructions. "Thanks, Dante. You're not coming up?"

"No, Miss." He flicked his cap again and returned to the town car. The cargo elevator ride was slow and jostling, and I held tight to side-mounted handles in the immense cage to steady myself on the climb. When the scissor gates arrived at an already opened freight door on the top floor, I found Stephi Chase, stilettos dangling from her fingers as she padded toward me bright-eyed and friendly.

"On my way!" Stephi shouted into her phone, then grabbed me by the chin. "Thanks for the great date." She kissed me with an open mouth and eager tongue, then whirled past me, pushing me out of the lift and into the apartment. "God, I love that guy. Hey, take the key." She tossed me the chain before clicking the gate closed. With a flirty wave, Stephi Chase descended into the night as the freight door slid shut.

Disoriented by the provocative reception, doubts regarding the evening's rash detour came on hard and fast. Woozy, I stood in an open-concept space that comprised a large living room, dining room combination with a bright white and stainless kitchen beyond it. Mortar-smeared brick surrounded window after window down the longest wall. Lighting glowed low, mostly from the under-cabinet fixtures in the kitchen. Distant street noise rumbled, but inside, the place was dead quiet, doing little to help my growing unease.

The beautifully decorated room, split into three distinct spaces, was colorful though masculine, with enormous Rothko-esque artwork hung in those spaces that weren't window. The floors were wood plank, worn and uneven, and evidently old, but the contrast with the sleek white kitchen and low-profile furniture showed an understanding of good design. It was an impressive home, but nothing like I imagined. It didn't feel like Andrew.

As I took it all in, barefoot steps approached from down a hall I wasn't far enough in the apartment to see. Andrew appeared through the opening and headed to the kitchen. Wearing nothing but long drawstring pajama bottoms low on his hips, he stretched his arms wide, and I watched his back muscles flex as his shoulder blades met in the middle. He gave a quick check of the phone sitting on the expanse of white quartz before walking around the large kitchen island to pour a glass of water and turning off the under-cabinet lights. The water went down in four long gulps, and I admired his silhouette in the semi-darkness. Streetlamps outside, plus a small light on an entry table next to me, allowed the view.

"Hi," I said, planted at my spot near the elevator.

Andrew set down his glass as I spoke. It tipped over, nearly rolling into the sink. He caught it and spun around in one smooth move.

"Hi. You're—here."

"I am." I gave a meek wave, far less flirty than Stephi's. He placed the glass upright and walked around the island where I could see him in better light. He stopped, still several feet from me. "You startled me. I didn't think you were coming."

"I see." I eyed his casual attire. "I saw." My head pointed to the elevator, implying his recent guest.

"No, I mean, I called and texted and got no reply." He leaned against one of the support poles lining the middle of the apartment, arms folded against his shapely bare chest.

"So, you got naked with your school chum?"

"What? No. She waited for Dante to take her to her *next* date. I figured if you were coming, you'd have been here an hour ago, sooner even. But after no word from you, I got ready for bed. Alone."

"I don't have my phone." I shrugged, my gaze squarely on him.

"You should always carry a phone, Calliope."

"I've been told." We stood in awkward silence, but when a car honked down below, I jumped to speak again. "Sooo, this was an error in judgment. I see that now." I put my hands on my hips with a sudden interest in the crystals adorning my Manolos.

"Because you think I slept with Stephi?"

"No, I believe you didn't."

"Cuz she'd sooner sleep with you than with me."

"Yeah, I got that impression." I reflexively brought my fingers to my lips.

He chuckled. "She's friendly."

Dwelling on Andrew's fake date's friendliness wasn't high on my to-do list. "If you could get in touch with Dante or order me up a rideshare, I'll be going." I turned to face the elevator, then back around to him. "Oh, and here's the key."

He caught it one-handed without stopping on his route to

where I stood. Without missing a step, he tossed it onto the industrial chic metal table beside me. The *clang,* as metal hit metal, jarred the stillness. I flinched. My sweater shrug had fallen, resting in the crook of my arms, allowing his warm hands to clasp my bare shoulders. Then his lips were on mine. Tumbling into the pleasure of it, my hands slid up his chest and around his neck. Still cool from the water he'd drunk, his mouth tasted of mint. I wobbled on my heels, and he knocked me into the elevator door.

Barely an inch from me, he asked, "You okay?"

"Yes—wait." The sound of our breathing bounced around the entryway as he stepped back. I flung off my shoes and emptied my pockets on the entry table, then grabbed his face before anyone changed their mind. His grip tightened around me, drawing me toward him and deeper into his apartment. Neither of us spoke, but his body leaned, implying we should move down the hallway I knew must lead to a bedroom. Instead, I pulled toward the living room and the, to-my-mind, safer blue suede sofa.

Sitting on the couch, he held my hand as I stood over him, peeling off my sweater. In the dim light, his dark blue eyes grew darker still—midnight blue, but heated with want. I twisted my hair over my shoulder and straddled his lap, sliding down to kiss him again, making clear the desire was mutual. A twinge in my knee ached, but when his hands skimmed up my exposed back, the pain vanished, but not before a soft moan escaped my throat. Andrew's mouth released mine, kissed my cheek, and continued down to that spot below my ear. A gentle nip aroused a flashback to my hotel suite all those weeks ago. My stomach tightened as I whispered, "Andrew" into his dark curls.

Hearing his name, Andrew stopped and nudged me upright to look me in the eye again. There was no boyish grin now. Nothing *boyish* at all. We stared while his hand ran the length of my arm, then brought my palm to his lips. Another kiss on the underside of my wrist made me see stars, and I closed my eyes to combat vertigo. Enjoying the sensation, I emitted a low hum. A gentle pull on my neck brought our mouths together again. I pushed in, unable to get close enough, greedy for more. When his fingers tugged on one end of the bow knot of my halter, another wave of dizziness hit, and I emitted an airy squeak with a sharp inhale. After the briefest hesitation, I sighed "yes," and kissed him harder.

But, as if on cue, the phone on the island lit up and pinged. I gave another quick gasp as his hands dropped to my thighs. Determined to ignore the interruption, my mouth collided with his while my hand encouraged his fingers to resume their magic on the tie at the nape of my neck. Again, the phone chirped. I rested my forehead against his.

"Andrew, *please* don't answer that," I whispered as my thumb stroked his lips. "*Please* do *anything* but answer that."

Those hands that had lost their way returned to my hips and slid up my back again. But as soon as he met flesh, the phone lit up and signaled, again. All momentum ceased.

"I'm sorry," he exhaled a sigh, chin to his chest. "I've got drivers on the roads tonight, and it's late. It could be a sister or my mom, someone who needs me." He gripped my sides.

"Well, speaking of needs—*uh*, no, of course. Right." I rolled off his lap, sucking air through gritted teeth as my knee made itself known again. Noticing my wince, he hesitated to stand, but I waved him off, not wishing to draw attention to it.

The bluish tint of the phone screen illuminated his face. The grimace was unmistakable. Another ping sounded as he read. His fingers ran through his curly mop. "Dammit." He tossed the phone with a *smack* on the kitchen island.

I draped my arm over the back of the low sofa, resting my head in the bend of my elbow, staring at Andrew's bare back. He'd turned around, placing both hands, arms spread wide, on the counter. His head hung while I waited for him to speak. He didn't. Pulling my wrap around my shoulders, I slipped my arms through the sleeves. A chill settled around me. I thanked the universe that he faced the other way as I stood and took three old lady steps before my knee cooperated with my asking it to move. My hand caressed the smooth, tight skin of his muscular arm, and I placed a gentle kiss on his shoulder. His body tensed with a held breath.

"You need to go somewhere?" I couldn't stand the quiet any longer.

"No. But we need to get you out of here."

"Don't tell me your wife is on her way." I felt a modicum of relief when his shoulders relaxed with something bordering on a brief chuckle.

"The texts. They're from Laney. *Ogler* posted again."

"I'm sorry. But we knew this might happen, right? Wasn't that sort of the point? I mean, Stephi knew what she was getting into." I wrapped my arms around his waist, determined not to call time-of-death on the night, and rested my head against his back, breathing in his heated scent.

"Not Stephi and me. You and me."

"What?" My own heat left me, sucked out along with the air in my lungs. "But there *was* no you and me." I wheezed with the last ounce of oxygen and let go of him.

"Well, the art says otherwise."

"Pictures? Let me see."

Andrew handed me his phone. I clicked the link.

OGLER.COM– The Greek God and Gimpy No More
Ogled! She's baaaack! It's been since

early March, but this brunette would-be
Helen of Troy has ventured back on
the scene with everyone's favorite
Greek-flavored playboy. At a space-themed
celebration of the new and improved Luna
Network, the mystery lady landed, looking
ravishing in black, turning the heads of
media types of every species. We're looking
at you, [a particularly well sought-after
EP rumored to be hitching his star power
to a new hush-hush Luna Network original
series]. Does this out-of-this-world woman
have some connection to that? And where
has she been these past weeks? Maybe she's
a UFO (Unidentifiable Foxy Outsider). More
importantly, is she looking to take a piece
of the Meatpacking District's Grade A Prime
off the market? Tune in. Ogler will go
where no one has gone before to get the
scoop.

"Seriously. Who writes this shit? I mean, it's just bad writing." I scrolled to view the photos.

"I'm not sure that's the point." Andrew reached for my cheek, but I shrank from his touch.

"And these photos. They're from when we said hello. You kissed my cheek. Lots of people kissed my cheek. You kissed lots of cheeks. *This* is the photo they post? Okay, you with your hand on my shoulder at the coat check—well, that could have been worse, *much* worse. And weird how none of them really show my face. The last time, too."

"I'm sorry, Calliope. I shouldn't have touched you."

"And this one—wait. This one is..."

"What?"

"That. There." I pointed to the edge of the zoomed in photo. "That's Dante. That's Dante flicking the brim of his cap. Someone took a picture of me without you anywhere around. This was after I left the party. Dante took me to the hotel. They followed me to my hotel?"

Andrew hung his head.

"This isn't about you, is it?" I set the phone on the counter next to him as a sudden wave of sickness hit me.

"Laney doesn't think so. She thinks the first one was to stir up talk, and when it didn't go anywhere, they doubled-down this time. Someone is trying to find out who you are."

"That's dumb, and it wouldn't be hard to find out my name. I was on the guest list. It wouldn't take much at all to find out. I don't get it."

"Exactly. Which means whoever is doing this knows who you are and thinks everyone should, too. And probably who *else* you are."

"To what end?"

"I don't know. Laney's working on it."

"And why is Laney contacting you?"

Drew picked up the phone, pulled up his texts, and handed it to me to read.

Laney Li: *Our girl is asleep, but she's going to wake to this in the morning. This isn't her world. She doesn't get it. You need to help her get it. Please... help her get it.*

There was more to the message, but I couldn't read any further. My eyes wouldn't allow it. I asked for directions to the bathroom. When I returned to the living room, Andrew had lit another lamp and wore a t-shirt, arms crossed in a rigid lean against a pole again.

"Dante's downstairs. He'll get you back to the hotel, take you in through the garage. Cisco will meet you at a freight elevator only used by employees. He'll be sure you get to your room."

I nodded at the instructions. No point in contesting. After I slipped into my shoes and gathered my things, Andrew wrapped his arms around me in a powerful embrace.

"You okay?" He whispered in my ear.

"I just wanna get home."

"This time of night—fifteen minutes—"

"No, my home. Charlotte. It's simpler there." The elevator door opened as the scissor gate rose out of the dark. I pulled from his hold to contract the metal grid enough to enter the cage. "What's next? I mean, what happens tomorrow?"

"I don't know." He stepped toward me, but I put up my hand to stop him.

"Andrew, I swear to God, if you touch me again, I'm not leaving." Fear and longing tangled inside me.

He took his frustration out on his curls as the freight door slid closed between us.

The return to the hotel went as Andrew had described. Dante saw me to Cisco; Cisco saw me to my suite. I pushed through the door, thanking the young man for his help and offered the second twenty I pulled from my pocket. He refused it. With no more fight in me, I let the door shut.

I kicked off my shoes on the way to the window to see the view I hadn't taken the time to enjoy when I first checked in that afternoon. The Empire State Building glowed red. I couldn't tell you why, but it didn't feel like a good omen. In fact, quite the opposite. Dread shot through me as I slipped off the sweater shrug and trudged to the closet. My whole body ached as I pulled the end of the bow knot at my neck. It hung, still half undone from an hour earlier, before Andrew's phone lit up, bringing the night to a crashing halt. I washed and dressed for bed, and true to form, my head hit the pillow, and I was asleep. But the last words on my lips were, "Tex, I need you."

23

RAIN FELL HARD ENOUGH to blur my view, and thunder boomed with angry crashes that shook the building. Turning from the window, I did something I hadn't done since I wrote book number two. I crawled back into bed and pulled the covers over my head.

A knock on my door woke me sometime later. I threw the covers off, waiting to hear housekeeping enter. Nothing. Another rap sounded. Louder this time. Swinging my feet to the floor, I howled with the first step on my bad leg. Damn my knee and the rainy weather. By the time I reached the door, all was in working order again. Through the peephole, I eyed Laney, winding up to bang on the door for the third time. I opened it and walked away with no greeting.

"Figured you weren't much for going out for brunch, the weather and all—so I brought brunch to you."

"Why?"

"Why? Why *what*?"

"Evidently, I don't know much in this world, Laney Li, but I know two things for sure. One, you don't do hugs; two, you don't bring me food. Ever. So, I ask again. Why?"

Laney ignored me. Rain droplets flew as she fanned out her coat over a chair to dry. In continued silence, she pulled paper napkins and wooden cutlery from one of the paper sacks, arranging them like a formal dinner party. The smell of fresh, warm bagels wafted from the brown wrappings. A momentary distraction.

I flopped on the sofa as the realization hit. "Oh, jeez. You know. Fine. You know, and what? You're *pissed*? Because there's no reason to be pissed. Anything having to do with *Ogler* had nothing to do with my post-party field trip. I didn't give them anything they didn't already have, and I got back here using some serious cloak and dagger shit. It's a wonder I didn't end up in the trunk of a car at some point. *Ridiculous.* You're pissed," I scoffed.

"Someone's pissed. Pretty sure it's not me. Bagel?" Laney spoke with unusual sweetness, which only riled me more.

"And the first photo? Come on! How many cheeks got kissed last night? That photo could have been anyone. And another thing, if you thought I was the target from the get-go, you should have said. So, you hold some blame too, Miss Li."

"It's Laney or Laney Li, never Miss Li. And you mean to tell me there was anything that was going to keep you from going to him last night, short of a shock collar? I don't think so. And I'm on your side, and I am not pissed, so let's eat some carbs and make a *damn* plan."

"How'd you find out?"

Laney busied herself with a coffee: six creamers, six sugars. She handed me a cup, black.

"Oh, my God. He told you? That *jackass*. What did you do? You probably glared at him and he folded like a lawn chair, didn't he? *Wow*. Did *not* see that coming."

"We *texted*, and he did the right thing. I can't control the story without all the facts. It's not the crime, it's the cover-up. He's smart. He gets it. And he cares what happens to you, which will always win points with me."

"That's right. I don't get it, but he does. Glad you two can team up to teach the rube a lesson in smear campaigns and the destruction of the love lives of the rich and not-so-famous."

"Love lives, *huh*? Alright, I see where this is coming from. I get it."

"No, you *don't*. Don't read into my witty banter."

Laney laughed in her straight-faced way. "It's fine to be mad at me. Don't be mad at him. He feels awful. He also said nothing happened last night, and I kinda believe him."

"For the record, I think it's *super* cute how you two are text besties now, and I wouldn't say *nothing* happened." I grabbed a bagel and a large container of cream cheese.

"Oh, yeah?"

"Stephi Chase kissed me. On the mouth. With tongue, so—"

"I KNEW it! My gaydar is still good. Up top." We high-fived and dug into brunch.

I spent the rest of the day alone, snuggled up with books and room service. Any other time, this would be heaven on earth. The three texts I composed to Andrew sat idle until I eventually deleted them instead of hitting *send*. I didn't know what to say, and since he hadn't reached out either, maybe no contact was the best plan. Besides, tomorrow was a big day of table reads. My focus needed to zero in on that, and I didn't know how to manage my expectations. As the day wound down, I checked my phone one last time before calling it a night. Andrew had emailed.

Calliope:
Per advice from your agent, I didn't call or show up or even text, but by the end of the day, it didn't feel right, so here we are. I kept busy

enough, I suppose. After nine oil changes and a mess of paperwork, it was time for dinner at my Mom's. It's not as childish as it sounds. One Sunday a month, the whole extended family gathers for dinner. The crowd is big and loud, with a ton of kids that climb all over me like I'm a jungle gym. I gotta say, it's pretty great.

Anyway, I thought of you the whole time and hope your day was better than oil changes and paperwork, but nothing is better than my Mom's bougatsa.

Laney invited me to the reading tomorrow. She said it was a "safe space," and if I could get there under the radar, I was welcome. With all the work I did today, I could probably make that happen if you want me there. I won't show up without your say-so. So... say so?
-Andrew

I replied:

Andrew:

I say so. -Calliope

24

Monday morning, I flew out of the hotel, ready to get to The Luna Network disaster zone. Sure, I was eager to see all the hard work the production team had done in the hopes the *Tex* project would get off the ground, but that wasn't the real reason. I felt sixteen again, and Bobby Janko had asked me to the senior prom—jelly from foot to eyeballs. Teenagers are notoriously dumb, yet there I was, feeling like one all over again. And I loved every tingly moment of it.

Dante greeted me with a flicked brim and a broad smile on the gloriously sunny May morning. Everything gleamed cleaner and greener after the deluge of the day before, and life itself was better than twenty-four hours ago. Traffic moved fast, and I texted with Laney the whole way, thanking her for the invitation to Andrew and letting her know I was open-minded and eager to be impressed, knowing it would be an outstanding day. Her reply?

Laney: *Whatever they put in your coffee this morning... I need some.*

I met my agent friend in the lobby of Luna's building as we had twice before, but this time I hit the call button once and waited. A model of patience. When the doors glided open, we encountered our first surprise. The elevator glistened, completely refurbished. Floor-to-ceiling stainless-steel in a flashy grid pattern sparkled. A dramatic, high-shine zebra wood floor matched handrails, gleaming under a series of small, round halogens that dotted the car's ceiling while a laser-cut carbon-fiber sign emblazoned on the back wall told us we were riding in style with The Luna Network. Laney and I nodded to one another on the fast, smooth ride to the top floor.

The war zone was a war zone no more. The Luna Network buzzed, up and running on rocket fuel. More carbon-fiber, more halogens, and more glossy zebra wood met us when we stepped onto the tenth floor. They had removed all the ceiling tiles to show off some refurbished remnants of the original pressed tin and left the HVAC and electricals unmasked for an industrial feel that coordinated with the updated design. Shiny white tables served as desk space, and the bold furniture was modern but comfy in Luna's own crushed velvet. They picked a spacey midnight blue. Yes, The Luna Network had come to play, and they planned to be taken seriously.

"Hello, hello!" Cyrus kissed our cheeks.

"Where's Jason?" My focus darted from one shiny surface to another and all the people in between.

"Oh, throwing up somewhere. Boss-man has such a sensitive tummy. Let's get you settled." Cyrus led us to the open space where we first met. Gone were the mismatched sofas, replaced with a huge, sleek table and long, cushion-backed benches. The space theme continued with coordinating Egg Chairs on swivels around the room. "You choose. Sit at the table with the team and actors or separate."

"Actors?"

"How else can you hear the episodes, sweetie?"

I shrugged.

"Laney Li, could I bend your ear for one teeny, tiny, hot minute?" Cyrus wiggled his finger. I waved her off to take in the view. My forehead pressed to the window while I looked to the street below. Ten floors up wasn't so high, but I didn't see anyone I recognized.

"Who ya lookin' for?" Andrew asked.

My breath fogged a circle on the glass as I exhaled in surprise. We stood side by side, and I caught his faded reflection. He wore jeans and a well-worn Mets t-shirt, more casual than I'd ever seen him. *God, he made me swoon.*

"Bobby Janko." I leaned against the window again, and Andrew did the same.

"Who's Bobby Janko?"

"The first boy that ever made my heart race. I thought about him this morning."

"Because your heart was racing?"

"Maybe. I'm glad you're here."

"Once you said I could be, I don't think anything could have kept me away."

"Well, Laney is sizing us up for shock collars so—be careful." Arms at our sides, the backs of our hands grazed one another's. Fingers barely touched as we kept our gazes to street level.

"Calliope, can we talk? I really think we need to talk." Andrew asked with a new gravity to his tone.

A cleared throat interrupted the moment. We spun to see Laney like chaperone-busted teenagers.

"Slight hiccup. Missing participant. Appendicitis. Apparently, the show doesn't *always* go on." Laney gave a barbed look to our now parted hands, then our faces, with a silent but stern reprimand. But that severe look softened almost immediately. "Hey, Baby Driver. First. Mets, I approve." She pointed at his chest. "Second. You do it."

Andrew and I both replied with a snappy, "*Huh?*"

"Yale drama in the house. Grab a script. Save the day."

I stepped away, hands in surrender. "This is between you all. I'm just here to listen."

"Cal—?" Andrew gave a questioning look while Laney dragged him down the hall to some place called a "green room."

Laney and I opted not to sit at the table with the production team and actors. The young man who bragged about his top-secret writing gig at the Luna party chose a different arrangement, too. He seemed determined to wear a hole in the shiny new floors, pacing the corner in a sweat, chewing a thumbnail. Talk about green. I gave a quick wave—a wave that apparently pushed his stomach to its breaking point. He bolted from the room, and I could only hope Jason had finished so the writer could have his turn with the toilet.

Laney leaned over as the actors, binders in their hands, filed into the room to take their seats. "Drew's gonna rock the face off Tex Miller."

"What?" The color drained from my face. "He's reading the part of Tex?" Laney gave an excited head jiggle in the affirmative. The young writer and Jason had both returned, and if my legs could have functioned at that moment, I would have run for the toilet myself. Too late.

In the end, the writer had nothing to fear. It was good. Very good.

No question, hearing all the different voices gave a better feel for the story, and the actors made an impressive showing. I made every effort to keep my eyes on my own paper without making eye contact with Andrew and, to my knowledge, he only looked at me once.

                          TEX

  Are you going to keep on like this? The
whole time?

                         RUBY

Keep on like what?

                          TEX

The talking. The constant blather.

                         RUBY

  I'm nervous, Tex. And when I'm uneasy,
I blather and when you just lie there,
saying nothing at all, it only makes me
more nervous, so I keep—

                          TEX

  Talking. Yes, I see that. Quite the
merry-go-round you've got us on, isn't it?

                         RUBY

  The solution is a simple one, you know.
Talk to me. Tell me what's going on under
those curls there.

TEX

You scare the hell out of me, Ruby. It's not a feeling I'm familiar with.

RUBY

Scared of little ol' me? Why's that? Let me guess. It's cuz I'm the Admiral's daughter, isn't it?. I get that a lot.

TEX

Definitely not that. Don't get me wrong. I respect your father more than most anybody. But I can handle him. I'm guessing it's more to do with my recent realization that there's nothing I wouldn't do for you.

RUBY

Like what? Finally reading *The Notebook*? I'm telling you that Nicholas Sparks can write.

Tex doesn't respond.

Ruby turns serious.

RUBY (CONT'D)

You mean, like laying down your life for me?

TEX

Aw, come on. I'm Navy—from a long line of Navy men. Laying down my life is part of my job description. That and making quick work of buttons. Lots of buttons on those dress uniforms.

RUBY

I like all your buttons. And what's under them.

TEX

That, my dear, is where the 'quick work' comes into play.

RUBY

There's that stoic flirt I remember. Dying doesn't scare you?

TEX

No. Chancing death to protect my country, my fellow Sailors, you? That's nothing.

RUBY

So, what's this fear, then?

TEX

It's the other part. The unconscionable bit where I'd *kill* for you. If anyone or anything ever harmed you? I'd kill with malice and without remorse. No matter my orders, or who got in my way. No questions asked. My need for you to be safe supersedes all of it. Everything. That loss of morality scares the hell out of me. And

yet, here I am—not giving a damn. Now go
to sleep. We move out at dawn. And I need
my beauty rest.

*Tex pulls the brim of his cap over his
eyes, ending the conversation.*

When the scene ended, Andrew's eyes shot to me. I returned his
look with a fleeting smile he didn't reciprocate.

At the halfway mark, the performers retreated to that green
room, which, by the way, was not green, and the production team
stretched, giving sidelong glances while I wrote notes longhand.
Those exiting included Andrew, still without even a glance in my
direction.

Laney walked my way, leaving a muttering klatch of producers
huddled around the coffee service. "They're impressed," she
whispered.

"*Hmm*," was all I gave her.

"Aren't you?"

"I am." I continued scribbling notes.

"You good?"

"I am."

Laney sat next to me. "Is this some kind of hardball poker face
routine going on here, or do we have a problem? Cuz, if we need
to shut this down, we shut it down."

"You're not interested in hearing the rest, Laney?"

"Okay, what is this?" Her palm circled my face. "I don't know
what this is."

The actors returned. I bent to whisper in Laney's ear. "This is
my 'Oh, this is happening' face."

Laney's face broadened into her version of a smile. "Really?

That's—wait, *what's* happening?"

"*Shh.*" I pointed to the group ready to resume.

The second half proved as entertaining as the first. The storyline followed the book, mostly. They combined some minor characters to make one, and cut a mini-subplot, but I saw the logic in it. Truth be told, my first book wasn't my best, and the writing team had done wonders with the source material. They created laugh-out-loud moments, and when the dramatic scenes sprang up, the juxtaposition made them that much more poignant.

But the last-minute stand-in impressed me most of all. The impromptu understudy given no time to prepare. Already a fan of Andrew's in general, watching him act thrilled me. His comic timing was perfect, and the quieter moments made you lean in to catch every syllable. When he said he was good at it, it wasn't false bravado. Merely a fact. Andrew Statheros was a talented actor.

With the reading complete, discussion with the production team would follow. As the break in between began, I angled toward Laney, whispering, "I need a minute alone with Andrew."

Laney rolled her eyes and shook her head.

"I'm serious. Just a minute. Promise. Get him to the green room in like thirty seconds." I rose from my seat and beelined to the rendezvous spot.

Once in the cushy lounge, I was pleased to find a lock on the door. I paced, waiting for Andrew's arrival. A hesitant knock startled me, and I opened the door a crack to see his turned-down head. Grabbing him by the shirt, I dragged him into the room, kissing him at once. The door slammed too loudly, but I didn't care. I shoved him against it with one hand as I locked the knob with the other. Both hands groped his chest. My lips melted into his, a slow, deep kiss I could have stayed in forever. Andrew held me by my shoulders, at first squeezing, pulling me toward him, but then he gently nudged me away.

In a raspy whisper, I said, "We have, like, fourteen seconds before I have to walk out of here. Kiss me again and tell me you will come to my hotel tonight. I don't care how. Just get there." I kissed him again, noting more resistance before his uncertainty vanished, and he seized me in a fierce embrace. I hated to pull away. "Please get there," I murmured again, this time looking into his stormy eyes. With one more tender kiss, I unlocked the door and slid through a narrow opening.

When I picked up my notebook to sit in my chair, Laney didn't take her eyes off her phone. "All set there? You look a little flushed. That green room get warm?"

"Maybe a bit." My fingertips touched my tingling lips, already missing Andrew's. "We ready to talk about this thing or what?"

Just as I spoke those words, the Executive Producer asked, "Where'd our Tex go? Where'd you find that new guy? I want a screen test. Outstanding."

That new guy had bolted, and I would soon find out that new guy had zero interest in ever playing Tex Miller again, under any circumstances. Ever.

25

SUNDOWN CAME AND WENT, and the Empire State Building remained its ominous red. Primped and preened and dressed in a black, lacy chemise under a matching silk robe, I sipped a glass of wine. Not my first. Hopes that anyone other than me would see the lingerie dwindled as my foolish feelings grew. Replaying the clandestine minute in the green room, I realized Andrew never said he would meet me. Upon further reflection, it occurred to me that Andrew hadn't said a word in that room. Not one. Though not my typical behavior, I checked and rechecked my phone for voicemail or a text, an email even, to give some clue as to his whereabouts. I got no answers.

By eleven-thirty, I gave up. Wrenching one arm free from my robe, I called it a night. But a quiet knock brought new hope. With my robe back on, I hurried to the peephole to see Andrew in the hall. One deep breath, and I swiftly opened and closed the door—just enough time to allow him quick access. Like the green room earlier, it was a rush of mouths and hands and heavy breathing. In the dim, close-quartered vestibule of the suite, I wrestled off his jacket, tossing it onto the entry table. The force of the flying coat sent a lamp teetering. Andrew caught it before gravity had its way. In the commotion, I stepped back against a floor to ceiling mirror. Two feet apart, we watched one another.

"God, what are you wearing?" he murmured.

"Not much," came my quick reply. I rolled my eyes at myself. It sounded sexy when I rehearsed it earlier.

He pushed against me again and I gasped at the cold glass on my skin, then shivered as his thumb traced the line of my collarbone. He slid one of the negligee's lace straps off my shoulder, but a door slam in the hallway startled us both into stopping. A grunt of frustration exhaled in my ear, and Andrew stepped away.

I swallowed hard. "How about a drink?" I asked, steadying myself before I walked by him into the living room.

"I—I already had one. Two, actually."

"I could tell."

"I'm not drunk. It was two drinks."

"No, I could taste it, is all."

His agile lamp-saving reflexes assured me he was sober. Still, I poured myself another splash of wine, mostly to have something to do. "Did you need to throw back a couple to get up the nerve to come see me?" Surely, I meant it as a joke. Didn't I?

"I don't know. Did I need to spend the day acting like Tex Miller for you to get up the desire to be with me?"

Before I turned, I downed the swig of wine, letting the question hang. "What?" With a shaky hand, I set my glass on the credenza.

"Is that what this is about? Him? Because I guess I could just go along. I mean, why not, right? I get mine, and you get—what exactly? But I guess I'd like to know. Is—is he back? Or am I—?"

"Don't."

"Don't what? *Don't* ask the obvious question? *Don't* feel threatened by the competition, which, by the way, after today, has proven to be—*beyond* formidable. *Don't* ask where your head really is, or who it is you really want here because I'm not gonna like the answer? What is it you *don't* want me to do, Calliope? I mean, other than *don't* be seen with you, because *that* you've made crystal clear."

A buzzing invaded my brain. Not an alcohol buzz, a high-pitched pulsating hum boring through my temple. Eyeing my pedicured toes and my ridiculous get-up, I realized the foolishness felt earlier had been a profound understatement. How had I allowed myself to get here?

"This?" Andrew pointed skyward. "This dead air? It's the wrong answer." Andrew fell quiet. His whole being seeped hurt as he stood with his hands on his hips, sad eyes focused on the floor.

Somehow, kicking him while he was down seemed like the appropriate response.

"How about *don't* be a child. *Don't* talk about things you don't understand. And *don't* spend another minute thinking about this thing that never was because it's never gonna be. And last, don't let the door hit you in the ass on your way out." I spun on my bare heel and rushed straight to my bedroom, sliding the pocket door with a slam. It wasn't until he was out of sight that I noticed my inability to breathe. The tightness in my chest constricted further as the buzzing morphed into a roar. "Shit." I ran back to the living room, then to the hall door. Andrew had taken his coat and left.

I stumbled back into my suite, still begging to breathe. The panic grew until I counted. Inhale, two, three, four. Exhale, two, three, four. Inhale... The pattern continued as I dragged my feet back to my bed. There, sporting Hawaiian swim trunks with snorkel gear wrapped around his forehead, Tex relaxed against the headboard on one side of the king bed, flippered feet crossed at the ankles. I took the same position on the other side.

"You know what this reminds me of?" Tex asked, while looking through the end of his snorkel like it was a handheld telescope.

"What's that?"

"Book seven. When I go swimming in that little cove on the

island that no one has ever heard of."

"Yeah."

"I get—what was it? A cramp?"

"Stung by a jellyfish," I reminded him.

"That's right. And the water comes up over my face. I can't breathe, and I'm tired, feeling the end near. What is it I think at that moment?"

"Gee, Tex. Why don't you tell me?"

"Nah, I think it's better if you say it."

I flashed to a scene from two months earlier. Andrew in my favorite room, sitting on a well-worn leather sofa in front of a fire. *Am I water in this scenario?*

"You think, 'Wow, who knew this beautiful, warm, inviting body of water would turn out to be so scary? Such a drowning hazard?'"

"Yep. That's it." We sat side by side as the temple-boring buzz subsided. "Now what?"

"Wanna write?" I flexed my fingers in front of me.

"I thought you'd never ask."

26

Nearly three hours and six thousand words later, I made a cup of coffee. The clock read three a.m. Sipping my single pod brew, I skimmed what I had written—what *we* had written—and before I even finished reading, I emailed it to Laney. Tex had gone again, but I knew he'd be back. Still, the words flowed.

An hour later, my phone pinged a text from Laney.

Laney Li: *Car coming 4pm. Meeting with Celeste. Maybe get some sleep?*

I didn't reply. I didn't need to. Then it pinged again.

Laney Li: *It's the best thing you've ever written, and I couldn't be prouder.*

I smiled at the phone screen because I knew she was right. I wrote more.

Four o'clock on a Tuesday afternoon, the elevator doors opened and the hotel lobby stood vacant. The flower arrangement on the pedestal table bloomed in vibrant jewel tones. At first, I thought for sure it was an imitation. Further inspection told me otherwise. Everything appeared more vivid: the patterned ceiling, the striking grout between the smooth tiles that clad the unlit fireplace, the stitch pattern detail on the hem of my summer sweater. When it occurred to me that my new visionary outlook resulted from sleep deprivation, I snorted a laugh no one else was around to appreciate. I hoisted my messenger bag, loaded with my computer, onto my shoulder.

I wore light blue jeans, cuffs rolled to capri-length, with a white cotton sweater and my Nikes. Hair pulled back in a ponytail—all that time would allow. It was not my usual Celeste meeting attire, but this was not an ordinary Celeste meeting.

I had held off long enough, distracted by a TV show, a cracked patella, and, well, *other* things—devastatingly sexy things. I hadn't said yes to Luna yet. Wasn't sure I would. Still, thinking Tex's time had ended rattled me, knocked me off balance. But now that he was back, ready to help me work in a new way, the idea of my reinvention seemed more possible than ever. Then again, maybe I could do both. Maybe I could write something entirely new, something female-centric, introspective, something that didn't include pirates or ancient curses or nuclear launch codes—but also keep Tex's story alive. Why couldn't I have the proverbial cake and eat it too? All I knew was it was a conversation worth having. Was I sleep deprived? You bet. Did my heart ache? And how. But today was the day, and Callie Austin was getting her life back on track.

Outdoors, two things greeted me: a mild breeze carrying the sweet scent of Wisteria just beginning to bloom on a nearby trellis, and my man Bernard, who stood at the rear door of a black town car, wearing his black suit, black cap. My heart leapt, overjoyed.

I kissed his slimmer, but still cherubic cheek, but then took him in a bear hug.

"Alright, Miss. You have a meeting to get to."

"You look good, Bernard. Are you up for driving, though?"

"Just for today, but yes, I feel very well, thank you." He opened the car door for me. I kissed his cheek again and hopped into the back seat. The trip to Watermount Publishing didn't require a car, even less so on a beautiful May day, but the delight at seeing Bernard more than made up for my missing a stroll through Madison Square Park. But fatigue and the wisteria perfume had distracted me from asking Bernard the reason for his unexpected visit.

When he took my hand to help me from the vehicle, I asked, "Is everything alright, Bernard?"

"I'll see you when you are done, Miss." Bernard's expression said now was not the time. We exchanged another hug, and despite the weighty impact of his dismissal, I bounded into the lobby of Watermount's building. Laney waited at the elevator atop the short flight of stairs.

"Well, I've heard of Taco Tuesday but not Casual Tuesday," Laney quipped. I blanched at the second blow. "What? I'm kidding. Why the face? Like I sucker-punched you."

"Nothing." I waved off her concern and the fond memory of tacos in a town car the Tuesday I met Andrew.

"You ready for this? I don't know what you plan to say, but you've got my full support."

"I know I do, Laney. Thank you."

Yet another fresh face greeted us at Watermount's reception desk. Laney stated our business, and soon Intern Elsie welcomed us with a gesture toward the conference room. The Waterford crystal sparkled, more dazzling than ever in my bedraggled high, and the smell of books, furniture polish and Chanel No. 5 made me smirk in a manner that may have given away my mental state. Yep, I was definitely too old to be pulling all-nighters.

"Alright, alright, alright," Tex mimicked another iconic movie line, feeling the stoned sensation. Dazed and confused, he half leaned, half sat on the cabinet below the shiny display of Watermount's awards. I let another snort go. "Okay, Callie G, you're gonna need to straighten up and fly right. Focus. This is your commander speaking."

"I got this." I saluted and gave myself a gentle smack on the cheek.

"I'm not worried," Laney said, entering the conference room after a private word with Elsie. Some impromptu mentoring, no doubt. I put my finger to my lips, telling Tex to keep quiet. He answered with an enthusiastic thumbs-up.

"Callie. Welcome. Can we get you anything? Fizzy water? Cappuccino?" Celeste began our ritual.

"God, yes," I whooped with an eagerness that surprised everyone. "Cappuccino, please."

Celeste flinched at the new reply and intercommed to some unseen minion to have a cappuccino delivered to the blue conference room and be quick about it.

Laney's eyes snapped to me as she declined when Celeste offered her the same.

"So, word on the street is there was a table read at Luna, and it went very well." Celeste busied herself with her tablet and small talk while we waited for my caffeine boost.

Laney set down her phone. "Sure as hell better *not* be word on the street, because any talks between Luna and us should only be between Luna and us, and *us* does not include you, Celeste."

"Settle down, Laney. A little good buzz is good for everyone. And the bigger the circle gets, the harder it will be to keep a lid on it. That's the business." Celeste sat back in her chair with confidence. I patted Laney's arm—a thank you for taking on the role of Bad Cop, again.

A young woman balanced an oversized, white cappuccino cup

brimming with foam on a saucer to match. Her concentration laser-focused, she was determined not to spill. "Over there, Madison." Celeste pointed to me. The assistant stopped, and her fair complexion paled further. She dropped the hot beverage.

When I was nine, my father and I attended a father-daughter Valentine's Day dance at my elementary school. I wore a red taffeta dress with a crinoline underneath and a black satin bow around the waist. New black patent leather shoes finished the ensemble, and I remember my excitement because the shoes didn't have a buckle. They were not the Mary Jane style I'd worn most of my life, but a slip-on flat. To my mind, they made me very grown up. Yes, my shoe obsession began early.

To make the evening more memorable, my father allowed me to sit in the front seat of our 1979 Oldsmobile Cutlass Supreme four-door sedan. On the drive home that cold February night in upstate New York, the roads were exactly as you would imagine.

It happened in an instant. Over the dash, a deer appeared in the headlights. The high-beams bounced off its eyeballs, bright like two round mirror reflections rebounding back at us. The intense stare mesmerized me. Then came the whirling. Dad slammed the brakes on that icy patched road. Tires on pavement gripped with the deceleration, but those on ice continued sliding at a higher velocity, forcing the veering car to rotate once, twice, three times, and another three-quarter turn before we came to an abrupt stop. Dizziness and nausea consumed me. My chest hurt from the impact of my father's arm as he desperately held me to the front seatback. The deer didn't move from its spot in the middle of the road. It stood frozen, simply staring like it wondered what we'd do next.

Madison and I were having a deer versus Oldsmobile Cutlass moment. As bile rose and the aroma of strong Italian coffee hit my nose, I swallowed hard. For me, the room would never smell the same.

Madison and I had met twice. Once here, in March, when she was a receptionist, and then again, a few days later in The Bar at my hotel, when Madison had a sudden yearning to take a picture of a particular liquor bottle. The tall one.

"Jesus, Madison. Don't just stand there," Celeste scoffed.

"*Shut up*, Celeste." Stunned by the epiphany, I stood, hunch over the table for support. As my gaze moved from my editor to Madison and back again, Celeste caught up to speed. She'd been caught. Her color morphed to the opposite of her ill-used, ashen assistant. A deep red seeped almost purple, telling me all I needed to know. Knowledge *was* power, and my new acquisition might just have the power to oust Celeste from Watermount, maybe out of publishing altogether. I pushed myself upright, grabbed my bag, and staggered to the elevator.

Laney, instantly at my side, waited for me to speak. I whispered, "Get me to Andrew's, please. Make sure we're not followed."

Laney replied, "I need a few minutes to make some arrangements." The doors opened.

"Do it. Bernard is here. We can ride around until you think it's safe." We stepped into the elevator. "And Laney, thanks."

In true Bernard fashion, we didn't need to wait long before he swerved to the curb in front of us. We were in the back seat before he ever got his driver side door open.

"No worries, Mr. Pierce. Just drive, but stay in the area, please." Laney's thumbs blurred in a typing flurry, or maybe my tired eyes lost the will to focus.

I rested my head, my lids shut, but then I knew better. I couldn't fall asleep now. Sleep now meant I would be out of commission for the next eight hours. No. Pushing through was the only option. I reached across the bench seat and squeezed Laney's forearm.

"You don't have to tell me now." Laney remained calm, whispering. "Whenever you're ready. You know where to find me."

"Promise me—"

"Anything."

"Promise me you'll keep your cool. I know you, Laney Li, and you're gonna wanna burn the place to the ground. You can't. Promise me."

"Jesus," Laney muttered. "I promise."

"It's Celeste. *Ogler*'s informant is Celeste. And she used a poor assistant to do her dirty work."

Laney sat, head back, stock-still, with her eyes to the car's ceiling. Trance-like. But her phone vibrated her to life again, and with a glance at the screen she said, "Mr. Pierce?" Laney typed as she mumbled, "Burn it to the ground, *ha*."

"Yes, Laney Li."

She looked up, calmly speaking to Bernard's reflection. "Not in any hurry, but we can head to your boss's home now. Through the garage, please."

"Yes, Laney Li."

She returned to her text. Thumbs flew as she growled, barely moving her lips. A multitasking marvel. "Burn it to the ground?

Burn it to the—*freaking* napalm the whole damn— *Burn* it to the ground...” Laney clenched her jaw, trying to contain her rage. She was going to need a minute.

It took twenty minutes before we pulled into the underground parking area. Bernard removed an elevator key on a familiar chain from the inside breast pocket of his suit coat.

“I’ll be opening the lift for you, Miss.”

“Thank you, Bernard.” I exchanged a nod in the rearview as he exited the vehicle. “You coming up, Laney?”

“*Ha*, no. Any fixing that needs to happen up there does not include me.”

“What do you know about it?”

“Nothing, except this,” she pointed to the elevator, “is worth fixing, so fix it. It’s real, tangible. Messy? A little, but real. Life isn’t always tidy. But we can figure out the messy bits. Plus, I’ve got this thing where I need to get my hands on a flamethrower and then find out where Celeste is having dinner tonight. Oh, and along with a few other things, we need to talk about those pages you sent me.”

“There’s more.”

“Send me everything.”

I kissed her cheek, leaving her to say my goodbyes to Bernard.

“You look good, Bernard.” I wiggled the knot of his uniform tie. “I don’t know what’s waiting for me up there, but I hope I didn’t put you in an uncomfortable spot.”

“I like the spot I’m in just fine, Miss. This spot pleases me very much. I wish we’d gotten to this spot sooner. Hadn’t occurred to me it was an option. Should have, though. Two of my favorites, you and Mr. Drew. If I may be so bold.” Bernard didn’t look in my eyes as he spoke about such personal things. He blushed. It was sweet.

"Well, let's not go getting ahead of ourselves, but I am happy to have your approval. Is there something else? The reason you're here today?"

"Funny how things make their way to being. I wanted to be sure you got here today. Now, here you are. Don't reckon it matters how." Bernard flicked his brim. I kissed his cheek and stepped into the big cargo lift to begin the rickety climb to the sixth floor.

It was a little like déjà vu. The gate opened, and Stephi Chase wandered in my direction.

"Take off your clothes." She placed her hand on her hip with a devilish grin.

"Stephi, I'm flattered, but I couldn't be less in the mood."

"*Ha*. Maybe another time, in another place, but I have a rule about not having sex with women my friends are in love with, so... *Strip*. The clothes are for me. I'm wearing them out of here, and I'll be sure to get seen if anyone is looking." Clearly, Stephi Chase enjoyed the use of shock and awe tactics and meant to deploy them on me. If she intended to knock me off my axis, she was late to the party. I'd been off-kilter since Monday.

I looked around for Andrew and some privacy to change. Stephi noticed my rubbernecking. "He's not home. Not yet. Bathroom down the hall. Here." Her offensive continued as she pulled her flowing maxi sundress over her head, handed it to me, then stood in the hall wearing nothing but a bra and panties, and heels. A faded black heart tattoo inked the flesh stretched over her protruding hip bone. I rolled my eyes. Not at her exhibitionism, but at the idea anyone would believe we were the same person. Dress in hand, I trudged to the bathroom.

"Bye, twin!" Stephi waved over her shoulder, wearing my jeans and sweater, her hair in a ponytail. As she got on the elevator, she tossed me the key.

"Wait. What about Andrew?"

"Well, since you're asking. I'd get wise if I were you. Recognize the amazing man offering himself up. And if you're looking for insight, I suggest you take a tour of the joint. See what his life was like before that—*woman* broke him. He built this place. I think he built it for everything he wants."

"*Uh*, I just meant, when will he be back?"

"Oh, no clue. But I heard he was in Astoria today. One more thing. You know how you've got Laney?"

"Yes." My reply sounded more like a question.

"Well, Drew's got me. Do we understand each other?"

"Laney Li doesn't need to protect me from Andrew. And you don't have to protect him from me. Retract your claws, Stephi."

"*Meow*." Stephi closed the elevator door between us.

The quiet should have felt serene. In the daylight, the loft was airy and open, with its enormous windows and colorful furnishings. But exploring any further felt like an invasion of privacy, breaking and entering where no one had invited me. Except someone had. Sort of.

The hallway included three doors, but also floor to ceiling bookshelves packed full. No real aesthetic here. Simply for housing books and lots of them. It was the only aspect of the place that felt like Andrew's.

Skipping the half bath, I opened the next door. Small in comparison, the dark and windowless room contained wall sconces that revealed a large screen hung on the far wall and a projector mounted on the ceiling. It was a man cave if ever there was one, but I had never known Andrew to watch television.

I yawned and my weighty eyelids struggled to stay open. Closing the door, I moved to the next: an inviting bedroom with its own bath.

An opened door clearly led to the main bedroom, large with a king bed and windows on two sides, but I didn't dare cross the threshold. It wasn't a place I cared to venture without Andrew's consent. I remembered his comment on the smell of my library and I took a deep inhale to enjoy his scent permeating the stylish room. A woozy feeling accompanied the fatigue beginning to overwhelm me. I left the door open as I found it.

Relaxing on my self-guided tour, I rounded a corner to find a fourth door. I should have guessed there would be a surprise. As I inched open the door, my stomach tightened as I took in the space. It too was another beautifully decorated bedroom, again with large windows in an exposed brick wall. Low-profile furniture filled it, but the difference came in the décor itself.

Someone had obviously designed the quarters with a child in mind, not a baby, but someone's young child, probably a young daughter. Bright orange, yellow, and fuchsia flowers splashed across the bedding and onto Roman shades at the window tops. Built-in shelves held classic books: L. M. Montgomery, E. B. White, and Lewis Carroll should have been no surprise. *Hello Kitty. Paddington Bear.* A pair of small white ice skates propped against one another. The large rug repeated the bedding colors in a geometric pattern while two bean bag chairs rested in the corner, sad from lack of use. Quickly closing the door, I pressed my forehead to it. *I think he built it for everything he wants,* Stephi said.

I wandered back to the first bedroom and opened the door again. Tex sat on a wooden slat bench at the end of the bed.

"What are you doing here?" I was glad to see him, though he looked as tired as I felt.

"Thought you could use some company. You know. Until he shows up. Why don't you lie down, Cal?"

"That's nice of you, Tex. Thanks." I lumbered to the bed and sat, practically falling over as I pulled up a throw draped on the end of the bed.

"Sorry I took off on you."

"I know." I tucked my hands under the pillow.

"I'm back now. We'll be alright."

"He wants children, Tex. That's not—"

"I know. Rest awhile. He'll be here when you wake up." I'm not sure who said it, Tex or me, but it was the last thing I heard before sleep took control.

27

THE NEXT TIME I recalled moving, daylight glimmered. Desperate to block out any sign that a new day had dawned, I squeezed my eyes closed, only to fall victim to the allure of coffee wafting from some unseen place in the massive loft. Flat on my back, I looked at the ceiling with the mechanicals and conduit circuiting it, wondering about the time.

Sitting up, I still wore Stephi's sundress but had somehow crawled under the covers into the most amazing bedsheets. I stretched and buried my head in a down pillow, but when I heard the *clank* of silverware, I knew I couldn't stall any longer. Towels and toiletries sat on the sink counter in the ensuite. Someone graciously made the uninvited guest feel welcomed. I freshened up before padding out to face whatever came next.

"Good morning." I cleared my throat after my first out-loud words of the day.

"She lives." Andrew hid behind the open refrigerator door. "Eggs?" He held up a carton as he elbowed the Thermador® closed. Dressed in familiar pajama bottoms and a dark gray t-shirt, it seemed he wasn't ready to look at me.

"Sure." I sat on a stool at the kitchen island. A moment later, Andrew slid a cup of coffee in my direction, still not meeting my eye. "Thank you." I savored a sip of hot and rich goodness that definitely didn't come from a pod.

"I brought tacos last night. It being Tuesday."

"I crashed. It's been a wild couple of days." I took another swallow.

Traffic on the street below increased. An early morning sanitation truck screeched and groaned as it compacted trash, while empty receptacles bounced and skidded on curbs. A quick whistle blew, and the garbage collectors moved down the block.

"I'm sorry," we blurted in unison.

"Apology accepted." I half-smiled over the rim of my mug, relieved he finally met my gaze.

"Yours too."

I don't think either of us breathed as we stared, rigid in the sudden void.

Twisting in my seat to look at the living room in the daylight again, I collected myself and pushed through the tension. "I neglected to say the other night, but your home is beautiful." Small talk, but full sentences. I'd call it a win.

"Wanna buy it? It's for sale."

"What? Why?"

"I got in pre-High Line, and it was nothing but a shell. It's too valuable now for me to hold on to it. Gotta know when to let go." He cracked an egg into a stainless-steel bowl.

"We're still talking about the loft, right?" I crossed the worn, painted floors to see the view, regretting the quip.

"You should let Laney know you're safe."

"Did you design it for yourself?" I ignored his suggestion and pried deeper for information.

"The hard surfaces, yes. I guess some of the décor, but no, there were others in mind when it came to the softer stuff."

"Others?" I forced out the question while looking through a window.

"Why are you here, Calliope?"

"What?" The trite response served as a stall tactic.

"Why are you here?"

"Well, the coffee is first rate."

"*Why*, Calliope?"

"Should I go?"

"I'm not asking you to leave. I'm asking why—of all the places you could have gone yesterday: your hotel, *any* hotel, to Laney's, the airport even. Why here?"

"Because I thought you'd be here."

"And why was that important to you?" Andrew waited, but I didn't speak. "It's not meant to be a tough question. Is it—"

"Because I wanted—" I interjected.

"Because he's still—?" He tried to continue.

"*No.* He's back," I interrupted with a bit too much enthusiasm. *Now* Andrew kept quiet. "He is," I repeated, more somberly. "But he didn't come back until after you left the other night. And he stayed, and I wrote, and it was good, I mean *really* good, and then he left, but I kept writing, and it was still good, and then I went to Watermount, and he was there, and he was funny and supportive and—" I took a breath. "Is this what you want to hear?"

Andrew stayed silent.

"I watched you on Monday. Listened to you. And you were terrific. *So* good. You should—well, you're incredibly talented. But you were not—Tex Miller. Not *my* Tex Miller, anyhow. I'm not knocking your performance. Not at all. But I tried so hard to reconcile it with my brain, but it was impossible. And you know why?"

Andrew waited for my explanation. Unblinking.

"Because all I could see was you. All I saw was Andrew Statheros, and it was like—I'd been holding this cumbersome armload of rocks for my whole adult life, and you said, *'What's with all the rocks? Let me lighten the load.'* And you did. See, Tex stepped in when my last rock holder couldn't do the job anymore. She'd been doing it since my dad died, and I know she didn't wanna quit, but I had to take all the rocks, except I didn't because *Tex* took some. And that worked for a while. A long while, but then you showed up and blew the ruse right out of the water. Because I realized I'd been holding all the rocks the whole damn time."

"Calliope—" Andrew moved around the kitchen island, but I put up my hand to stop him.

"No. That's not the end of it. *Jeez,* I wish that was the end of it. I've still got rocks. Rocks are a part of life, and I get that. But I realize now, you've got your own armload, and it's a *heavy* one. And while I would love nothing more than to help you carry yours, there are some rocks I can't take on."

"What's that mean?"

"It means we are back where we started. Back to *the* rock. The one obstacle you said wasn't an obstacle, and maybe you were right because an obstacle implies there is a way around it, over it—hell, through it. But this rock? It's insurmountable. This rock *sinks* us."

"Again, with the age thing? God, Calliope. Stop. Why? How can I prove to you—?"

"I've seen the proof, and I'm sorry for crossing that boundary, but Stephi—no, she was looking out for you. Protecting you—from me. I've got to go." I walked toward the hall to the guest room.

"What did she say to you?"

I stopped. "She said I needed to get wise. To recognize the amazing man offering himself up. And I do. I see you so clearly. And everything you sacrificed—" I breathed a jagged inhale. "I get it now. I get why he's back. He knew."

"He knew what? *You* knew what?"

"That I was going back on solo rock duty." I lifted my chin as a tear ran down my cheek. "I've been playing pretend for a long time, and you know—it's really not that bad. So let's just pretend this next part won't hurt so much."

"Don't go. Not yet." He stepped toward me again.

"Andrew, it matters how this ends. And I'd rather guess what staying would have been like than have an actual memory of it. My imagination won't hurt me. But memories? They'll break my heart into more pieces than I could ever put back together." I reached for Andrew's hand, pulling him close for one last kiss at the same time I pushed him away, knowing any more touching threatened to change the ending. "That might be a lie. But if it is, it's a good one." I trudged to the guest room to collect my things before the long walk to my hotel.

I pulled the elevator gate closed between us.

"Aren't you worried about being seen?" Andrew's red-rimmed eyes avoided mine, and his voice strained. The usually tall man displayed slumped shoulders, another sign of the weight of *his* rock load. But a flash of little white ice skates also reminded me that my walking away would one day allow him the opportunity to replace some of that burden with a happiness I could never give him.

"*Hm.*" The reality of what was about to happen hit me squarely between the eyes. Every ounce of me fought any physical reaction to the blow. "Actually, I'm afraid I'll never be seen again." I pushed the button to begin my descent. "Goodbye, Andrew."

28

Laney stood in the doorway of my hotel room, much like she had on Sunday, minus the raincoat but with instantly wide eyes. "What? What is happening? In twenty-two years, I have never—you have never—what the hell is happening here?"

"I know, you don't *do* tears. But that's why I asked you to come. If you don't *do* tears, then I can't *cry* tears. Ignore this, and I'll stop soon. Just fix me a bagel." I blew my nose for the umpteenth time and went to splash cold water on my face.

"I should have known something was wrong. You texting this early in the morning when you should have been basking in the glow of all the hetero boot-knocking. Dammit. I do not understand you people. Us, we—never mind. But you—"

"Talking about it won't help, so let's forget my non-existent love life and focus on saving my career. What have you found out?"

"Oh, well, I was so engrossed with the pages you sent, I mean, really, Callie. So good, but then—you won't believe this."

I gestured for her to continue while I skipped the bagel and ate the strawberry cream cheese with a spoon.

Laney grimaced. "Well, before all hell broke loose yesterday afternoon, I handed over a thumb drive with your pages on it."

"NO!" I nearly choked on a dollop of schmear. "But, but, but I told you Celeste is the leak! You gave her—oh my—"

"No, that's the beautiful thing. Of course, I was pissed

when—who am I kidding? I'm *still* pissed, *so* pissed, but my therapist says I really need to find an outlet for my anger. Like knitting or underground cage-fighting. I'm looking into it. Anyway, the thing is, I gave it to Elsie."

"Intern *ELSHEE*?" Between my snotty nose and the dairy stuck on the roof of my mouth, pronouncing Elsie proved a challenge.

"Guess what she *didn't* do with it?"

"She didn't *gib* it to *Sheleshte*!" I smacked Laney's arm. "I knew I *lubbed Elshee*."

"Now, guess what she *did* do. Guess. Never mind. I'll tell you. She freakin' edited it. Brilliantly. The kid is like some editing savant. Her notes are good. And you know how sometimes you do that thing with—"

"Yeah, yeah. I know," I interrupted.

"But sometimes it really works and sometimes—not so much, but she nailed it. Every time. She saw your style, knew when it worked, when—not so much. I'm telling you, Callie. You're gonna love what she did with it. And I know she's young, but she's gifted, and just what you're looking for. I know it. And I was thinking, where the heck was this kid when you were starting out, but she wasn't even born yet!"

My eyes bulged, and I snorted my sip of coffee.

"Yeah. Don't think about it too hard. But can you believe it? She's a damn prodigy."

"What about Celeste?"

Laney sat back, breathing away sudden anger. Finding restraint, she continued. "Up to you. We can nail her to the wall, or we can politely tell her boss we demand someone else, *ahem*, like Elsie. Totally unconventional, but what the hell, and if they balk, we nail Celeste to the wall. Or, we can leave Watermount entirely, and if they balk, we nail her to the wall. That's bad press the organization cannot abide, so you've got the power. I'm guessing if she holds any responsibility for this train wreck I see before me," she waved her hand in my face, "we are definitely nailing her to the wall, and I'm one hundred percent on board."

"She doesn't." I got up from the sofa, already regretting my cream cheese binge.

"Then who? Who do I get the privilege of destroying today, because—"

"Down, Laney Li. It's nobody's fault. It's Andrew, and it's just bad timing. Timing we could never have fixed."

"Timing? Because of your age difference? That's bullshit. I don't believe that for a minute."

"Not the age difference. My age."

"I will *rip* his face off. God dammit. What is it with men?"

"No, it's not like that. He just wants things I can't—things I don't—"

"Whoa. That escalated. You've known each other for a few months, you're taking it very slow compared to the industry standard. Like *super* slow." She gave me a sidelong glance. "Then boom, he's all 'Let's have kids'? Surprising."

"He didn't say it. He didn't have to."

"*Oh*, mind-reading now. That's cool and *always* works out the way we think it will."

"No, I didn't have to do that either. Look. He has a room—before he got there I looked around the place, and there was a bedroom in his home for a little girl. Apparently, his last—whatever had—has a daughter. And he has a room for her. A beautiful, sweet room, full of precious things..."

"So he's just waiting around for them to come back?"

"Well, not exactly. He's selling the place."

"But when you asked him about it he was like, *'Kids? Yes,*

absolutely. Total deal breaker."

"*Uh*, no. I didn't *ask* him. But he has mentioned how much he adores his nieces and—"

"So it couldn't possibly be that having a room decorated for a child in a three-bedroom loft near the High Line is a selling point. A marketing tool. A staged space to induce buyers with children to consider purchasing the home. Jesus H. Christ, Calliope Grace Austin. What is wrong with you?"

Laney grabbed the bag of bagels and assorted cream cheeses and shoved it into the trash bin. "One question and then I'm going to leave here and clean up your mess. Why? Why would you snoop around behind his back? Go looking where no one asked you to? That doesn't sound like you. You're such a private person, and you have always treated others' privacy with such respect. Why would you sabotage yourself like this?"

"Snoop? Sabotage? I opened a few doors, I didn't pick locks, besides, Stephi—"

"*Ah. Stephi, huh*? Excellent." Laney typed on her phone. "Clean yourself up. Between your snot, raw nose and the six thousand calories of sugary dairy you just ingested, you are not fit for public today. Don't leave your suite. Read the prodigy's notes. Send her more pages. The two of you are going to make a beautiful book together. Oh, and I noticed Tex was back."

"Yeah, only just though. How'd you know? Wait. How'd you *know*-know?"

"You talked to him at Watermount. Last time too. And at The Bar. You lack a little subtlety sometimes. But I cover for you. I know you think I'm always on my phone, but I notice stuff. It's been twenty-two years. Plus, I know everything."

"I love you, Laney Li."

"It's because I'm so charming, but I'm taken." She flashed her two-carat diamond and wedding band. "But I know this great guy. Greek. A real catch."

"Nope. Don't. There's more than you know. It's too much." I fought more tears.

Laney's chin dropped. "I hate to ask, but what about Luna?"

My insides burbled, full of cream cheese and sadness. And while my best friend showed worry and grief for my broken heart, my *agent* stood ready to go to battle for my career, and she needed a win.

"Let's do it."

"Really? Do the show? Put Tex on screen? For real?"

"For real. Make it happen." I gave a definitive nod. "I insist on a damn fine script, Laney. And the kid from Monday has got the stuff, but I want final approval. Other than that, I'm out. It's time. Tex Miller is ready for his close-up."

"Whoa, so that's it. Just like that? No more Tex? For you?" She had a look of panic.

"No. Tex isn't going anywhere. Not my Tex. But the world will have to get its own, and Luna can give it to them. With my blessing. My Tex and I have our own work to do, and I'm not sure what that will look like, but I'm eager to find out. Something tells me Tex Miller is going to be just fine. Cockroach that he is. But right now, I've got to get out of this town. I'm leaving today."

29

ONE YEAR LATER...

LATE IN MAY, CHARLOTTE, North Carolina means SpeedStreet Festival. For the uninitiated, the SpeedStreet Festival includes a series of NASCAR races, lots of bands, beer, and breakneck partying. Which also makes it a time I often leave town. No offense to race fans, but for me, it's best to skip the raucous enthusiasm of thousands of out-of-towners. Plus, this year, I had an opportunity to witness another kind of *wild* altogether.

New York City in May is perfection, probably my favorite month to visit. The heat of summer hasn't yet descended, and spring blooms bring a technicolor addition to the concrete jungle. This year I was particularly eager to get there because I hadn't visited in over a year, and it had been decades since I'd stayed away so long.

My jam-packed year had meant avoiding the Big Apple. But no one mentioned my absence except Laney, who brought it up at every opportunity she could muster, and that was a lot. Dodging a stay any longer was not an option, but with a busy schedule for my visit, I'd hardly have a moment to think about any specific resident of the eight-and-a-half million who called it home.

Foremost, depending on who you ask, was the annual *ActionCon*. *ActionCon* is one of many versions of conventions where fans from multiple genres dress up, attend panel discussions, view movies or episodes of television, and a whole host of other activities. All that takes place in the confines of some enormous venue crammed full of people from every walk of life. These extravaganzas brim with creativity and zealous fandoms, and I couldn't imagine a more appropriate place to debut The Luna Network's *Tex Miller* series—or a more terrifying proposition.

Luna kept any buzz about the new original series under wraps. Bumps in the road included some weather-related production delays, a stunt double injury, and wranglers underestimating the time and patience needed when filming more than a few felines. Yes, trouble arose with the actual herding of cats.

The decision came down to the wire. An episode would air at *ActionCon,* followed by a question-and-answer panel with some members of the production team and principal actors. Tickets to the one-night-only episode watch party and Q&A were exclusively available through *It's Tex Miller Time,* the official book series fan club, a robust association with a well-organized governing body that held the reins as moderators in the Tex Miller online universe. The event sold out in minutes.

Once the scripts satisfied me, I relinquished control of other production aspects. Keeping Tex off the screen was no longer a priority for me. He'd changed. *We'd* changed, and I had renewed confidence in who and what he was to me, no matter the alternate public version. The television show was just pretend. I would attend the convention as part of The Luna Network contingent, merely a background player on the convention's first day. In a well-negotiated deal by Laney, all the Tex Miller books would be available for purchase, of course, and in a gesture of goodwill, I offered to sign copies before we displayed them at the Tex Miller swag kiosk. Calliope Jones continued to live her reclusive lifestyle.

Second, my latest book debuted a week earlier. *Former* Intern Elsie and I worked long and hard. Thrilled with the finished product and more nervous than I'd ever been about any book launch, I eagerly awaited the next and—new to me—steps in marketing a debut novel.

Watermount was still my publishing house, and even though the new novel was a stand-alone book, released under my real name with little fanfare compared to the kind Tex Miller garnered, the powers-that-be put some muscle and speed behind it, hoping to bridge any divide caused by the Celeste shenanigans of last year. I don't know what became of Celeste, but in my defense, I still don't use the Google.

A celebrity book club endorsement gave us a boost, and there were already discussions about film rights. So, while Laney busied herself writing contracts, I planned to do my first-ever in-person book signing. The novel hit bookstores Tuesday of the week before, but Laney said people would like to meet the writer. They would connect with it that much more to see me face to face, and it would be a great way to introduce this "new" author to the masses.

Chances are, there would be far more *Calliope Jones* signatures written than of the *Callie Austin* variety, but I was fine with that. I had written for myself in a way Tex Miller didn't allow, and it gratified me.

I also planned to put in some face time at Watermount to rave about my editor, Eloise Murray. Young Elsie possessed a genius unlike anyone I had ever known, and we clicked, I believe, from the day we'd met in front of that elevator fifteen months ago. In that time, Elsie graduated from Columbia and had a little-talked-about meteoric rise in the ranks at Watermount Publishing. As mentioned before, we were an unconventional pairing, but under the circumstances, all parties agreed to give it a shot. The result pleased everyone involved, and everyone did *not* include Celeste.

The Luna Network sent a plane for me like they had for their relaunch party, and I landed on a balmy Thursday as the sun set. Grateful to see the city gleam in the low glow on my landing at Teterboro, I approached my waiting ride into Manhattan. Nerves ricocheted in my gut.

Dante waited at the end of the carpet roll at the rear passenger-side door of the black town car. Dressed in his black suit, black cap, the former linebacker flicked his visor and gave his kind smile.

"Evening, Ms. Austin. Welcome back. It's been a minute, hasn't it?"

"It has, Dante. But it's good to be back."

"You've been missed, Miss." He gave a short laugh at his word choice.

"That's kind of you to say, Dante."

"Oh, not just by me, to be sure." He took my bag.

"Bernard?"

"Oh—" He cocked his head and opened my door, "him too, I suspect."

I slid into the pleasantly cool and, as usual, pristine vehicle. From the driver's seat, Dante turned to face me, holding two business cards. "Before things get too hectic, as I hear you have a busy few days planned, we should go over some of the scheduling. Of course, I'll drive you tomorrow, both to and from the convention, and anywhere in between should you need me. I'll be at your disposal throughout, if you need anything. Just to get out for a breath of fresh air or what have you. Text me at this number."

"Thank you, Dante. Around Town sure knows how to take care of their clients." I took the card.

"We do, I'm proud to say, but some of our clients are more special than others, Miss." His small but sincere smile grew tighter.

"Which brings me to Saturday. I hear you have an important event in Midtown, but Around Town is closed for business. But for you, we've made arrangements."

"Closed? On a Saturday?"

"Company-wide, yes, Miss. But don't worry. In this profession, we all know one another, and your driver is a great guy. Name is Chet. He used to work for us but got scooped up for a private driving gig some years ago. A nice family in Connecticut. He's doing us a favor. Rest assured that he'll take right good care of you. Get you where you need to be and when. This is his card, in case you need to communicate. We apologize for any inconvenience, it's just the way the date fell."

"Oh, sure. I understand," I said, but I didn't. Why would the company shut down for a day? A Saturday in late spring? It would take some indirect interrogation of Laney. She'd know.

My stomach roiled, a mix of nerves and excitement as we made our way into the city. We drove a different route than the last time I visited, and I was glad not to have the reminder. Clearly, Andrew Statheros was in no way on my mind.

Despite this, my heart quickened with the pleasure of being back in one of my favorite places. Under my breath, I professed, "It's good to be back."

"Early start to the day, Miss. And a long day too. Get a good rest, and I will see you at eight tomorrow morning." Dante flicked his visor. "It is good to see you, Miss. Shall I pass along your regards?"

"Thank you, Dante. Yes, please tell Bernard I hope he's well. And I'll see you in the morning." I wheeled my bag into my usual Flatiron District hotel.

At check-in, a new face greeted me. When she saw my name, she asked if I wouldn't mind waiting a moment. Her boss wanted to have a word. Stepping aside, I watched the big-city bustle of the hotel lobby looking no different from a year ago.

Tofer exited an office behind the sleek front desk. New hipster glasses and a goatee adorned his youthful face, and he met me with a firm handshake and, at my instigation, a kissed cheek.

"The boss, is it? Congratulations."

"Well, *a* boss. I'm just starting back after a stint at a Las Vegas property, so I'm still detoxing, but I couldn't be more pleased to be home or to see you, Ms. Austin."

"It's kismet because I haven't been here since you saw me last. A busy year. But I'm happy to be back, too."

"I've seen to all your usual requests." He moved behind the desk. "Just the one key?" The question sounded more loaded than one might expect, but I let it slide.

"Just the usual, Tofer. Thank you."

The suite, my suite, remained the same also, and as the sun set, the view did not disappoint. To the right, the Empire State Building glowed with Memorial Day patriotism, red, white, and blue. The park below bustled. Joggers and dog walkers, plus the occasional frisbee toss, added color to the landscape. This weekend kicked off summertime in the city.

A text to Laney informed her of my arrival and my desire to stay in to rest up for the big days ahead. She obliged me, and we planned to meet at the convention center the next morning. I plugged in my phone and drew a bath.

No sooner had I slipped into the thick suds of the soaker tub, when a light knock tapped on the bathroom door.

"Enter," I sang.

"*Me and Mrs. Jones...*" Tex *da-dee-dah-ed* as he swayed into the bathroom. "That song never gets old. You know what this reminds me of?" Back in his hotel bathrobe, Tex took his perch on the sink counter.

"No, Tex, what?"

"That moment in all the books, that—*lull* before something exciting is about to happen."

"Lull? My books have lulls? *Ouch*. Good to know." I bristled at the remark, then grinned. "I'm glad you're going into this with such a positive attitude."

"*Hm*?" He raised his brow and cupped his ear.

"We. I mean *we*. I'm glad *we* are going into it with such a positive attitude. It's a new dawn. I'm glad you're here. Now leave me be. Good night, Tex."

"G'night, Cal. I'll be around."

I sank deeper into the tub, closing my eyes while I relaxed away the travel stress.

30

As planned, Dante and I met at eight o'clock on Friday morning to head to the *ActionCon* venue in Hell's Kitchen. The irony was not lost on me. News outlets predicted more than one hundred thousand participants would attend over the four-day run of the holiday weekend event. Dozens of panels and screenings in every subgenre of action-adventure, be it historical fiction or sci-fi, anime, and even reality television, filled the schedule. The notion of all those people had me mildly panicked. Anyone who knew me would know this introvert would avoid anything like this. Callie Austin had left her comfort zone.

"You have my number, Miss. Anytime at all, and I will meet you at this spot or any other that suits you better; I will be there. I'm told this isn't exactly your type of thing, so if you need a break or a quick escape—"

"I'm sorry if Laney Li has been wearing you out with the care and feeding of me, Dante, but she shouldn't. I'll be fine. Thank you. And I will see you later today. And stay up there. I'm also fine to open my door."

"Yes, Miss. But—" Dante gave a quizzical look, but I was gone.

We met at the entrance for credentialed participants: Laney, eyes to her phone, a pale, almost green Jason Steinman, and Cyrus, all kisses and pouts.

"What's with the sour face, Cyrus? I hear the cosplay will be quite the spectacle."

"Don't I know it," he scoffed, sneering at an oblivious Jason. "But *someone* wouldn't let me dress up." Seeing the Luna duo made me smile, but I had no plans to get in the middle of any tiff. I had one of my own, and it'd been brewing for a year.

Three different lanyards hung around my neck gave me access to all I would need throughout the day. Jason said it would be thirty minutes before crews unloaded the books, so I had time to explore before it got crowded, and I needed to start scrawling my John Hancock—or *Calliope Jones*.

"I'm going to need you to lighten up on Dante, Laney Li."

"Um, o-kay."

"He's doing a fine job. Always has."

"O-kay."

"And I'm a big girl and can take care of myself. And later, we should talk about the change-up in Saturday's transportation." Evidently, I opted for a more direct approach in my Around Town reconnaissance.

"I have had zero contact with Dant—never mind. Got it. Don't know where this ass-chewing is coming from, but message received." She never looked up from her phone.

"Oh, and hello. Good to see you. You look great." I kissed her cheek.

"Thanks. You look good too. Great, even. It's been a year—something I should know?"

"Yeah," I walked away, calling over my shoulder, "airplanes fly *both* ways, Laney Li."

The monstrous venue would be shoulder-to-shoulder with costumed action-adventure fans in less than two hours. The echoes bouncing about now wouldn't be for long, and the thought made my head spin. "Laney, let's find coffee."

"Amen."

Crowds funneled in, and they did not disappoint. The time and expense these cosplayers invested were remarkable. Replicas of out-of-this-world costumes and make-up you've seen on the screen, both large and small, were even more impressive in real life. I couldn't stop gawking. And to make the day more enjoyable, the camaraderie, the joyful atmosphere surprised me. Sure, there were put-on rivalries and faux-warring factions, good guys and bad, but respect and amity abounded.

Late in the day, I signed more books out of public view, behind the curtain at The Luna Network's *Tex Miller* booth. A shocking number of hardcovers sold. When Watermount predicted we would do another print edition, I hadn't believed them. Today I did.

Balancing a stack of books, I slid through an opening of our booth curtain and backed into a statuesque gladiator. The scantily clad man towered over me, wearing a full face-masked helmet and platform thigh-high boots. His skimpy costume shimmered burnished gold, and consisted of a well-ventilated skirt, a glittering chest plate with matching elbow pads, and a long, sheathed blade. Impressively muscular limbs, and lots of dark bronze skin glistened with a metallic sheen.

"Whoops. Excuse me, Mr. Gladiator." I grabbed at my book tower, placing my chin on top of the pile to hold them upright. A few hit the floor.

"That's *Galactic Gladiator*, ma'am." His voice had a deep, affected tone befitting an otherworldly warrior. "Hey, I know you." His tenor changed to one more earthbound.

"Pretty sure we travel in different solar systems, sir." I set the books on the table while the alien space fighter picked up those on the floor. He had no inhibitions about what his shiny loincloth would or would not hide while squatting to assist me, but I averted my eyes.

"*Uh*, what was it? Martini, just a little dirty, *extra* dry, with three olives. I never forget the drink order of a beautiful woman." The cosmic gladiator handed me the books and then removed his mask. "Jonathan. We met—"

"Yes, at The Bar," I chimed in. "I'm Callie. Wow. Didn't recognize you without your—pants. How are you? New gig?"

Jonathan showed his toothy grin at my teasing. "It's just for the convention, but the pay is ridiculously good, so I can't complain. Of all the places to run into you..."

"Yeah. Weird." I looked around to find only an unknown salesclerk at the booth. None of my associates wandered nearby to run interference. Better yet, bail me out.

"How long's it been?" Jonathan looked casual in his over-the-top get-up.

"Oh, over a year, I think." I knew full-well it had been fourteen months, three weeks, six days, and nearly twenty-two hours, but who's counting?

Jonathan scanned the booth over my shoulder.

"I, *uh*, do some work with a publishing house." I thrust a book toward him. "And they provide the books for the vending booth here for The Luna Network. I guess it's a sort of crossover promotion for book admirers and future TV fans."

"Ah. I see. So you're not here for the—I just mean this weekend is—well, I heard anyway—the big event?" Jonathan fumbled.

"*This* isn't the big event? I've never seen anything like it."

"No, I meant the *wedding*."

"Wedding? No, I'm not here for any wedding."

"Oh. Well, I guess it's gonna be small. Rumor has it they had to rush it a bit." Jonathan grimaced with a shrug. "If you know what I mean." His large hands pantomimed a round belly before he nudged my arm with his sparkling elbow pad. "You'd think in this day and age it wouldn't be a big deal, but a big Greek family like that? They can be a bit—*traditional*."

"Yeah." The rumble of the event crowd felt closer, louder and my scalp prickled with the start of a sweat.

"I really thought you and Drew—"

"No." I interrupted with a strained, high-pitched yip. "We didn't. There was nothing... I've got to get back to my books. Best of luck with future invasions or whatever."

"Are you okay?" Concern flashed in his anxious search for help. "You've gone pale."

"I'm fine. Missed breakfast. And lunch. Need some water. Good seeing you, Jonathan." I stumbled through the backdrop slit, falling into a metal folding chair. An unopened carton of bottled water taunted me. With a burst of unexpected aggression, I grabbed a pair of scissors and stabbed at the industrial plastic-wrapped bundle.

"What the hell is happening here?" Laney appeared, grabbing the metal shears from my swinging grip. "Jesus H. Christ."

"I'm thirsty. Very, *very* thirsty, and if I don't get water, I'm—" Back in the chair, I bent, letting my head hang between my knees. Everything went black except the light explosions flickering in the corners of my eyes. I was glad for the curtained-off hideaway, but the crowd noise, coupled with the roaring in my ears, disoriented me. Overhead, a loudspeaker boomed the announcement of the next panel discussion about to begin in the *Wars and Westerns*

Hall, startling me to my feet again.

Laney handed me an opened bottle of water rescued from my vicious attack. After a few sips, dizziness hit again, and I flopped into the chair and over my lap.

"What's come over you? It's a little late for second-guessing your choices here." Laney knelt next to me.

"Truer words, Laney Li, you have no idea," I grumbled from my semi-fetal position.

"They've got half the season in the can. We are committed here, Callie."

"In the can. *Ha.* That's an expression Hollywood should reconsider." Tex flapped around in tights and a cape, his physique exaggerated, muscles bulging. "*What* am I wearing? It's fan*tastic*!"

"Not now," I begged.

"Yes, now. This thing is going to launch in October. They plan to make the announcement at the panel tomorrow," Laney explained further.

"Not you—Laney." I hyperventilated.

"You need a paper bag," Tex said matter-of-factly while still making swishing noises with his cape.

"I need a paper bag." I seized Laney by the wrist.

"A paper bag! A paper bag! My alien universe for a paper bag!" Tex howled his Shakespeare parody while galloping in a circle, then came to a sudden stop. "*Oooh*, can I *fly*?" He leapt without success. "Aw, *dammit*."

Laney grabbed the bag of bagels Cyrus brought but had chided us for even considering the carbs. She dumped them on the floor and handed me the paper sack. I breathed into it once, twice, three times, then guzzled more water.

"What is happening?" Laney gritted, wide-eyed.

"I'm fine. But I have to go now."

"Go where?"

"Anywhere." I held my head at the temples.

"You should stay seated. There's medical on site. We should get you checked."

"No, just a panic attack. Did you know, Laney? Did you know and not tell me? Because I don't know how you'd think I wouldn't find out."

"I don't know what you're talking about. Not about this or about any instructions for Dante. I may keep a thing or two from you every now and again, but nothing that would ever provoke this. Hand to—"

"Fine. I believe you." I grabbed my bag to find my phone and text Dante. "They're gonna need more books. Messenger cases of them to my suite for me to sign. I'll see you tomorrow morning at the Midtown book signing." I downed the rest of the water bottle and kissed her cheek, but I felt nothing. Numb, head to toe. Zombie-like, I jostled my way through the convention center display aisles that teemed with extravagantly costumed action heroes and villains. I registered little of it. Tunnel-vision led me to the exit where Dante waited and into the back seat where I asked to be taken to my hotel.

"You alright, Miss?"

"I will be, Dante. But if you could hurry?" My head bumped the headrest as his heavy foot did its job.

We swerved into the drop-off at my hotel. The trip was fast, or I had zoned out shortly after Dante's speedy take-off.

As I stepped out of the town car, he held the door. "I am sorry—about tomorrow, Miss."

I let loose a brief sigh. Numbness wearing off, the ache in my chest mushroomed. "Me too, Dante. Me too. As long as he's happy, that's what's important." I gave Dante's forearm a squeeze.

"Miss?"

I forced a smile. "I look forward to meeting your friend Chet tomorrow. I'm sure he'll do a fine job. Enjoy the day. The—celebration. It's wonderful how it will be such an Around Town family event."

"Oh, yes, Miss." Dante's expression shifted from concern to something near joy. "We're all looking forward to it, but I gotta say, I think the boss just wants it to be done and over with at this point." Dante put an abrupt stop to his low bellow when I cringed at his comment.

Nausea sloshed in my water-filled stomach. "Sorry, Dante. I have to go." I bolted for the hotel lobby. Several pushes of the elevator call button finally yielded the ride to the thirty-eighth floor.

Entering my refuge, I flung my bag with more force than I meant. It skidded, hitting a leg of the dining table several feet away. My phone spilled onto the floor. I remembered flinging my purse once before, losing my phone in the back seat of Andrew's car. When I kicked off my shoes, my balance failed, and I stumbled into the entry table. The lamp lurched before I caught it with a cat-like reflex I didn't know I possessed. Another memory flashed of the same wobbling light fixture. The room flooded with triggers, recollections of a man I walked away from, gave up. Did I expect he wouldn't move on? Evidently, I had. My hope was he couldn't possibly, because I hadn't, couldn't. My flair for playing the fool never ceased to amaze me.

I called room service to have a burger and fries delivered, regretting it as soon as I ended the call. Was there any aspect of daily life in this city that wouldn't call to mind his face? With a snort, I thought SpeedStreet seemed like a far better alternative to the one I found myself in now.

"Really, Callie? Not sure we could make this fly, even with

our adoring followers." Tex perched on the sofa in the colorful, ad-splattered fire suit of a professional racecar driver, his helmet in his lap, the midnight blue Luna Network logo adorned each sleeve and across his chest and back.

"But consider all the *new* fans," I replied, comforted to see a friendly face.

"You think *our* groupies are fanatical. Imagine. I can get sponsors, do celebrity endorsements. I've always wanted to know what confetti shot from a cannon would feel like, beer and sports drink spray flying. The smell of high-octane fuel in the air, thousands of screaming fans. Ooh, maybe *I* can get shot from a cannon!" Tex shouted as his excitement exploded. "Forget what I said before. Let's *do* this!"

I laughed as he strutted about the suite, flexing and stretching to read the patches sewn all over his racing costume. A knock on the door startled me to quiet as I blotted the combination of laughter and crying tears and hurried to receive my dinner delivery. Looking back over my shoulder, I put my index finger to my mouth, asking for Tex's silence but hoping he would stay. He pantomimed zipping his lips.

Classic blunder. I neglected to use the peephole, so Cisco surprised me with his hand-truck loaded down with book cartons and Laney in tow. The two stood stone-faced. Cisco leaned to see inside.

"You're not dinner," I chirped, then cleared my throat.

"You alone in there?" Laney's head cocked in an unfamiliar fashion.

"Alone?" I asked and walked away, deciding to be done with that line of interrogation.

Laney took the hint. "Delivery from the publisher. Elsie planned to bring it herself, the *mensch,* but I told her I'd do it. Thanks,

Cisco." Laney tipped him and ushered him to the door while he continued rubbernecking to see who else was in the suite.

"Don't feel you need to stay, Laney. I've ordered dinner, and my hand is just about un-cramped from all my earlier signing. I'll get right back at it."

"Subtle," she jeered.

"Wasn't trying to be." I opened a box of books as Tex snickered from his spot on the sofa.

"Are you losing it, Callie? Is this the mental breakdown? Now? Right when everything is coming together? The TV show will be huge, and you're safe from exposure. Your new book is so good, and such a beautiful way to introduce my brilliant and talented friend to the literary world, and now you crack? *Now*?"

I had never seen Laney lose her composure, but she teetered on the brink.

"Jeez," I muttered, then took a deep breath. "Laney Li. I'll be fine. As a matter of fact, any distraction that might have existed has been eliminated. I just need tonight to grieve. Mourn. Get over it. Tomorrow, I will be your resolute, single-minded client again. The silliness will be over."

"What silliness?"

"It doesn't matter. Sorry I bailed today, but I think I've done my part for the Luna folks. I'll sign more books, but then I'm—"

"From the Luna folks." Laney pulled a DVD from her bag. "It's the episode they'll screen tomorrow night. I knew you couldn't see it for the first time in a room full of people—or figure out how to download it from—whatever. Sealed in plastic, very hush-hush."

"Super," I groused. "Sorry. Thank you. I'm not sure I can watch it in a room by myself either." I took the jewel case.

"Then I should stay?" Laney's tone rang more hopeful than it should have.

"No, you should go. I need you to go."

Laney didn't fight it. "Tomorrow is going to be a better day. *Your* day. I can't wait to share you with the world. I can't wait for you to finally be seen."

The last words twisted in my heart, and my eyes stung. Laney caught my reaction, and I knew she regretted saying them. She left without another word.

Tossing the DVD on the sofa where Tex sat, he stared at the cellophane-wrapped package. "*Plastics.*"

"What?" I opened the rest of the book cartons.

"There's a great future in *plastics.*"

"If you are referencing a movie because of the older woman seducing the younger man trope, you are *not* my friend."

Tex tsked. "Not that trope. The end. Consider the end."

It had been a while since I'd seen *The Graduate*. "When they sit on the bus and realize, *Oh crap, what have we done?* Yep, bullet dodged."

"Well, that scene is up for interpretation, but no, I mean, before that part."

I belly-laughed again. "Crashing a wedding? Yeah, that sounds like something I'd do. *Ne-ver.*"

"I'm just saying we've got *options.*" Tex leaned back, crossing his ankle and knee.

I wandered to the minibar. "Let's just get drunk instead."

When Cisco delivered my dinner, I tipped him too well, wishing him a good night. The DVD remained in plastic all night long.

31

THE NEXT MORNING, TEX sat propped against the headboard with a lampshade on his head. I snorted, forcing him "awake."

"Jeez, Callie, you can't even get drunk right."

"I know. I fell asleep. You know I can't do today hungover. I may be a fool, but I'm rarely irresponsible."

"Funny. I excel at both."

"Get out of here. I've got yet *another* new driver to meet." I crawled from bed. Tex disappeared. The cases of books I signed the night before cluttered the living room, waiting for their return to the front desk where someone would fetch them for *ActionCon*. Today was about my newest novel. The fresh start to my "new" career. Callie Austin's career.

Dressed in a colorful sundress and a poncho in blue pulled from the dress, I strapped on sandals and approved my reflection. I felt pretty, feminine, and creative, everything I wanted the readers of my latest labor to see. Stepping out to the sidewalk, wisteria scent wafted to me. I closed my eyes, sucked down my lingering sadness, and breathed deeply, ready for the next adventure.

"Ms. Austin. Chet, your driver for today." A middle-aged man with kind, dark eyes approached me from the curbside town car. I offered my hand to shake his, and with a polite nod, he took it.

"Good to meet you, Chet. I understand you are pinch-hitting today."

"Ah, yes, ma'am."

"Callie, please."

"Yes, Miss Callie." Chet gave another polite nod. "Happy to help the Statheros family anytime. They are good people. I've known Drew and the girls for a long time. Since they were kids. Drew more, since he hung around the garage some. You must be quite the family friend for him to be taking such special care on an otherwise busy day."

"I don't really know them, the family. Andrew, *um*, Drew I've—met, but not the sisters." My pulse raced. "Big day."

"Oh, yes." Chet gave a pensive sigh and opened the car door for me. Sunlight hit his thick dark hair, highlighting gray just beginning to invade his temples. I was relieved to have the conversation end.

As Dante predicted, Chet delivered me where I needed to be, and in good time, so I ducked into the coffee shop next door to the bookstore to order a venti, nonfat, no whip, double shot, white chocolate mocha, extra hot. There was little question I owed Laney a peace offering.

The first friendly face I saw belonged to Elsie. From a distance, the young woman appeared her usual calm and poised self. But up-close I noted a stiffness and a little extra perspiration.

"You nervous there, kiddo?" I asked, sidling up to her.

"Callie. Between you and me? *Yes.* Aren't you?"

"I'm not now, strangely. I'm so stinking proud of the work we did. Nothing is getting in the way of that today. How about you take it down a notch or two? Lose the blazer. Roll up your sleeves."

"Yeah?"

"Definitely." I put my arm around her shoulders in a side hug. "Relax. Today's gonna be fun. And let's be extra nice to Laney Li."

"Oh, *alright.*" Instant disappointment. "And why are we doing that again?"

"Just to mess with her." I elbowed Elsie's ribs as she took off her jacket. "Speaking of. Where is the tenacious one?"

"Upstairs. She's already bossing around my new summer intern. I had to come out for air to save me from the flashbacks." Elsie quirked her lip, her posture easing with her cracked joke.

I squeezed the handrail and swallowed hard on the escalator ride, desperate to greet my future while still feeling the pangs of regret I'd been dodging for more than a year. Onward and upward, I told myself.

We found Laney directing furniture placement. The table angle displeased her. Harsh light reflecting off a stack of newly unwrapped books on display wouldn't do, and she complained about the bookstore's use of fluorescent bulbs when halogens or even LED were plainly better choices. I didn't recognize her behavior but felt confident it had to do with some nervous excitement and her desire to have everything perfect for me.

I asked Elsie to intervene while I pulled Laney aside. "Peace offering." I presented the extra hot sugary coffee drink with a bowed head.

"Were we at war?" She sipped it immediately. I had long guessed asbestos coated her tongue.

"Think of it as preemptive." I grinned at her wary eyes over the rim of her cup. "You have been the best agent, best *friend*, any writer could ever dream of having. I know none of this would be possible without you. I also know I have been absent and busy and difficult, and for that, I am sorry. Truly. Thank you for putting up with this year of change, and even though you think Manhattan is the center of the universe and can't get your ass on a plane, and you sometimes cheat at Scrabble, and maybe—well, I know how lucky I am to have you in my life, business and personal, and I won't shut you out again."

"You've got a *real* interesting apology style there, Austin," Laney sneered, holding a copy of my book. "But if you keep writing stories like this, I can handle some more cold shoulder." She took another sip of her drink, looking teary-eyed. "Sign this? To me? Your first Callie Austin signed novel?" She handed me a book and a pen.

To Laney Li: The best damn agent in the biz and the best damn friend in the world. Love always, C.G. Austin.

"Thanks. What about the preemptive olive branch?"

Ignoring her use of a Greek allusion, I said, "For this, and I promise never to do it again. Ever." I wrapped my arms around her in a bear hug, rocking her back and forth. I kept it brief and scurried away as soon as I released her. She stayed in her spot, adjusting her clothes. Then, with a slight shrug, she launched into ordering around an unsuspecting bookstore employee.

Display reset, tables realigned, books restacked to optimize the lights, the bustle of activity settled. Social media and emails announced the event, and a festooned sandwich board at the street told passersby of the book signing, and so we waited. Having zero expectations, I smiled when a chic, petite blonde, I'd guess to be my age, approached my table, setting a newly purchased book in front of me.

"Hi, I've never heard of you, but I've heard this book getting some talk. You know, on the socials and stuff. I hope it's good, but I'm really buying it, hoping to spur more women like you to write books about women of a certain age."

"Yes. This genre is new for me—"

Across the aisle, Laney gave a slow headshake, mouthing the word, "no."

I stopped myself. "What I mean is, I hope you enjoy it, then tell your reader friends, then tell the rest of them, too. What's your name?" I got a thumbs up from Laney.

"Miriam, but people call me Miri. M-I-R-I."

I signed the book:

To Miri: From one woman of a certain age to another. Happy reading! C.G. Austin.

As the morning ticked by, a few more women approached me with similar remarks, and I confided to each of them they weren't alone. After another kind chat with a forty-something female reader, I looked up to find my first visitor, Miri, standing before me again. This time with tears in her eyes and a tissue to her lips.

She began slowly. "I've been *sniff* in the coffee shop next door *sniff* reading for the last hour. I had to come tell you—well, first of all, how long are you here today? My entire book club knows they should come get this. *Now.*"

I grinned at the excited woman in front of me. My heart pounded to see the reaction my words elicited from her. And while all my years of writing anonymously were worth it, this was the moment I wanted as a writer, a genuine connection, a meaningful bond. A connection I never thought I would know with a Tex Miller fan.

"... and in the restaurant, when she feels like she is being seen for the first time—well, I—my goodness, I almost dropped the book."

"Wow, you read fast. That's a good way into the thing." My brow arched in disbelief.

"I'm headed home, and I know I'll finish tonight. Look for my reviews, and for my friends. Some will get here today."

"I'll sign a couple and have them put aside in case we miss each other," I suggested.

"Well, aren't you the kindest?" Miri blew her nose as she walked toward the escalator. "Buy this book," she half-shouted at two strangers coming off the moving staircase. "Just buy it! And no, I don't know her, but I love her."

My heart overflowed with gratitude. Laney sat across from me. My home-base. I mouthed "thank you" and not for the last time. Down the stairs and out of sight, Miri, at a near-yell, told other shoppers to "*buy this book.*" The two women first accosted by my newest fan also, to my surprise, bought the book, but more on the word of the celebrity endorsement that one of them recalled upon hearing the title. No matter, I'd take any sale in any old or new way.

By lunchtime, bookstore traffic in general increased, and friends of Miri showed up with books in hand. Feeling the need, and, frankly, the desire to speak with these women as long as they wished to talk to me, encouraged a line to grow. A line piqued more interest, and then, as they say, we were off to the races. The store manager dispersed a second bookstore employee with another credit card cube to help expedite sales. The store manager grinned ear to ear, and Elsie had gotten her full-fledged confidence groove back. Giving a thumbs up, she left with her summer intern.

Nearing the end of the signing event, the line still a few deep, I signaled Laney for water—parched from hours of chit-chat. She pointed to the floor at my feet, where she'd placed two bottles for easy access. Bent over to crack open the cap of one, I took a big swig and sat up to resume my work. But, like something out of a Mel Brooks film or maybe Jerry Lewis—some iconic slapstick scene—water spewed from my mouth, barely missing the next woman in line.

"*Hey, laaady*! Clean-up on aisle one," Tex sang out. "That's one hell of spit-take, Mrs. Jones."

"Oh my, ma'am. I am so sorry. Truly." I lurched toward the two shocked women in front of me.

Laney rushed to my side with a wad of napkins, wiping up the water and whispering in my ear. "What's wrong? Is Tex here?"

"*Uh, Austin*, we have a problem." Gravity-light, Tex floated by in a slow-motion bounce, wearing full NASA lunar-landing gear.

"Not just Tex. Look. By the escalator," I coughed into a napkin. From her squatted position at my knee, Laney peered over the table spying Andrew.

"Jesus H. Christ. Breathe."

"Try-ing," I wheezed.

"Nope. I don't see it," Tex jeered, no longer in a spacesuit. "We look nothing alike. I mean, sure, he's tall, dark curly hair, piercing blue eyes, that chiseled chin... oh yeah. Okay. Now I see it. *Damn*. He is a fine-looking young man. A real tall drink of wat—"

"*Hush*," I implored.

Tex leaned against a book display, laughing at his own joke.

Laney cleared her throat and forced her scary smile, handing me the next woman's book to sign.

"Who should I make this out to?" I sputtered.

"Shelby. I'm here visitin' from North Carolina, and here you are from Charlotte. Small world, isn't it?" Shelby's drawl provided a sweet reminder of home. I'd have done anything to be there now.

"Isn't it? Thanks, Shelby. Enjoy the book." I cooed as Laney ushered the woman away.

"Well, bless her heart, folks! Apparently, we have now entered the speed-signing portion of today's program. Get 'em in, get 'em out!" Tex whooped with too much southern twang and a lively two-step.

"Not helping, you *son* of a—"

"Hey, who's next?" Laney interjected. "Our author is getting a little punchy. Maybe she needs a break?"

"She's *fine!*" Tex chortled in an exaggerated tone.

"I'm *fine*," I mimicked, not that anyone else would know.

"Did I hear you say you're from Charlotte?" the next patron asked. "My sister lives in Raleigh. Is that close?"

"*Uh*, no—no, not real-ly." My sentence-making skills diminished as Andrew approached, last in line.

"Charlotte's a wonderful city, though." Andrew leaned in to fill the void while I tried to gather myself. "Street art, great theater, fantastic dining. No Putt-Putt, though, as I recall."

The woman did a double-take, then blushed with wide eyes and an even wider grin at the Greek god speaking over her shoulder.

I stared.

Laney punched my arm to break my trance.

"And your name?" I finally asked.

"It's Linda. I'm Linda." Linda continued to engage the handsome man behind her in our conversation. "Such a fan of these celebrity book club picks, you know. Any of them. They *never* disappoint."

"This one won't either." Laney tried to move the woman along, but I was the impediment.

"Whoops! We're gonna need another copy." I slammed the book closed and leaned on it. "I wrote the name wrong. Maybe it *is* time to call it a day."

"Really?" Linda rolled her eyes with a flirty elbow to Andrew. "Who messes up *Linda*?"

Laney scrambled to toss another book in front of me to sign. "So sorry, Linda. Long day. Thanks, enjoy." I passed the book I mistakenly signed *Calliope Jones* to my agent. The baffled Linda craned her neck for a last glimpse at the tall, dark stranger as Laney escorted her to the escalator.

All I saw was Andrew standing over me. He gave a sheepish wave, then slipped his hands into the pockets of his jeans. God, he looked good. A spring tan browned his skin, and the black button-down he wore highlighted that glow. His uneasy expression relaxed as he took one more step toward me. I moved to stand, ready to scramble across the table and climb him like a tree. But in my graceless rush, my thighs slammed into the table. The collision knocked over the display in front of me, spilling water, and sending books and a tabletop sign to the floor.

"Oh, Lord, Callie. Get it together, woman." Covering his eyes, Tex chided over my shoulder, peeking through split fingers.

Fearing any more movement on my part might set the building on fire, I sat back in my chair. Keeping still would be safest for everyone.

"I'm your biggest fan, but it seems like you're the nervous one." Out of nowhere, a young woman I hadn't noticed scampered up behind Andrew. She giggled and pushed him aside with a playful hip check. "Hi!" she squealed and thrust her hand to shake mine.

The striking brunette was clearly younger than Andrew, maybe as much as I was older than him. She was tall, though not as tall as me. Her curls reminded me of Andrew's, but hers bounced off her shoulders. Sparkling eyes were big, with eyelashes anyone would consider breaking the law to have.

"Callio—Callie, this is my—"

"Ana," the woman interjected. "*Oh. My. God*. I cannot believe I am meeting you. Best. Day. Ev-er."

I breathed some relief that only the two of them remained. The conversation came with some privacy, but Andrew tried to shush the woman.

"Oh, stop. No one can hear me," she whispered, giving Andrew another mischievous shove. "But seriously, Ms. Jo—Austin. I've read all your books. More than once. Then, of course, when Drew told me he knew you—don't be mad, he just tells me stuff—and I was like—*what*?! *You know her?*" Her whisper was gone.

The moment ranked as *the* most surreal of my life. And that's saying something. "What are you doing here? I mean, aren't you—isn't today your—" I ping-ponged from her to him and back again.

"Yes," Ana squealed again. "Tonight. We were just taking care of some last-minute details at the Yale Club. It's just a block up. That's where the reception is. But when I read online you were going to be here, in person, signing a new book—I couldn't believe it. I said I don't care about the rest. *This* is the wedding present I want!"

Andrew forced a chuckle. A strangled, sad sound. "She did. She made me bring her here to meet you. With everything we need to take care of today. This is priority one." He swallowed his exasperation and lovingly declared, "Wedding gift delivered," with a gesture to me.

I faked a smile.

"This, and the fabulous wedding, and the incredible honeymoon! He's sending us to Santorini!" She wrapped both of her arms around one of his and kissed his cheek. "He's the best."

"Yeah, the best," I choked out and took another sip of water.

"These last few weeks have been crazy, what with all the—" Ana waved her hand around. No one could miss the dazzling diamond solitaire. "I don't even know what this book is about. Do you, Drew?" The young woman tugged Andrew's arm, and her adoring look ripped a new hole in my heart. But Andrew only had eyes for me. He shook his head.

"Well, it's—it's a bit different. I wrote it under my real name so... um, it doesn't have anything to do with you-know-who." I gestured over my shoulder to Tex. Their eyes followed my thumb, but of course, no one stood there. I slowly put my hand back in my lap.

"Smooth, Cal," Tex groaned.

"Can you give us the SparkNotes' version?" Ana pleaded.

"*Hm.* Let's see. It's about a woman's journey to find a way to finally be seen in the world. A bit *Eat, Pray, Love* meets *Wild* meets *Still Me.*"

It occurred to me Andrew might deserve a heads up on one particular plot point. "Yeah, so there's *one* section, not a *big* part, it's pretty *small* actually, well maybe not *so* small, but anyway—the woman meets a young man, the only son of a big, tight-knit—*Italian* family." Thank God I'd changed some details.

I sipped more water. It only seemed fair to warn him.

"He's, well, he's very talented. Wants to be a concert pianist. And he is very good, so good he goes off to Juilliard to study." I glanced up at Andrew's fallen face. "But when his father dies, he goes home to run the family business. The dutiful son—you know—even though he could have been a professional musician. Turns out, he excels in other ways. Makes an enormous success of himself, does his family proud."

The fluorescent lights buzzed like the start of locust season. And why was it so hot in here?

"Anyway, the woman, she's old-er, beyond, you know—a certain point in life, and when she realizes the sacrifices the man has made—throughout his young life—the *music* life he gave up out of duty, out of love for his family—she lets him go so he can have that family experience she knows he must want and could still have, but she could never give him. Domestic happiness he'll find with someone else. Someone younger." I almost pointed to Ana, but then fidgeted, straightening an already straightened, short stack of books. "*Other* stuff happens too. Lots and *lots* of very *fictional* stuff, but—" I frowned and took another swallow.

Andrew freed a little cough, and I chanced a look. His tan had lost a few shades.

"Wow. That *does* sound different." Ana paused. "Oh well," she chirped. "I'm gonna get it, anyway. Be right back." She thrust her hand at a motionless Andrew. Realizing Ana waited for his credit card, he fumbled with his wallet, struggling to remove a card. Giving up, he handed her the whole billfold. She skipped away to buy the book.

I took a long swig of water. The crinkling crunch of compressing plastic filled the quiet as I sucked the fluid from the bottle. When I finished, I said, "She's lovely. Very sweet."

Andrew sighed. "She's a handful, to be honest. But she gets what she wants. Always has. How are you? You look beau—"

"*Don't*—don't you dare say something kind." Hardly any voice came with my plea. "Please—I'm sorry. Just—"

"Got it!" Ana exclaimed. "Make it out to 'Ana,' of course. *Ana* like *wanna*, but only one *N*," she snickered, sliding the book to me.

To Ana: Congratulations on your wedding day. I wish you all the happiness in the world. C.G. Austin.

"Can I hug you? Tell me I can hug you." Ana had already rounded the table, wrapping me in her arms as she made her request. Karma for my sneak attack on Laney? I took the assault in my chair without any fight, then watched her jog around the table to grab Andrew around his waist, resting her head against his shoulder. She kissed his cheek before she gasped. "*Oh. My. God. You should totally come.*"

"What?" Andrew and I asked in unison.

She smacked her hands on the table between us. "Yes, you should totally come to the reception! Eight o'clock at the Yale Club."

While Ana kept talking, I said *no* repeatedly. *Thank you, but no.* The words came out as calmly as I could make them. My brain spiraled as Tex rejoined the scene reprising, *Plastics. There's a future in plastics,* while doing the two-step in an astronaut's helmet.

"Drew! Make her. It'll be so much fun. We'll have a blast. I swear." Ana had more energy than anyone I had ever encountered in real life.

"Remember the Energizer Bunny?" Tex asked. "Now we know where it got off to. Right up her—"

"*Don't*—you two have someplace you need to be?" I glared at Tex, then at Andrew in a way that meant to say *please leave.*

Andrew shrugged. "Of course, you're welcome to join us. I'd welcome your company anytime, anywhere. Feel free. You know the place."

I couldn't believe he spoke to me like that, in front of Ana, no less. Her response? "See! You should *totally* be there." She pulled on Andrew's arm, dragging him toward the escalator. "Eight o'clock!" she shouted.

"I—I don't know what to—" Andrew's glassy blue eyes crushed my heart.

"Just *go.*" I mouthed, unable to look away.

He stared, too, until the escalator carried him below my line of sight. I dropped my forehead to the table.

Laney had been standing guard at the escalator to protect our privacy. She crept to where I crumbled in exhaustion.

"Who the hell was she?"

Tex and I spoke in unison, "His bride. His *pregnant* bride."

"Jesus H..."

32

"You know, you imagine certain moments in your life—I mean, you prepare yourself the best you can. You know the moment will come eventually, that moment when your legs just get *unceremonious-ious-ly* taken out from under you, leaving you flat on your back in a pile of dog crap." I fished cashews from the nut bowl and set them on Laney's cocktail napkin. "But nothing, *no-thing* prepares you for hearing those soul-crushing words—whatever those words turn out to be—from a seven-foot-tall, sword-wielding, golden-hued, Galactic Gladiator. Nope, did not see that coming. That's for *damn* sure." I snorted, then emptied my martini glass and signaled for another.

"And *you're* cut off." Laney sat next to me at The Bar and shook her head at the bartender. "Three, and you're out."

"I'm not *drunk*, Laney Li. Just sad. God, I'm sad—and maybe a little *dur-runk*. And how does he stand there, in front of her, and say he'd *welcome my company anytime, anywhere*? I mean, what *was* that? *Feel free*, he said. That was not like him."

"Maybe he's gotten stuck. It happens. Maybe he's trying to be a stand-up guy but then saw you again and—"

"Stop. Stop talking. It doesn't matter. I should take solace in the fact I was right. And now he's getting what he apparently always wanted, and I could never give him. Right? *God*, she was so young. So, so—I gotta go, Laney." I slid off my barstool. "It's Saturday night. Go be with Genevieve. Go home to your wife."

"What will you do?"

"I'm gonna lay my head down and fall asleep, for eight hours at least, and then I think I'll walk to Central Park, where I hope to catch the end of the tulips at the Shakespeare Garden." I kissed her cheek and wobbled to the elevator and thirty-eighth floor.

The Empire State Building continued its patriotic glow scheme while a smattering of Memorial Day weekend fireworks exploded over the distant Hudson River. My pacing quickened. Panic rose. I didn't know what to do with myself.

"How about a soak in that tub? You always relax in a tub." Tex appeared and watched me walk the length of the suite. "A glass of wine?"

I eyed the minibar. "No. None of that will make this alright, Tex. Thanks for trying, though."

"You know what this reminds me of?"

I stopped in my tracks. I couldn't imagine his answer. "No, tell me."

"I don't know. I've never—we've—*you've* never felt this way before." Tex looked at me with sad eyes. "I don't know how to help you, and I don't like it."

"Guess I'm on my own with this one. Good night, Tex."

I hadn't been in bed long when my phone lit up on the other side of the room. It did it again and a minute later, again. I considered letting it go; leaving it unchecked until morning, but when I realized sleep was refusing to come in its usual way, I tiptoed to see the messages.

There were three texts from three different numbers, and each said the same thing.

Laney Li: *Tex Miller is a hit!*
Jason: *Tex Miller is a hit!*

Cyrus: *Hey, gurl, Tex Miller is a hit!*

"Way to go, Tex," I spoke the words aloud, but they weren't for my Tex, and my Tex wasn't around. My Tex had disappeared to nurse some serious heartache. Turning off my phone, I crawled back into bed, and in three deep breaths, I escaped that same pain for at least eight hours.

33

True to form, I slept eight hours, but eight hours was all the escape I allowed myself. The earliest morning light snuck over the horizon, reflecting off the steel and glass to the west, while I sipped weak pod coffee. Long shadows stretched across Madison Square Park as locals began their Sunday dawn exercise regimens and breakfast-themed grub trucks set up for the impending brunch patrons keen on morning meal picnics. With a holiday weekend and beautiful weather forecasted, they were right to get a jump on what would surely be a good business day.

Despite last night's suggestion of a relaxing soak in the tub, I hadn't even showered off the day I'd spent signing books. The early hour gave me time to do it now. A quick pick-me-up before taking the hour-long stroll to Central Park.

It had been more than a year since I wandered the city I loved, and I wasn't sure when I'd be back. My bruised heart might always hurt with regret in this place. It lost some of its luster, but that was understandable. Maybe in time, that would change. It was naïve to think a walk in the park to see petal-dropping tulips would be the cure to anything, much less a broken heart, but it would be a hint that seasons come and go; life goes on.

Joggers and a matching zip-up with my favorite sneakers made up my Sunday best. With another couple of slurps of unsatisfying single brew, I slipped my phone into my back pocket with my key card and some cash, ready as I'd ever be to face the day.

The hotel lobby stood vacant, not unexpected for daybreak. I nodded to the desk clerk I didn't know and pushed through the glass door onto the sidewalk to cross Madison Avenue, cutting through Madison Square on a pathway exiting onto 5th Avenue. A just-opened coffee shop supplied a stout pour-over to help clear the fog I hadn't been able to shake. Turns out caffeine isn't a cure for an emotional hangover. Time is the only true panacea, but for now, over-priced, fancy coffee would play the placebo.

No matter how many times I've made the trek up 5th Avenue, I'll always marvel at the Empire State Building. One hundred two stories of Art déco beauty. And as a writer and a reader, it can't be a surprise that another favorite highlight on this path to Central Park would be the New York Public Library's Main Branch. The colossal building was over a hundred years old, and the marble façade and ornate details on the 5th Avenue side boasted Patience and Fortitude, a pair of stone lions, the icons of the impressive public-private partnership. Those cats with their apt names may have smirked at me as I walked by.

A few blocks further, I passed Luna's headquarters and the bookstore that, until the end, had been such a bright spot for me the day before. I would need to make it a point to tell Laney to schedule more book signings in the future. Anywhere but New York City. I might have guessed I missed out, living the anonymous writer life with all my years of work on Tex Miller novels, but I knew it for sure at the book signing. A one-on-one moment like the kind I had with Miri was a gift, and I selfishly wanted more. The notion of "want" almost made me smile, and I was quick to point out to myself that smiling might still be possible. All was not lost.

The earliest Mass, the first of seven given on Sundays alone, let out at St. Patrick's Cathedral. Attendees trickled from the Roman Catholic Church, while half a block earlier and across the street, Rockefeller Center, another tourist destination popular throughout the year with its flags and fountains, a seasonal ice rink, and more, stood nearly empty. Fancy hotels and upscale shopping lined the Midtown area, with the Museum of Modern Art half a block to the left of me, and finally, the Pulitzer Fountain ahead.

Once in the park, I kept to Park Road, walking by the zoo. The tree-canopied path wound around statues and playgrounds, and I was happy to have the shade as the temperature climbed while the sun did the same.

When I veered onto the park's East Drive, my heart raced at my first glimpse of the now-shuttered Boathouse. Memories of a sunny day in March were inescapable, though I'd have given anything not to linger on them now. Maybe that wasn't true. Perhaps I was a glutton for the ache that came with all this sightseeing. Deviating from my intended route all but proved it. I rounded the model boat pond where I'd find the bronze sculpture of Alice, the Mad Hatter, and their tea party. Surrounded by leafing trees and the lavender-colored blooms of catmint gave the scene a lush, woodsy backdrop, so unlike the stark bare sticks on that March day more than a year ago.

Now, without crutches and no one around to see me, I climbed the famous statue like the toddler who scrambled up the toadstool steps and table on my last visit. Higher than I thought, the idea of merely hopping down onto the concrete gave me pause. Four or forty-something, taking a leap would always be daunting.

"Are you gonna do it? Are you gonna jump?" The man's voice mocked me, tinged with spite. It carried through the trees along the curved path opposite the direction from where I had entered the roundabout. "Can't say for sure, but I don't imagine whatever it is it's worth risking, say, oh, I don't know—maybe a hairline fracture to the patella. I hear that smarts."

Frozen to my spot and facing away from the heckler, I steadied myself with my hand on top of Alice's head, begging my heart to slow and dizziness to subside. Maneuvering my way around Alice's splayed legs, I turned to face Andrew's raised brow.

"What? Cheshire Cat got your tongue?" He continued a laid-back stroll with his hand outstretched. "Why don't you let me help you off there?"

I didn't let go of Alice's head but collected myself enough to speak. "What are you doing here?" Banality won over droll. If clever wit was my superpower, Andrew Statheros proved to be my kryptonite. Again.

"Looking for you. Are you gonna give me your hand?" He bore an edgier version of his crooked grin with all the boyish charm. Still, it was a wonder I didn't fall right there.

"Not yet." I gripped the bronze that grew slick with my sweat. "You're looking for me? Here?" I shook my head. "No, the Andrew I know wouldn't do this. He wouldn't shirk responsibility, wouldn't abandon someone who needed him."

"I appreciate you think so highly of me, Calliope. It's—a relief, actually. And I agree. I also think I have more than lived up to my responsibilities, and the only one I shouldn't abandon right now is the woman climbing statues all alone in the early hours of a Sunday in Central Park. And—speaking of *alone*," he shrugged with a faux frown, "I should probably ask. *Are* you? Alone, I mean."

I snorted at Andrew's teasing despite myself, and his rigid grin relaxed. Snapping back to the seriousness of the situation, I recalibrated, balancing myself with the help of the bronze tree limb shared with the Cheshire Cat.

"I suppose your refusal to come down from there works in

my favor. You can't walk away. Now, what have I told you about carrying a phone, Calliope?"

"Don't patronize me, you pompous—I have my phone. Thank you very much." I reached into my back pocket to prove it.

He shook his head as his condescension grew. "Is it—*on?*"

I looked at the black screen, then at him while I pushed the power button. "No," I admitted.

"That's fine. I'll wait for it to boot up." Andrew rocked back on his sneaker heels, taking in the sights. Birds sang an early morning back-and-forth in the surrounding trees, and on the far side of the model boat pond, clinking chains echoed as a park employee readied for a day of remote-control rentals. Focused back on me, he asked, "Miss any calls, by chance? Texts, maybe?"

Powered on, the phone and message icons on my home screen both indicated I had—well, let's say, a *few.*

"Just for fun, read the first text Laney sent you this morning. Out loud, if you don't mind." He stared up at me, still perched on the damn statue.

I opened my message app but then swallowed hard at the sight of the first text, reading it to myself.

"Take your time. I've got all day. Is it long?"

"No," I mumbled. "Three words, is all."

"And which three words would those be, Calliope?" he asked in an exaggerated lean.

"He's. Not. Married," I punctuated the message.

"*Hm,* now that's interesting reading."

I returned the phone to my pocket and spun away from him. With one hand gripping the Mad Hatter's hat, my feet found one toadstool, then another, eventually landing on the ground. I wiped my hands on my thighs, still confused, but until I knew more, I planned to keep silent.

Andrew had a different strategy in mind. "So, that list of things I think about you starts off a lot like yours for me: funny, smart, kind, sexy as hell, loyal—"

"I never said that," I interjected, goaded to respond.

"Loyal?" He nodded with a furrowed brow. "It's been a while, but no, I'm pretty sure you did."

"Not that one. The one before."

"Sexy as hell? *Hmm*, thought I'd slip that in. Can't blame a guy for trying. Well, it's on *my* list, anyway. But I'll add strong-willed, obstinate, stubborn."

"Lookout, Andrew, you just used three words that basically mean the same thing. Seems like overkill."

"Welp, that's just how strongly I feel about it. How about we add self-righteous, needlessly insecure, and frankly—just plain wrong-headed sometimes?"

"Wow. This is fun. If your little plan is to act like an ass to ensure I realize I'm better off without you—bang-up job. I'm good now. Thanks." I stepped away; the sculpture still loomed large between us. "Nope," I rotated back. "I don't understand. Forget about me, I'll be fine, but that poor girl—and when I say girl, I mean *girl*, that *'handful'* as you so vividly described her yesterday. What about her?"

"What about her? As of about, oh, seven-thirty last night, she's someone else's handful now and on her way to Santorini as we speak." Andrew made his way around the tea party, his grin gone, and his striking blue eyes read hurt. "Ana, short for Ariana, *is* a girl, I agree. She will always be a girl. I'd just turned twelve when my parents brought her home from the hospital and she's had me wrapped around her little finger ever since. She's my baby sister, and there isn't much I wouldn't do—*haven't done*, to see her happy. And she is—which almost makes up for how utterly miserable I've been since you walked away from me last May. She was the one bright spot in a year of awful. But now I learn you think knocking up a twenty-five-year-old is something I could—I *would*—do, and *Jesus*, Calliope, the hits just keep on coming."

"No, I didn't. Al-alright, I did, but I figured—shit happens, and you were stuck. So surely you'd do the right thing by her because the Andrew I know is honorable, principled, moral."

"*Uh-oh*, Calliope. You just used three words that basically mean the same thing. Seems like overkill."

"Yeah, well, that's how strongly I feel about it."

Neither of us spoke, but the sounds of the park coming alive with Sunday morning activity grew. Andrew's pained expression delivered a gut-punch, and my explanation wouldn't bring relief to either of us.

"Please understand, Andrew, when I heard—what I heard, it validated *everything* I thought a year ago. You wanted a family, and that wasn't in the cards for—"

"*You* never asked, Calliope," his abrupt interruption thundered.

I jerked in surprise. "And you never *said*, but you had that room. That darling room with *Hello Kitty*, ice skates, and *Anne of Green Gables*." My volume matched his, then escalated. "And I'm not exactly sure how a woman of a certain age goes about asking a younger man she's only known a few months, but is desperately falling for, his opinion about raising a family."

"I don't know *either*, but you do. You ask, you sure as *hell* ask before you walk away because you weren't the only one in free fall." With that confession, he looked away. Our sudden quiet underscored the disruption we'd stirred in the peaceful setting. "Made for some great chapters in your book, though, *huh*?" Those last words came at just above a whisper.

"Are you upset about the book? Because hurting you was never my intention. Ever."

"No, you wrote a beautiful story," he paused as his head made a slight side-to-side motion, "Not—wild about the ending, but..."

"*Ha*. Hollywood might have an issue, too—wait, you finished it? Already?"

"Started yesterday afternoon. Had to break for a couple of hours because I had a *thing*, but then read all night. Laney texted and called this morning. A bit frantic. She saw the wedding announcement. I've been out here looking for you since then. She said you were going to see the tulips. I took a chance you might come here." His hands rubbed his face before he gave his curls a workout. "*God*, I need some sleep."

"Kinda far from home."

"I'm not now. Got a place east of here." He gestured toward 5th Avenue.

"The High Line place sold?"

"It did. To a family—with daughters."

"Nice." I meant to be congratulatory. "Well—the tulips are *west* of here," I pointed beyond him, "so I won't keep you—from your sleep."

"Right." Andrew shook his head with his eyes to the ground. When I walked past him, he reached for my hand, barely grasping my fingers with his. I stopped, our two arm-lengths apart, and tightened the grip.

"I should probably ask, so I don't regret *not* asking later," I spoke over my shoulder.

"What's that?"

"You got an opinion on tulips?"

"I might. I could come up with one on the fly and tell you all about it while we walk to the Shakespeare Garden."

"Yeah? I'd like that."

"And maybe I could—hold your hand while we walk?"

"*God*, I'd like that too." My insides slowly unknotted, easing with relief.

With synchronized, deep breaths, we wandered under black tupelo trees, half-leafed out with their yellowish-green blooms filling in the branches while the spring leaves sprouted their way to full summer foliage. In the distance, music played with the echoing acoustics of a solo violin under the Glade Arch, a wide tunnel providing an overhead walkway to Fifth Avenue. A well-known Bach movement floated through the air, giving my nerves a break with something other than talk to fill the anxious quiet. For two people who, only a moment ago, said so much, our silence hovered now like unwelcomed clouds. Maybe a year was too long. Injury left unattended could be beyond healing, and I knew the blame lay at my feet.

As we walked by the violinist, I tossed dollar bills and coins into the musician's instrument case—the change from my fancy coffee earlier in the morning. I owed her more than that for taking up our wordless space, if only for a few moments, but it was all I had to give. Her soundtrack to our awkwardness was exquisite, but truth be told, I would have gratefully tipped a kazoo player for doing the same work.

Once far enough away from the distraction, I knew the conversation had to begin, or there'd be no hope for us.

"I should have made you a violinist," I spit out the words faster than I intended.

"What?"

"In the book. Instead of a pianist. Maybe a violin?"

"A little late now, though, right? The book being in stores and all." He flattened his grin.

"Yes. Good point." Fingers still interlaced, I took hold of his arm with my free hand, leaning into him as we strolled. Would closing the physical gap between us be enough to help repair the emotional rift? Two women in about as many years had kicked this man's heart around, so any skittish behavior on his part would be understandable.

"It's still cute how you get nervous when things get quiet."

"Again, with cute?" I hid my face in his upper arm.

"That's what this is, isn't it? You're nervous?"

It took five slow strides before I confessed. "Can you blame me? I messed up, and not just once." We walked through the Cedar Hill picnic area where, in an hour, visitors would have blankets staked out in prime spots for later in the day lunches and sun-soaked naps. "I am sorry. Truly. I'm sorry for all of it."

"I'm sorry too." He let go of my hand and wrapped his arm around my shoulders. No space between us now as we climbed the slope edging the Met.

"What are you sorry for?"

"Let's see. I'm sorry I didn't fight harder. Sorry for not opening up sooner, so you knew where I stood. I should have been braver, more trusting. I hold plenty of blame, and I've had an entire year to examine each misstep I took along the way. And there were a few. This time? This time we'll do it better."

"This time?" Hope sprang and with it, a glimmer of possibility.

Andrew stopped us in front of Turtle Pond. Belvedere Castle stood above us. He let go of his one-armed embrace to face me. Hand outstretched to shake mine, he said, "Hi, my name's Andrew, and I have a private car company and some parking lots, but that's not really important. I just read your book, Ms. Austin, and I'd love to talk to you about it over dinner sometime."

"Are you—asking me on a date?" I took his hand in a cordial greeting.

"Yes, I'm asking you on a date, Ms.—"

"Please. Call me Calliope," I filled in the name in jest. "I'd like that, but maybe after you've gotten some rest. You're no good to me asleep at the table."

"Wow. You've got some high expectations for a first date, but I'll be sure to rest up. Take my vitamins. Stretch." He winked.

His flirty joke forced an unstoppable snort. One hand tried to hide my blush, the other pulled the crook of his arm. "Let's go see the wilting tulips."

After an hour's stroll, catching up on the last year, I caught Andrew mid-yawn and knew he needed sleep. The remorse that came with all the time we'd lost fueled our reluctance to part ways now, but I had responsibilities, and he had—exhaustion.

"You need to rest, and I need to let Laney know I'm alive."

"She knows you're with me. I texted just before I rescued you from your Alice in Wonderland swan dive. And we have more talking to do. Talking we *need* to do." We sat on the steps at Bethesda Fountain.

"I agree we have more talking to do, but you look like a truck hit you."

He nodded. "Probably not in the best headspace for talk, but I hesitate to let you walk away again."

"How about we agree we're merely going our separate ways for a short while so I can check in on my work life, and you can sleep. And when you are in the right headspace, we'll reconvene to resume the talking."

"For such a rational, clear-cut plan, it's hard to believe you write such romantic, heartbreaking stories." Elbow to his knees, Andrew blinked bleary-eyed.

"Hard to believe you'd think walking away is anything close to what I want to do right now. But—" Frustration grew. Too many things to say. So much I wanted to do.

"But what, Calliope?"

"But nothing. When can I see you again?" My nerve surprised me.

"Come home with me now."

You'd think I'd jump at the offer, but I froze as the warm day got warmer. "I—I thought you asked me on a date." My arms hugged my shins, chin to my knees as I absorbed the implication.

"You're right. I shouldn't have suggested that. Out of line. I'm sorry." Andrew ran his hand through his curls, then pinched the bridge of his nose.

"No. Don't be. Please." I tilted my face to his. "Kiss me."

"What?" Andrew squinted as if he might have misunderstood.

"Kiss me," I repeated.

He hesitated, then gently pounced, eager for the opportunity. Or maybe afraid I'd rescind the offer. His tender kiss gave me life and stole my breath all at once.

I clutched his shirt collar when our lips parted. "Now, kiss me again, and then I'm walking back to my hotel. Call me for that date. I'm free tonight." I lifted my chin for him again. This time the kiss was more—more heat, more promise, more desire. I fought pulling away from him, wishing I could stay in that kiss but stood and walked toward my hotel, hoping I didn't let slip how faint I felt. In ten paces, my phone rang. I answered, "Thought you'd never call."

"Sorry. Got sidetracked. Turns out, watching you walk away isn't all bad."

34

"And why didn't you tell me about it sooner?" I stepped off the hotel elevator on the thirty-eighth floor, talking with Laney on my walk to my suite, ready to get off my feet.

"I figured you might be nervous, so as little time to dwell on it seemed like the best course of action." Laney had a frankness about her I didn't always enjoy, particularly when she was right.

"And it didn't occur to you I might have other plans?"

"No. When do you ever have other plans, or unalterable plans, anyhow?" Again, she wasn't wrong—except this time.

"Well, Laney, this time I do." I kicked off my sneakers with great satisfaction.

"I hear you, but this time, the unalterable plans are the ones I made for you. Cancel the other."

"Don't you want to know what the other is?"

"I can guess, but like I said—cancel."

"I will not. Whatever is going on with Andrew is shaky at best, and I'm not canceling. I'll postpone."

"Potato, pot*ah*to."

"How about I have him meet me there?" I reconsidered.

"Bad idea on a couple of counts."

"What counts?"

"One, you're reading from the book. Two, he attracts attention you don't need."

"The first one doesn't matter. He's read the book. The second one—well, we need to figure that out because, well, we need to figure it out."

"Well, kudos to him for putting in the work. But have you changed your mind about going public with Calliope Jones?" The question felt black-or-white.

"*Uh*, no." I hadn't thought about Calliope Jones at all today and failed to see what one had to do with the other.

"Are you willing to take the chance? I'm telling you, the minute he pokes his head up, the fleas will pounce. And you don't want fleas. So Drew needs to stay away. And I will tell him so. We also need him to sign an—"

"*No*. You will not present him with any sort of NDA again. Is that understood? And I don't need you running interference with him."

"My job is to protect you. NDAs and running interference are necessary tools for me to fulfill my duties."

"What about the part where you're my friend, Laney?"

"I was your agent before I was your friend, and as your agent, I promised to protect your anonymity. Other than selling your books, that was your number one request, and until you tell me otherwise, it is my number one objective. If you don't want me doing that job anymore, *change* my objective, or *fire* me."

"Laney? Where is this coming from? I thought you were Team Drew."

"I will *always* be Team Callie. You stayed away for a year. I blame him."

"Whoa. And the book? I thought you loved the book."

"Maybe I just liked it more when you were in love with your damned imaginary cockroach of a muse—*Jesus*... Callie?"

"I'll see you at the gallery. Park and Seventy-what? Never mind.

I'll find it."

"Callie, I'm sorry."

"*Save it*, Laney." I hung up. I'd never hung up on Laney. A text pinged almost immediately.

Laney Li: *I'm sending a car for later tonight*

I didn't reply. Instead, I ran a bath. Stepping into the steamy bubbles, music sounded through the small speaker under the bathroom counter. The haunting melody the Glade Arch violinist had played filled the stone tile room, and my tension dissipated with a knock at the door.

"No robe this time?"

Tex, dressed in street clothes, took his leaned perch at the sink. "Guess it's not a robe kinda talk."

"What is happening, Tex?"

"It's called change, my dear, and it could be a great thing. Just maybe not everyone handles it as well as you do."

That obvious misjudgment made me laugh.

"I'm glad to see you've got your sense of humor."

"Am I being selfish? Do I want too much?"

"Maybe we should start by saying *what* you want. Out loud. How will anyone know if you don't say it?"

"I want my career. Both the C.G. Austin and Calliope Jones career. I want you and I want him. Do I have to choose? Is that what it comes down to? *No.* I choose me."

"*Ah-ha.* Well, then. You know what needs to happen, and maybe not today or tomorrow but at some point. Just don't let the choice get made for you. And that's what our little badass is trying to do. Laney's keeping your options open. And as always, she has your—"

"I know. Thanks, Tex."

"Don't thank me. I just say the words I'm given." Tex's words had always been my words.

"I know that, too."

"Speaking of words, when are we—?" He wiggled his brows.

"Soon. I think. I've got an idea percolating. Quick question. How do you feel about wearing a banana suit?"

"*Pfft.* Bring it, Jones." Tex pushed off the counter to leave.

"See you tonight?"

"If you need me, I'll be there."

"Wait. What does that mean?"

"It means someday you might not."

"Get outta here. That's never gonna happen."

"If we've learned anything today, it's never say never."

I threw a washcloth at Tex as he walked out of the bathroom. But when the Bach ended, I sat in a brief silence as the idea sank in. After a long, hot shower, I bundled up in the cushy hotel robe and hurried into the suite in search of my phone.

Callie: *Not canceling. A slight change in plan. I'm doing a reading at a gallery in your neck of the woods. On Park. 7pm. Laney's not keen on you being there. Meet at the planned spot when I text or feel free to show up because I am keen on seeing you.*

I hoped no reply meant Andrew was sleeping, and I settled in for some reading before I dressed for the evening. Laney sent word when to expect my ride, and I was ready at the appropriate hour. A Madras midi sundress with wedge sandals and a denim jacket felt right for a boho-chic art gallery talk about literary fiction with women of a certain age. To be honest, I hadn't a clue, but I felt fantastic.

"Good evening, Miss," Dante greeted me, black suit, black cap, and a broader than usual smile.

"Dante. Thank you for Chet yesterday. He did a fine job.

Uneventful."

"Not how I heard it, but we can go with your version of events, Miss," Dante snickered as he opened my car door.

"Are you getting comfortable with me, Dante?" I squinted at him.

Dante's massive frame went rigid. "No, ma'am. My apologies."

"Stop. I'm giving you a hard time. Let's go. I've got a date after work tonight. With your boss."

"Yes, Miss." His shoulders lowered. "Upper East, here we come."

The gallery was lackluster, to say the least, but I think that was the design plan. A blank canvas with a typical storefront housed mobile screens on lockable casters so the gallery owner could reconfigure the displays as she saw fit. The evening's art also had a woman-centric theme. Earlier, I questioned my excerpt choice, but I no longer had doubt. The subject of women being seen, no matter their age or social standing, whether in moments of pure joy, profound grief, or merely sitting at a table with a grilled cheese sandwich—is a universal longing. We all want to be seen.

A nice-sized crowd of onlookers wandered while a small staff dressed in black served wine and canapes. Laney spoke over the event noise, including a jazz trio playing in a corner.

"Callie, I don't want to get in your head before you do this, but I need to apologize—for what I said." She had never behaved with such contrition.

"Okay." I walked toward theater-style seating for a few dozen. A podium stood center with a plinthed microphone.

"Okay, what?"

"Okay, apologize." I gave her a blank stare.

"I thought I just did. Can I get you a glass of wine?"

I sighed. "I'm not sure drinking on the job is a good idea."

"You're a writer. Drinking is part of the job, no?"

"I see what you are trying to do, but I'm pissed and nervous, so I'm going to *stay* pissed a while longer, so I'm not just nervous."

"Don't be. Jason and Cyrus are here. And Genevieve."

"Genevieve? Here? Oh, wow." I grinned. "You're in the doghouse," I sing-songed.

"Well, it happens I told Genevieve about our little dust-up, and she took your side. Yeah, I'm in the doghouse."

"Did you tell everyone to stay away? Why is no one coming to see me?"

"So you can do your thing, and then they will come heap praise. After, though."

I shrugged. As my butterflies grew rambunctious, I reconsidered the wine. I should have asked Andrew to be there, told him outright I wanted him there. Screw Laney's opinion. Tex was right. I needed to stop letting people make choices for me. "Go socialize, Laney. I need to get in the zone—or whatever."

"The gallery owner will introduce you. She's the woman in the black dress by the water fountain. You read. That's it. They'll break, so maybe mingle a bit. Then there will be a poet and a photographer, I think. Have a drink. Signed books are on display. You look great, by the way," Laney rambled.

"Go away now, Laney Li." I shooed her as I went for my phone. No message from Andrew. My heart sank, and I cursed under my breath while I texted.

Callie: *I messed up. Again. I should have asked you to be here. I wanted you to be here, and I didn't say so outright, and I should have because if I don't ask for what I want, how will anyone know? I'm sorry.*

I hit send and struggled for a deep breath. My phone pinged as I sipped from a water bottle.

Andrew: *Back of the room, stage left. Don't look.*

Slowly, I lifted my gaze to the room. The phone pinged again.

Andrew: *The other left.*

Andrew: *I see you, and you're amazing.*

A calm washed over me. Breathing got easier, and my rapid heartbeat slowed. Someone had just taken a few rocks from my armload. The gallery owner met me in the center aisle to thank me for coming to speak. The crowd gathered. Some sat, others stood, still others continued exploring the artwork displayed around the room.

I hadn't expected the applause. I hadn't expected anything, but when I finished the excerpt, it was as if we all took a collective breath. Clapping followed, and a few raised hands. Questions? I looked at Laney. She signaled I should call on someone. I pointed to a woman seated in the middle of the pack.

"The section about her and Tony—Anthony, was my favorite."

Others in the crowd agreed.

"He seemed so real? Is he? Real? And if so, please tell me he has a brother. Maybe a cousin?"

People laughed.

I chanced a glance at Andrew. Clad in jeans and a heather gray Mets logo t-shirt, he stood in the back, casually leaning against a pillar, arms crossed. With the slightest headshake and a crooked grin, he looked at his sneakered feet crossed at his ankles.

"It's a novel. By definition, it's a work of fiction. But, no. Just the sisters, I'm afraid. So—next?" Eager to move on, I pointed to a woman seated down front.

"Ms. Austin. What took you so long to write a book? Why'd you wait?

"Actually, I've been writing a while. This is just the first time I've wanted to put my name on something."

Laney gave a nod of approval for the reply.

"How about you, sir?"

An eager gentleman, veiled in the shadow of a display, asked, "Has anyone ever compared your writing style to any other authors? Do you have a favorite? Something about your prose reminds me of—"

"All writers have their influences." I hurried to cut off his comment. "Imitation and flattery, you know the rest. I'm sure you can find similarities throughout literature. Take Shakespeare and Kit Marlowe. Thackery and Dickens..."

Laney was already in the gallery owner's ear, who quickly interrupted the Q&A to move the program along. Crisis averted. Spectators rose for more refreshments, and a small, friendly crowd descended upon me. Cyrus, Jason, Genevieve, and Laney were an obvious buffer, if only to me, from any more uncomfortable inquiries. Andrew slipped out, and the irony of the *being seen* theme knocked the wind out of me. A glass of wine appeared in my hand, and Cyrus kissed my cheek. "You okay, honey?"

I forced a smile and nodded.

Laney's wife, Genevieve, a stunning, tall blonde, took me by the arm to assure me I was right, Laney was wrong, and I should not let her off the hook too soon. Genevieve's throaty voice, tinged with a hint of Long Island, made her someone you definitely wanted in your corner. She and Laney made a fierce pair.

"I'm not exactly sure what she told you—" I eyed Genevieve with some suspicion.

"She said you were growing, and she was afraid you didn't need her like you used to because of a certain young man—this *Tony* character I presume, and that she hit you with something too personal and totally off-limits even for her and then mumbled something about *Agent Academy* which I'm pretty sure isn't really a thing. In her defense, your absence this year left a big hole in her world. Then again, the woman needs to learn to share."

I raised my chin, suggesting Genevieve wasn't far off. "I missed her too. Think you could do me a favor?"

"Name it, even better if it fires up Miss Hothead in hot pants over there." She leaned closer with a fiendish leer.

"I need to sneak outta here. Can you help me with that?"

"Done and done."

I slugged back the wine, kissed Genevieve's cheek, and went in search of my messenger bag.

Callie: *Tell me where to meet you.*

Andrew: *North on Park, third right, I'll find you.*

Using display canvases as cover, I bolted for the gallery exit. Genevieve gave me the high-sign, and I blew a kiss before hurrying up Park Avenue. Three blocks north, Andrew perched on the low iron pipe railing of an upscale co-op building. I stopped to catch my breath from my rush to get there and the pleasure of seeing his beautiful face in his screen's glow. A stroll brought me to his spot in the dark, his eyes glued to his phone.

I cleared my throat. "Know where a girl can get a drink around here?"

He bounded to his feet. "Hi." He gave me a distracted peck on the cheek. It was a little disappointing. "Sorry. Your agent is giving me the business end of—"

"That didn't take long. Ignore her."

"I can't do that. Besides, she says you're ignoring her. What gives?"

"She said something cruel, and she didn't mean it, but she said it, so I'm letting her think about it for a bit. And I don't mean to make any assumptions here, truly, but this time, I hope when it comes to you and me, it can be less about her and more about—you know—you and me." Saying the words was another rock lifted from my load.

Andrew put his phone in his pocket. "This asking for what you want thing?"

"Yeah?"

"It looks really good on you."

"Yeah?" I couldn't look away.

"Yeah."

I smiled. "In that case, I'd like you to take me on that date now."

"You got it. It's chillier than I thought it would be. Mind if I grab a sweatshirt first?"

"Is this you?" I pointed to the building.

"No, over this way and another block north." He offered his hand. I took it gladly as we walked down the sidewalk. "You were terrific tonight. Hard to believe you'd never done that before. You're a natural."

I blushed at his flattery. "You didn't mind the excerpt?"

"The excerpt from the novel, which, by definition, is fiction?" He smiled when he repeated my Q&A reply, but then stopped under a corner streetlamp with a serious face. "No, I didn't mind it. Interesting your memory of it and how it compares to mine."

"You agree it was memorable?" My body tightened with the question.

"Oh, yes." His eyes brightened at the recollection. Riveted by the talk and still astounded that I held his hand at all, I barely noticed the other pedestrians push past us to cross the street. Before long, we entered a building, then an elevator. Andrew inserted a key into the lock next to the button labeled "PH." This smaller elevator had a smooth ride, unlike his last home. A whirring hum was the only sound as we climbed to the top floor. I let go of Andrew's hand, adjusting the weight of my messenger bag on my shoulder.

Andrew cleared his throat. An attempt to ease the growing tension? "I won't be a minute. Just gonna grab something with sleeves." The doors opened.

"You don't want me to see it? Your apartment? Maid's day off?" I followed him off the elevator.

"*Ha.* No. I mean, I don't have a maid. That was a joke. You were—you were joking." He grinned as I nodded. "I'd love for you to see it. When I was looking for a new place, there were features here, I thought—never mind. Come see the view."

The secured elevator opened twenty floors up and into Andrew's foyer, much like a small, personal gallery. The large, colorful modern art pieces that decorated the loft were gone. Instead, this space featured expertly hung and beautifully lit black and white photography. I stopped to admire each framed shot. Farther in, the apartment gave way to a large dark living room. Beyond that, a far wall was an expanse of windows flanked with a glass door on each end. Andrew flipped a switch. Recessed lighting illuminated the room.

"The terrace wraps around three sides with access here, the main bedroom, and the dining room. I caught balcony-envy in Charlotte."

"This room is stunning, Andrew. Your other place was great too, but this one, it seems more—"

"Me?"

"Yes, it's you. Understated and still uniquely you. Comfortable but with flawless style. Did you take these photographs?" I pointed to the display behind us.

"*Uh*, yeah. I did. A project I did over the last few months." A shyness I hadn't seen in a long time flickered in his look.

I took his hand. "I could tell. Something about the way you see the world. You captured it. They're outstanding." I squeezed his fingers, considering the pictures again. "Show me the view?"

Across the living room, he held open a wide iron-framed glass door to a deep, long verandah. I gave a bashful smile and walked past him. The smell of cedar floated from planter boxes teeming with lush greens, looking almost black in the nighttime light. Patio furniture, arranged in both directions, offered places for sitting, lounging, and dining. Beyond the flora, a city view glowed.

"*Wow*. Is there nothing you can't do? You garden, too?"

"Oh no, for now, they're cared for by a trained professional. I never owned plants before, but I'm learning and getting tan in the process. Another project."

"*You've* been busy."

Andrew bowed his shaking head. "I've been filling time." A chill racked his sturdy frame, and I stroked the suntanned gooseflesh on his arm. I, however, felt warm all over.

I pulled my bag strap over my head. "Wanna get that sweatshirt?"

"Yes." He stepped toward me but stopped short. "I'll be back in a sec. We'll go get that drink." Andrew went inside, and I followed, watching him jog past the gallery to a hall that led to his bedroom. Setting my bag near the sofa, I bent to unbuckle and step out of my sandals, then removed my denim jacket, laying it across the arm of a modern wingback chair. With forced bravery, I slipped from another garment, tucked it in my bag, and tiptoed in Andrew's direction.

A light inside the room guided me through the dim corridor, but Andrew flipped a switch before I met him as he exited. His arms were overhead, with his head still inside the well-worn hoodie. He bumped into me.

When he poked his face free of the neck with a flinch, he said, "Oh, there's a bathroom here." He pointed to a closed door behind me and moved to pull the sweatshirt to his hips.

I stopped him.

"What are you doing?"

"On second thought, I don't think you need this right now." With my help, the new extra layer found its way to the floor.

"Where's your jacket, Calliope?"

I tilted my head to the living room. "Don't think I need that right now, either."

"Looks like you lost your shoes, too." We both looked at my bare feet.

With my palm pressed to the NY in the center of his chest, I shrugged. "No shoes. Care to kick yours off?" As soon as he had, I grabbed a fistful of t-shirt and pulled him to me. A distinct lack of tenderness accompanied the kiss, precisely what I wanted at that moment. Fingers groped and pulled hair, tongues were soft but eager, and low moans whimpered out in the heated scuffle that found me pressed against that powder room door. His hands on my skin played tricks with time, and I wanted everything to move slower and faster all at once.

"Andrew?" I asked when my mouth found the moment, and my lungs, the air to speak.

"Yes?" He rasped into my neck.

"Can we—talk?"

"*Huh*?" He stopped kissing me and clenched his jaw. "I mean, yeah—of course." His head jiggled as he exchanged his grip on me to that of the door frame. He took a step back, and I recognized his efforts to focus.

"What are you doing? Don't pull away. Why are you moving away?" I tugged at his shirt again, afraid I had discouraged our progress.

"I'm not sure, but I imagine I'll do better, you know, *listening* to you if I'm not—*touching* you."

"Oh. Smart." I swallowed hard.

"What's up?" he asked as he ruffled his curls and caught his breath.

"What? Oh, talking. Yes, so, I'm wondering your opinion on—foreplay." My hands petted his buff arms, my grip tightening on his shoulders as he resumed his firm hold on the decorative molding.

"Big fan. *Super* important." He gave a sideways glance with his succinct, husky reply.

"Good answer." I rose on my tiptoes with a vigorous nod and kissed him hungrily, briefly concerned he might tear the millwork from the plaster. "Just wondering if—" I continued to assail his mouth, "maybe—just this once, we could—skip all that?" Again, with help, one quick yank over his head, and I tossed Andrew's t-shirt into his pitch-dark bedroom. I bit my bottom lip at the sight of all that glorious skin, knowing horticulture had fast-tracked its way high on my list of new favorite spectator sports.

"Is this—a test?" He eyed me with skepticism as I made quick work of his belt buckle. With a jerk, metal clunked against the wall and then jangled across the terrazzo floor when I chucked it.

"Shut up and—" I grabbed at his waistband and nuzzled his neck, dizzy from his scent, "Wait. No—*don't* shut up. Keep talking. I like the talking, and don't second guess," I pleaded in his ear.

"Well, now you're just getting bossy."

"Please, Andrew, take me to—"

"Yes, ma'am." He grabbed me again, lifting and pulling to guide me into the darkness of his room. His kiss devoured me, unyielding as I fumbled with the zipper and the removal of his jeans. But then he stopped. Slowing the frenzy, he sat on the edge of his bed and leaned to click on a low bedside lamp. He nuzzled my stomach through my dress, breathing me in from his righted position.

"What are you doing?" I stood between his bare thighs.

"Getting some light." His palms slid from my shoulders to my fingers and squeezed.

"Why?" I exhaled.

"Because I want to *see* you." Those warm hands found my knees and traveled under my dress, up the backs of my thighs. "*Calliope Grace*?" Andrew's eyes grew wide with a gulping grin. "Where—are your panties?"

I eyed the living room, then hid my face in my hands. Mortified. "Jeez, Andrew. Could I be *any* more awkward? It's been a very long time since—"

He pulled at my wrists to reveal my blushing scowl. "You couldn't be any more beautiful."

My scowl vanished.

"Hey, remember that night, getting you out of the car and into the wheelchair?"

"*Uh-huh*." I stifled a laugh with a nod and cupped his cheeks to give him an encouraging kiss.

"Talk about foreshadowing." Andrew flipped me flat on my back as I squealed with more laughter.

His crooked grin beamed above me. "You ready?"

"Yes. I'm—*oh my God*, Andrew," I gasped. "Kiss me." And he did.

35

A VERY SHORT TIME LATER...

"Well, that was—"

"Every man's worst nightmare," Andrew interjected. "Now who's awkward?"

We lay on our backs, side by side, ninety degrees of the typical bed-lying position. Andrew hid his eyes with one hand and patted my thigh with the other. We snorted.

"I thought the nightmare was not being able to at all."

"Hold on. I could defend my performance—the unexpected nature of the encounter, the amount of time since my last encounter, the surprising though thoroughly appreciated lusty pursuit by my incredibly hot partner—"

This brought on more laughter as I raised up on one elbow and gave Andrew a playful punch in the arm. I looked down at our prone bodies. The skirt of my dress pushed up to my mid-thigh. His long, lean muscles sprawled, sculpted like Carrara marble, even in their relaxed state. He showed no inhibitions about being undressed. But then, why would he?

"Is that a tattoo on your pelvic bone there? A black heart tattoo?"

Andrew's hand instinctively covered the taut skin on the front of his hip, the first sign of any humility. "It is. Funny story."

"I bet. Since I've seen Stephi Chase's matching one." I countered with raised brows.

"Whoa, now that raises questions. If you tell me your story, I'll tell you mine."

In a move that seemed choreographed, Andrew rose on his elbow as I lay flat again.

His expression grew serious. "It's not what you might think."

"I don't really care," I shrugged, meaning it. "But if you want to add it to our list of things to talk about, we can." Restless, I sat up and traced the inked heart with my index finger, upside down from my vantage point. His skin twitched in response; his body stiffened. The mere mention of *talking* made us go mute. Twisting to face him, my palm skimmed his grooved torso, eyes focused on his. After a sharp inhale, I said, "I'll be back," and took three steps to the bedroom door. I glanced at him, still propped on his elbows, wearing nothing but his socks. "I'll be back," I repeated with a timid smile, and hurried to the hall powder room, closing the door behind me.

Cool water wetted my mouth and face, and I dabbed the droplets on my cheeks with a soft hand towel. Movement rustled on the other side of the door. A not-so-subtle stirring in Andrew's room. After fingering my tousled hair that rested around my shoulders, I wiped away smudges of eye make-up with a tissue. My deep inhale only riled the butterflies already running riot around my insides as I slipped out of my bra and smoothed my dress. "You can do this," I told my reflection and lowered the lever handle to exit.

Andrew had turned down the bed, removed his socks, and now wore pajama bottoms. The acrid whiff of a freshly struck match lingered from the lit pillar candles arranged on a bureau. The soft glows danced against the walls, bathing the room in dim light and shadows that I'd appreciate soon. He noted my assessing the scene from his spot on the far side of his bed and bolted up, suddenly flustered. "We should talk in the other room. I have water. Wine? Beer? Anything stronger?"

"Don't get up." I extended my hand, and he tentatively relaxed against a smooth upholstered headboard, a masculine tweed, fitted in a foot-deep recess just the width of the king-sized bed. "Liquor would probably help, but I'd like to do this sober—I think." I appraised the room again.

Anxiety mounted. "Candles too much? It feels like I've started with a negative balance here so—"

"The candles are perfect," I interrupted. "And your—*ledger* is just fine." I moved to his bedside, and he inched toward the center. "You trying to get away from me?" Our unplanned evening had us both nervous and unsure.

He shook his head with a short laugh while I climbed astride his lap. I gently stroked his tanned chest, admiring the result of his urban gardening efforts. The backs of my fingers traced under the ridges of his effortlessly firm pectorals. Dark hair swirled the shapely bulges and trailed the hard centerline to his navel. My hands moved to the fitted sheet at his sides as I bent to place a delicate kiss on his lips with a single soft flick of my tongue. Andrew gripped my hips in reply.

"I know we need to talk. And I promise we will—" Another kiss like the last one carried on a moment longer. "And that talk really needs to include you telling me where the hell you buy your bedsheets, because—well, they're fan*tas*tic, so add that to the list."

"The *talking list*?" Andrew's hands slid under my dress, grasping my bare thighs. My nod meant to encourage his bravery, and I pushed in for another, more demanding kiss, hoping to prove mine.

"We might want to find a more clever name for it, but yeah."

"That list is getting long." His fingers tucked my hair behind my ear and caressed my cheek.

Closing my eyes, I tilted my head into his palm, loving his touch and wanting more of it. "I've got time, I mean, not right this minute, but—later." I knew the moment was close, and my stomach tightened at the thought. His thumb stroked my bottom lip as our eyes met again.

"Later," he agreed. "What now, then?"

Looking at the ceiling, I forced a ragged inhale and reached behind my neck to pull my dress over my head. Shaky hands pressed the garment to my chest, desperate for the courage to let it drop. Andrew's eyes sparkled in the candlelight, locked on mine. Slowly, the dress clenched in my fists lowered to his stomach.

"What are you thinking right now?" I forced the question through my knotted throat.

"Three things—*four*, actually."

I dipped my head, signaling he should tell me.

"One, I lied before. You just got more beautiful. Two, I'm wondering what exactly I did *so* right to get to this moment in my life. Three, I'm running through this season's Mets lineup and their spring training batting statistics."

With a loud laugh, I found myself on my back again as Andrew pounced with a smile, landing with his full weight upon me. My dress was nowhere to be seen. I yanked at the waistband of his pajamas while his tongue grazed my earlobe, and his teeth nipped my neck.

"What's the fourth thing?" I squeaked as one of his now-bare knees adeptly parted mine.

While one hand had a firm hold of both my wrists on the pillow beyond my head, his other delicately stroked the flesh between my breasts before cupping one and taking it into his warm mouth.

Stars flashed, and the world fell away as, I swear, he said something about needing to stretch and take more vitamins.

36

I woke with a start in a strange bed in an unfamiliar room. It wasn't until I rolled over and felt the sumptuous sheets on *all* my skin that I recalled my current situation. A tingle shot through me. I grinned. It was pitch dark, the middle of the night, so being awake was a curious thing. No way had I slept for my customary eight hours, considering what time I fell asleep—whenever that was. I grinned again. A stretch in all directions told me I was alone. My eyes adjusted to the darkness, but Andrew had drawn the window and balcony door shades, leaving little ambient light to help me see.

Finding the top sheet already freed from the mattress by earlier activities, I wrapped it securely under my arms and around my torso. The remaining train of material rested in the crook of my arm to avoid tripping. A low squeak from the bedroom door hinges sounded as I opened it to find a computer screen's telltale bluish-white glow emanating from the living room. Andrew sat shirtless on his sofa, feet propped on the coffee table, laptop open on his knees. I tiptoed toward him, and without looking at me or saying a word, he simply reached for my hand. He kissed the back of it and pulled me to sit at his side. With a subtle tilt of his head, he kissed my bare shoulder, then resumed clicking through colorful spreadsheets and continuously fluctuating finance indices that meant nothing to me. Silently, I returned the favor, kissing his shoulder, then nestled into the cushions. My head settled against his warm skin as my fingers glided back and forth on his pajamaed thigh until his hand stopped me. Message received, I withdrew, but seconds later, he returned my hand to his upper leg in a wordless invitation. I kissed his shoulder again as the screen powered down. When Andrew leaned forward to put the laptop on the coffee table, I traded stroking his thigh for the length of his spine. He stalled, bent forward, muscles flexing as he enjoyed the gentle back scratch.

The window wall allowed the city's gleam to throw long shadows across the room as its faraway street sounds added sporadic background noise to the apartment's calm. He proved his considerable strength, pulling my hips so my sheet-clad thighs crossed his legs at right angles, and cradled my face in his hands. Our noses brushed once, twice, and he placed a gentle kiss on my lips.

We sat in the nighttime light, foreheads touching, while his fingers explored the curves of my ear, the line of my jaw, the rise of my collarbone. His mouth traveled the same route until my lips insisted on enjoying more of his, another non-verbal message. This one said he hadn't sated me yet. I stood, urging him upright, too, and led him back to his dark bedroom. With an easy shove, he sat on the edge of his bed. I bent to turn on the low bedside lamp once again, then unwrapped my makeshift toga before straddling his now bare lap. Turns out, waking in the middle of the night has its perks, and I'd grown fond of being seen.

My eyes opened to daylight seeping through the window shade edges into the still well-darkened bedroom. Andrew slept on his stomach, hands under his pillow. His subtle sleep smile shone in my direction. I wanted to kiss it but resisted so he could sleep. Careful not to disturb him, I inched out of the bed that groaned with my movement. I empathized, suppressing my own groan as aches in places I hadn't exerted in a very long time reminded me of their lack of use.

Andrew's Mets t-shirt was the first piece of clothing I found. I slipped it over my head before opening the door to the rest of the apartment. It, too, expressed some achiness, and I hunched my shoulders, hoping the hinge creak didn't bother the sleeper. He didn't stir. In the hall, I nearly tripped over his strewn sweatshirt. I said a silent *thank you* for last night's cool temps, the Yale hoodie, and the excuse to come to the penthouse. Pressing my nose to it sparked a twinge in my pelvis that begged *more* and *not yet* both at once. The far-flung belt reminded me of my brazen behavior as I set it on the sofa arm along with the hoodie. The underwear I'd tucked into an inside pocket of my messenger bag earlier provided some modesty under the longish tee while provoking an eye roll at my moxie.

In the kitchen, I considered making coffee, but to keep noise to a minimum, settled for some much-needed water instead. Bathed in the morning sun, the living room balcony lured me. It was too chilly for me to sit in the shady spots, but in the direct sunshine, the cool air felt refreshing, and the sweet smell of dirt and foliage almost allowed me to forget my urban locale until a delivery truck's reverse-gear alarm, stories below, brought me back. Someone wasn't enjoying a day off on this early Memorial Day Monday. A wind gust told me the t-shirt alone wouldn't be enough to stay outdoors. I crept inside to snag the cozy cashmere throw I had noticed draped across the sofa.

As the heavy verandah door clicked closed, Andrew stepped

from his bedroom. Still drowsy-eyed, he wore his pajama bottoms, his curls wild.

"Good morning," I said, rooted to my spot.

His eyes shot to me, and a sleepy grin appeared as he pressed his hand to his stomach. "Good morning. For a minute, I thought it was all—"

"It was all a dream?" I interjected.

"The *best* dream. Yeah." Neither of us moved.

"Hope you don't mind about the t-shirt." I tugged at the hem, feeling exposed. Silly, considering our activities before sunup.

"You in my living room, wearing nothing but a Mets t-shirt, might just be *the greatest* thing I've ever seen in my whole life." One hand rose from his stomach to his chest while the other grasped the nearest door frame.

My butterflies were awake now, too. I blushed. "You know, Laney is a season ticket holder. I bet she'd give up her seats for you sometime."

"Oh. Maybe."

"You already have seats, don't you?" I don't know why I thought otherwise.

"I do, yes. Do—*you* like baseball?"

"I like beer and men in snug pants, so yeah, I *love* baseball."

A smile stretched across his face. "We should catch a game."

"We should. It could be our second first date or—our second, second date if last night counts as a date."

"I think after last night, it all goes out the window."

"*Ah*," was the only reply I could muster. "So—I'm guessing this uncomfortable morning-after thing is typical, right? Kinda hoped we could skip the weirdness, but..."

"I hear that," he said with a pensive frown. "And I'm just spit-balling here, but it could be the daunting task of getting through that *talking list* we avoided while having all the mind-blowing sex." He gave a nonchalant shrug.

"Mind-blowingly *good* sex, right?"

"Oh, God, yes." His nod bobbed with enthusiasm while my knees buckled, and I almost toppled over when the patio door handle rotated as I grabbed it for support.

"Phew. Just wanted to be sure we were on the same page." I leaned with my hand on my hip, knowing full-well I wasn't kidding anyone with my casual act.

"And how about that page with the *talking list* on it?"

Like a dog with a bone, this guy. "Wow, we really should have come up with a much cooler name for it." I got the impression my stall tactic wouldn't work, and for an instant, I considered stripping off the t-shirt to buy me time. The glorious but unforgiving sunshine and Andrew's determined face convinced me otherwise. "Over coffee?" I winced with a sigh.

"Sounds good."

"I'm gonna go find my dress."

"*Aww*," his remark had the high pitch of genuine regret, but then he shook his head. "No, good call. Probably best."

I crossed to him and pressed a finger to his chest, "And if you're as serious about this *talking list* as it appears you are—"

"I am," he interrupted.

"Then I'm gonna need you to do me the courtesy of putting on a shirt." I patted his cheek and winked before heading off in search of my own clothes.

37

It's said, memories triggered by scent create the strongest emotional connections and emerge more intensely than any other memory prompt. If I hadn't already been a believer, the smell of Andrew's freshly ground coffee as it jarred free the memory of our morning a year ago in his High Line loft would have converted me. The overwhelming recollection ripped sadness through my chest, reminding me of the difficult conversation we'd started that May dawn. That sadness morphed to dread as I contemplated how that talk could end *this* May morning. I pushed away the steaming mug.

"You don't like it? I thought you did." Andrew sat in an armchair adjacent to my spot on the sofa. I guess discussing the *talking list* called for distance.

"Maybe in a little while." I waved it off and curled up on the sofa, trying to look relaxed when I felt anything but. How was this going to work? Would we blurt out uncomfortable, private confessions? Ask probing, personal questions? And then answer them? No, the *talking list* was *dumb*. Worst. Idea. Ever.

"I don't want kids," Andrew blurted.

"What?" I asked, startled by the blunt kickoff.

"I don't want to have children. I mean, I love kids, but I don't need—Look, I'm an uncle eight times over, and now Ariana makes nine, plus I'm the godfather to four other children of cousins, which is kind of a big deal for Greeks. Basically, I'm already staring down a baker's dozen of kids, and I'm the oldest, so chances are my sisters aren't done—by a long shot—so I'm good on that score."

Andrew sat back with a vague look of pride for taking the proverbial bull by the horns. I sat unmoving while I considered my response.

"You could change your mind. What if you change your mind?"

He didn't know it yet, but that was the easier question.

"I'm thirty-eight, so I don't see it happening, but I suppose you're right, I could. But I don't think it's like a clock that goes off like it does with women—*some* women." He hurried to revise his generalization. "I think, for men, it's about wanting a child with a certain someone at a certain time. Not just having a child. It's less chemical for us. I'm not trying to paint with too broad a brush here."

I appreciated his attempts at explanation and the gentle tone of his delicate approach. But now, as if on cue, he unwittingly brought us to the tough question.

If only I had found a way to take the same care.

"So, you would have had a child if you stayed with your—socialite. I mean, maybe more than one, but you were starting with a ready-made family. And you wanted that, right? *Charlotte's Web*? Little white ice skates?" Anxiety had me diligently pressing out dress wrinkles with my sweaty palms.

"Wow." The exclamation carried little sound but propelled Andrew to his feet.

I tried to quell the ratcheting tension. "Yeah. The *talking list* is no joke."

Andrew paced, his expression near shock, and I wished I'd just taken off the damn t-shirt when I had the chance. But the floodgates had opened, and I pushed forward.

"I don't care about the woman. I mean, I guess I'll wonder about her from time to time for a little while, anyway. Unless, of course, I've already blown up whatever is happening here." I paused but got no reassurance, and the silence terrified me. "But there was a child involved, and you were in it for the long haul, so that raised the stakes, and its shattering to bits had to put you through the wringer a bit. More so than if it had just been the end of a romantic relationship—which is hard enough. So..." Fingers pressed at my temples, then groped my forehead, and eventually, both hands were in my hair, pulling at the roots. "Jesus, Andrew. Say something."

He stared out the veranda door. Seconds ticked by in a quiet unlike any I had ever experienced. When he returned to his chair, I was afraid to look at him.

"Okay, one. Nothing is blown-up here." He squeezed my skirted knee. "*Here* is—incredible, and not just because of last night. But last night—I mean I never—it felt right, real, meant to be, like no other time—" Andrew stopped for us each to take in some air.

I clutched his hand in both of mine, hoping to make clear I agreed.

"*Here* is different for a whole host of reasons, not the least of which is you care enough to have this conversation in the first place. It's not what I expected, but I guess I should have." He pulled my hands to his lips. "Regarding Lucy. That's her name. I knew Lucy from age five to seven, and she was a terrific kid. Precocious, artsy, tough, and I liked her a lot, no—I *loved* her. And it hurt—worse than hurt—when she could no longer be in my life. But her mom would not be in my life anymore, so that's how it goes. It wasn't fair to Lucy—or to me, but she wasn't mine. Thankfully, she has a great dad, so I know she's okay. It's been almost three years since I've seen her. But I do *not* have any desire to fill that void with some other child. It wasn't about having a daughter, it was about having *Lucy* as my daughter, and that was no longer possible. And I am as okay with that as any feeling person can possibly be."

"And making it work with Lucy's mother wasn't an option?" I pressed my luck.

"It was not." He shook his head with calm adamance.

"May I ask why?" Why couldn't I keep my mouth shut? What if I pushed him too far, or learned something I didn't want to know?

Andrew didn't skip a beat. "Because I take fidelity seriously."

"*Ah.*" I nodded, not surprised by his answer, but then he said more.

"So hearing another man's name at—shall we say, an *intimate* moment—was not something unfamiliar to me. That it happened *again*, with the first woman I dared to—well, it did a number on me." He leaned, forearms on his knees.

"Oh, shit," I muttered and pressed my palms into eyes, wishing I could disappear.

"How's that for a seamless segue? Next item up?" He asked with a gently coaxing grimace.

"Andrew. I am so sorry, but you have to believe me. Tex Miller is no one for you to worry about. Not someone to envy or feel threatened by, certainly no one who compromises my faithfulness. Ever."

"I know," Andrew whispered while I spoke over him.

"He has been in my life for a very long time. A hugely important part of my life. He will continue to be in my life. That's just a fact."

"I *know.*" Andrew held my hand and smiled.

"But he's like a child's imaginary friend. He's my muse, my Jiminy Cricket, my secret keeper. He's my sounding board, a totem, and if I'm honest—"

"*Please.*"

The more animated I got, the wider his smile grew.

"He's been my savior, and he's—"

"He's *you,* Calliope. He's you."

"And—he's me." I stopped. "So, I couldn't get rid of him even if I tried."

"I know, and I wouldn't want you to."

"You get that? I mean, you understand and don't think I'm—not well?"

"No more *not well* than my mom with her prayer rope or people who meditate while breathing through their eyelids or run ultra-marathons. People cope the way they cope. And if I'm honest—"

"*Please.*" I ventured a grin, astonished he grasped the notion that took me years to understand.

"I think you're lucky. I am curious, though."

"Oh no," I interjected, my grin vanishing.

"I know. This *talking list* is no joke," he mocked my earlier snark. "Has he ever been around when I've been with you? In the same room?"

"There have been some close calls, but only twice. Two times."

"At the bookstore?"

"Yes! Oh my God, do you see him too?" I laughed.

"Ha-ha. I'm pretty sure you gestured to him when you were explaining how your new book is different."

"Yes, I did." My eyes rolled, remembering the scene two days ago. "Speaking of *handfuls,* he was particularly rowdy at that moment."

"Makes sense."

"How so?"

"I can see how you would have—needed him, considering what

you thought the circumstances were. Me with a young, pregnant bride-to-be."

"Nah. It wasn't a big deal." I frowned and shrugged through that lie.

Andrew rose from his seat, kneeling on the floor in front of me.

"I was fine. Didn't I look fine?" I avoided his gaze but smiled, unable to keep up my straight face.

He pulled me toward him, his body nestled between my thighs, placing his nose inches from mine.

"You looked so beautiful, and it broke my heart all over again." He kissed me. "And the other time?"

"The day we met. In the car from the airport." My jaw clenched recalling that day.

"When you found out Bernard had—"

"Yes." Eager to push past the memory, I leaned in. "You know what I need?"

"Name it."

"A shower and food. I'm starving."

He pulled me to my feet. Leading me by the hand, we walked toward his bedroom.

"*Whoa,* where are you taking me?" I pulled back in mock alarm.

"To the shower. We Manhattanites are serious about the sustainability of our natural resources. Water conservation, in particular."

"How noble. The self-sacrifice."

"I'm nothing if not—what was it? Honorable, principled, *moral*?"

"*Hmm,* the mischievous glint in your eye makes me wonder. And what about the *talking list*? Black heart tattoos, and the sheets? I *have* to know where you get those bedsheets?"

"Oh, don't you worry. We'll revisit the sheets. Promise."

38

"You know I can have your things brought here, right? This is New York City. Anything can get delivered." Andrew picked up my empty plate and refilled my coffee cup.

"Am I being held hostage?" I twisted my damp hair over my shoulder.

Andrew pretended not to hear me. "And besides, what could you possibly need? You have towels and toiletries, food, and drink."

"*Um.*" I plucked at the sundress I'd been wearing since the day before, except not exactly. "I need clothes."

"Do you, though?" He gave a sidelong squint. "My Mets t-shirt collection is—huge."

I threw my napkin at him, never feeling so good. "Nope." I sprang from my seat, prying away the phone he'd picked up, and held it behind my back. "No phones. If anything pressing happens out in the world, someone will call. It's a holiday. You can go one day without getting immersed in that e-world."

"People are still driving and parking on this holiday."

"And you've got my man Bernard on supervisor duty. If he has a problem, he will send out a bat signal."

"It's a mystery how you have no attachment to a phone." Andrew pulled me to him.

"Well, see when I was young—"

"No, the age excuse won't fly this time. I think Laney has hers surgically affixed."

"Let's not talk about her." I stepped away, wiggling the phone over my shoulder. "And surely, we can find a better use for your hands than fooling around with this thing." In three quick strides, Andrew snatched the phone, tossing it on the sofa. He scooped me under one arm and carried me off, like a snorting sack of potatoes, to revisit those sheets.

For the second time in less than twenty-four hours, I woke in an empty bed. It was just past noon, so I hadn't napped long, but evidently, my new favorite pastime meant to disrupt my usual sleep cycle. I couldn't care less. Stretching across the bed, I considered closing my eyes again, but talk came from the living room. The conversation sounded one-sided. My heart sank with the guess someone had sent a bat signal. I lay waiting to hear what would end my best Monday ever. But when Andrew's volume climbed with an unfamiliar agitation, I threw on my sundress to investigate.

"... look, Laney, your end-run around Calliope to me—has to stop. She's tougher than you think, and her relationship with me doesn't necessitate an agent... I will... I *do*... I am." Andrew looked at his phone. "*Uh*, bye?"

"She's not into hellos or goodbyes." I hadn't meant to sneak up on him, but Andrew flinched when I touched his bare back. "Sorry. What's going on?"

He wrapped his arm around my shoulders, kissing the side of my head before handing me his phone. "No, I'm sorry."

OGLER.COM- Greek God Goes Solo

Ogled! It appears, like a Phoenix reborn, our favorite Herculean hottie is out of hiding, but where we found him might surprise you. Ogler spotted Andrew Statheros, tri-state parking Greek God and NYC's hunkiest single of a certain age, at, of all things, a small Upper Eastside gallery night aimed at female-focused art. Get this. We found no sign he was there *with* anyone. Has it come to this for our aging eligible bachelor? So sad. Trolling venues where the women meet? What's next? Crashing baby and bridal showers? The handsome heartthrob, scrumptiously laid-back in jeans and a t-shirt [#LetsGoMets], went missing as quickly as he materialized. Maybe he wandered in by mistake. Whatever the case, we Oglers are glad to see him out and about. His hiatus has gone on long enough. He's our Achilles' heel and how we love him so.

"Again, seriously, who writes this shit? The Greek cliches? And the Phoenix wasn't in hiding. Everyone knows it burned—*uh-oh*." I returned his phone as he gave me a curious look. "What's the problem? Is it the age reference? Aww. They still think you're pretty," I teased. "Scrumptious even. Guess I can't disagree." I patted his scruffy cheek in pseudo-solace.

"Are you upset?"

"No. Certainly not with you. It seems silly."

"Laney doesn't think it's silly. She's a bit pissed."

"Oh, I'm sure, and no doubt she blames you entirely, which puts you on the wrong side of a formidable badass." I gave him a playful poke in the chest.

"She doesn't want you to get caught up in it."

"Maybe I want to get caught up in it." I poured a glass of water to keep my nervous hands busy. Unsure if I was ready for the next leap.

"What's that mean?"

"Maybe the way to make it stop is to let the *Oglers* know Andrew Statheros is officially off-the-market. Unless, of course, that's not true." I drank a sip, avoiding his eye.

"*Ha.* If I ever considered myself *on*-the-market, and I did *not*, I am most definitely, and quite happily, *off* it now." He took me in his arms.

"Good to know." A quick kiss escalated. His hands gripped my hips, and I clung tight, unsteady from his touch. I hoped that reaction never stopped. Catching my breath, still in his embrace, I asked, "So if you happen to be seen with a woman of a certain age, an up-and-coming author with a recent debut, you'd be okay with that?"

"Okay with it? I couldn't be prouder. I'd take out a full-page ad, hire skywriters. Tweet it to the entire world, but are you sure?"

"Yes." I thought so, anyway. "Don't you think they'll get bored with this pretty quick?" I indicated us. "I don't see why anyone would dig any further. And maybe C.G. Austin sells a couple more books. Win-win."

"Calliope Grace, are you using me to promote your fledgling writing career?" Andrew feigned shock.

"No. I would never." My lips climbed from Andrew's chest, up his neck, and nipped at his ear. "But it's possible I'm using you for the mind-blowing sex."

"*Huh.* For the moment, I think I'm okay with that."

With the day slipping away, part of me wanted out of Andrew's penthouse, if only for a short while. We had no plans to be overtly public, but we agreed if anyone saw us, it wouldn't be the end of the world. With zero intention of feeding the social media beast, what harm could a trip to my hotel for a few things do?

How Andrew and I disagreed was whether to inform my agent of our new strategy. He was pro. I was con. But in the end, it was my choice, and he respected it. I should have known that would bite me in the ass. Agents and mothers: they always find out.

The compromise? A nondescript Around Town black town car to run my luggage errand rather than Andrew's sportier, more identifiable personal vehicle. We would go from one garage to another and back. A quick venture. Baby steps. The new normal might take some getting used to, but I felt emboldened, deciding not to live in the shadows. Still, I loved every moment in the bubble made for two in a penthouse on the Upper East Side.

As we pulled into the garage at my hotel in the Flatiron District, the attendant bolted from his booth, frantically waving his cap before donning it. "Sorry, sir, this is for hotel valet only—Oh, Mr. Statheros. I'm sorry. I wasn't expecting you today."

"No problem, Pete. And it's Drew. Everything quiet down here?" Andrew leaned out the driver's window as Pete ducked his head to speak to his boss.

"A-okay here, Mr.—Drew. Ma'am." The young man flicked his brim like Bernard and Dante as I gave a nervous wave, needlessly adjusting my denim jacket.

"We're just popping in for a bit. Keep up the good work." Andrew and Pete shared a fist bump. The window went up, and we drove deeper into the garage.

"This is—the garage is yours, not the hotel's?" I asked.

"It's mine, but for their use only. I provide the staff and maintain it. They pay me a rate, then charge hotel guests what they will. A typical arrangement. I always have space available should I need it. Like I said, not sexy, but it's a living." We parked. "Ready? We'll take the employee elevator like you did—"

"Yeah, I remember." The details of last May's cloak-and-dagger routine depositing me safely back in my room when *Ogler* prowled after the Luna party became clearer. The quick access to the secure entry was easier than I knew. Easy, because Andrew owned it.

The elevator stood at the far end of the clean, well-lit garage that was not for public use. Valets and hotel employees were the only ones to walk the aisles of the underground parking lot. My bag hung across my body as we held hands on our approach to the doors that would lead us to the hotel above, but we let go when Andrew pulled a card from his wallet and slid it through an electronic reader. He also entered a six-digit code on a keypad, then placed his thumb on a black square.

"What? No retinal scan?" I joked. It all seemed excessive to me.

"Hey, garage security's important. One bad incident kills business."

As he uttered the words, the shuffle of hard soles scuffing on concrete echoed behind us. The elevator doors opened, but we turned when, far away, Pete shouted, *"Mr. Statheros! Trespasser!"* The footsteps scraped and sped up, and the blur of a man appeared between two parked cars, then ran toward us.

"Miss Austin? C.G. Austin? Are you Calliope Jones?"

"Shit!" I lurched forward.

With nimble speed, Andrew hit a button, pulled me into the elevator, and gave a swift shove in the chest to the fast-moving assailant before the doors closed.

I barely heard the loud mechanical screech of the cargo elevator over the roar in my ears. My eyes closed tight, and the tang of metal permeated my mouth. Heat rose under my jacket as I instinctively threw off the strap of my messenger bag and tore out of the denim. Bent over with my hands on my knees, I blew out a long breath but jerked away and stood straight when Andrew touched my shoulder blade. He pulled back, hands up around his shoulders, mouth moving, except I couldn't make out what he said. Slowly, he reached toward my face, his thumb swiping near my mouth. Three words became clear, "Calliope, you're bleeding."

I pushed his hand away. "I'm okay. Are you okay? I'm okay. Why am I talking so loudly? Dammit. I—I bit my tongue." My fingers brushed the corner of my mouth, wiping away a dribble of bright red blood. "I'm okay." I wiped my fingers on my dress. "We—we have to call Laney Li," I sputtered.

He exhaled relief. "Yeah, we'll call her when we get to your room. The police are on the way too."

"What? Why police? No police."

"Someone trespassed on my property. No one violates what's mine. I'm calling in law enforcement."

"You sure as *hell* better be talking about your garage, mister."

"Well—you're back. Sense of humor and all." He shook his head at my cracking jokes.

The doors opened on the thirty-eighth floor. Rounding the hall corner, we found a frazzled Tofer outside my door, a walkie-talkie in hand. He bounced and paced, his breathing labored.

"Pete called. Are you alright? Is she alright?" Tofer's eyes bulged wide as he pushed his glasses up the bridge of his nose.

"Right here, Tofer. I'm right here, and I'm fine."

"Police are on the way. I'm having them come through the garage and the cargo lift. No uniforms will walk through the lobby." Andrew reassured Tofer with a shoulder squeeze. "Don't worry. No lights and sirens. Promise, Tof."

"Can I get into my room, please?" I elbowed past the two men, eager for a moment "alone."

Tofer stepped aside. "Thank you, Mr. Statheros. No need to draw attention, right?"

"We'll need to see the security footage, and Pete will make a statement..."

I left Andrew and Tofer to talk in the living room and kicked off my sandals in my rush to the bathroom, stripping off my clothes along the way. Leaning against the stone counter, I cinched my bathrobe belt tight and spat into the sink. More bright red splattered against the brilliant white basin, then swirled down the drain when I opened the faucet full blast. One glance in the mirror allowed me a deep breath. "*There* you are."

"And there *you* are. *You're okay.*" Tex leaned against the door frame, arms folded.

"I know I'm okay. Except, we're—not okay." I shook my head at him.

"What do we do?" Tex's look was genuine concern.

I backtracked to my strewn jacket, pulled my phone from its pocket, and dialed. "Laney Li? We might have a problem."

39

MY HOTEL SUITE GOT very small, very fast. With Andrew, Laney, a police detective, and a uniformed officer, it was a full house. Tex made it *extra*. He sat in the corner wearing a colorful coned hat with elastic under his chin and crunched potato chips I wished he could share. "Worst. Party. Ever. *Callie*," he groused and offered me the imaginary bag. I snorted. Andrew and Laney both looked at me askance. A knock on the door pulled everyone else's attention.

"*Hot* damn. Tell me it's a stripper," Tex cheered, clapping.

Pete entered with a laptop.

"*Never* mind." Tex rolled his eyes. I covered my guffaw with a cough.

Pete, lacking anything in common with an exotic dancer except a heartbeat, set up the computer in front of Andrew and the detective. Andrew clicked the keys until he found what he needed. Access to surveillance footage.

"Can we take this with us?" the uniform asked.

"It's on the cloud. We'll make a copy."

"Ooh, you know what this reminds me of?" Tex jumped.

"*Uh-huh*," I muttered.

Andrew's eyes shot to me again. I winked at him.

"Book eight. God, what a year that was," Tex waxed on. "All that research into the cloud. Digital data, logical pool storage, the hosting companies. The technical detail was *so* good, and Celeste went and cut it all. What a waste. I do *not* miss her."

I bit my tongue to keep from laughing but nipped the spot I had bitten earlier. "*Ouch.*" I jumped this time. "Excuse me." I tiptoed to the bathroom for privacy.

"You know who it is, right?" Tex and I both paced the stone floor.

"Yeah. I'm pretty sure. Hey, I got this. You should probably go." I sat on the edge of the tub while Tex shrugged in his lean on the counter.

"What? And miss all the fun?" He gave an exaggerated yawn. "Alright, but if it comes to arm-wrestling, put me down for twenty that Laney Li beats them all."

Laughing, I agreed, "Will do. Now shoo." I slid open the pocket door. Andrew sat on the bed, elbows on knees, fingers interlaced.

"What's up?" I nonchalantly sat beside him.

"Laney's a little worried about you."

"Then why isn't Laney in here checking on me?"

"Maybe I'm concerned too."

"Don't be." I kissed his cheek. "Got security footage?"

"We got enough for a decent still shot. Maybe the police can do something with it."

"Let's see it." I took his phone. "Yep, that's him."

"Yeah, we know it's him. The time-stamp tells us—"

"No, I mean, it's the guy from last night." I handed the phone back. "That's the guy I called on at the Q&A after the reading. Sorry, it took us—me—a minute to figure it out."

"Wait, so this guy is really following you?" Andrew ran his hands through his curls.

"Yes, and no."

"We need to tell the cops."

I squinched up my face. "That opens a can of worms I'd rather keep closed."

"I don't understand." Andrew's angst drove him to stand.

Leaning back, my bare foot nudged his shin. I wanted to reassure him, calm him, but kept mum.

"*Jesus*, Calliope." Exasperated, Andrew walked to the door to the living area and stared. His hands gripped his hips. Chin to his chest, he sighed, then trudged back to me and skidded down the side of the bed to sit on the floor at my feet. "For the record, this is me not walking away. And I don't feel threatened or jealous, but *he* can*not* be the only one you speak to when it comes to your safety." The poor guy's curls got a workout. "And if you can't talk to me—then let me get Laney in here so you can talk to her. But, *God*, I wish you would talk to me."

The backs of my fingers stroked his cheek. His dark stubble had grown thick without a shave since Ana's wedding. He took my hand and kissed it. Tex cleared his throat in the bathroom doorway, telling me to talk to Andrew before making himself scarce.

I slid to the floor next to Andrew, still holding his hand. "His name is Linus, at least online. He's a Tex Miller fan, and he's pursued Calliope Jones for years. And somehow he thinks he figured something out, I guess. The way some of these readers pore over the material, parsing words, examining sentence structure, comparing dialogue cadence. It would be impressive if it weren't so *obsessive*. I doubt he means harm. I think he just wants to know. But he has gotten belligerent in the past. *It's Tex Miller Time* forum has put him in *'Miller Time-out'* more than once. Usually for coming to Calliope Jones's defense, but he just does it with—gusto. Think Laney Li, but on social media anonymity steroids, except he uses his actual face on his avatar, apparently. He's not hiding who he is." I turned ninety degrees, crossing my legs over Andrew's, and kissed his cheek. "Now, about who I speak to, and when. These last twenty-four hours have been a lot. And I regret nothing, but—"

"*There* it is," Andrew interrupted. His head flopped back onto the mattress with his eyes closed.

"There *what* is?"

"The *but*—the *but* I should have seen coming."

"Wow. I'm gonna steal from your list this time. What was it? Needlessly insecure and just plain wrong-headed sometimes? Though you are sexy as hell."

Andrew opened his mouth to speak.

"Nope. Not done talking." I pinched his lips between my fingers. "I appreciate you being patient with me, and you have been, in so many ways, but that has to include letting *me* get my head around the fact I have someone else to talk to now, while *you* understand what a monumental change that is for me. My rocks don't have to be mine alone, but they have been for a very long time, which means—that independence, my self-reliance—doesn't just go away. And *frankly*, it never will. But I will do better. I promise." I kissed his cheek again, then whispered in his ear, "Ok, you can talk now." I snickered.

"Calliope?"

"Yes." I turned my head, my cheek pressed against my knees, hugging my shins. Bending a fraction, he brushed my nose with his once, twice, then placed a delicate kiss on my lips.

"I lo—"

A firm knock rattled the door.

"You kids alright in there?" Laney called through the crack.

"Yep!" I straightened, shouting over the edge of the bed. "*Go away* now. We'll be out in a minute." I nuzzled close to Andrew again. "Sorry. You were saying?"

Andrew kissed me again, then slid his legs out from under mine to stand. "This conversation will wait." He helped me to my feet.

"Are you sure? It seemed kind of important." I could have throttled Laney.

"It is, so it'll keep. Coming, Laney." Andrew pulled me toward the living room.

With a glance back, I watched Tex bang his forehead against the door frame. I snorted.

40

I held a piece of paper, the note Linus left for me at the hotel front desk, before he coincidentally spied Andrew and me entering the garage. "I say I text him. Offer to meet."

"*NO*," Laney and Andrew spoke at the same time in resounding agreement.

"Someplace public, and you can come too." It's funny when I'm the voice of reason. "Let's hear him out. What's he going to do? Extort me."

"Extortion? That's the least of my worries. He found your hotel, Calliope," Andrew groaned. With a vigorous rub, he ran his hands over his eyes like he meant to scour away some unpleasant vision in his head.

"*I* say we set a meeting. *Only* Drew and I show up, and we break every bone in Linus's body." Laney stomped the length of the suite after she learned the identity of our problem fan, still angry that she failed to recognize him at the gallery. Andrew *hmphed* with a gesture that said he was all in on Laney's plan.

"*Ooh*, I want in." Tex shadowboxed around the room.

"Sit," I hissed in Tex's direction but smiled when Laney obeyed. I shared a deliberate look with Andrew. He knew I meant the command for Tex, and his understanding pleased me, as did having both men in the same room at the same time.

"Let's give peace a chance, guys. Bring him in. Praise him for his diligent detective work, his mad semantic skills. Find out what he knows and how he knows it and then slide him one of your famous Genevieve-made NDAs and welcome him to our little club—the club of those in the know. He'll feel on the inside, and we'll have some leverage over him if he does say something. But truly, I believe the opportunity to be heard is all he needs to keep quiet."

Andrew and Laney looked at one another across the hotel suite dining table, brows furrowed.

"And what if he talks? What if he spills it, anyway?" Laney asked, always the pessimist.

"Then—then we get out in front of it, and Calliope Jones gets freed. As a matter of fact, it's probably time we make a plan to do that."

"Seriously?" Laney looked at both Andrew and me. Andrew shrugged and pointed in my direction. This would be my call.

"While the decision is still mine to make—yes."

Andrew took my hand in support.

Laney appeared less certain.

"Come on, I'm old enough and wise enough, and, let's be frank, rich enough to make this work. All the things I wasn't in my twenties. That fear, the fear of being discovered, has ruled my life. My privacy, my success? Somehow, my anonymity became the linchpin. I don't know how I let it happen, but it ends. Maybe not today or tomorrow, but soon. It ends soon. It's time, and I can do it."

"One more thing," Laney added.

"What's that?" I took Laney's hand.

"You won't do it alone." Laney reached for Andrew's forearm, letting me know I had her blessing. "And with that, I'm out! Where can I find you tomorrow?"

"Uh—don't know. Haven't gotten past today yet." I raised a

shoulder at Andrew.

"She hasn't said yes yet, but I'm hoping she packs up and comes home with me." He kissed my hand. "Tomorrow is Tuesday. I'm in Astoria on Tuesdays, so I hope you'll hang with me at least through lunchtime. Oh, and did I mention it'll be Tuesday? So, there will be tacos. Tacos that I haven't even considered for more than a year."

Hearing Andrew had avoided his favorite food truck since I left last May was sad and sweet, but seeing his delight at the prospect of visiting it again made me smile.

"And Laney, rumor has it, you're a Mets fan. The boys are back in town tomorrow, so we should catch a game. I've got some club seats. They're pretty good. Bring your wife. Double date."

Laney bowed her head in a way I had never seen before. Speechless, she jumped from her seat and wrapped her arms around a surprised Andrew, while I wiped away a tear.

Tex grumbled, "Oh, Callie, there's no crying in baseball."

41

Andrew and I enjoyed twilight on his verandah, lounging on cushioned chaises. The chilly hour found his urban oasis mostly shaded with the sunset behind us. I read a book while he tapped on his laptop, and we shared a bottle of wine. Snuggled in the cashmere throw, I watched him type while the light faded from the day. Forty-eight hours ago, I thought he was getting married; in just over another forty-eight hours, I was supposed to fly home. Home. How was I going to get on a plane to fly six hundred miles, unpack my bags, and live my life in Charlotte when my heart stayed in Manhattan?

After reading the same paragraph three times, I gave up and closed the book in my lap. Andrew, hunched in his Yale hoodie, was rapt with his work. It was easy to see how the young Mr. Statheros had found his success. The man worked hard for it. I tiptoed inside with my blanket and wineglass.

Wandering around the apartment, I took in the differences between Andrew's new home and his previous one. First, the current residence measured half the size of the huge slaughterhouse loft and only had two bedrooms. It was a pre-war building erected in 1928, but you would never know from the remodel. Gone was the man-cave, or any sign of high-tech entertainment, while each room housed a bookshelf packed with reading material of all kinds, classics to pulp, plus some academic, but also every title I had written, including editions published in Greek.

"Ονειρα γλυκά, Ariana." Andrew entered from the balcony, smiling with a headshake. "There you are. I looked up, and you were gone."

"I just came inside. Got restless. Didn't want to disturb your work."

"Sorry."

"Don't be. Hardworking. It's on my list, remember? It also reminds me I need to get back to work again, too."

"And what does that look like?" He held up the opened wine, and I slid my glass toward him as I hopped onto the kitchen counter. He emptied the bottle.

"You mean after I touch down in Charlotte?" I watched him pause a moment before he tossed the dark glass into a recycling bin with a sharp *clink*. He faced away, but a slight head tilt registered his dismay at those words. I hurried to change the subject. "Were you speaking Greek on the phone?"

"Yes, Ariana called. Leave it to my baby sister to get homesick two days into her honeymoon."

"I saw the translations of my books. How did I not know you *speak* Greek? Your whole family speaks Greek? All the time?"

"Not all the time. And after Dad died, Ariana fought it. She was eight and defiant, so she stopped for a time. I was off at school, but I would take the train home weekends after that, and refused to speak English to her or listen to her English, but because I wasn't around day-to-day and she wanted to speak to me, I was the only one she would take the Greek from. Everyone else—it was English only. *Ironically*, she was in her, θέλω να σε παντρευτώ, 'I want to marry you' phase, so that helped." He winked as I rolled my eyes. "Aww, what? Too soon?" He flinched when I gave a playful shove.

The notion of an eight-year-old girl having a crush on her big brother in the wake of her father's death endeared Ariana to me, and I hoped for the opportunity to get to know her better.

"It was a relief to Mom. She worried Ariana would lose the language."

I stroked his whiskered cheek. "I—it's sweet how you are with one another. Is it like that with all your sisters?"

"More or less. They may be *less* sweet when they meet you."

"Why?"

"They're a bit overprotective of their μεγάλος αδερφός. 'Big brother.' At least you're not blonde."

I laughed. "Do they know about me? All of them?"

"Ariana did first, but just that you were a client. Then she met you and figured a thing or two at your book signing. She's pretty intuitive for her age. That's why the impromptu invite to the reception. She grilled me all the way to Queens. God, it was brutal. I told her everything and made my baby sister cry on her wedding day. Word got around to the rest of the family by the reception. Ariana was pretty disappointed when you didn't show at the Yale Club."

"Just her?" I offered him my wineglass with a cheeky grin. He took a sip in lieu of an immediate reply.

"At the time, we didn't know what *you* thought the situation was, of course. In hindsight, that must have been surreal. Anyway, she knows you're here now."

"Oh." Heat rose in my cheeks. "You buried the lead. And?"

"She's happy. Wants *all* the details that she definitely won't be getting. She is disappointed to miss you meeting Mom. Oh, and actually, by now," he looked at his watch, "all my sisters probably know. There's some mystical Statheros women text chat they've never invited me to join." Andrew busied himself, rearranging lemons and limes in a bowl as he said the last bit.

"Whoa. Back up. Meeting your mom? And when is that happening?" I tugged his arm to catch his eye.

"Tomorrow, lunchtime."

"And when were you planning to tell me?"

"About the time I said, 'Mom, this is Calliope; Calliope, this is my mom, Thea.'"

"Is this a big deal?" My foot nudged his leg.

"No. Maybe. Yes." His head hung down as he looked up, failing to curb his boyish grin.

"Are you nervous?"

"No, she's gonna love you." Andrew walked out of the kitchen.

"Why? Because I'm not blonde?" I joked.

"No," he chuckled over his shoulder, then pulled his sweatshirt over his head.

I hopped off the counter. "Because my name is Calliope?" I spoke louder as he crossed the living room.

"Not gonna lie. It doesn't hurt, but no." He disappeared into his bedroom.

"Well, what makes you so sure, then?" I hollered from the kitchen.

"Because I do," he called from inside his room.

Motionless, I stared in his direction. The sudden thudding in my chest overpowered the silence of the penthouse. Andrew's head popped out from the doorway with a curious grin. "You wanna—come in here and—talk about that?"

I nodded, set down my wineglass, and beelined to him.

The next two days were a whirl of garage tours and family introductions, baseball games, and exploring parts of the city I'd never visited. Nights were long, with more passionate adventures in fantastic bedsheets and very little sleep.

Rico's Diner was a favorite breakfast spot for Andrew and his Queens crew, located a quarter-mile from their Jamaica Hills maintenance garage. Chrome stools lined a stainless-steel counter featuring a view of the short-order cooks on one side and on the other booths tucked into the slanted windowed wall of what used to be a gas station mid-last century. The sweet and savory combination of maple syrup and sautéed onions hung in the air as the tarnished brass bell dangling over the door chimed a new arrival.

In an extraordinary example of life imitating art, Linus Rohrbach tripped over an invisible something and stumbled into the greasy spoon. If you've ever seen the Peanuts comic, you've seen a two-dimensional Linus Rohrbach in what I'd swear was his namesake Linus van Pelt. Long since thinning wisps of mousy-brown hair did little to cover a lumpy head that seemed a smidge too big for his squat, stocky frame. He wore a khaki-colored Members Only jacket and well-creased dad jeans, carrying a bouquet of near-fluorescent-dyed daisies the Kwik-Mart likely threw in their alleyway trash earlier in the week.

Laney honked a laugh but quickly righted herself with her game face firmly affixed.

I glared at her with a behavior warning, then half-stood, waving at the befuddled man, who still tried to figure out what had snared his feet a moment prior.

"Mr. Rohrbach?"

"Hello, Miss Jones. It is the honor of my lifetime to meet you." He offered the wilting flowers with great fanfare.

"Oh my," I took the cellophane-wrapped bundle. "Please, call me Callie."

The little man gasped as his cheeks reddened. "I could never, *never* do that."

"Then, Miss Austin. Please." I gestured for him to sit in the booth I shared with Laney.

"Yes, of course." He attempted an exaggerated wink, delighted to be privy to the nom de plume ruse, but couldn't quite close only one eye.

Laney cleared her throat. "Mr. Rohrbach. Linus. I'm an associate of Miss Austin's, and as you might imagine, she is a *very* busy woman with strict time constraints, and she has a *crucially* important meeting—"

I stepped on Laney's foot.

"*Ow. Uh, another* important meeting after this one, so we would like to get down to business."

That *next* important meeting included beer, club seats, and Laney's beloved Mets. Her wife Genevieve, Andrew, and I would also attend, but I didn't think Laney cared about that part one way or the other. Eager to get to the ballpark, my agent took over, thoroughly explaining the special Genevieve-made NDA and ensured Linus signed it properly. In triplicate.

"This? This is the big bad wolf everyone is so afraid of? Gee, Cal. Getting a little skittish in our old age, aren't we?" Tex brought along his own cup of diner coffee but grimaced when he took a sip.

I pursed my lips, then grinned at my prized protagonist, careful not to engage.

"Nah. Scratch that. I think old age is treating you just fine, Calliope Jones. Why—you're positively glowing." Tex walked away but flashed his crooked grin and called over his shoulder, "Don't forget. You and I've got writing to do. See ya 'round, Cal." He wiggled his fingers and disappeared.

Laney handled Linus, and as I guessed, he happily obliged us, signing that NDA prepared specially for him. My "punishment" for choosing to manage the situation in the kinder, gentler manner meant having to endure a strictly-timed, thirty-minute chat about possible future plots for Linus Rohrbach's favorite literary character. But I felt confident I sealed the clandestine deal when I shared with him a peek at the copy of my latest standalone novel accidentally signed *Calliope Jones*. That tickled him.

We said our goodbyes, and Linus bowed and retreated from our booth before turning to leave. I'd swear he stood a little taller, his chin higher than an hour earlier. But the hunky Greek God that held the steel-framed glass door for the puffed-up Linus to exit quickly distracted me. Andrew showed *his* crooked grin, but then looked to the parking lot. His index finger asked me to wait while he followed the unsuspecting Calliope Jones fan across the pavement. I twisted and ducked for a better view, but all I could see was Andrew, hands on his hips in what might have been a menacing pose. Linus cowered in Andrew's tall shadow for a full minute.

When Linus slunk away with one quick backward glance, Andrew's sweet face headed back inside and joined Laney and me at our booth.

"What was—?" I hadn't gotten out the question when I found myself in a firm embrace and a kiss rapidly heading north of PG-13.

"Get a room, you two," Laney groused, while also giving Andrew a furtive fist bump.

"Andrew? What was that all about?"

"That was a kiss. A kiss, hello. A kiss that said I've missed you since this morning. A kiss that said I can't wait until later tonight." Andrew grinned as perused a menu he surely knew by heart.

"I meant the parking lot. With Linus?"

"Oh, I just explained to Linus how Miss Austin is a very dear friend of mine, and as her *very* dear friend, I hope there is never, *ever* any trouble for Miss Austin online or in real life. And if there is trouble, Linus would find his own—trouble."

"Andrew." I scowled now.

Laney raised her hand for a high-five. "This guy. Up top, Baby Driver."

Andrew indulged her.

"God," she sighed. "If I was any younger and not already married—or a lesbian."

That stand-alone C.G. Austin book became a bestseller that week, and while it didn't hit number one like a Tex Miller book always did, I beamed with pride to see my real name make the list no matter how far down I needed to scroll to read it. The first Tex Miller book also had a sizable sales spike after *ActionCon* and The Luna Network's announcement of the first season air date beginning in October. That debut seemed like a good time to free Ms. Jones, and a strategy to unmask the recluse took shape.

"So, what about *Good Morning America*, says low-key? What about sitting down with *Vanity Fair,* says low-key? Oh my God, Laney Li. Annie Leibovitz? Come *on*." I tossed the print version of Laney's media plan for outing Calliope Jones, and it slid to a stop in front of her.

"What?" She looked up from her phone. "Nothing but the best for my bestie."

"Your bestie said *low-key*."

"My bestie doesn't always know what's good for her. What did you have in mind? A blind item on *nooneisevergoingtoreadthis.net*?"

"Is that a thing?"

"Callie. Look. I get this is scary, but to my thinking, we flood the landscape, get all the information out with one big boom across multiple outlets, one explosion that will die out quickly—lost in the media blitz the TV show will no doubt create. Give them everything, so no one has questions, and eventually, the public will leave you alone."

"*Hm*. I see the logic in that. I do. And I have time to prepare myself for it." I paused to consider. "But here are my stipulations. One. One outlet. A single outlet gets the story, and under no circumstances do they spend even a moment teasing the news, and two, the story breaks *with* the premiere. Not a month, a week, a day before. *With* the premiere, so it is just one sound-bite in a whirl of Tex Miller noise. And as a reward for your capitulation, I will do the silly midnight blue carpet thing that already has poor Jason turning sickly green."

Laney set her phone on the table and folded her arms. I could practically hear and smell her brain gears grinding. Her chin lifted, and I thought she'd speak, but she kept mum a moment longer. I waited. Whether or not she knew it, my part of the negotiation was done.

"You'll do the red carpet? *Blue* carpet—whatever."

"I will."

"With Drew?"

"Andrew will attend the premiere, but I don't need him for the media gauntlet. I would like you with me. And if he wants to be my arm-candy, that's fine, but my guess is he'd rather avoid the limelight. And like I said. I don't need him—not for that."

"Proud of you, *Miz* Jones. You got yourself a deal."

We shook on it.

"Oh, I'm also going to send you my thoughts on the next book. Before I get Elsie in on it."

"Are you a plotter now? Say it ain't so."

"*Ha*, hardly. Just some thoughts. Tex is getting eager. He wants to come out and play. I think I'll let him."

"A *Tex* book?" Laney had her unusual ear-to-ear grin on display. It would frighten small children.

"Yes, a Tex book, and don't gloat. It's unbecoming."

"What? Who's gloating? Ah, who am I kidding? I'm totally gloating. And I couldn't be happier."

Tex appeared, kicking his feet onto the vacant table beside us with his hands clasped behind his head. "We're back, baby."

"How are you feeling?" Andrew kissed my hand, keeping his eyes on the road.

"Sick to my stomach," I whined, watching his serious face in profile.

"Then why are you leaving?"

"Because I have this plane ticket. Because I only packed for a week. Because I have an oddly personable philodendron missing me at home—and it's my home. Let's not make this any harder than it already is, please?"

"Pretty sure that's not possible." As usual, Andrew took his frustration out on his curls. "Screw this. I'm coming with you," he blurted.

"*Ha.* No, you're not. You need me to get out of here so you can get back to normal life. Your employees, your clients, your family."

"Normal life? You mean the fog I bumbled through this last year? No thanks. And besides, my employees have enjoyed the improved mood of their boss this last week. Now, they'll bear the brunt of your absence," he teased. "My family is over the moon about you and thrilled you'll be back for Ana and her husband's return party. And my clients are well-cared for by your man Bernard, who is thriving in his new role as my number two. Which happens to free me up to do other things."

"Things like me?" I blushed at my suggestive quip.

Andrew gripped the steering wheel and growled, finding no humor in our situation.

"I will be back in two weeks to meet the honeymooners. Two weeks is nothing."

"Two weeks is a lifetime when I've had you for less than five days."

"You may not have known it, but you've had me a lot longer than that, Mr. Statheros." I held his hand to my lips.

42

NEARLY ONE YEAR LATER...

"You look handsome." I sat in a rocking chair at Charlotte-Douglas International Airport amid fellow passengers waiting to hear their flight numbers announced.

"I *am* handsome. But you..." Tex wore an elegant suit with a white tulip and acanthus leaves on his lapel.

"But me, what?"

"Don't look at me. That's your job."

Flight 515 to JFK, New York. This is the final boarding call for flight 515 to JFK, New York.

"There's my ride. See you on the other end?"

"I never miss a party, Callie G." Tex did the *stir-the-pot* dance move with a firm bite on his bottom lip.

I hurried to my gate with a muffled giggle, scanning my phone app to board. A quick glance back, and Tex waved from the end of the gangway.

The flight attendant gave a flash of recognition as I took my bulkhead window seat in first class. "Cocktail?"

"Just water, please." My phone buzzed in my hand. "On the plane. Gotta turn off my phone, Laney."

"Yeah, yeah, just doing my duty, making sure you are where you're supposed to be. I'll see you when you get here. Now get here." She ended the call.

"Are you—?" The flight attendant handed me my water, holding up the backside of a book adorned with my picture.

I smiled, surprised by the novel in her hand. "I am." More often than not, I found myself signing *Calliope Jones*. Not today.

"Would you sign my copy, Ms. Austin?"

"Gladly. What's your name?"

"Natalie. I keep hoping you'll write a sequel where she meets up with that Tony and they end up happily ever after."

"I get that a lot, but if you're a Tex Miller fan, keep your eye out for something new soon." I returned the book and pen.

Natalie gasped. "Gosh, I just love that Tex Miller."

I met her adoring grin with my own quirked lip. "Me too, Natalie. Me too."

Two hours later, I descended the escalator at JFK and couldn't help but grin and wave at my driver. Wearing a fancier black suit and black cap, holding a white placard with C. AUSTIN in neat block lettering, my man Bernard waited for me.

"Hello, Miss. Don't you look lovely?"

"Thank you, Bernard. You look snazzy yourself." I bent to kiss his cheek. "I'm so pleased you could come to get me today." We stood at the baggage carousel. I tapped my toe and craned my neck, looking for my suitcase.

"You alright, Miss?"

"Oh, yes, just eager to get going." I pointed to the bag approaching us on the beltway.

"Yes, I imagine so." He snagged the luggage and offered me his arm. "Shall we?" We headed to the car.

Climbing into the pristine black town car, I found a small envelope on my seat and slid a card from it:

Calliope,

Hurry!
Love, A

I tapped the missive on my smiling lips as butterflies ricocheted.

"There is a bit of a backup on 495, Miss."

"Of course there is. Oh well. We have time. Besides, they can't start without me." I winked into the rearview.

"Surely not, Miss."

It was mid-May in Manhattan, and weather professionals promised glorious sunshine for the day. The sky did not disappoint. I leaned back in my seat and reread the card.

Stop-and-go traffic on the multi-lane interstate played the part of the literary last hill to climb, the final wall to scale before reaping the reward at the end of some metaphorical rainbow. Somehow, it seemed appropriate there would be an impediment. It didn't matter, though. By the end of the day, I would be exactly where I was meant to be.

Bernard entertained me with a recap of the last couple of weeks, and an hour later, we pulled up to the Yale Club. Laney waited under the blue awning. As she helped me out of the vehicle, Bernard rounded the car for my bag.

"You're dressed." She eyed under my coat. "Smart though. Cutting it close. I told you it wouldn't wrinkle. You look great, by the way. Let's get you settled in. Your suite is nice, not as big or as high as your usual, but—"

"I'll barely need it. I'm going home tonight but thank you."

"I'll see you in one hour, Miss. At your suite." Bernard gripped my hand as I kissed his cheek.

The two-room accommodation sported the traditional decor of striped wallpaper, floral draperies, and Chippendale style furniture. Arrangements of white tulips and more acanthus dotted the room in simple, clear glass vases, and a sterling silver High Hat with iced champagne stood near a bistro table and chairs.

"Bubbly?" my *best person* offered. Laney refused to be a *matron* of any sort.

"No, thank you. I want my wits about me for now."

"In case you decide to make a run for it, you mean? Good thinking. My suggestion? I know you love your shoes and all, but if we're running, kick those puppies off."

"Any running will be down that aisle, but thanks, Laney Li. Everything all set?"

"Sure. Not exactly a *traditional* deal, but all is as you've requested. Though I think I should put my foot down about this next part."

I shook my head as a knock sounded at the door. "Too late. Now scoot. I'll see you soon."

Her look said she disapproved, but I knew she really didn't care. She opened the door and reached up to pat Andrew's cheek and straighten the flower in his suit lapel. "Hubba, Hubba. You've got thirty—" she checked her watch, "seven minutes. Don't you dare wrinkle her."

Andrew stood in the doorway in a stunning blue suit, white shirt, and tie. His eyes were closed, but I knew they too would be brilliant blue when I would finally see them open.

"I'm not sure this is such a good idea. We Greeks are a superstitious people. Now, I don't care that it's Tuesday or we're at the Yale Club, but seeing you? Why tempt fate?"

"Well, I'm only Greek on my mom's side, and—it's not *fate* I'm trying to tempt." I pulled him near as the heavy hotel door clunked closed behind him. "Besides, they say it's unlucky to see me in my *dress* beforehand, and I'm not wearing a dress. It's a jumpsuit, so *lawyered*."

Andrew laughed. "Well, if the writing gig doesn't pan out, you should definitely reconsider law school."

"Nah. I landed me a rich, young hottie who's going to keep me in the manner to which I've become accustomed."

"Young, *huh*? He'd need to be to keep up with you. Lucky guy, though."

"Truth be told, I'm the lucky one. But if you don't want to see me, keep your eyes closed. That's fine, but you haven't kissed me in two weeks while I was off packing up my Charlotte apartment, and I'll be damned if I'm gonna wait another minute." I brushed my nose against his once, twice, then gently placed my lips on his. He smiled. I pressed in for more as his hands cradled my face and mine slid up his chest and tugged at the nape of his neck. When I pulled back, he held tighter, but then relented.

"What are you thinking right now?"

"Two things—*three*, actually."

"Yes," I prodded.

"One, I can't wait to see what you're wearing. Two, I can't wait to see you *not* wearing it." He held me close as I laughed. "And three, I'm wondering what etiquette says about how long a couple needs to stay at their own reception."

"Why do you think I picked a Tuesday?"

"*Uh*, for the tacos." He gave a closed-eye, incredulous shrug.

"Yes, of course, the tacos," I snorted. "But also the early bedtime. Who parties late on a Tuesday?"

"*Hmmm*. You've met my family, right?"

"Speaking of. You should go be with them now, because later, you are all mine." After one more kiss, I turned and guided him toward the door. "I'll be down as soon as Bernard and Laney come to fetch me."

"*Aww*. O-kay." Andrew took slow steps, arms outstretched to feel the way to his exit. "You better hurry, though. I'm pretty eager to marry you."

"Andrew? You know I love you, right?"

"Oh, I know it for sure, Calliope."

"And you know I'm...?"

"I love you and your brand of... Give Tex my best." Andrew left.

"*Hellooo*. I can hear him. It's like he doesn't even know how this works," Tex scoffed from his seat on the sofa. "You know what this reminds me of?"

I looked south from my window on the twenty-second floor, enjoying the city view. Despite the late daylight, I could see the Empire State Building lit in my favorite signature white. "Tell me."

"That part at the end of all the books. The slow creep up the steep track just before the coaster cart is about to crest, whooshing into the next big adventure."

"It's sort of like that, but different. Why?" I kept my eyes on the cityscape.

"Easy. This time you're holding someone's hand. A real-life, tangible hand."

"But you're coming too, right?" I asked the dashing adventurer.

"Wouldn't miss it for the world." Tex lifted a glass of champagne in my direction and disappeared.

When the *little* big sister I'd always wanted and the gentleman who had been the closest thing to a father I'd had since I was twelve arrived at the door of my Yale Club hotel suite on a clear Tuesday evening in May, I was ready.

Bernard needed a handkerchief and came prepared. Laney

needed a drink and flashed me her flask, but I declined. No liquid courage necessary. I had never been more certain about anything in all my life.

The crowd gathered for the day's unconventional nuptials was small. As small as we could make it when the groom comes from a family that could field a baseball team. Both dugouts, actually. The stately room with Palladian windows was not new to me. It was the same room where I spied a certain chauffeur who wasn't a chauffeur, reading a newspaper. Today, we had replaced the matching sofas and coordinating wingbacks with Chiavari chairs, white tulips, and the promise of a new adventure.

When the doors opened, a familiar Bach suite movement, featuring a violin, played. We even found the young violinist from Central Park to play it for us.

Laney kissed my cheek before beginning the walk down the configured aisle. I trained my eyes on the dark brown curls of the man in the brilliant blue suit facing away at the end of the white runner and tightened my grasp on Bernard's arm. As the music ended, I took a step, but Bernard pulled back on my elbow.

"Not just yet, Miss. Eager now, are you?" he asked with a fatherly squeeze of support.

"Never more so, Bernard." I bent to kiss the old man's cheek.

As the next song's opening chords began, so did a smattering of snickers around the room as the guests stood. Andrew's head bent back as he looked to the ceiling with a shoulder shake. Just as the first lyric sounded, Bernard patted my arm to tell me it was time to take our first step.

Me and Mrs. Jones... Andrew turned as I lowered the tulip bouquet I briefly hid behind for one last deep breath before the start of my biggest adventure yet. His crooked smile with all the boyish charm radiated, and I never felt more seen.

OGLER.COM Opa! It's a Teeny Tiny Greek Wedding

Ogled! Another one bites the dust as the Upper East Side is down one eligible bachelor, and on a Tuesday, no less. Everyone's favorite Greek catch Andrew Statheros has been plucked from the market as he and Charlotte, North Carolina author Callie Austin [aka Calliope Jones of Tex Miller book and The Luna Network mega-hit series fame] said, *'I do'* at a private ceremony with friends and family at Midtown's Yale Club tonight. Why Tuesday? Why not? Ogler is proud to say we caught this love affair from the get-go when the duo first got together in March two years ago. Rumor has it the couple will make Manhattan their home, and why wouldn't they? But if anything changes, you can be sure we'll ogle it for you and spill all the dirt.

THE END

ABOUT THE AUTHOR

Kelly Elizabeth Huston grew up in some pretty idyllic small northern towns playing "Let's Pretend..." with anyone who would take her direction. Through dance studios, community theaters, and college, she found her way to the stage, both on and behind it. So while she wasn't the kid who kept boxes of journals brimming with stories, the later-in-life leap to writing wasn't huge. There's more than one way to tell a story, after all. And what a wonderful way to continue enjoying the *Let's Pretend* game.

In real life, she is a boy mom to two and the proud wife of one of the hardest working men she knows. These three guys have been the best cheer squad a gal could want, especially since her family began making a life in the South.

Kelly still adores the theater and travel and looks forward to an ACT II that includes more of both. But most days, she is happy to sit in her writing nook with all the words at her fingertips, playing more "Let's pretend..." with laughs, some tears, and a surprise or two along the way. And love, there will always be love.

For more information and updates, sign up for Kelly's newsletter at www.kellyelizabethhuston.com.

Other books by Kelly Elizabeth Huston:

A Very Crowded House, October 2023; A Girl, Stuck, March 2024; See Sadie Jane Run, August 2024

ACKNOWLEDGMENTS

Many of the writer friends I've made on this roller coaster ride called 'publishing' felt compelled to write from a young age. They still have boxes chock full of old stories, poems, and journals that offer a blow-by-blow account of middle school and beyond. That was not the case for me.

My story began in the spring of 2018 with an unfriendly medical diagnosis and the even ruder awakening that I didn't have the patience for knitting. I'm well now—well enough, anyway, but my less-than-stellar health will be a lifelong pebble in my shoe. *Dems da berries.* And yet I can't help but be grateful for this weird and wonderful vocation I've discovered in the mess of it all. Like Andrew so eloquently said, you cope the way you cope. Running ultra-marathons or breathing through my eyelids held little promise; neither did knitting.

And oh, what a weird and wonderful village this vocation provided, too. Yes, writing is a solitary life if you want it to be (and one facet I like most about it), but going it alone isn't advisable. Just ask Callie. And I would be remiss if I didn't make a few shout-outs here to be celebrated on the page until the end of time.

I'll start with my *firsts*. My first alpha/beta readers were my mother, Suzanne Huston, and my best friend, Aly Gimbel. They have read more words than I had the right to ask of them and told me from word one to keep going. My first editor Ash White got in on this nuttiness early too, and when I came back to her four and a half years later, she quickly agreed to fix my comma situation. My first agent, Rebecca Strauss, fell in love with Tex Miller and helped me dig deeper by asking the right questions. She also provided that inside-the-industry thumbs-up I needed to keep at it, even when we kept hearing no. She took a chance on me—and my not-quite-traditional stories. Thank you, Rebecca.

The next names are more genuine friends, some writers, all readers, and the collective cheer squad someone like me needs. Critique partners who decimate with love: Gwynne Jackson, Paulette Stout, and Kyle Ann Robertson. My in-town betas, whose enthusiasm for the *Kelly Verse* (trademark pending) gives me strength for days: Heather Ross and Michaela Pennebaker. Your willingness to read, read fast, and then dish about it all has provided more encouragement than you will ever know. And a few other writers in various stages of *'the life'* that just clicked with me, and I don't click easily: Sheila Athens, Lisa Roe, Robin Facer, and Shelby Reilly. We don't see each other often but watching you do your thing, get some wins, take some hits, and get back up again, inspires me in ways I can't express. A pretty epic failure for a writer, but I thank you nonetheless.

Lastly comes my family—in more ways than one, some days. I've mentioned my mom. The number of hours I've droned on about the ins and outs of every aspect of writing—well, it's a lot. I love her for that and more. She deserves a medal. My dad, Otis Huston, thinks I'm the greatest thing since sliced bread and, luckily, gets to read after all the blood, sweat, and tears. He doesn't get involved in how I make the sausage, but he *loves* it every time. My guys Hal, Jack, and Henry have watched from the sidelines as this adventure grew into something none of us imagined. Hal: You never let slip even a smidgeon of doubt that I could do this, and I couldn't do it without your support. To my boys: I hope I have shown you an example of tenacity and forging your way when roads close before you. Take the leap. And if you get banged up along the way, those scars will only make you a more interesting character in your story. That's called a metaphor, so please, no more broken bones.

What's Next: A Very Crowded House

PROLOGUE

It was the summer I learned to tie my shoes because my big sister Genevieve refused to do it for me anymore. I conquered riding a bicycle without using training wheels because training wheels were for babies. My two front teeth fell out, and I saw my sister kiss a girl for the first time, but not the last. It also meant the beginning of my love for fireworks and the unfortunate start of the Monsters finding their way to our summer safe-haven.

We were suffering the hottest day of our summer stay so far, and nighttime brought little relief. Despite the fully opened windows with drapes pushed wide, the night air, too thick to move, hung in the eaves of the upstairs bedrooms. It suffocated us in the dark with the added cruelty of the screeching tree frogs and their unique brand of rhythmic torture. I lay atop my sheets and considered sneaking to the end of the hall, where a sunroom offered windows on three sides and perhaps a chance of a mild crosswind.

Rules about leaving our rooms once we were sent to bed had been clearly outlined, but the night's heat smothered us, and my eyelet-trimmed Raggedy Ann nightgown clung to my belly; my blond curls stuck to the back of my neck. Dangerously dangling my feet off the side of my four-poster, I assessed the benefit to harm ratio of breaking those well-defined bedtime tenets. Having weighed my options and determined the possible consequences, I slid down the mattress until my bare tiptoes hit the wide planks of knotty-pine floors, prepared to suffer the penalty if it meant a breath of fresh air.

At the moment of impact, when flesh met wood, everything changed.

Frozen to my spot, the stifling heat of the night no longer my concern, I held an inhale in the hopes I had misinterpreted the sound, but I knew I hadn't. A door slammed, and a door slam marked how it always began. My new hope was for another door to slam, the front-entry, the backdoor, any portal that let him exit the house before things escalated. But someone had lifted the charm thanks to me and my yearning for a gentle breeze. The price would be paid. The Monsters had found their way to our once-peaceful summer sanctuary on Market Street. Life, as we wished it, was no longer.

To be clear, until that long ago summer, the Monsters had never come to the Hamptons. At least I never heard them until that swampy July night. Maybe we could chalk that up to a solidly built shingle-style "cottage" of five thousand square feet or that summertime in Amagansett meant running free dawn until dark and then sleeping hard after all the sun and sea air. But I had long believed guardians had enchanted the big, old fairy tale house with its mullioned windows, cedar shake, and bright white trim. Keeping it protected on an expanse of the softest lawn bare feet ever scampered across, while tiny pixies glimmered around nearby greenery in a dreamy twilight dance show. The magic hour. Then again, I was only six. Whatever the reason, until that July, summers in Amagansett were the best weeks of the year, the best weeks of our lives.

That sweltering airless night, as the thumping on walls and the smashing of glass amid shouts and screams commenced, I burrowed under my bed with down-filled linen wrapped around my ears to block the horrifying noise.

A firm yank on my ankle startled me out from under the pillow, and I swallowed my scream.

"Jojo," my sister Genevieve beckoned in a loud whisper.

"Don't grab me, Gigi." I swatted back and shimmied out of my makeshift foxhole. All my curls stuck to my head, matted down, sweat-soaked from hiding under the pillow.

"Come look. Plug your ears but come see." Genevieve walked to the double-wide casement window, and I watched my sister remove the screens to sit on the windowsill. Her version of blonde lay straight in the nighttime light. Four years older, she knew everything and had no fear. Fingers, firmly in my ears, muffled the Monsters thrashing below us. I tiptoed to where she sat. Fireworks brightened the distant sky with white, red, and blue. Colorful sprays of fire arced through the air, overlapping, popping, and whistling in the moonless night.

"Gigi." I watched the colors reflect on her glistening face. "Gigi," I repeated, then bit my bottom lip, waiting to make my confession.

"What, Jojo?"

"I broke the magic, Gigi. I'm sorry, but I broke it."

Genevieve smeared the sweat and tears across my cheeks and shook her head. "It was bound to happen, Jojo. No one to blame but the Monsters. Now, no more tears and stop biting your lip.

Watch the fireworks."

1

JOCELYN DURAND

I remember the days when the racket wouldn't stop. Neighborhood kids running through the house, plastic light-up toys, powered by vicious Energizer Bunnies, squawking constant noise, blared music or television, and the phone ringing twenty-seven times a day, at least. Sure, when earbuds arrived on the scene, and my son Gabe got a cell phone, things quieted some. Still, the tromping up and down the wooden stairs, beckoning shouts through closed doors, and a near-constant thump of a basketball, soccer ball, or a tennis ball on the driveway—too often a bedroom wall—inundated our charmed existence. And did I mention the drum kit I could still kill his Aunt Genevieve for buying him?

Those were the moments I dreamed of quiet, wishing for Calgon to take me away. Naturally, I also loathed the nights when I lay awake, desperate to hear the rumble of Gabe's rusted muffler pull into the garage, telling me he had survived another night of teen driving. So yes, some quiet you don't want to relive. But to tell the truth, I've longed for this day, the stage of my life with few disruptions, no persistent noisemakers or usurpers of my time and attention. The day when I'll pick up my writing career again and *surely* it will be as easy as that. *Think again, Jocelyn.*

Of course, the landscape had changed since those chaotic days of carpools, sports practices, and after-school clubs. The 1920s four-bedroom, three-bath Tudor outwardly looked the same, though we completely renovated the indoors. But I hadn't imagined I would be alone in this more serene chapter. My ex-husband Will had always starred in that movie-in-my-mind of what Act II would look like. To be fair, he still plays a role in my life since the *Second Act* began, but as a background player, maybe a somewhat regular walk-on, but certainly no longer the leading man.

Don't cue the violins. They aren't necessary. I married extremely well, but I divorced even better. Will and I remain close friends. And the change in the *figurative* landscape I mentioned became quite literal, compliments of the man Will left me for. A landscape architect, Raphe, built and continues to maintain an outdoor paradise behind my house that flourishes beyond compare. No doubt to assuage his guilt for stealing my husband of twenty-four years. And if it makes him feel better, who am I to get in the way of that?

As I sat on the flagstone patio in my Westchester oasis, I enjoyed a cup of coffee and my New York Times crossword. The coo of mourning doves with the low hiss of the in-ground sprinkler, watering the luscious green space, accompanied the quiet in my meticulously cared for backyard. See? I'm doing *just* fine. It was early morning, but in an hour, the June sun would shine high enough to make the lounging spot untenable until Happy Hour when wine on the then-shaded terrace served as the perfect end to a summer day. I breathed a sigh of relief when a ringing phone interrupted my wistful thoughts of five o'clock.

"Gigi, little early, isn't it?" I answered my big sister's call on the first ring.

"To start drinking? Yes. To call my kid sis? Also, yes. But I know you're *always* up at the crack of dawn, Jojo." Gigi possessed an uncanny knack for knowing when to call and what to say, and she purred it in a low, sexy Kathleen Turner rasp with a hint of Long Island I had long since lost.

"Guilty, counselor. But why are *you* up this morning?" I sipped my coffee, relaxed on a cushioned chaise.

"Laney is beside herself. It's rare, but never a good look on her. Her bestie had the gall to marry, then jet off on a honeymoon to Greece with no discernable return date. Plus, the bride is notorious for never carrying a phone."

"No phone? I'd be lost without mine. My whole life is in this thing."

"Yeah, well, Laney is driving me nuts, so I gently encouraged her to go to the office and foster some other needy writer's career." Gigi's wife, Laney Li, was a five-foot-nothing spitfire of a literary agent.

"Gently, huh?" I gave her a verbal poke.

"Not really, no. Speaking of, are you writing these days?" She returned the favor.

I sighed, "Not really, no." We sat in a comfortable but long silence. "Gigi?"

"Hm?"

"You know you don't have to call me all the time, right? I mean, I'm fine. Alone? Yes, but fine. Between you, Gabe, and even Will, it's like constant surveillance." That's how it had always been. Like they've been in cahoots, on a check-in rotation. 'Cahoots.' Now, there's a great word more people should use.

"I have no use for that ex-husband of yours, but hey, when's my *brilliant* and *gorgeous* nephew getting home?" My sister side-stepped my observation, but the new topic wounded my heart.

"He's not. My *fair-to-middling* son got an internship for the summer. In North Carolina. Yaaaay." I joked, of course, but the late change in plans disappointed me.

"Can't help but notice your less than enthusiastic cheerleading routine, Jojo. That's not like you. And stop biting your bottom lip. I can practically hear it from here." She wasn't wrong.

Summarily chastised, I released my lip and adjusted my attitude. "It's fine. I thought Gabe and I might have some time. Head out to the summer house for one last family hurrah. Whatever. He said I should go anyway, but I assured him I wouldn't." I paused before asking the foolish question. *Don't suppose you've considered going out there? To the summer house?* I knew better than to ask. Gigi conveniently begged off, unable or unwilling to make the two-hour trip to East Hampton most times. If she did, the visit never included an overnight. The sleepy little hamlet of Amagansett was either too quiet with no traffic noise, too loud with its tree frogs, or had too much green grass Gigi swore exacerbated her allergies. It didn't.

"Nope. No plans for that," she dismissed the notion. "But you should definitely go."

"Are you and Gabe in cahoots?" *Ah-ha.* "I'm not going out there by myself, Gigi. Raphe will take care of the grounds. Some of his crew, anyway. It's fine if no one goes this season."

"Good lord, Jo. *Cahoots?* And really? Poor Raphe and his guilty conscience. How long are you going to milk the home-wrecker routine?"

"Shut up. Raphe loves me. And if he and Will ever split, I think I'll side with Raphe just for the landscaping perks."

"See, there's a joke in there somewhere, but it's too damn early for me to find it." Her laugh hinted the joke might be dirty, but as usual, I didn't get it.

"Okay, why'd you call, Gi? Is there a problem, or you just bored?" I set my lukewarm coffee on the stones at my freshly pedicured feet and stepped out to feel the cool fescue still damp with morning dew.

"Bored? As in-house counsel at a talent agency, life is never boring, Jojo. Surreal? Often, but never humdrum."

For years I clamored for any tidbit of celebrity gossip and, attorney-client privilege aside, Gigi shared it, but these days I had enough of my own small-scale scandal to reflect on, so the chinwag had lost its appeal.

"Then what?" I asked, distracted by the tickle of my foot, the soft blades of grass grazing it.

"Hold on, incoming call... *Huh*, it's Laney. She never calls. I should take this."

"Okay."

"Hey, go to the summer house." Genevieve pushed once more.

"For the last time, I'm *not* going."

"Fine. Then write something."

"Love you, Gigi." I brushed over her suggestion.

"Love you, Jojo."

I returned to my crossword only slightly agitated my sister had ruined my timed speed, but in three more clues I'd complete another puzzle.

Twenty years ago, I wrote a book. A fluke in my opinion, but if I've learned anything about the publishing business, it's that my opinion isn't worth much. Writing stories wasn't something I did as a child, but when Will and I met during freshman year of college, he encouraged my creative side, though I never thought I would do anything about it.

We married young, right out of school, and traveled the world, in love *with love*. Then, when it came time to start a family, we had a tough go getting pregnant. The inconsistency in our sex schedule was likely the culprit and, in hindsight, should have been one of many red flags. Many, *many* red flags. Anyway, it finally happened, but not without a price. Doctors confined me to strict bed rest from eight weeks on. I stood to shower and use the toilet—nothing else. And while Will doted on me like the devoted husband and proud papa-to-be, it was a maddening time. I found solace filling blank pages with words. Hopped up on pregnancy hormones with nothing but time, I wrote like wild, and in the end, a highly regarded, critically, and then commercially acclaimed novel emerged. No one was more surprised than me.

The book launched a brilliant start to a young writer's career, or so the industry thought. In reality, I wrote the proverbial one-hit-wonder. Maybe that's going too far. Failed attempts at another success would be necessary to prove true lightning in a bottle, and those attempts never happened. Not in earnest. Nope, I took one look at my son Gabriel's baby blues, and *that's all she wrote*. Literally. To this day, Jocelyn Atwater's debut novel (published under my married name), having won notable prizes and awards, is a perennial, highbrow book club favorite, and an often-studied work in university Modern American Literature classes. The tale of two young sisters growing up in an outwardly idyllic existence, when their picture-postcard life is anything but ideal, told a very adult story, rife with symbolism, magic, and monsters. Smart people said so, anyway. Again, no one was more surprised than me.

A crack of thunder startled me out of my trance. To the west, a storm I hadn't seen brewing roiled with dark, angry clouds and a sudden uptick in the wind. At the edge of the patio stood a two-hundred-year-old white oak, its trunk over three feet in diameter with impressive leafy limbs that spanned wide and high atop the house. The crown jewel of my garden of Eden. The whitish undersides of the bright green, round-lobed leaves bared themselves in the abrupt, gusty breeze. A sure sign of an imminent downpour. I should have guessed. Inches of rain had fallen every day this week, and my left arm had that bothersome barometric ache, but the morning sunshine duped me into thinking the unusual spate of days upon days of showers had run its course. No such luck.

When the first splat of fat drops darkened the blue-gray slate, I darted to grab my crossword and coffee mug before I found shelter indoors. Catching the screen door with my foot to avoid its slam, I witnessed the skies send down yet another deluge. For the fourth time in as many days, I chided myself for neglecting to turn off the automatic sprinklers that continued to soak the already well saturated grounds around the house. To make matters worse, the chaise cushion would also get waterlogged since I failed to grab it in my rush to stay dry. It had been the soggiest June I could remember.

"Aww, poop." I watched as the hydrangeas took a beating for another day. It may have been the morning's sunny tease, but the downpour looked harsher than any of the others that week. I closed the door and poured another cup of coffee. My phone signaled a text from Genevieve.

Gigi: Work emergency. Left coast variety. I'd tell you all about it, but I'd get disbarred. ;) Out-of-pocket for the next few days. Laney too. I'll call when I get there. Tmrw, latest. Hey, so about the summer house?

Me: STOP! Quit calling me for no reason. And seriously, I'M NOT GOING!

Gigi: Good. Don't.

I rolled my eyes and tossed my phone onto the quartz counter. It landed with a *smack*. Taking another sip of coffee, I trudged the basement stairs to swap laundry from the washer to the dryer. It wasn't a California celebrity legal crisis, but it was my life.

2

ASHER CRAY

It happens to *everyone* eventually. Isn't that the lie we tell ourselves? The first time we can't— I mean, you reach your mid-forties, and things don't always work like they did in your younger days. Back in my twenties, I could go all day and night, it seemed. Nothing slowed me. Even in my thirties, my drive surged, relentless. And if I felt my performance waned, the shortest of breaks... a quick shower, maybe a snack, the occasional catnap, and I rebounded right back at it.

The reasons for my sudden— incompetence could be any number of things: lack of sleep, stress, hell, it could be the summer heat for all I knew. I hadn't imagined it would happen like this, not that I dwelled much on this particular scenario. Who would? But it seemed to me there would be a slow decline, a petering off, not an abrupt inability to—perform. And now I couldn't get out of my head, which only made matters worse. The memory of my last time ran on a loop. The last time? Jesus Christ, not *the* last time. Was it?

I looked at my watch and then ran my fingers through my graying hair. A vigorous scalp rub provided momentary relief to my throbbing— The elevator dinged, and I launched out of my chair, eager to see the only woman I knew could help with my little *um...* problem. Instead, a custodial worker appeared as the doors slid open. I stayed on my feet and gave a weak salute with a nod. He returned the non-verbal greeting and pushed his garbage bin and tool caddy by me. My chin hit my chest.

Plodding down the hall toward a wide window offering an

impressive view of Lower Manhattan, I waited for my savior. Despite the early hour, traffic inched through the Financial District. Thirty-eight stories gave a dizzying perspective. My stomach lurched, and I stepped back from the glass. "Jesus, Ash. Get a hold of yourself, man." I strained for a deep breath but forfeited that exercise when another mellow *ding* announced the elevator's return. I jogged the carpeted hall to meet my ace in the hole.

"Asher Cray? Did we have an appointment?" Laney Li exited the elevator, ubiquitous phone in hand. Her frenetic thumbs almost blurred with their speed as she spoke. "Pretty sure I'd remember if we did. Sorta pride myself on keeping up with my clients, my favorites, anyway. Joking, of course. Wait. Aren't you supposed to be in L.A.?" She continued to text while I stood paralyzed in front of her. Phone to her side, Laney craned her neck to meet my pleading eyes. I stood more than a foot taller than the pint-sized woman, but I trusted no one more when it came to...

"I can't write," I blurted.

Laney's brows raised as she sidestepped me and hurried to her door down the hall. "Okay."

"No, not okay. I mean I. Can't. Write." I punctuated the confession. "There's nothing flowing here, Laney. Nada. Zip. Like for a while now." I took long strides to keep at her fast-moving heels.

"I see." She unlocked her door and flipped the switch to light the foyer of her office suite.

"*Uh*, your casual tone makes me think otherwise, Ms. Li."

"Asher, it's going on twenty years now, and we've been over this. It's Laney or Laney Li, *never* Miss Li, and this may surprise you, but— not the first time I've heard this from a writer client. Other popular authors who have written longer than you, more books than you. Trust me when I say, while your CV shows you to be an incredibly talented and prolific novelist who spends more time *on* the New York Times bestseller list than *off* it, you are not exactly unique, big guy. This, too, shall pass." She busied herself around the office, opened the blinds, booted up her computer, and flipped through junk mail.

I sank onto a smooth black leather sofa across from her sleek glass and chrome desk. Laney Li in furniture form. My palms pressed into my eyes. "When a man comes to you, practically on his knees with a—performance problem—a creative muscle dysfunction... I'm not sure telling me I'm *not special* is really the way—I mean, far be it from me to tell you how—"

"Hey Ash," Laney interrupted. "I'm your agent, not your fluffer." Laney stared, steely-eyed.

I threw back my head with a laugh, finally able to get that deep breath. Elbows to knees, I held my head again, massaging my temples.

"We good?" My agent rocked in her desk chair. Smiling didn't come easily to Laney, but she did her version of it now.

"We're good. Better anyway. Thanks."

"And what about L.A.? Thought they were going to woo you into script approvals."

"Aw, Laney, I couldn't give a crap. I'm a writer, not a movie maker. And if I can't write, then I don't know what the hell I am. You're welcome to make the deal on my behalf. I trust you. But the window's closing. End of business two days from now, I think. Sorry. Guess I dropped that ball too."

"I don't care about the flick biz, but really, Asher. How bad is it?"

I stood, feeling caged. "I don't know what's happening. I've never—"

"Never?" Laney gave me a side-eye look.

"There are two things I have never had a problem doing. And the second one is writing." I paced in front of her desk.

Laney let loose her loud honk of a laugh. "Says the man I know has been single for over a year and even then… Glad to see you're keeping up the persona, outwardly anyway. Maybe you just need to get—"

"All right, Laney Li," I jumped in. "I think it best we stick to one problem at a time, and I pick the writing. I can handle the other one on my own."

"I'm just saying, maybe your handling the other one *on your own* isn't—" My agent's hand gesture wasn't Disney-approved.

"Jesus, Laney Li. You're on fire today." I resumed my head massage.

"You know what I think you need, Ash?"

"Yes, Laney. You've made that clear."

"No, seriously."

"Please don't tell me to go to *shul*." If an award for world's most-lapse Jew existed, I'd be a frontrunner.

Laney rolled her eyes. "Give me a minute." She reached for the phone, never more than an arm's length away, and dialed. "Genevieve… what do you mean, I never call? I call sometimes. Did I interrupt something?… Jojo, *huh*? That can't be a coincidence. How about you and I hop a flight to L.A. to hammer out a lucrative deal for Asher Cray? Wanna bat around some movie producers?… Um, today… No, I'm not kidding. We'll be back in two days, three tops. Now here comes the big ask…" Laney pulled out a bottle of dark liquor and two short glasses. It wasn't eight a.m.

Nope. No one I trusted more.

AVAILABLE NOW